MOTH *and* FLAME

MOTH *and* FLAME

JOHN MORGAN WILSON

ST. MARTIN'S MINOTAUR
NEW YORK

www.minotaurbooks.com

Library of Congress Cataloging-in-Publication Data

Wilson, John M., 1945–
    Moth and flame / by John Morgan Wilson.
      p. cm.
    ISBN 0-312-30984-8
    EAN 978-0312-30984-8
    1. Justice, Benjamin (Fictitious character)—Fiction. 2. West Hollywood (Calif.)—Fiction. 3. Real estate development—Fiction. 4. Freelance journalism—Fiction. 5. Journalists—Fiction. 6. Gay men—Fiction. I. Title.

PS3573.I456974M67 2004
813'.54—dc22

                                   2004051019

First Edition: December 2004

10 9 8 7 6 5 4 3 2 1

For my beloved sister, Penny Thayer

And in memory of my great friend Bertha Joffrion

ACKNOWLEDGMENTS

Many people assisted in the research and writing of this novel. First and foremost, I must thank my editor at St. Martin's, Keith Kahla, for his guidance and wisdom from start to finish. At various West Hollywood agencies and departments, I must acknowledge Helen Goss, director of public information; Tatiana Rodzinek, Russian community outreach specialist; James Kampas, marketing manager, West Hollywood Convention and Visitors Bureau; Fran Solomon, deputy to council member John Heilman; and a special nod to Roz Helfand and Corey Roskin for their dedication to the annual West Hollywood Book Fair. The ONE National Gay & Lesbian Archives (www.oneinstitute.org), its staff and volunteers, deserve heaps of praise. I must also mention Alan L. Gansberg of Gansberg Productions, Ltd.; Greg Klein, bell captain at the Argyle; and Ryan Gierach, author of *Images of America: West Hollywood,* which proved to be an invaluable resource. Other helpful resources included *Los Angeles: An Architectural Guide,* by David Gebhard and Robert Winter, and the city-published brochure *A Guide to West Hollywood Historic Sites and Cultural Resources.* I need to include two organizations, Mystery Writers of America and Sisters in Crime, for their continuing support. And, of course, special thanks to my longtime agent, Alice Martell, and my steadfast companion, Pietro Gamino.

AUTHOR'S NOTE

While much of the history portrayed in this book is based on research and fact, it is, after all, a novel. With the exception of actual celebrities and other public figures identified by their real names, all characters herein are purely fictional. In addition, a few details, such as dates of certain events, have been altered for dramatic purposes. One street, Paul Monette Avenue, is pure fiction, but all other streets exist as portrayed.

It should also be noted that the northeastern border of West Hollywood is blurred, in this book and in the public's mind. Technically, the border along Sunset Boulevard between West Hollywood and Los Angeles (Hollywood) city limits ends a few feet west of the Chateau Marmont Hotel, which sits west of Crescent Heights Boulevard. Even the map printed in this book, used by permission from West Hollywood's archives, includes at least two blocks east of that northeast border that actually belong to Los Angeles. It's a reminder of how often West Hollywood and Hollywood are confused, and how the pasts of both are so heavily shrouded in myth.

WEST HOLLYWOOD, CALIFORNIA

MOTH *and* FLAME

PROLOGUE

Every place, like every person, has its own character, its own history, its own secrets.

West Hollywood, where I reside, is no exception. For more than a decade now, I've been telling myself it's time to move on, time to leave a town I never much liked to begin with, for all kinds of reasons. But here I am, still torn over a place where I've experienced my greatest joys and sorrows, my deepest friendships, my darkest moments.

It's a lively little city, a busy, vibrant, cultural patchwork situated between the garish sleaze of Hollywood and the posh veneer of Beverly Hills, with some of each seeping across the borders to give West Hollywood its special flavor. The town teems with people, roughly thirty-six thousand residents packed into slightly less than two square miles, most of them renters who pay outlandish sums to live here. Through the decades, WeHo has become a haven for artists, designers, entertainers, homosexuals, Russian Jewish immigrants, and single heterosexual women who feel more comfortable residing in neighborhoods where gay men predominate. On the map, it's shaped like a tommy gun, its muzzle poking Hollywood in the gut, a reminder of the town's more freewheeling and lawless days, when bootleg whiskey and prostitution were the chief attractions and gangsters like Bugsy Siegel and Mickey Cohen ruled the Sunset Strip.

That fabled section of Sunset Boulevard still thrives, although the denizens these days tend to be club-hopping straight kids and youthful Hollywood glitterati, at least when the clock is closer to midnight than noon, and most of the tourists and well-heeled lunchtime ladies have abandoned the Strip to a younger crowd immersed in a heady brew of music, booze, drugs, and sex. Down the hill, along Santa Monica Boulevard, lies bustling Boys Town, the heart of the city's gay night life, where all of the men and most of the women are assumed to be queer unless there's strong evidence to the contrary, and condoms are dispensed with HIV tests along the sidewalk, while the midnight hour transforms certain dance floors into throbbing cauldrons of crystal-driven sensuality and foreplay. There are families throughout the city, to be sure, and thousands of retired folks on fixed incomes, and blue-collar working people who stay because of apartments subsidized for low incomes or still protected by rent control, but they tend to be less visible, or at least less noticed. West Hollywood is the kind of community outsiders like to call colorful, a place where fantasies come to life, dreams are bought and sold, and the streets are filled with hungry souls looking for an identity, an opportunity, a connection. More than most cities, WeHo attracts the bored and the lonely, restless dreamers, men and women looking for something different, or someone, to make them feel alive and less alone, if only for the night. It's a seductive mix of lust, culture, and commercialism, where surface trumps substance and longing and temptation permeate the air.

Secrets never die. That's what Harry Brofsky, my old newspaper editor, gone for years now, told me once. *Secrets never die. They lie buried and dormant, waiting for someone to dig around beneath the surface, deeply enough to stir them back to life.*

I came here roughly fifteen years ago, loathing the place. I detested WeHo's fake glitz and glamour, its frantic, artificial fun, its accent on image and superficiality, where youth and looks and fashion were displayed and worshipped with such fervor, and still are. I came because I'd fallen in love with someone who lived here, a gentle, joyous man with a poet's soul named Jacques, who embraced all those things I despised in his sweet and cockeyed way while I improbably loved him. Long after death had taken him I remained, residing in the modest garage apartment where he'd spent his final days, haunted by his memory but clinging desperately to it at the same time, unwilling to move on. Year after year, I fretted about getting out, hitting the road, finding a place more suited to my reclusive and melancholy nature, a place where I didn't feel so alien and out of sorts, or at least where I might be left alone.

Secrets cast a spell, Harry told me. *Long after they should have crumbled to dust and blown away they whisper to us, demanding to be heard.*

Why do we settle and stay in the places that we do? What is it that draws us to a particular city or neighborhood and holds us there, year after year, often for a lifetime? Why is it that so many of us keep telling ourselves we need to get out, go somewhere else, make a fresh start, but never seem to?

For years I pondered questions like these, as I entered my forties and began to count more years behind me than ahead, concerned that I still lived in a place where so much had gone so wrong for me in so many ways. I had history here, but much of it was ugly and shameful, the kind that follows you like a shadow down through time, along the rough, uneven streets of your life, no matter how many corners you turn, trying to lose whatever's chasing you.

I kept running but going nowhere, sensing that persistent shadow, until I turned an unexpected corner and faced a series of violent events that caused me to see the city in a different light. Or maybe it was me I was seeing differently, refracted through a prism in which the past illuminated the present, shining its light into the heart of a troubled young man accused of murder who reminded me so much of myself, and thus casting its light into the darkest corners of my own soul.

Secrets have a life, Harry Brofsky told me. *They live and breathe and grow, like creatures underground. Only they don't die. They never die. Our pasts are like cemeteries of the undead,* he said, *filled with buried secrets.*

ONE

On a Saturday, the first of May, a man named Bruce Bibby was murdered in his apartment on North Flores Street.

Neither Alexandra Templeton nor I was aware of this as we met the next morning for brunch at La Conversation, a charming corner café on North Doheny Drive, roughly a mile west of the crime scene. It was a balmy, pleasant day in West Hollywood, the kind that's good for forgetting one's troubles, which dovetailed nicely into our intentions. It was certainly not a day for discussing murder—*anyone's* murder—if you could help it, so we didn't. Instead, we tiptoed carefully around the land mines of our lives, looking for safe paths to lighter subject matter.

"Things are getting better," Templeton said, after I'd inquired how she was feeling without really wanting an honest answer. "Day by day, I'm getting my footing again." She smiled in that rigorously reinforced way that people do when they're faking it. "Thanks for asking."

We'd taken a sidewalk table in the shade of an umbrella, our usual study in contrasts: a fashionably dressed black woman of thirty-three, statuesque and with regal bearing, but without the spark and sparkle that had animated her striking face and dark eyes in earlier years; and an unglamorous white man twelve years her senior, with no fashion sense whatsoever, a fringe of blond hair around his bald spot, and some recently regained muscle on his six-foot frame. We'd tried to convince ourselves that we had no more on our minds than Templeton's hunt for a new home somewhere in West Hollywood; she had her eye on the historic Lloyd Wright house just up the street, a miniature architectural gem that was on the market for about a million dollars. But as we sipped our espressos and munched our fresh pumpkin muffins, each of us was aware that just below the surface of the other lay a vulnerability too fragile to be exposed; it was our shared secret, a special knowledge about each other that bound us while also keeping us apart, because getting any closer might rub open and make raw the wounds again.

Without asking, Templeton passed me the little pot of fruit jam, knowing how much I liked it after all the breakfasts we'd shared. "I hope to find a place soon," she said. "Before the end of summer, anyway. I'm really looking forward to moving. I'm prepared to rent if I don't find something I want to buy."

"Be patient, Templeton. Some things you can't rush."

"Funny, isn't it?"

"What's that?"

"You—advising *me* to be patient. It used to be the other way around, remember?"

I smiled mildly. "I've got an advantage now—forty milligrams of Prozac."

"It seems to be working. I haven't heard you ranting and raving since Christmas."

"I always rant and rave at Christmas, you know that. All that holiday cheer—it's enough to drive any sane man crazy."

Her old smile came back, the real one, which was good to see. "You haven't punched anyone, either," she said. "At least not that I'm aware of."

I feigned a couple of jabs in her direction. "I miss that part, but I suppose it's for the best. I'm getting too old for the rough stuff."

She laughed a little, which was like wonderful music, since I heard it so seldom these days. Then she glanced around the corner and up the street. "I think I'll like it here, Justice. If nothing else, I'll be closer to you." Her eyes slid cautiously in my direction. "That won't bother you, will it? Having me around so much?"

"Not at all." I winked. "You can take me out to eat more often, with that convenient gold card of yours."

Our breakfasts arrived—a fresh fruit plate with yogurt for Tem-

6

pleton, a big bowl of almond-and-raisin oatmeal for me, with heaps of golden brown sugar—and we basked in the friendly and civilized atmosphere for which La Conversation was known to locals in this end of town. Nearby, the actor Leonardo DiCaprio chatted with pals over plates heaped with Kugoloff French toast and Belgian waffles, while dogs lolled in the shade of nearby tables; inside, the actress Sharon Stone sipped sparkling water with two sturdy-looking female friends whose hair was as short-cropped as hers, while Nubia, the patient waitress, took their order; a number of older faces about the place looked vaguely familiar—either performers whose celebrity had faded or agents and executive types who didn't register all that high on the power scale. It was an "industry" crowd—at least partially—but with a neighborly feel; despite some high profiles, one's privacy here generally went undisturbed, safe from rude fans, paparazzi, and prying eyes, which were part of the landscape in other quarters of the city.

Maybe it was the proximity to genteel Beverly Hills that made the difference. The little café sat beneath towering palms at the westernmost edge of West Hollywood, looking across North Doheny Drive, where the zip code suddenly changed from 90069 to 90210, and the property values doubled, before escalating to even more ridiculous heights with the rising hills and spectacular views, where mansions sometimes sold for tens of millions of dollars. Doheny Drive was the demarcation line between the two cities, between the fashionably comfortable and the filthy rich. From our table, we could watch the pretty people jogging toward the nearby park or walking their pampered dogs or whizzing by in their convertible Mercedes and Beemers with the tops down, their well-tanned faces promising no shortage of business for the dermatologists and cosmetic surgeons who plied their trade so profitably along the avenues that intersected Rodeo Drive a mile west.

Templeton had money herself, of course, which she enjoyed without flaunting. Or at least she *came* from money—a corporate attorney father who made sure his only child had everything she might want or need—supplemented by a decent salary as a first-rate reporter for the *Los Angeles Times*. But money doesn't buy happiness, as the saying goes, and in that respect, lately, Templeton had been painfully impoverished. Not quite six months earlier, she'd lost her fiancé, Joe

Soto, in a diabolical murder plot that had engulfed us both, leaving Templeton bereft and me mutilated and missing my left eye, with a prosthetic one in its place, and deeper emotional wounds that hadn't healed as easily. Templeton's vehicle for recovery had been a hiatus from work, a grief support group, and the embrace of her loving parents. Never one for groups, and with no living relations that I knew of, I'd opted for a monthly therapy session provided by the nonprofit Shanti and a potent daily dose of Prozac covered by my medical plan. Thanks to the popular antidepressant, nothing much bothered me anymore; I was one of those fortunate souls for whom the drug worked, rather than the smaller percentage who reacted badly to it—some very badly, if the news reports were true. Prozac had eliminated my emotional highs and lows, as it was intended to do; I existed now somewhere in the tranquil middle, able to deal with setbacks and crisis in a calm and rational manner, which was new for me.

"I enjoy the beach," Templeton went on, with that slightly distant air she'd taken on for self-protection, even after Joe Soto's murder and the horrific events surrounding it had been sorted out and solved. "But Santa Monica's become saturated with twenty- and thirtysomethings desperate to entertain themselves between six in the evening and two A.M. Clubs, clothes, being seen—their existence seems to revolve around it. God, what a waste of time and energy."

"West Hollywood's not exactly a sleepy village," I reminded her. "And you shouldn't expect any less emphasis on the trendy and meaningless."

"No, but it's got its pockets of quiet and taste. I also like the fact that you can walk here. You can be out on the street and run into friends and neighbors and actually know their names." She glanced around again, first toward busy Santa Monica Boulevard to the south, then up toward Sunset Boulevard to the north. "You have everything you need within a few blocks." Her brown eyes, softened a bit by mischief, found my blue ones. "They do allow African Americans to rent and buy here, don't they? The neighborhood's not exactly swarming with black folks."

"In West Hollywood," I said, "green is the only color that matters. And you've certainly got plenty of that."

Her face clouded over. "I want this move to work, Justice. I need some new scenery, some new friends. I'm not too proud to admit

8

that." She reached across, took my hand. "And being closer to the friends I already have, the ones who matter."

"You used to have plenty of girlfriends for company."

"Most of them are married, or have moved away. It's different now." She didn't say it, but we both knew what she was thinking: *Joe was my company, my soul mate, my future, and he's gone. Somehow, I have to fill that void, rebuild, and move forward.* She squeezed my hand tighter. "You're sure you don't mind—my encroaching like this?"

"I think we can find room for you." I raised my glass of fresh-squeezed orange juice in a toast, unwilling to tell her that it would take more than a new residence and zip code to put behind her a murder that was wedged so deeply in her psyche and so close to her heart. An agreeable toast, a bland smile—and my dependable Prozac coursing through my system—and we'd glided easily past that uncomfortable subject. Even when Templeton mentioned that she was thinking of making a career move from newspaper work into local TV news, I reacted with diffidence and detachment.

"If you're dead set on turning yourself into a pretty talking head," I said, smiling amiably, "who am I to argue? You've certainly got the looks. Might as well exploit them."

She raised her chin defensively. "I'd continue to work as a serious reporter. That would still be my top priority."

"Of course you would, Templeton. When you weren't spending time on your hair, wardrobe, and makeup, and fighting for that extra fifteen seconds of airtime to flesh out your story with all the nuance and complexity it deserved."

She showed me the tip of her tongue, I grinned, and we cleaned our bowls, finishing off with another order of espressos to fuel us on our way. When our waiter arrived with the check, I directed it to Templeton. Like so many West Hollywood waiters, he was easy on the eyes—slim and doe-eyed, with dark, Italian looks, probably an actor or a wannabe—the kind of man I would have homed in on like radar in the old days, when I'd still had the urge. My manner now was polite but disinterested, even though he had that puppyish quality so many younger waiters exude, as if they're ready to lick your hand and follow you home. It had been a while since anyone had followed me home, or I'd tried to follow them. Thanks to my Prozac, my libido had gone south for the season.

When the waiter had left with Templeton's credit card, she said carefully, "He was very pretty, Justice. You didn't even give him a second look."

"I doubt that he'd fall for a washed-up reporter who's facing middle age, with a receding hairline and bank account." Although I had a contract to write my autobiography, I desperately needed short-term work to see me through the next few months, until I could complete the first draft and collect the next portion of my advance from the publisher. My health insurance had only covered part of my recent medical bills—the surgery to remove my damaged eye and the prosthetic that replaced it—and I was seriously broke. The problem was the Prozac again; while stabilizing me mentally, it had dulled my creative drive, just as my therapist had warned me it might. Months had passed with nothing to show in the way of a manuscript except a few chapters of lifeless prose. My deadline was less than a year away, and it had occurred to me that I might never get the book written at all. Finding work, even temporarily, wasn't easy for a guy like me. I wasn't just a washed-up reporter but a ruined one—Benjamin Justice, the notorious reporter who'd won the Pulitzer Prize for a series of articles he'd fabricated, before being exposed and forced to give it back, resigned to a life of infamy and shame. It was an old story I was tired of repeating, but if a publisher was willing to pay me a decent advance to tell it again, why not? Now I just had to get the damned thing written.

"Anyway, I'm HIV-positive," I said, still on the subject of the dreamy waiter. "Not the best calling card, is it?" I swallowed my morning meds with water and offered Templeton a carefree Prozac shrug. "Probably just as well. Getting romantically involved always seems to get me into trouble."

Just then, our handsome waiter returned. He handed Templeton a tray with the check and a receipt, which she signed. He had beautiful, fine-boned hands—I'd always had a thing for hands and forearms—accentuated with delicate, dark hairs that looked like the finishing strokes of a master painter. Just as quickly as I noticed I glanced away, unable to feel or register anything deeper. Templeton thanked him, and he departed, but not before finding my eyes, just long enough to deliver a silent message in that secret language known only to homosexual men. Templeton slipped her credit card into her wallet, watching him go.

"You see, you've still got it," she said. "Even with your bald spot."

"He probably mistook me for Bruce Willis."

"I think he's interested, Justice. I really do."

"There must be something seriously wrong with him then." I stood, cranking up my smile. "Shall we go house-hunting? See if we can find a palace worthy of L.A.'s top crime reporter?"

She stood, grabbing her handbag. "I put my condo on the market, by the way. I've got it priced to sell."

"You are serious about moving, aren't you?"

She nodded. "I'm looking at rentals, just to be safe." She smiled at the actor Robert Duvall, who was coming out the door with his younger wife, who carried a bag of La Conversation's popular pastries. Duvall, ever the courtly gentleman, dipped his head slightly in return.

"Thank goodness he's married," Templeton said, watching him go. "Or else I'd probably make a fool of myself."

I took that as a positive sign, but said nothing. Templeton slipped her arm through mine, and we strolled up Doheny in the direction of Sunset Boulevard.

During the night, showers had cleansed the air and left the streets sparkling. Bells clanged from the tower of the First Baptist Church up on Cynthia Street, where Templeton had attended the early service. White clouds scudded across a sky of vivid blue. It was a perfect Sunday morning for a walk with a good friend, the kind that lulls you into feeling that life is good and all's right with the world.

Halfway up the hill, we stopped for a look at the tiny but fascinating Lloyd Wright House at the corner of North Doheny Drive and Vista Grande Street, one of twelve buildings within the city listed on the National Register of Historic Places. Built in 1923 of precast concrete block and now covered largely with vines, the two-story home incorporated touches of art deco and Mayan, blending the primitive and the futuristic. Inside, its most distinct feature was a great hall—surprising in so small a dwelling—with an impressive fireplace and hearth fashioned out of the raw concrete.

"Interesting, but too stark," Templeton whispered, as the agent stood discreetly at a distance. "I need more warmth and charm."

"Don't be so hard on yourself, Alex."

She slapped lightly at me, laughing a little. "I'm talking about the place I'm going to live in, and you know it."

We thanked the agent, made our way out of the famous home, and retraced our steps one block to Norma Place, where we turned east into the heart of the Norma Triangle, a small area formed by the angles of its bordering streets. The leaves were damp, and puddles glistened at the curbs. Neighbors were out walking their dogs, which sniffed wildly at the fresh odors; the males repeatedly lifted their hind legs, anxious to leave new scents, marking their territory. Mourning doves were all about, nesting in the thorny bougainvillea and under the eaves of houses; we could hear their cooing and the musical flutter of their wings as they brought twigs and pieces of string to meticulously build nests in places they hoped would be safe. Squirrels chattered at us from tree limbs as we passed, and all along the street jacaranda blossoms drifted down like lavender snowflakes, carpeting the lawns and pavement.

"It's a good time of the year to go house-hunting," Templeton said. "A time for growth, for renewal."

Every so often, we came upon a FOR SALE sign, and once or twice Templeton paused to scribble the address in a notebook. We meandered past cozy houses that had gone up early in the last century, when the local farms and ranches were being carved into small lots as the movie industry burgeoned, and housing was in sudden demand. West Hollywood had been part of Los Angeles County then, a remote and unincorporated railway town called Sherman that was often overlooked or ignored by sheriff's deputies, allowing it to develop a reputation for vice and other lawlessness. Even after WeHo had become an independent city in 1984, forged by a coalition of renters, seniors, Jews, and gays, its reputation as a contrary and iconoclastic community had survived. The politics were liberal, strong on social services and renters' rights, with a bent toward diversity, self-expression, and personal freedom. Even if the cost of life here excluded most people of color, the shade of Templeton's skin would barely draw a second glance, as it might in some of the sniffier suburbs.

"I've always liked Norma Place," she said, studying one of the quaint Craftsman bungalows that had started appearing after 1910. Designed for comfort, efficiency, and affordability, they featured porches, big windows, and plentiful garden space, with long driveways and detached garages, fusing nature with more modern living. Here and there, we passed larger, more contemporary homes—imposing, impersonal structures that had recently replaced the tear-downs—but not many. My landlords, Maurice and Fred, had purchased their Craftsman on this street in the 1950s for ninety-nine hundred dollars. Today, with its garage apartment in back, where I stayed, it was worth close to a million.

"It's such a lovely street," Templeton went on, "so quiet and neighborly. And you're here, and Maurice and Fred. Who knows? Maybe I'll find something nearby."

I understood Templeton's need to put the past behind her, to move on as soon as possible. But I also knew how difficult it could be, how rarely it happened quickly, and sometimes not at all. "Take your time," I said, as gently as possible. "Somewhere, down one of these streets, just the right place is waiting for you."

She took my hand as we sauntered along the bumpy sidewalk, where the roots of older trees pushed up through the concrete, forcing cracks, tilting the slabs, the way they did here and there around the city. One had to be careful to avoid tripping, so we stepped carefully over and around them. A minor inconvenience, I thought, on a balmy spring morning when everything looked green and fresh, and promise was in the air.

Really, things couldn't have been more pleasant.

TWO

"Benjamin, thank goodness you're back!"

Maurice dashed from the house and down the walk as we approached, clad in his usual Sunday morning kimono and open-toed rubber sandals. His long, white hair was drawn back and secured by a lavender silk scarf into a ponytail, and he looked freshly shaved, showered, and powdered. All around us, his well-tended flower beds were heavy with buds, while several wind chimes draped the gnarly limb of a California oak. Through the open windows, we could hear the grandiosity of *La Boheme*, complete with scratches on the old vinyl LP. As Maurice got closer, the faint scent of French cologne came with him, and an array of bracelets jingled on his slender wrists.

"If you hadn't returned just now," he went on, his hands fluttering like a butterfly's wings, "I swear, Fred and I were going to go out searching."

"Take it easy, Maurice. What's going on?"

"Something you badly need, Benjamin—possible employment!" Maurice took my elbow and turned me toward the house. "But we need to move quickly, get you in the door while it's still open. They'll be meeting about it in City Hall tomorrow, but I think you should talk to one or two people today, the ones who really count. I've already called Cecelia Cortez, the city's director of publications, and put in a good word. It's just temporary, but it could lead to more work, possibly something steady." Maurice paused, looking aghast as he glanced back at Templeton, who followed us up the walk. "Forgive me, Alexandra. I'm such a rude old man!" He left me to embrace her, kissing her lavishly on the cheek. "It's just that this opportunity sounds so perfect for our boy, just what he needs to bring in a little money and get back on track in the working world, while he finishes up his book."

"So he can start taking *me* to breakfast," Templeton said, feigning resentment.

"And catch up on his rent," Maurice added, teasing me with a playful eye. "Come inside, dear ones, and I'll tell you all about it."

Templeton begged off, saying she had an appointment with another real estate broker, to look at homes south of Melrose Avenue, below designer row. She was anxious to get there early and spend some time alone getting a feel for the neighborhood.

Maurice clasped his pale hands theatrically, clutching them to his chest. "Could you spare just a few minutes, Alexandra? I believe this might interest you as well—in the professional sense."

Templeton perked up. "Something newsworthy?"

"I do believe it qualifies, because of a certain individual who's involved—and the awfully sad circumstances."

The record finished playing, and the turntable shut down as Maurice herded us up the steps of the house, past cats lounging behind the porch rails or up on the swing. Just before we entered, he stepped past us, cupping his hands to his mouth and calling ahead. "Fred! Company approaching, lady included. Cover your big, furry body, sweetheart!" Maurice glanced back, lowering his voice. "Fred's in his old boxers, the ones with the rip in the back that he won't let me fix—says he likes the fresh air back there. Not a sight that company should be subjected to." He rolled his eyes dramatically. "That man! I gave up trying to civilize him decades ago."

"You mentioned a particular individual, Maurice," Templeton said. "Who exactly is involved?"

"Does the name Bruce Bibby mean anything to you?"

"Rings a bell," Templeton said. "Can't place it, though."

We stepped across the threshold, into a living room crammed with kitsch and photographs, most of them of close friends, living and dead, whom Maurice and Fred had made during their forty-odd years as a couple. They'd spent most of those years together in this two-bedroom Craftsman, which smelled faintly musty, the air further laden with the musky aroma of incense that Maurice burned on occasion. In the kitchen, remnants of a pancake-and-egg breakfast littered a dining table, along with sections of the Sunday *L.A. Times*. Fred appeared from the hallway, a burly man nearing eighty, tucking a T-shirt into the size thirty-six waistband of his trousers. We greeted each other in an affectionate but perfunctory fashion—Fred was a man of few words—before he turned into the kitchen to begin cleaning up.

Maurice sat Templeton and me on the sofa and took a rocker facing us, while he directed his attention at her. "Bruce Bibby—adorable child, had a part for several years in that television series *Those Crazy Carltons,* back in the late seventies. Cute program, if you like those saccharine family sitcoms, where all of life's problems can be taken care of with a pat solution and a group hug at the end." Maurice shrugged apologetically. "I've always been partial to them myself."

"I vaguely recall the show in reruns," Templeton said.

Two of the cats wandered in, jumping up on the couch in synchronized motion before parting ways to settle into our separate laps.

"Bruce Bibby never worked much as an actor after *Those Crazy Carltons* went off the air in the early eighties," Maurice went on. "Appeared on *Hollywood Squares* and made a few guest appearances on *Murder, She Wrote* over the years, but that was about it. Got into drugs along the way, then a terrible automobile accident about ten years ago. As I recall, he lost control of his car and went into a ditch. Wasn't wearing a seat belt, poor lad. Ended up in a wheelchair, paralyzed from the waist down."

I sat back, scratching a cat between the ears. "This is all very interesting, Maurice. But what's it got to do with me finding work?"

"After his accident, Bruce Bibby took up writing. He also had a keen interest in history and research. He settled here in West Hollywood, made some friends, eventually started getting freelance assignments at City Hall, working on special projects. His great love was West Hollywood history—so much so that he became our unofficial archivist, taking over for someone who was getting on in years. I understand his apartment is crammed floor to ceiling with photos, documents, and memorabilia."

I raised my hands, smiling affably. "About the job, Maurice?"

"Charming young man, by the way." Maurice's incessant chatter had begun to sound like deliberate procrastination. "I first met him as a volunteer at a city function, not more than a year ago. He seemed to have gotten his life back on the straight and narrow." Maurice smiled impishly. "Well, not necessarily straight. My impression was that he was as queer as most of the men employed at City Hall. Nice-looking young man, very personable."

I nudged the cat from my lap and sat forward. "Maurice, what about the job?" I tapped my watch. "You said that time is of the essence."

At that moment, a grandfather clock in the house struck the hour of noon, as if to underscore my complaint. That seemed to get Maurice's attention, because he said quickly, "Bruce Bibby was researching and writing some brochures connected to the city's twentieth anniversary this year. He'd completed all but one, which is due in a few weeks. It had to do with local landmark protection. West Hollywood's Historic Preservation Plan has been hailed as a model for other cities. Because of my interest, I was somewhat involved, helping to point Bruce to the right places and the right people." Maurice grimaced. "I'm afraid he won't be able to finish this last brochure, which may provide an opportunity for you, Benjamin."

"They fired him for some reason?"

Maurice drew in a deep breath, looking pained. "A friend found Bruce dead in his apartment late last night. Over on North Flores Street. Just thirty-four years old! Can you imagine?" Maurice shook his head, and I saw tears welling in his rheumy eyes. "He had so much ahead of him, that boy. It's so terribly, terribly sad."

Templeton was opening her purse, pulling out her reporter's notebook. Bruce Bibby might not have been a big star by Hollywood standards, but he'd had a run on TV, which made his passing at such a young age worth at least a short news piece in the morning *L.A. Times*. "Bibby died?" she asked. "From complications of his paralysis?"

"I'm afraid it's not that simple." Maurice swiped at a tear. "Oh, my, this is so distressing." He stared at the hardwood floor for a long moment before looking up; his tears spilled over, streaking his wrinkled face. "Why would someone want to kill a nice young man like Bruce Bibby?"

"It was homicide," I said.

His voice trembled. "I'm afraid so."

"More specifically, murder. Is that what you're suggesting?"

Maurice covered his face and began to weep audibly. Fred came from the kitchen without a word, handing Maurice a tissue and standing over him with a meaty hand on his partner's narrow shoulder. Maurice dabbed at his eyes, blew his nose, and patted Fred's hand tenderly, glancing up with a grateful smile. Before he spoke again, he pulled himself up with a sense of strength and composure, as he tended to do when his softer emotions had given way to indignity. His words came crisply now, etched with anger.

"Yes, Benjamin, that's exactly what I'm suggesting. Someone wanted Bruce Bibby dead, so they murdered him. Someone took the life of an innocent young man, and I hope whoever did it rots in hell."

THREE

Shortly after nine the next morning I began reading Templeton's account of Bruce Bibby's death in the *L.A. Times,* while taking my caffeine at Tribal Grounds down on Santa Monica Boulevard.

At a nearby table, a male cast member from TV's *Queer as Folk* shared a Danish and coffee with one of the boys from *Queer Eye for the Straight Guy,* and by the moony looks in their sleepy eyes, I guessed they'd just crawled out of bed together. As I scanned Templeton's six paragraphs, it became quickly apparent that Maurice had added a touch more drama to the story than it perhaps deserved. Judging by the brief article, the sinister intent and premeditation Maurice had suggested the previous day—*someone wanted Bruce Bibby dead, so they murdered him*—seemed at least an exaggeration.

Former Child TV Star
Found Beaten to Death

Bruce Bibby, a former child actor who costarred in the CBS series *Those Crazy Carltons* from 1978 to 1984, was found dead in his West Hollywood apartment early Sunday morning, the apparent victim of a homicide, according to sheriff's deputies.

Bibby, 34, had suffered a blow to the head from a blunt instrument, possibly after surprising a burglar, investigators said, although there were no signs of forced entry.

According to authorities, computer equipment was missing from the first-floor apartment where Bibby had resided since an automobile accident a decade ago left him paralyzed from the waist down and dependent on a wheelchair for mobility.

Bibby, who lived alone at the time of his death, appeared in several TV guest roles after the cancellation of *Those Crazy Carltons* in 1984, but was unable to sustain an acting career, according to a 1992 interview in *People* magazine.

The former actor later overcame a drug habit and had worked in recent years as a freelance researcher and writer for West Hollywood, while serving as the city's unofficial historian and archivist.

According to the sheriff's department, Bibby's death was the first murder this year in West Hollywood, which has been experiencing one of its lowest rates of violent crime in many years.

Selfishly, I felt some relief in this new version of the incident. If I were going to replace Bibby as a researcher and writer, or at least be considered for the job, I wasn't keen on coming in with a murder investigation under way. I'd been involved in enough of those as a crime reporter and, later, as an unwelcome snoop, which had kept my name in news stories long after I'd ached for anonymity. Now, with a 10 A.M. job interview at City Hall, I found the notion that Bruce Bibby had died at the hands of a common thief an odd blessing. At this point, I had two clear goals in mind, to help me get my life back on track: land this assignment with the city so that I might pay some bills and pave the way for future work, and complete my autobiography and collect the remainder of my advance. The last thing I needed was a complicated murder mystery hovering over my efforts or presenting a distraction, which made me thankful that Bruce Bibby's death fell into a more routine category of crime.

Accompanying Templeton's news piece was a photograph of the victim from his *Hollywood Squares* period, probably the most recent file photo the *LAT* had on him. It was a standard Hollywood glossy, showing an attractive young man with curly hair on the lighter side, a winning smile, warm eyes, and scattered freckles in a pleasant, open face. Bibby's chin wasn't strong, but his cheeks were dimpled, which fit the appealing, boyish look. Studying the picture, I could see how the camera must have favored him in his early years, and how he must have stolen more than a few hearts as a child actor in a family sitcom. It was sad that he was gone so young, I thought, yet it literally happened every day in a county that registered nearly two thousand homicides a year, most of them in poorer minority neighborhoods, which got scant attention from the media. Since Bibby was a celebrity—never mind how minor—and video clips would be available to illustrate his middling career, his murder would no doubt serve as a lead story on the local evening TV newscasts, while the day's more mundane homicides went unmentioned. I could almost hear the afternoon promo: *Shocking murder claims life of beloved Hollywood actor! Killer remains on the loose! News at five!* I shuddered to think that this was where Templeton might be headed as a journalist, although I forgot about it just as quickly.

My mind now was on my job interview, and what it might mean to my future. I washed down my forty milligrams of Prozac with the last of my coffee and set out on the mile walk to City Hall, determined to make the most of an employment opportunity that might not come my way again soon, if ever.

West Hollywood City Hall occupied an ultramodern, three-story structure with lots of glass situated at the corner of Santa Monica Boulevard and Sweetzer Avenue. Stretching out on either side were cafés, hair salons, pet boutiques, and gay bars, interspersed with thrift and secondhand clothing stores catering heavily to young men who constantly rediscovered retro looks that triggered new fashion trends almost as fast as the last ones disappeared. I entered the lobby of City Hall, making my own retro fashion statement in pleated beige slacks, a white dress shirt, a navy blue blazer, and black penny loafers. The ensemble had somehow survived from my working days at the *L.A. Times*, through the drinking binges and lost years following Jacques's death and the Pulitzer scandal that had cost me my reputation and career.

When I met Cecelia Cortez, the city's director of publications, in her third-floor office, she quickly dispelled my concerns about my troubled past.

"Obviously, we're aware of your unusual background, Mr. Justice. I have some questions, but I don't really see it as a serious problem."

Mrs. Cortez sat behind a broad desk, putting aside a half-eaten bran muffin and dabbing at her red lips with a paper napkin. She was a large woman, dressed in a business suit of light gray with a rainbow lapel pin as an accessory, whose dark hair and eyes were in sharp contrast to her alabaster skin. By today's standards, she'd be judged much too plump, an ideal candidate for Weight Watchers or Jenny Craig. But put her back in the seventeenth century, I thought, exchange the bran muffin and business suit for a piece of luscious fruit and a carefully draped garment, and Rubens would have begged Cecelia Cortez to sit for a portrait, capturing a classic female form for the ages. As we talked, I noticed a small diamond on her ring finger and, on the credenza behind her, a framed family portrait in which she posed with her husband and three small children, all of them as well fed and pleasant looking as she was.

"Frankly," she went on, "under other circumstances, we might have second thoughts about hiring you, given how many qualified writers are looking for work. But the fact is we don't have time to post the job or search for other applicants. We need someone who can do thorough research, write fast, and handle the pressure of a tight deadline. From all accounts, your journalism experience makes you an ideal candidate."

I smiled thinly. "Up to a certain point, you mean."

"One mistake doesn't necessarily negate everything that went before, Mr. Justice."

"I appreciate the sentiment."

"We feel fortunate to find someone with your skills on such short notice." She informed me that Maurice—highly regarded for his extensive volunteer work and community activism—had given me a stellar recommendation. My checkered past was well known at City Hall, she said, but hadn't seriously raised eyebrows. West Hollywood was noted for its tolerance, she reminded me, as well as its tendency to give people with problematic pasts a second chance. Bruce Bibby himself had come with a history of drug addiction, she pointed out, and had never once caused anyone at City Hall to regret hiring him.

"We'll need you to turn in a first draft within three weeks," Mrs. Cortez said. "We want the brochure finished and ready for distribution prior to Gay Pride weekend in late June. I'm assuming you can start immediately."

I arched my eyebrows in surprise. "I'm hired?"

"I'm sorry. I thought I'd made that clear."

"I guess I didn't expect it to go so smoothly."

Her smile was supportive, while holding just a little back. "Let's hope it continues that way." She opened one of her chubby hands and extended it across the desk, the long points of her red nails leading the way. "Welcome to our family here at City Hall." A frown darkened her round face. "I just wish it wasn't under such tragic circumstances. We're a very tight-knit group here. Bruce's loss has been a blow to all of us."

She handed me some papers to fill out and sign, stood, and suggested she get me started on my assignment right away. I followed her from her office to an elevator, where she punched the DOWN button. While we waited, she told me that Bibby had worked at home, by choice, but that I'd be coming to City Hall each weekday, since I was new and would need special support as I got oriented to the job. All of Bibby's notes and research materials for the final brochure had been on his home computer, she said, which had been stolen during the burglary.

"He kept a backup copy on a CD," she went on, "but that was in his console when it was taken."

"So everything was lost? I'm starting from scratch?"

The elevator doors opened and we stepped in. "Fortunately, there was another backup system. Trang Nguyen, one of our systems managers, created it especially for Bruce, because his data was so extensive and because he worked at home." The doors closed, and she pushed a DOWN button. "Trang linked Bruce's home computer to our systems here at City Hall, so everything Bruce saved was backed up here."

"Smart move."

"It was Trang's idea. He's a very resourceful young man. You'll meet him soon enough."

Trang Nguyen's cubicle was located in the building's basement, where the City Hall communications systems were operated and maintained. As we entered, his back was to us as he worked furiously at a keyboard, deleting lines on his computer screen. I could see an entire block of highlighted text disappear as we approached.

"Excuse me, Trang," Cecelia Cortez said.

He quickly switched off the screen, which went dark, and jumped to his feet to face us. Nguyen appeared to be in his midtwenties, perhaps older, and was on the tall side for an Asian man—probably five-ten or five-eleven—with a lean, sleek look, unblemished tawny skin, and a face that seemed cut like a diamond. A swatch of thick black hair fell boyishly across his forehead, above dark eyes that regarded me keenly but gave little away. His beauty was striking, yet I found myself responding to it in a detached and cerebral way, as if I was gazing at a fine painting rather than a breathtaking man of flesh and blood.

"I'm sorry, Trang," Cecilia Cortez said. "I should have called ahead. We can come back later, if you're busy."

Nguyen's eyes darted in my direction, but only momentarily. "Is he the one who take over for Bruce?"

"Yes, this is Benjamin Justice. He'll need to have copies of Bruce's files."

"Fine. I take care of it." Nguyen spoke as if I wasn't there. His English was passable but chopped, suggesting emigration as a boy, probably with parents who continued to speak the native language. The accent was surely Vietnamese, I thought, like his name. "I have them ready in two, maybe three minute. I working on them now."

"It looked like you were deleting some of the text," I said.

"Because some things, maybe Bruce not want everybody to see. Private stuff."

"Perhaps the police might be interested in seeing all of it."

"I make copy for them earlier," Nguyen said sharply. "I do my job right."

"Trang and Bruce were good friends," Mrs. Cortez said to me. She laid a hand on Nguyen's arm. "We've told everyone to take whatever time they need, Trang. Perhaps you should take some time off. I know how close you and Bruce were."

"Maybe not so close." Nguyen's words were curt, almost cold. Mrs. Cortez smiled sympathetically as he turned away to sit at his computer again. His back remained to us while he spoke. "I copy the files to you when they ready."

Mrs. Cortez nodded in the direction of the door, and we left. When I glanced back, Trang Nguyen watched us warily, the computer screen still dark, waiting for us to be gone.

"Trang's a very private person," Cecelia Cortez told me, as she gave me a brief tour of City Hall. "Don't mistake his sense of privacy and dignity for rudeness. He's actually a very sweet man, and an excellent employee. He just keeps a lot to himself."

With the exception of the City Hall meeting rooms, each floor appeared to be a maze of offices and cubicles crammed into every inch of available space. Most of the cubicles were occupied, and employees occasionally looked up, but the atmosphere was generally subdued. Here and there, workers had gathered to huddle and talk; a few hugged and cried, and others sat alone, staring disconsolately into space. Mrs. Cortez apologized for not introducing me to people along the way.

"It's just too soon," she said. "People are still in shock. It's a bit awkward, replacing Bruce like this, only two days after his death."

"That might explain Trang's reaction to meeting me."

"I'm sure that's part of it, yes."

The cubicle I'd been assigned was a Spartan space on the second floor equipped with a PC, shelves, and file cabinets built in beneath the desktop. Thankfully, the cubicles on either side were unoccupied at the moment, allowing me some time before I had to begin the ordeal of smiling, shaking hands, and trying to remember names.

Mrs. Cortez picked up a handful of colorful brochures from the desk—the first four brochures that Bruce Bibby had produced over the past several months, with one remaining to be completed. Beginning in early February, she said, a new brochure had been introduced each month for four months, with the fifth and last one due out in early June, in time for the city's annual Gay Pride celebration later that month. That one—which now fell to me to complete—was to focus on the city's Historic Preservation Plan and its many historic sites and cultural resources protected by local, state, and national designation.

"We wanted these to be special," Mrs. Cortez said, handing the brochures to me. "This year is a true milestone in our history—November twenty-nine marks our twentieth anniversary as an independent city."

"You mentioned three weeks for a first draft." I glanced through the brochures, surprised by the density of the text and the plentiful graphics, all with detailed captions and some cross-referenced to illustrations on other pages. "That's not a lot of time."

"I'm afraid it's all we've got. You'll need to go through all of Bruce's data, deciding how you want to put the brochure together and write it up. At least your project will be heavy on photographs, which will save some writing time." She indicated the finished brochures with a nod. "You'll find that Bruce did a very professional job. The brochures also reflect his feeling for the city, both past and present. Naturally, we hope you'll continue in that same spirit. Do you know the city well?"

"I've lived here close to fifteen years."

"Wonderful! You must be very fond of West Hollywood then."

I smiled tightly. "If not, why would I still be here?"

She handed me a list of names, telephone extensions, and internal e-mail addresses of City Hall employees I'd be working with, and left me to study the brochures. Bibby had done a first-rate job, both in the writing and the selection of the illustrations. His eye for detail and passion for city history were obvious, and I realized that measuring up to the standards of the first four would be a challenge. He'd broken them down into four subject areas: First, the city's early history, as a rural railway stop called Sherman, when homes started appearing around the turn of the century to house railway workers, followed by the town's development as an adjunct to Hollywood, including the colorful Sunset Strip; second, the political movement of the early eighties, spearheaded by an alliance of gays and seniors, that had led to West Hollywood's city charter in 1984; third, the city's strong commitment to human rights and social services, especially for the elderly, gays, political refugees, and persons with HIV and AIDS; and fourth, West Hollywood's emergence as "The Creative

City," an important commercial, tourist, and cultural center for the new century. I thought I understood why they'd saved the subject of historical preservation for last, bridging as it did the past with the present, while looking to the future and planned architectural projects that might one day need landmark protection of their own.

"You must be Benjamin Justice."

The deep and mellifluous voice drew my attention toward the doorway, where a broad-shouldered man in a nicely tailored olive suit leaned against the frame like a smug Casanova in an *Esquire* fashion spread. He was a handsome guy with curly dark hair and lashes, solidly built, roughly my height, and a few years younger. It took me a moment to place the familiar face before I pegged him for Tony Mercury.

"I didn't realize the City Council would be giving me a personal welcome," I said.

He grinned, showing perfect teeth, and stepped forward, offering a big, well-manicured hand, which I shook. "I've taken a special interest in the work you'll be doing for us," he said. "I thought I'd drop around and give you my perspective on it."

Tony Mercury—born Odessa Mercouri—had been a successful porn star until a few years ago, known as the Greek Stallion for his dark good looks and prodigious male endowment. He'd also made a name for himself by pushing for safe sex in the gay adult film industry in the eighties and nineties, while the heterosexual segment of the trade had carried on pretty much as usual, leaving its performers ravaged by HIV, Hepatitis C, and other sexually transmitted diseases. Once Tony Mercury had insisted on condoms in all his films, it had become a staple in most gay porn flicks, while the straight hard-core trade had lagged foolishly behind until a recent HIV outbreak among straight performers had rocked the industry. Late in the game, as he faced forty and a decline in his lucrative career, Mercury had gone back to school, earned a law degree, then run for West Hollywood City Council, which could only be a boon to his budding law practice. A background as a well-hung porn star might not be a political asset in most cities, but West Hollywood wasn't like most cities. On his first try four years ago, Mercury had been among the top three .winning election, finishing behind a popular lesbian incumbent and

27

an eighty-six-year-old retired rabbi but far ahead of the rest of the pack. Currently running for reelection, Tony Mercury was considered a shoo-in for a new term.

He was standing over me, close enough that his muscular thigh was inches from my shoulder. "I see you're going through Bruce Bibby's brochures. He did nice work."

"More than nice—I'd say excellent."

"Although I'm not sure Bruce was the right person for this last brochure."

"Really?" I glanced at the first four. "I thought he was doing a terrific job."

Mercury lodged his butt on my desk, facing me at an angle. "Are you experienced with City Hall politics, Justice?"

"City Hall was never my beat when I was at the *L.A. Times,* if that's what you mean."

"Every city has its own brand of politics, its special issues. Historical preservation is a charged subject here in West Hollywood. Writing about it for the general public, as you'll be doing, needs a keen sense of objectivity."

"Something you feel Bibby lacked?"

Mercury briefly touched my shoulder. "Don't get me wrong. Bruce was a nice guy and good at his work. I'm just not sure he understood the need for a balance between preserving the old and building for the future. Especially here, where we have one of the highest density rates in the state, a huge social services budget, and a constant need for new development as a tax base."

"Meaning space is limited," I said, "and something's got to go."

Mercury laughed, squeezing my arm affectionately as only a porn-star-turned-politician might. "We should go to lunch soon, talk about it when we have more time." When I didn't say anything, he asked carefully, "Are you familiar with the Sherman cottages, Justice?"

"The old houses on Paul Monette Avenue, in the west end?" He nodded. "I've passed by them plenty of times, like everyone else. Always wondered why they were boarded up, looking so abandoned, given how valuable property is in this city."

Mercury sat back, folded his arms across his chest, and looked me in the eye. "The Sherman cottages are termite-infested shacks and public eyesores. They should have been torn down years ago, so we could use the land more productively."

"Perhaps I'll read about them in Bibby's research materials. I understand he was very thorough."

"I'm afraid all his files were lost in the burglary, including his backup copy. At least that's the scuttlebutt."

"Apparently, there was another backup made. I'm waiting for it now."

Mercury cocked his head in surprise. "You're getting a copy of his files?"

"So I've been told."

Strain crept into Mercury's voice and manner. "How fortunate." He tried to loosen his tight smile. "I guess that makes your work considerably easier, doesn't it?"

"It would seem to."

He glanced around, leaned closer, lowered his voice. "I don't mean to sound insensitive, Justice, given what's happened. But Bruce was a nostalgia queen—loved old movies, old clothes, old buildings, you know the type. He had a badly distorted view of the historical and architectural value of the Sherman cottages. I hope you'll take that into account as you do your work."

"He wanted them protected?"

"Bruce and a few others. A small group of vocal militants who object to the destruction of just about anything built prior to 1950. They'd get old outhouses listed on the National Register if they could. I've been concerned that they've been influencing Bruce unduly, that in his brochure he might give more weight to the Sherman cottages than they really deserve."

"Is this brochure really so important?"

"A copy goes to every resident of West Hollywood, and quite a few important people who live outside the city. For many, what you put in that brochure will be all they know about the issue of the Sherman cottages."

"You'd prefer they see the cottages as worthy fodder for the bulldozers," I said.

"I want them to see the cottages for what they are—insignificant relics hindering municipal progress."

"And if they get torn down, what goes up in their place?"

Before Mercury could answer, Trang Nguyen came through the door, clutching a CD in one hand. The moment he saw us, he pulled up, tension further tightening the lines of his angular face, while his dark eyes flickered distrustfully from Mercury to me.

"I bring you the files," Trang said, holding up the disc. He stepped over, keeping his eyes on Mercury as if he was a coiled rattlesnake, and placed it on my desk before quickly retreating.

"I thought you'd transfer them to me through the system," I said. "Wouldn't that have been easier?"

"You not signed on yet. I got nowhere to send them."

I shrugged. "Of course, I hadn't thought of that." I asked Trang if he could give me a quick tutorial, guide me through the system. "When it comes to computers, I'm afraid I'm still in the Dark Ages."

But Trang was already at the door, his eyes still on Mercury. "I come back later, help you then."

"It's all right, Trang," Mercury said stiffly. "I was just leaving."

As he moved toward the door, Trang backed through it. "No, I come back." An instant after that, he was gone.

"Jumpy kid," Mercury said, underplaying it, while he stared at the empty doorway.

"From what I hear, he's smart as a whip. He certainly was wise to create a backup system for Bibby, wasn't he? Otherwise, all Bibby's notes and research would have been lost."

Mercury continued staring into the corridor, as if he hadn't heard me. Briefly, he glanced in my direction. "I'll get back to you about lunch. Give you my view of things."

"You've done a pretty good job of that already."

Mercury's smile was as slick and sweet as flavored lubricant. "Then I guess we'll have more time to socialize, won't we?"

He let his suggestive eyes linger a moment, then turned quickly in the direction Trang Nguyen had fled moments before, as if giving chase.

By the end of the day, Trang Nguyen had familiarized me with the city's computer system, to which I had limited access tailored to the special needs of my assignment. He remained cool and distant through my tutorial, as if he wanted as little contact with me as possible, physically and otherwise. Only once did he broach anything personal, when he asked if Tony Mercury and I were friends. When I told him no, that we'd just met, he seemed to relax a little, though not much.

At 5:00 P.M. sharp, most of those who still remained in City Hall left nearly en masse, ending a day that had started for them at 8:00 A.M. I could hear them emptying from the spaces around me and shuffling down the corridor. Cecilia Cortez stopped by to tell me I should go home. When I suggested working late because of my looming deadline, she laughed.

"We want you to do a good job and get it done on time, Benjamin. But we aren't a sweat shop. If necessary, we'll reconsider your working hours as you get closer to your due date."

By the time I packed up to go home, the building was nearly empty. On my way out, I became lost in the confusing maze of corridors and cubicles, my sense of direction completely undone. I found myself in a strange hallway and was about to turn back when I heard voices from an open office door down the hall, and moved that way instead, intent on asking directions.

As I approached, I heard what first struck me as a man's voice, the timbre husky, the cadence terse and forceful.

"It's safe to say, then, that you and Bruce Bibby were not on the best of terms. Is that correct, Mr. Mercury?"

Tony Mercury looked up from behind his desk as I appeared in his doorway. His mouth was set firmly without a smile, and his arms were folded like armor across his deep chest. Across from him sat a trim woman in a dark, no-nonsense business suit, her hair cropped short and severe, her makeup minimal, her speech and manner on the curt side. I put her age around forty; the gray streaks in her hair struck me as premature. Displayed at her waist was a Los Angeles County Sheriff's Department detective's shield. She glanced up and kept her eyes on my face, as if she might know who I was.

"I beg your pardon," I said to Mercury. "I got lost, wondered if you could point the way out."

The detective rose before Mercury could speak, grabbing a

strapped bag from the floor. She slung it over one shoulder, while turning to face me. "You're Benjamin Justice, aren't you?" I nodded, accustomed to people recognizing my name and face, and linking them to my notorious past. "You have business here in City Hall, Mr. Justice?"

"I'm filling in for Bruce Bibby, finishing up his work."

"How interesting." She glanced at Mercury, then back to me. "Mr. Mercury and I are finished now. I'll walk you down." She extended a hand. "Detective Mira De Marco, sheriff's homicide. My partner and I are investigating Mr. Bibby's death. He's off chasing forensics at the moment."

"From what I gather, it's a case of a burglary gone bad."

Her tone was noncommittal. "That's possible."

I accompanied her down the hall until we found an EXIT sign, then an elevator. When it was clear that we were alone, she asked me if there was anything else I'd heard about Bruce Bibby's death.

"Not really," I said. "I don't have any interest in it, to be quite frank. I just want to do my work and collect a paycheck."

The elevator doors opened, and we stepped in. When they closed, she said, "While you're being so diligent, it's possible you might see or hear something."

I cocked my head curiously. "You think someone at City Hall might be involved?"

Her smile softened the sharp contours of her face. "You see, you're more interested in Mr. Bibby's death than you want to admit." When I said nothing, she continued. "You come with a history, Justice. You've been involved in some of the more fascinating murder investigations in Southern California. You have a way of finding them, don't you?"

"Sometimes they find me, Miss De Marco." I hadn't seen a ring. "It is Miss, isn't it?"

She ignored that and pressed on. "You're known as someone with exceptional skills of observation and deduction, going all the way back to your days as a reporter."

"Like I said, Detective, I just want to do my job here at City Hall."

"Keep your nose clean, get on with your life?"

"That about sums it up."

The elevator doors opened, and we stepped out.

"Still," she said, "I hope you'll call me if you come across anything that looks like it might be worth checking out." She opened her bag, found a wallet, and opened that; inside, as she removed a business card, I glimpsed a dog-eared, black-and-white photograph displayed in a clear plastic window. It was a head shot, a twentysomething man with crew-cut hair on the dark side and a stubbly, chiseled face, handsome in a tough sort of way. De Marco didn't strike me as a woman likely to carry a boyfriend's picture so prominently in her wallet, unless she was in the closet, using the photograph for cover; that didn't seem likely, because the sheriff's department regularly hired and even recruited gays and lesbians as deputies. On the other hand, trying to figure out who was gay and who was homosexually challenged these days was getting more difficult, and I'd guessed wrong on that score before. The guy in the snapshot might have been a younger brother, I thought; there was a slight resemblance, although the crew cut looked dated by a few decades. At any rate, the face of the stranger disappeared as the wallet was closed.

De Marco held out the business card, and I reluctantly took it. The front entrance was locked after hours so we crossed the lobby to the rear entrance on the building's south side. A security guard opened one of the glass doors, tipping his hat as we passed through and out to the parking lot, where De Marco asked if I needed a lift home.

"Thanks, but I like to walk. Part of my fitness routine."

"I'm a jogger myself." I kept my silence, so she said, "Have a nice evening then."

"You too, Detective."

De Marco turned toward her unmarked car, and I started the other way, in the direction of Sweetzer, which would connect me to Santa Monica Boulevard. Behind me, I heard her husky voice, calling my name. I turned to see her standing with her strong legs slightly spread and her feet planted firmly like a soccer goalie, her hands on her hips, striking a sturdy, athletic pose.

"I forgot to mention that we're narrowing in on a suspect," she said.

I took a step back toward her, almost as an involuntary reflex. "A suspect? No kidding?"

"But I don't imagine you're interested in that, are you? Keeping your nose clean, the way you are." Mira De Marco turned on her low heels and climbed into her car, while I cursed myself for taking her bait but chuckled with admiration for the way she'd played me.

On the walk home, I tried every trick in the book to think of something other than Bruce Bibby and how he died. Not a damn one worked.

FOUR

By noon the next day, I still hadn't made my way through all the notes, documents, and photos in Bruce Bibby's files, and I realized just how much work I had to do in such a short time.

Going over all of it and making sense of it was the first challenge. After that came the organization, writing, fact-checking, and polishing. I didn't care what the city's policy was about overtime; I intended to put in as many hours on the project as it took to meet my deadline and do it well, short of working myself to utter exhaustion and triggering a decline in my immune system, always risky for someone with HIV. It wasn't that I was a selfless, noble worker, devoted to my masters. On the contrary, my motives were purely selfish. For a guy like me, who had screwed up so much in his life, including his ability to make a living, this brief but forgiving freelance assignment was like a lifeline to a drowning man.

That work ethic didn't mean skipping meals, however—not yet, anyway—and when Alexandra Templeton called to invite me to join her for lunch up on the Strip, I accepted. She told me she was meeting Dr. Roderick Ford, a psychologist and university professor who specialized in genetic research into the criminally violent mind. This included neurological studies of the human brain that had generated controversy, less for their basis in science than in what the results might mean to standards of individual responsibility and the application of the law, should the research prove conclusively that certain individuals were genetically predisposed to predatory behavior. I recalled an interview Templeton had done with Dr. Ford a couple of years back, shortly after he'd joined the university. I also remembered her telling me that, although married, he was a flagrant womanizer, and her resistance to his advances had only spurred him on.

"So why are you meeting him for lunch?" I asked.

"He's got a fascinating angle on a current murder case, connected in some way to his research. Says he'll give me an exclusive if I promise him decent play in the paper. I told him no promises. But if it's as good as he says it is, that should be no problem."

"Which murder case are we talking about? There's no shortage of those in Lotus Land."

"He's being coy on the specifics, until we actually meet."

"Crafty old lecher, isn't he?"

"Not so old, Justice. About your age, actually. Quite attractive, too—if you like the George Clooney type."

"I seem to remember you drooling over Clooney once or twice."

"That's not why I'm meeting him, if that's what you're suggesting."

"Never crossed my mind, Templeton."

"I'm getting a chance to break the story, before he talks to the evening news shows. He says the piece has a nice visual element that will work well for TV. He's bringing photos no one else has seen. Says I can use those, too, before the TV people get hold of them."

It sounded to me like Dr. Roderick Ford was using Templeton in lieu of a publicist, getting his story out in a major newspaper where other media couldn't miss it. From the *L.A. Times* to the local news shows to the national network—it could hardly miss. It was no secret that every morning all the local TV news directors scanned the morning *L.A. Times,* looking for material for their afternoon and evening newscasts. Often, the local stations simply condensed what the *LAT* had printed, using little more than the headline information, supported with file footage and maybe—if they were really ambitious—a couple of sound bites and fresh footage grabbed by a field producer and camera crew on the run. In the world of serious journalism, most local TV news programming had become a sad joke, a troubling symptom of a culture that was becoming increasingly less literate, addicted to moving images, and satisfied with facile analysis and the quick sound bite, as long as there was something eye-catching to look at. The local news directors would no doubt respond to Dr. Ford's images like Pavlov's dogs, and Templeton had to know that.

"I'm not sure why you want me along," I said, mildly annoyed. "Won't I just get in the way?"

"I want this exclusive, Justice, but I don't want Dr. Ford putting his hand on my leg. Having you there should provide a buffer and force the horny professor to behave like a gentleman."

"You sure he'll want me there, privy to this scoop he's giving you?"

"I already told him you'd be joining us. He wasn't thrilled about it, but I didn't give him a choice. He knows all about you, by the way, from your past exploits. If he could, he'd probably like to have *your* brain for his research."

"If he's nice, I'll will it to the university."

"Half past twelve OK? Chin Chin, up at the Plaza?"

The thought of Chin Chin's shui mai and garlic tomato chicken already had me salivating. "My appetite and I will be there," I said, "as long as your credit card is there to meet us."

"Benjamin, I'd like you to meet Dr. Roderick Ford. Dr. Ford, Benjamin Justice."

Dr. Ford extended a hand but barely looked at me, and withdrew it almost before I could shake it. He and Templeton were sitting at one of the umbrella tables that were so popular out front, where Chin Chin's diners could sit in the polluted but rarefied air of Sunset Plaza, trying to look as chic and blasé about it as the fashionable patrons lodged outside the other cafés clustered along this tony section of Sunset Boulevard. Studying them, one might suspect that barriers had been erected at either end of the Plaza's three-block stretch, to keep everyone but the most beautiful people out. Not more than fifty feet from us, at the next bistro, the actress Salma Hayek was being seated with two male companions who had the fine suits, power ties, and self-important looks of agents or entertainment industry lawyers. Templeton craned her neck for a better view.

"God, I love her shoes," she said. "I'd kill to know where she got them."

"I'd kill for the money she paid for them," I said.

37

"You and plenty of others," Dr. Ford said, a bit pompously. "Which is why my work is so essential."

The first response that came to mind was: *Forgive me while I puke.* Instead, I said mildly, "Just a figure of speech, Professor."

"Yes, Justice, I realize it was a figure of speech." Dr. Ford's smile was half amusement, half condescension, and I realized he must have seen me as competition, or at least a nuisance. "I was just having a bit of fun with you."

I picked up the menu. "Mind if we order? I'm on a tight schedule."

"Justice has a freelance gig with the city," Templeton said.

"How interesting," Dr. Ford said, scanning the appetizers without another word. He took his time, so I spent a couple of minutes studying the street, where gangsters had once rubbed elbows with movie stars in legendary nightclubs like the Mocambo Room and the Café Trocadero. From the background material I'd scanned in Bruce Bibby's files, I'd learned that most of the structures in the Sunset Plaza district had been designed in the mid-1930s and since restored and rebuilt in their original Neoclassical, Regency, and Colonial Revival styles. The stately Ionic temple, shimmering white with its dramatic pillars and colonnades, served as the crown jewel, sitting directly across from us at the intersection of Sunset Plaza Drive.

"I believe I'm ready," Dr. Ford said, setting aside his menu as if he were the only one ordering. He was in his midforties, a good-looking guy with easygoing sex appeal who knew it. There were the strong jaw, the distinctive streaks of gray in his wavy hair, the crinkles at the corners of his clear brown eyes when he smiled in a self-deprecating way. Even when he began explaining his complicated research, he did it confidently and with command, as smoothly as a skilled actor working from a memorized script.

"During the nineteenth century, we knew very little about the criminal mind," Dr. Ford intoned, after we'd placed our orders. "People were bad or they were good, and the bad ones were punished. Or they were punished for making bad choices, when they might have made good choices. During the last century, we began to look more closely at the connection between heredity and behavior, with statistics our most powerful analytic tool. Still, we were operating virtually in the Dark Ages, relying on a good deal of theory and guesswork. Fortunately, that's changing."

"Molecular biology and neuroscience are revolutionizing the academic field of criminology," Templeton said, picking up his thread and showing off a little. "New technology, new techniques that were unheard of a few years ago."

Dr. Ford touched her wrist, before showing me his devilish smile. "This woman is as smart as she is attractive." He turned his attention back to Templeton, gazing at her with his crinkly George Clooney eyes. "Which is why she's the one who's going to deliver news of the most important scientific breakthrough yet regarding the link between genetics and predatory behavior."

Templeton withdrew her hand and switched on a recorder sitting next to her bottle of Evian water. "I'm all ears, Dr. Ford."

"There's a lot more to you than your ears, Alexandra."

"Let's stay with the ears for now, shall we? And the eyes—I believe you mentioned you had some illustrations?"

Dr. Ford talked as he opened a satchel and rummaged among numerous files and documents inside. "Fifty years after the discovery of DNA structure, scientists are now able to directly scrutinize the biological causes of human behavior. There's no doubt—no doubt, whatsoever—that genetics influence personality. We know that tens of thousands of genes working together have a profound effect on the mind, which in turn affects behavior—including, of course, criminally violent behavior."

"If that's true," I said, "it means that none of us is responsible for his or her actions. We're not to blame for thrusting the knife or pulling the trigger. We were genetically programmed for it. Our biomolecular structure made us do it."

"I believe you had a violent father, didn't you, Justice?" Dr. Ford's thin smile was like a slap in the face. "From what I've read in various published accounts."

"Then you probably also know that I killed him when I was seventeen," I said, "in defense of my little sister."

"Yes, I seem to recall that part as well. But let's not get ahead of ourselves, shall we?" Dr. Ford withdrew a file, opened it, and removed a set of photographs. "Through studies of identical and fraternal twins, we know that genetics is behind a lot of what we do or don't do as individuals. Again, that applies to violence, including rape and murder. We just haven't been able to find, isolate, and identify the specific genes that are responsible."

"And when you do," I asked, "it becomes a defense in court, during a rape or murder trial? A rapist's father passed along his genes to his son, so the son can't be held accountable? Is that your theory, doctor?"

"Is your concern professional, Justice, or more personal? Of course, it wouldn't be professional, would it? You're no longer in the journalism trade, are you?"

Templeton took a deep breath, and said evenly, "Perhaps we should leave the more difficult questions until later, after Dr. Ford shows us what he's got."

Ford smiled like a snake that had just swallowed a rat. "Very sensible, Alexandra."

He placed the photographs in two rows, three photos on top, two on the bottom; they appeared to be images of brain activity, marked by various color patterns of red, green, yellow, and blue. "A few years ago, with the old technology, we might have been able to study one or two genes in a month. Today, with new gene sequencers, researchers are able to study the action of tens of thousands of genes in a single afternoon. Advances in brain scanning allow us to measure the blood flow and metabolic energy of thought while it occurs, and find direct links to the corresponding activity of genes. The progress in recent years has been nothing short of astounding. It's only a matter of time before specific genes that generate specific behaviors are identified, patented, and even altered."

"Genetic engineering," Templeton said. "Identifying potential murderers at birth, even in the womb, and changing their genetic structure so they don't grow up to be Charles Manson or John Wayne Gacy."

"That's not my immediate concern," Dr. Ford said. "You'd have to talk to legal and medical experts about that—and perhaps the families of the victims of Mr. Manson and Mr. Gacy. At any rate, we also know that environment and life activity at the earliest stages—how we grow up—can induce biochemical changes in the way a gene behaves. Loving maternal interaction and parental bonding, for example—lots of hugs and kisses, consistent nurturing—may override the genetic predisposition to criminal behavior."

"While child abuse and other childhood trauma may stimulate it," I said.

Dr. Ford tossed me another smile like a penny thrown to a beggar. "Yes, Mr. Justice, that's correct."

"You mentioned a breakthrough," Templeton said pointedly, attempting to silence me with a sharp glance.

Dr. Ford indicated the three photographs in the top row. "These are the results of a new technology I've been using. It's called positron emission tomography, or PET, which measures differences in neural metabolism. Combined with computerized tomography, or CT, which captures detailed images of the brain's soft tissue, I'm able to measure, catalog, and analyze patterns of mental activity—to actually see how the brain works, and compare it with other brains."

"And you've been doing this with violent offenders," Templeton said.

Dr. Ford nodded, tapping each of the three photographs in turn with his forefinger. "I've now done enough controlled studies to know that certain brain activity patterns signify a murdering mind. These images reveal the neural activity of three different people—a normal person, an impulsive killer, and a premeditative murderer. You can see a marked difference in the normal brain from the other two. Now, look at the distinct patterns in the mind of the impulsive killer. These same patterns then increase dramatically in the mind of the premeditative murderer. There's no question that all three brains are behaving quite differently. We see similar brain patterns again and again in violent criminals, linked to the chemistry of neurotransmitters."

"Such as serotonin," Templeton said, "which to some extent controls our levels of aggression and depression."

"You've been doing your homework," Dr. Ford said.

"She's been observing me," I said, with a wry smile.

Dr. Ford ignored me, staying fixed on Templeton. He leaned so close to her that their heads were only inches apart. Templeton, engrossed in the photos, didn't seem to notice. "Now look at the two images on the bottom," he said, after stealing a glance at Templeton's face. "You'll notice how similar the patterns are."

"Almost identical," Templeton said.

"Some subtle differences," Dr. Ford countered, "but not enough to mean much."

Templeton looked up with astonishment. "These were different subjects?"

"Yes." Dr. Ford sat back, placing his fingers together like a teepee under his chin, looking quite pleased. "Different—but related."

"Related?" The astonishment rose in Templeton's voice. "They must be fraternal twins then, with a genetic similarity this striking."

"You'd think so, wouldn't you?"

"That would be incredible," Templeton said. "Two different people, with brains that behave almost identically."

"Even more incredible," Dr. Ford went on, "when you factor in the relationship between them."

"Twins," Templeton said again.

Dr. Ford shook his head with undisguised self-satisfaction. "Father and son." Templeton looked up, startled. Dr. Ford met her eyes directly, holding them there. "Alexandra, you're looking at the first images that prove scientifically that the genes for murder can be handed down from one generation to the next. A killing gene, if you will, that has never before been demonstrated with anything close to this kind of clarity." He shifted his eyes in my direction, rebuilding his insulting smile. "That doesn't necessarily mean that you're the violent, predatory individual that your father was, Justice. Merely that there's a predisposition for it."

Had it not been for my Prozac, I would have thrown a punch across the table that would have knocked him halfway to The House of Blues. Of course, that would have only given his theory more support.

"Oh, look," he said, turning away. "The appetizers are here."

While we munched on finger food, Dr. Ford rummaged again through his satchel. By the time lunch had arrived and Templeton had studied both photos in the bottom row several times, he'd found the file he was looking for and had it open in front of him.

"Hopefully, this story will get top priority in the *Times*," Dr. Ford said. "Especially when I give you a local hook—a very timely local hook."

"It always helps," Templeton said.

His voice sharpened. "I'll be frank, Alexandra. I'm looking for page one."

"I told you before, Dr. Ford—the editors make those decisions. It really depends on what you've got, and what kind of stories are breaking the day the piece gets scheduled."

His hand was on her wrist again. "I imagine how hard you fight for a particular story also has some bearing on its placement."

Templeton withdrew her hand and switched on her recorder again. "Why don't you show me what you've got, Doctor?"

He winked. "Nothing would give me more pleasure."

I spread my hands. "And who said the clever double entendre was dead?"

Templeton shot me another sharp look. Dr. Ford shrugged to let her know how childish he found me and riffled through the papers in the file. A moment later, he was placing two more photographs in front of her. One was a black-and-white head shot of a rough-looking, middle-aged man, with ruddy, pocked skin, dull eyes that looked unfeeling, and unruly hair on the dark side, like his eyes. The other was a color shot of considerably higher quality. Staring into the camera was a blond, sullen boy, possibly in his late teens, gauntly handsome in the manner of male models in edgy, Euro-style fashion spreads. His hair was buzzed short, making him look younger than he probably was; a soft, sparse beard covered his chin and upper lip. But it was his eyes that held my attention: blue and piercing, neither blazing nor icy, and difficult to read, as if he didn't want you to know exactly what he was feeling, or maybe wasn't so sure himself.

"The older man is Leonid Androvic," Dr. Ford said. "He was executed a few months ago in Russia for multiple murders—you may have read about it."

"We ran an article on it in the international section," Templeton said. "He was quite a big story in Eastern Europe."

"Leonid picked up girls, young women, probably prostitutes, then bludgeoned them to death for no apparent reason," Dr. Ford went on. "The authorities there linked him conclusively to fourteen murders, although they suspect he was involved in many more over the years. Fortunately, before he was put to death, I was allowed to include him in my PET and CT studies. I traveled to Russia to make sure it was done properly, with no room for error."

43

"Why so much interest in this one?" Templeton asked. "Don't we have enough serial killers and mass murderers in this country?"

"Availability, cooperation, access," Dr. Ford said, rattling off the reasons matter-of-factly. "I go where I must to broaden my study and make it as comprehensive as possible. Whenever I can, I find convicted killers who have children with violent tendencies."

"What induced Leonid Androvic to work with you?"

"In Russia, when you're condemned to death, you never know when you're going to die. You sleep in a tiny, cold cell, isolated, devoid of creature comforts. One night, unannounced, the guards come, drag you from your sleep, march you straightaway to the scaffold, slip the noose around your neck, and drop the trapdoor. Some prisoners say the worst part is the waiting, never knowing when they'll hear those footsteps in the middle of the night or if the footsteps will stop outside their cell. By cooperating with me, Leonid Androvic bought himself some extra time, a few weeks when he could at least sleep through the night."

Templeton drew the picture of the younger man closer, studying it keenly, as if trying to see more deeply into those alienated, unreadable eyes.

"That's his son, Victor Androvic," Dr. Ford said. "Lives here in West Hollywood with his mother, about a mile southeast, in the Russian section. They immigrated a few years ago, after Leonid was convicted. The mother's name is Tatiana. A good woman, hardworking, kindhearted, who happened to marry a very bad man. She was in her late thirties when she became pregnant with Victor. Both she and her son had a rough time of it. Leonid was brutally abusive, to both of them."

"How did you find the mother and son?"

"Traced them back here though government channels, offered them money to get involved in my research studies. Promised Tatiana I'd try to arrange a scholarship for Victor at the university if his grades and SAT scores were up to snuff. He's a reasonably smart boy, speaks fluent English. Tatiana was hesitant at first, for reasons I don't fully understand."

"She probably wanted to put her life in Russia behind her," I said. "If I was in her situation, I'd want to forget about what my son and I had been subjected to and spare him any further memory of it."

"Yes, that was probably it," Dr. Ford said curtly. "At any rate, I convinced them how important it would be to science, and to society, to help us learn as much as we could about the criminal mind and its hereditary influences. Victor wasn't happy about that part of it, as you might imagine. But the cash and the possibility of a scholarship proved to be ample inducements."

"I imagine desperate people can be bought off more easily," I said.

"Are you opposed to scientific progress in this area, Justice? Is it really so threatening to you, because of your own problematic background?"

"Gentlemen," Templeton said, "if you don't mind." She placed the photo of Victor Androvic aside and picked up the two brain scan images that looked nearly identical. "I assume there's a connection, Dr. Ford."

"The neural activity of two brains—those of Victor and Leonid—show remarkably similar indicators of aggressive and violent behavior. There's never been a study like this made of a mass murderer and a son who appears headed in the same direction."

"The boy's been in trouble?"

"He pleaded guilty a few months ago to a smuggling charge—poached caviar, which was being sold here on the black market. It was his first offense, at least the first time he'd been caught. He got a suspended sentence and three years probation."

"But no record of criminal violence?"

"Not yet."

"You make that sound portentous."

"Yesterday, a sheriff's detective paid me a visit. They've placed Victor at the scene of a murder, through fingerprints they had in the computer database because of his previous conviction in the smuggling case. When they questioned him, he told them that he was with me at the time of the murder, which simply isn't true. He called me immediately after they questioned him and pleaded with me to provide him an alibi. I told him I couldn't do that, that the best thing he could do now was to get a lawyer."

"It's a fascinating story," Templeton conceded. "First, the results of your study on both men. Then the son's possible involvement in a homicide. But until convicted, or at least arrested—" She broke off, raising her hands in apology. "I can't really use this boy in a story like this. Not yet, anyway."

"I believe you can," Dr. Ford said. "You don't have to name Victor or his father. They can both be anonymous, kept off the record until Victor is arrested."

"If he's arrested," I said.

"You can tell the story of my findings," Dr. Ford went on, "linked to a local suspect in a murder investigation, while keeping his identity confidential."

"Why the hurry to do the story now?" I asked. "Why not wait until the boy's at least picked up and formally charged? Makes it a better piece, does a better job of validating your findings. Less risk for Templeton that it might not work out."

"Because I can't sit on what I've got," Dr. Ford said, sounding irritated. "If Alexandra doesn't want the story, I'll go elsewhere with it. I need renewed funding for my research, and I simply can't wait weeks or months for the boy to be arrested. The detective who spoke to me assured me they have a strong case. But the police often move slowly, methodically. My work is too crucial, too important, to suffer an interruption for lack of funding."

"Or to risk another researcher breaking similar findings first," I said.

Dr. Ford peered at me with steely eyes. "It's about science, not competition."

"I'd have to name the victim," Templeton said. "I'd have to peg my story to something at least that concrete. Otherwise, we lose our hook—a breaking crime story—and it becomes a story for an inside science page."

"Assuming the science editor approves it at all," I said.

"Naming the victim shouldn't be a problem," Dr. Ford said, "as long as you keep Victor's name out of it for now."

"At the very least," Templeton said, "I'd need to confirm with the lead detective on the case that Victor's a suspect."

"Yes, please, talk to her, by all means—Detective Mira De Marco. That's her name."

"I've met Detective De Marco," I said. "She spoke to me yesterday about the murder of Bruce Bibby."

"That's the case," Dr. Ford said. "The Bruce Bibby killing."

Templeton was staring at me wide-eyed. "You didn't tell me a detective had spoken to you about the Bibby investigation."

I shrugged. "She asked me to keep my ear to the ground since I'm working at City Hall. Said she had a suspect in her sights. That was the extent of it."

Templeton was glaring now. "And you didn't think I should know?"

"She tossed it out as bait, Templeton. That's all there was to it. Don't get your knickers in a twist." I swung my eyes toward Dr. Ford, speaking as blandly as possible. "Anyway, I doubt that Mira De Marco is going to name anyone as a suspect until she's made an arrest. She seems like the no-nonsense type. She doesn't strike me as a media whore, willing to compromise her investigation just to get her name in the papers."

Dr. Ford held my gaze for a chilly moment before turning to Templeton again and resurrecting his self-assured smile. "Alexandra is not without her resources. My guess is she's the type who enjoys a challenge. If she didn't, I doubt that she'd have the reputation she does as the finest crime reporter in Southern California. Which is why I've selected her to report this story."

Templeton's eyes were locked on his. "You're awfully kind, Dr. Ford."

"Please, call me Rod."

"You're right about one thing, Rod. I do like a challenge."

"So do I, Alexandra." His smile was smug, his gaze unblinking. "So do I."

I thanked Templeton for the meal and excused myself, explaining that I had a lot of work to do back at City Hall. Then I got out of there as quickly as I could, before I lost my lunch.

FIVE

Ordinarily, my disgust for someone like Dr. Roderick Ford would have had me grinding my teeth and tossing and turning through the night. But thanks to my Prozac, I slept that night like a contented baby.

The next morning, at eight sharp, I was back at my City Hall desk, where I found a lavish gift basket waiting for me: fresh fruit, several nice cheeses, fine Swiss chocolate, a fancy bottle of champagne, and two flutes that looked like genuine crystal. A small card was attached bearing a message in a graceful but confident script:

Dear Mr. Justice,

Welcome to your new job and a wonderful opportunity to serve the city and its citizens, and possibly pave the way for future opportunities for yourself as well.

Yours truly,
Lester Cohen

Clipped to the note was a business card identifying Lester Cohen as a developer and attorney-at-law, with offices in one of the more prestigious high-rise buildings up on the Sunset Strip. I didn't need the business card to know who Lester Cohen was; he'd made his early fortune running gay bathhouses in the freewheeling seventies and early eighties, before AIDS and a legal backlash shut most of them down, and had built a sizable fortune as a business developer in the years since. I hadn't had a drink in a couple of years, so the gift basket with the champagne would go to Maurice, as a thank-you for pointing me to the job. I tossed Cohen's card into a drawer, pushed the basket aside, and got down to work, plowing through more of Bruce Bibby's research material. Within the hour, the phone rang. It was Templeton, getting back in touch not quite twenty-four hours after our lunch with Dr. Ford.

"So," she asked straightaway, "what do you think of him?"

"Nice teeth," I said.

"Seriously, Justice."

"Erudite, full of himself, and intent on getting you into the sack."

"That's all you can say about him?"

"If it weren't for my Prozac, I'm sure I'd have different feelings. As it is, I don't feel much about him one way or the other. You seem to enjoy his company, which is nice, I guess."

"I'm after a story—a really good one."

"That's nice, too."

"Everything's so nice with you these days. How do you really feel?"

"Nice. So what's up, Templeton? I'm busy here."

"Doing what?"

"Sorting through photos of Schwab's Pharmacy, where Lana Turner was supposedly discovered sitting on a soda fountain stool back in the forties."

"Who's Lana Turner?"

"God, you're so young. So what's on your mind?"

"At lunch yesterday, you said you knew Detective Mira De Marco."

"I said that we're acquainted, and barely at that."

"I need you to talk to her for me."

"You're a reporter. You know how to reach her."

"I've left messages for her, yesterday afternoon and again this morning. She hasn't gotten back to me."

"She's probably busy, running around solving murders."

"Or maybe she doesn't want to talk to me about the Bruce Bibby case."

"If she's zeroing in on a suspect, the last thing she needs is press interference."

"That doesn't sound like a reporter talking."

"I haven't been a reporter for a long time, remember?"

Templeton changed her tone, opting for a softer approach. "She obviously respects you, Justice, or she wouldn't have connected with you the way she did."

"She's a diligent cop. She takes her leads where she can find them, even from jerks like me."

"You could at least ask her to return my calls."

"So you can get your confirmation that Victor Androvic is a prime suspect in the Bibby case?"

"Without that, I've got no story."

"If she wanted to call you back, she would have."

"Justice, please. This exclusive means a lot to me."

"Not nearly as much as it does to Dr. Ford, judging by the way he leaned on you yesterday to get it on the front page, ASAP."

"You heard what he said. He needs the publicity to help him secure more funding for his research."

"Maybe his research is suspect. Maybe that's his problem."

"I've checked him out. His work is controversial, but he's well-known and respected in his field. He's considered a brilliant researcher, a pioneer in the study of the criminal mind. He collects academic degrees the way I collect jewelry."

"What happened to your reporter's healthy skepticism, Templeton?"

"Are you going to help me or not?"

"Not."

"Haven't I always been there for you when you needed me, Justice?"

"Yes you have, and I'm grateful."

"All I'm asking is this one little favor."

"Try me again next week, with something more savory."

"You're refusing to help, just because you don't like Dr. Ford?"

"What I don't like, Templeton, is the idea of you fingering a kid as a suspect when he's yet to be arrested. You're a better reporter than that, with stronger ethics. Or at least you used to be, before you heard the siren call of television. This story has TV written all over it, and you know it—it's visual, sensational, easy to promote. It'll get you all kinds of attention from the TV news directors, maybe even a job offer."

Her voice grew chilly. "You're not in the best position to be lecturing anyone on journalistic integrity."

"You got me there."

"You really won't call Detective De Marco for me?"

"I really won't. But don't take it personally."

"Damn you, Justice!"

For the first time in the eight years I'd known Alexandra Templeton, she hung up on me.

My phone didn't ring again until half past three. I grabbed it hoping it wasn't Templeton, pressuring me again to connect her with Detective De Marco.

"Benjamin Justice?"

"That would be me," I said.

I cradled the phone under one ear while thumbing through Bruce Bibby's photos of the luxurious Garden of Allah, built in 1921 by the legendary silent screen star and unabashed lesbian Alla Nazimova, at the corner of Crescent Heights and Sunset Boulevard. Today, it was a tacky minimall anchored by a McDonald's.

"My name is Lydia Ruttweller," the voice on the phone said. "Former schoolteacher, community activist, and champion of historical preservation here in West Hollywood. Perhaps you've heard of me."

"Of course, Miss Ruttweller. You're quite a presence in the community."

"It's *Mrs.*, thank you very much. I'm a divorcée for more than thirty years now. Never remarried. Never saw the point."

Although I'd never met her, I'd seen Lydia Ruttweller on televised sessions of the monthly City Council meetings that were aired live on West Hollywood's local cable channel. She was known as a relentless gadfly, infamous for her abrasive remarks and tongue-lashing tirades at public hearings and council meetings, so tenacious in defense of her positions that she'd earned the nickname of Lydia Rottweiler. Although she seemed to have an opinion on virtually every issue that came before the council, from trash collection fees to parking meter hours, she was most vehement as a force for protecting West Hollywood's cultural and architectural treasures against what she considered rapacious developers. Some joked that if she could, Lydia Ruttweller would expand the city's Historical Preservation Overlay from border to border, encompassing anything with a roof on it.

"What may I do for you, Mrs. Ruttweller?"

"I understand you'll be completing Bruce Bibby's work."

"That's correct."

"No one will replace Bruce, Mr. Justice. Neither you nor anyone else. You might as well accept that right now."

I put the photographs aside, pushed my chair back, crossed my feet on my desk, and braced myself for more. "Go on, Mrs. Ruttweller."

"Bruce was a dear friend of mine. A bright young man, serious and socially responsible, dedicated to the cause of historic preservation. I doubt that you'll do half the job he would have, but if you can manage that much, I suppose we should all be grateful."

"I certainly intend to try. Now, what is it you want?"

"We need to meet, as soon as possible, so that I might give you the kind of insight and guidance you'll need to do your work properly. I'd also like to have copies of all of Bruce's files, especially those regarding the Sherman cottages."

"I imagine that would be up to the city and Mr. Bibby's family."

"I've already told you that he and I were dear friends."

"Are you officially involved with the work he was doing here, Mrs. Ruttweller?"

"In case you're not aware of it, I'm the founder and president of CUP—Citizens United for Preservation. It's a nonprofit organization here in West Hollywood dedicated to—well, the name says it rather well, don't you think?"

"Short and to the point," I said. "Something I appreciate, by the way."

"No one in this city knows more about the value of historic preservation or its implementation than I, Mr. Justice. I've devoted much of my life to—"

"I'm rather busy, Mrs. Ruttweller. What is it you want?"

"We have some vital matters to discuss. I'll meet you at the Sherman cottages at four P.M. You do know about the Sherman cottages, I assume, given their important role in city history." I told her that I knew where they were—on Paul Monette Avenue in the Old Sherman District—but not much more than that. "Never mind," she said, "I'll fill you in when I see you in precisely twenty-seven minutes."

"Mrs. Ruttweller, I—"

"Four o'clock sharp, Mr. Justice. I'm also quite busy, and my time is quite valuable. I place a high priority on punctuality, and I expect no less of you."

Thirty minutes later, I was striding up the west side of Paul Monette Avenue, the busy residential street named after the late gay writer and activist that ran north–south through the heart of Boys Town, connecting Sunset and Santa Monica boulevards. Just ahead, halfway up the hill, I could see Lydia Ruttweller pacing the sidewalk, glancing impatiently at her wristwatch. I quickened my step.

She was a tall, trim woman, at least six feet, with white hair drawn back into a practical bun and wire-rimmed spectacles that were as sensible as her baby blue warm-up suit and spotless New Balance walking shoes. I'd been told she was close to seventy, but her erect stature and assertive manner—shoulders back, chin in—made her look younger, and just a bit formidable.

"There you are," she said, surveying me with critical eyes. "You look better than your photographs in the newspapers some years back, when you made such a mess of your life."

"It wasn't the best of times," I said.

"We're not here to talk about you, Mr. Justice." With a sweep of one hand, she indicated a row of dilapidated cottages along our side of the street, badly weathered firetraps with the windows boarded up and weeds choking the yards. It was a strange sight in West Hollywood, where the parcels were generally well kept, and developable land was painfully scarce. "The issue at hand is these historic structures, which my group is fighting to save from the greed of one Mr. Lester Cohen."

"The developer," I said.

"Lawyer, developer, heartless businessman." She spit out the words like bits of putrid food. "Made his fortune operating bathhouses that fostered filthy sex and disease. Now that he's up in years, thinking about how he might be remembered, he wants to tear down all these lovely old cottages and build the most extravagant condominium complex on the west side. Casa Granada, he wants to call it. For Lester Cohen, that's some kind of achievement—destroying irreplaceable history for grandiose living quarters for the wealthy and privileged, at the expense of our city's priceless heritage."

"The cottages look awfully run down."

"That's what restoration is for, Mr. Justice."

"Who would pay for this restoration?"

"I can assure you, I'm gathering more funds every day. The tragedy is that we're having to spend so much money in court, fighting to save these precious buildings, money that could be going toward their renovation."

Mrs. Ruttweller delivered a crisp lecture on their history as she marched me up the hill to the first and largest, a corner cottage that she identified as Harrison House. Although frequently mistaken for Craftsman, she said, these houses were in fact "Plains Cottages"—pre-1910 and pre-Craftsman—which had served as the first worker housing when West Hollywood was only a train stop known as Sherman, situated between downtown Los Angeles and the beach. Harrison House had been the last of the cottages to be constructed, she added, named for the current owner, Colin Harrison, who'd occupied the cottage for more than a decade, beginning in 1967, with his friend, Ted Meeks.

"It was a darling house," she said, "with lovely touches from the past—stained-glass windows, old-fashioned wicker on this broad front porch, flowering gardens all about. It's a disgrace what's happened to it, and all the others, due to Colin's neglect."

A winding pathway of loose gravel gave way to a solid brick walkway as we made our way around the back, onto a brick courtyard that must have been charming decades ago. A fountain at the center had been vandalized and broken, and the lush landscaping had become a tangled mess of overgrown shrubs and vines. A side door of the cottage had been kicked in, probably by transients looking for a

54

place to sleep, and the air close to the house reeked of rancid urine. Floorboards sagged on the porches, while roof shingles hung loose or littered the yard. The only truly intact aspect of the old place seemed to be the well-laid bricks beneath our feet; here and there, facing up, the year 1896 was stamped into a brick, adding a touch of antiquity to what must have once been an enchanting oasis tucked away in a city on the brink of modern development.

"More than a century these treasures have stood." Lydia Ruttweller surveyed the ruined house, her nostrils flaring. "I knew Colin Harrison when he and Ted Meeks lived here. I considered them friends. They loved old houses like this, loved fixing them up, restoring them, renting them out. But as rental property in West Hollywood became more desirable, and Colin grew wealthier with the rising rents, it changed him. Greed—I don't know that there's a more destructive aspect to human nature."

"I guess wealth can do that to a person," I said. "Once you get a taste of it, you just can't have enough."

Lydia Ruttweller brightened. "You see? You do understand. I sense an ally in you, Mr. Justice."

"This Harrison fellow sounds interesting. You mentioned that he still owns the place."

"Colin Harrison must own half the city by now, at least the rental units. When the housing market exploded here in the seventies Colin began buying up properties left and right. Some of them were wonderful old places that deserved to be preserved for posterity. But what did he do with them? Tore them down and cleared the lots so that he could build apartment buildings and condominium complexes, squeezing every penny he could from the land. It was easier then, you know, before we got our city charter. The county was much more lax about historical preservation."

"I imagine he opposed secession from the county."

"Oh my, yes! Colin Harrison is the main reason I founded CUP—to stop Colin and those like him who place the almighty dollar above tradition and quality of life. The only reason the Sherman cottages are still standing is because we've fought him at every turn, through City Hall and the courts, to save them from the wrecking crew."

"And his friend, Ted Meeks—he feels the same way?"

She hesitated, then spoke more curtly. "Ted Meeks thinks what Colin thinks. He's devoted to Colin. Always has been."

I glanced from the yard, up and down the broad street, where a condominium complex of two or three stories would offer fine views of downtown Los Angeles in one direction and sunset views from the ocean in the other. "It's a choice location," I said, "in a city with few remaining lots. There must be a good deal of profit at stake."

"Millions, Mr. Justice." Lydia Ruttweller's eyes blazed. "Millions of dollars with which Colin Harrison and Lester Cohen would like to fatten their already bloated bank accounts. If nothing else, I owe it to Bruce to fight for these old houses. He loved them as if they were his own children. We shared that in common, Bruce and I."

"Bruce Bibby," I said.

She nodded. "He'd planned to feature the Sherman cottages prominently in his final brochure, to give them their rightful place. He was in possession of vintage photos, you know, taken when the cottages were still in pristine condition." Her lips curled with disgust. "Not like they are now, turned into crumbling slums."

At that moment, an old Mercedes station wagon, faded yellow, pulled into the gravel driveway alongside the house. Lydia Ruttweller took notice, tensed a little, then moved cautiously in that direction as I followed. A spry, wiry gentleman—wispy gray mustache, white hair poking from beneath a floppy golf hat—jumped from behind the wheel and scurried around to the passenger side.

"Colin Harrison?" I inquired.

"No, that's Ted. Colin's the frail one, I'm afraid. Ironic, since it was always Colin who was the warhorse, the one with the heart of a lion."

Meeks opened the passenger door, where a much larger, older man sat passively in the passenger seat.

"Tsk, tsk." Lydia Ruttweller shook her head. "I hadn't realized just how frail. Time eventually claims us all, even the most robust, doesn't it?"

Harrison was tall and broad-shouldered, his bald head shiny, his complexion ruddy, with a thick red mustache that might have been the model for his partner's wispier gray one. As he struggled to climb from the car with the help of Meeks and a cane, he didn't seem to fit his big frame; the wide shoulders sagged, and the body looked in need of more muscle and flesh, as if it were slowly wasting away, along with his vigor. Even the ruddy complexion appeared on the wane, with a hint of the ashen, as though the last of his fire was struggling to give off some heat, before old age or disease finally extinguished it forever.

"He was once such a hearty man, so full of spit and vinegar." Mrs. Ruttweller kept her voice low, surprising me with a smile and a hint of admiration in her voice. "We've had some memorable confrontations, Colin and I. He's a fighter, I'll give him that."

Meeks got Harrison on his feet, if unsteadily, and they began moving slowly along a pebbly path in our direction, still out of earshot.

"And Ted Meeks? What about him?"

"Colin's devoted companion for more than fifty years now. Serves as Colin's property manager and errand boy—collects the rents, deals with tenant complaints, makes sure the properties are maintained. That is, the properties they aren't deliberately allowing to deteriorate, like this one."

"Why would they let these places go to ruin? It makes no sense."

Lydia Ruttweller snorted "From Colin's perspective, it makes perfect sense. City laws protect neighborhood character by restricting demolition to structures that are uninhabitable or lack architectural distinction. The municipal code is quite strict about the upkeep of rental properties. But there are no laws that can force Colin to rent his properties out. So he leaves the Sherman cottages empty and untended, while the city faces a severe housing shortage. Since he's collecting no rents, the city loses revenue. In the meantime, these properties become eyesores, a blight on a municipality that's trying to attract tourists and new business. In short, he's forcing the city to grant him permission to tear down these houses for development." Her eyes fixed on Harrison with a mix of respect and loathing as he shuffled in our direction, still leaning on Meeks. "There's a method to Colin's madness, Mr. Justice. He didn't become as wealthy as he is without being clever regarding the law."

Ted Meeks pulled up when he saw us, regarding us with pale blue eyes that seemed cautious, even skittish, like those of a dog that's been raised by a cruel hand. Harrison's eyes, green but lacking much spark, took longer to find us. When they did, they had a searching look that bordered on the lost.

"Good afternoon, Colin, Ted." Lydia Rutweller sounded slightly embarrassed. "I didn't mean to trespass on your property. I merely wanted to show Mr. Justice the historic Sherman cottages—while they're still standing."

Harrison smiled feebly, without further response, as if she were speaking a foreign language he didn't understand. Mrs. Ruttweller mentioned to me that Bruce Bibby had been renting an apartment from Harrison, and thanked Ted Meeks for his cooperation and assistance following Bibby's untimely death.

"He was a model tenant," Meeks said, speaking crisply and without much warmth. "Never a problem with Bruce. Of course, anything you or his family need. Anything at all."

"We'd like to keep his apartment intact for at least a month," Mrs. Ruttweller said. "Until we can find a place for the archives and other research material." She turned in my direction. "Mr. Justice may need entry. He's replacing Bruce and writing up the brochure about the city's commitment to historical preservation."

"I see." Meeks's voice grew even cooler. "I trust that Mr. Justice is unbiased on the subject—that he'll keep the property owners in mind."

"I'll do my best to be evenhanded, Mr. Meeks."

"Of course"—he sniffed—"you're employed by the city. Hardly partial to landlords, despite the taxes we pay. Still, a young man's dead, isn't he? It's a tragedy, and that's a fact. If the family approves, and you wish access to the apartment, we'll certainly cooperate."

"I imagine it's sealed off as a crime scene at the moment," I said.

"For a few more days," Meeks said. "Or so I've been told. As you can imagine, it's been extremely upsetting for us. We've never had something like this happen in one of our rental units. A suicide or two, over the years, but never—" He broke off, looking distressed. "Never something like this."

"Murder," I said.

An uneasy silence settled over us, while Lydia Ruttweller studied Harrison closely. He regarded her with a blank stare, his feeble smile unchanged. "Colin hasn't said a word to me. I'm not sure he even knows who I am. Colin?"

Harrison's lips formed a stupid smile, but that was his sole response. Meeks tightened his grip protectively on the older man's arm. "Colin's fine. He's just tired, that's all." He tipped the brim of his floppy hat, then gently tugged at Harrison until the older man turned again up the path. We watched Meeks make his way patiently toward the more solid footing of the brick walkway in back, providing support as Harrison shuffled along with his cane.

"Now you've seen them," Mrs. Ruttweller said, "the old relics so symbolic of a forgotten time."

"You're referring to the cottages, I presume."

She regarded me sharply. "Of course, Mr. Justice. What else would I be speaking of?"

It was half past four when Lydia Ruttweller and I stood again on the sidewalk halfway down the hill, as the late-afternoon traffic began to thicken along Monette Avenue, and the long shadows of the palm trees slanted sharply to the southeast.

"Such a shame," she said, her keen eyes moving from cottage to cottage, as if drinking in their antiquated features for possibly the last time. "So much history in these old places, so much character, reminding us where we came from and what brought us here."

"So many stories within their borders and their walls," I said.

Her eyes glistened with emotion. "Yes, and they may all be destroyed if Colin Harrison and Lester Cohen and their ilk have their way." She swung her eyes in my direction, a sudden fire burning away their dewy sentiment. "But not as long as I'm alive to fight them, Mr. Justice. Mark my words—the only way they'll tear down these cottages is over my dead body."

SIX

The funeral service for Bruce Bibby was conducted on Thursday morning, five days after his death, at the Crescent Heights Methodist Church in West Hollywood.

To accommodate the many mourners from City Hall, the mayor declared it closed for the morning except for the most essential services. The city also provided shuttle buses from the parking lot to the church for anyone who wanted to catch a ride into a neighborhood where a parking space was as rare as a Republican. I rode from home with Templeton, who'd insisted on attending once she heard I was going.

Driving east on Fountain Avenue, she marveled at the variety of houses and apartment buildings around us, dating back to the twenties, when Hollywood's creative elite had occupied so many. "I'm definitely holding out for a view," she said, talking about her move from the beach. "I don't care if it takes me a year to find it, and I have to rent until I find what I'm looking for. I want a view, three bedrooms, and a yard, where I can grow roses and have a dog."

"In this neighborhood, you're talking at least two million dollars," I said. "And for two million around here, it'll probably be a fixer."

Her eyes were on the road; she didn't look over. "Money's not a problem."

"Daddy helping out?"

"Making it easier."

Coming from a blue-collar family, I resented Templeton's wealthy background and easy money, and the cycle of privilege and class it perpetuated; in turn, she resented my resentment. It had always been a sensitive issue between us, and there was no good reason for pushing it. Not until lunch was over, anyway, and it was time to pay the check. Dining with Templeton had become my personal form of socialism.

"That's the church up ahead, on the right," I said.

We got lucky and found street parking three blocks farther down and walked back to the intersection of Fountain and Fairfax avenues, where the church anchored the southeast corner. A lively breeze teased the leaves and cut the early May heat, just enough to make it pleasant. I was dressed in the same dark suit I'd worn to the service for Templeton's fiancé, Joe Soto, the previous October. She was turned out in a fine-looking silk dress of dusky maroon, with a wide-brimmed matching hat and a veil that obscured her classic face. She'd abandoned her weave and braids for a shorter cut with soft curls, a new look that probably had something to do with the new beginning she was hoping for.

"We haven't been to a funeral service since we said good-bye to Joe," she said.

I was surprised she'd brought it up. "How are you feeling about that?"

"I'm OK. It's one reason I wanted to come today—kind of a test, to see how I'm doing." She smiled bravely. "I'm glad to be back at work, getting my teeth into a real story again." Her eyes slid uneasily in my direction. "It would be nice if I could nail it down, before someone else gets it."

I didn't begrudge Templeton her ambition. Without some ambition and a competitive zeal, a reporter isn't worth much. And I certainly didn't begrudge her a need for healing. But I never expected to hear her using Joe's death, her grief, and my guilt to pressure me into helping her with a developing story about which I had serious reservations.

"You're nothing if not resourceful, Templeton. If it's meant to happen, I imagine it will."

She faced forward, walking stiffly with more purpose, and we didn't speak again until we reached the church. A crowd had gathered on the sidewalk outside, with some of the mourners already trickling in to face the inevitable. Built in 1924, Crescent Heights Methodist was a sandstone-colored structure in the stolid Mission tradition, with a bell hanging in a *campanario* that faced north and tall, narrow stained-glass windows on the north and west sides. I'd seen photographs and a description of it among Bruce Bibby's notes; he'd planned to include a brief mention of it in his brochure, since it was one of the older churches in the city and designated as a historic site.

We found Maurice and Fred out front, sheltering from the sun under the heavy leaves of a spreading ficus tree. Templeton lifted her veil to greet them, getting a warm embrace and peck on the cheek from Maurice and a more perfunctory hug from Fred.

"I plan to blubber like a baby," Maurice said, checking his pockets for tissues. "I'm just warning everyone right now."

I recognized a number of faces in the crowd, including those of Trang Nguyen, Ted Meeks, and Cecelia Cortez. I also noticed various council members in attendance, though I didn't spot Tony Mercury among them. Detective Mira De Marco was just arriving, in what looked like the same no-nonsense suit she'd worn the day I'd met her at City Hall, her jacket buttoned to conceal her badge and gun. Closer to us, not ten feet away, Lydia Ruttweller stood at the curb, separated from us by a group of mourners, looking impatiently from her wristwatch to the intersection. She'd dressed all in black, in clothes that looked decades old, with the hem of her dress well down her calf and the veil of her pillbox hat turned up, exposing her anxious face to the late morning glare. Under one arm, she clutched a small, black, beaded purse; in her other hand, a white hankie.

Suddenly, a Mazda RX-8 convertible careened around the corner on a yellow light. At the wheel was a thirtyish man in wraparound Ray-Bans, holding a cell phone to his ear with one hand, while he steered with the other. He pulled to the curb so fast and close that all the bystanders except Mrs. Ruttweller stepped back to give him room, while she held her ground as if it mattered. The driver was wearing a neon green tank top that showed off his thick neck, massive chest and shoulders, and swelling biceps, without an ounce of body fat in sight. Under his heavy stubble, his face was florid, while his elongated jaw suggested the distended bone structure of a man who'd been doing too many steroids for too long, without the desire or discipline to quit.

Mrs. Ruttweller bent her tall figure at the waist, leaning into the car, shaking a finger and scolding the man with words I could only intermittently make out. I heard her say, "Never again!" and "Absolutely the last time!" but that was about it. Then she opened her little purse, pulled out a wad of cash, and thrust it at him. He grabbed it, made a kissing sound, and sped off with his ear to his cell phone, while Mrs. Ruttweller stood shaking her head, watching the flashy sports car disappear into traffic.

"Chas Ruttweller," Maurice whispered, close to my shoulder. "The bane of her life, I'm afraid. Sad to say that about one's only offspring, but I'm afraid it's true."

"Son?"

Maurice nodded, keeping his voice low. "She never could decide whether to punish Chas or coddle him. The result is what you see—a spoiled, resentful adolescent in the pumped-up body of a chemically enhanced weight lifter. Works as a bouncer at one of the trendy clubs up on the Strip, but never seems to have enough money. I've often wondered what's troubling that young man so."

"Is there anyone in this town whose background you don't know, Maurice?"

Maurice feigned indignation. "Are you suggesting I'm a busybody, Benjamin?"

"Let's just say that you make it a point to stay informed."

"Information has a way of finding me. Keep in mind that West Hollywood is a very small town. Especially when you've lived here as long as Fred and I have."

Templeton approached, touching my shoulder. "We probably should go in. Service is about to start."

"Oh, my," Maurice said. He took a deep breath, emotion clouding his face. "I'm not looking forward to this—another young one making his transition much too soon. But it's got to be done, doesn't it? So let's just go in and help Bruce on his way."

He slipped his arm through Fred's, as Templeton did with me. As we started in, Lydia Ruttweller was already ahead of us, reaching up to lower her veil as she stepped briskly toward the church entrance.

The service for Bruce Bibby was unusually poignant, in part because of his youth and obvious popularity with the large crowd. His wheelchair was parked next to his open coffin, a reminder of the life challenge he'd faced with such resolve, only to lose that life so senselessly. We'd been handed a memorial pamphlet on the way in, and I studied photos of Bibby from infancy to manhood, while a minister droned on with his eulogy and mourners around me wept or blew their noses. The minister caught my attention when he spoke of Bibby's successful battle with drug addiction and the courageous way he'd come back from his car accident, coping with his paralysis and determined to get on with his life without feeling sorry for himself. As someone who'd lost too many years to the bottle and spent too many more wallowing in self-pity, I felt a special admiration for Bibby, a kinship that I hadn't anticipated. After the minister's remarks, nearly two dozen people came forward to remember the deceased, including several colleagues from his days as a child actor, some of them famous enough that I almost recalled their names. Lydia Ruttweller was the last to take the microphone, raising her veil to speak in a voice that quavered only slightly.

"Bruce was a dear, sweet, decent young man," she said, "whom I would have been proud to call my son. His dedication to preserving our city's history was unparalleled. I intend to carry on that commitment and honor his memory with every fiber of my being, until I've taken my last breath on this earth."

While she spoke, I surveyed the audience as discreetly as I could. Four members of the City Council had elected to sit together up front in a show of nonpartisanship and solidarity, with the fifth, Tony Mercury, conspicuously absent. Nearer the back, Ted Meeks sat on the aisle in an ill-fitting sport coat and rumpled tie, looking fidgety without the camouflage of his floppy hat, but Colin Harrison was not with him. Just behind me, to my right, Trang Nguyen sat stoic and without tears, his face as hard and cold as finely carved jade.

At half past noon, as we filed from the church, Templeton steered me around the corner toward Fairfax Avenue, for reasons I didn't at first understand. "The car's the other way, Templeton—back on Fountain."

Before I could say more, she'd maneuvered me nearly to her target—Detective Mira De Marco, who was having a smoke near the curb, away from the crowd. She looked up at our approach, her eyes moving quickly from me to Templeton, where they settled for a brief but telling moment before coming back to me again.

"Hello, Mr. Justice. How's your work coming at City Hall?"

"I'm barely started, I'm afraid."

De Marco's eyes had already moved on again, as Templeton thrust out a hand and introduced herself. "Benjamin's been telling me all about you, Detective, and how you might be making some headway in your investigation. I was hoping I might run into you. I've left several messages."

"How did you recognize me, Miss Templeton?"

"Yes," I said, "how did you recognize her, Templeton?"

"I ran your name through the *Times* database to see if anything turned up. The paper ran a feature a few years ago on openly lesbian deputies who were making their mark in the sheriff's department. You were among those interviewed. We also had a photo on file." Templeton smiled and shrugged. "Nothing very complicated."

De Marco's smile was warmer than I expected. "You're determined, Miss Templeton, I'll give you that."

"I need your help, Detective—with a story I'm putting together."

"Sorry, but I'm not ready to talk yet about the Bibby investigation, if that's what you're after."

"All I need is for you to confirm that Victor Androvic is a suspect." De Marco's smile disappeared the moment she heard Androvic's name. "I know he's the one you're looking at, Detective."

De Marco took a drag on her cigarette, letting the smoke out slowly. "No comment."

"I also know about the research he's involved with at the university," Templeton went on, "under the supervision of Dr. Roderick Ford." De Marco's face looked as if it were set in plaster, while her eyes stayed fixed on Templeton. "Dr. Ford gave me a detailed interview," Templeton went on. "I know that Victor Androvic is your prime suspect. I know he's got no alibi for the evening of the murder. And I know he lied when you asked him where he was that night."

De Marco took another hit of nicotine, stubbed her cigarette on a fire hydrant, wrapped the butt in a tissue, and tucked it into a jacket pocket. "Dr. Ford assured me that our conversation would remain confidential," De Marco said, in a voice that fit the hard set of her face. "Apparently, he has a short memory for promises."

Templeton smiled, keeping her tone light. "I'm afraid you'll have to take that up with Dr. Ford. In the meantime, I've got my interview on tape. It's a great story, the kind a reporter doesn't stumble on that often."

"I really wish you'd wait on this, Miss Templeton. The Bibby investigation is at a sensitive juncture."

"The Bibby murder isn't the focus of my story, Detective. My story is about Dr. Ford's groundbreaking research, which includes Victor Androvic. Androvic's connection to the Bibby case is merely a tangent, a coincidental link."

"Then you don't need any comment from me," De Marco said.

"If you were willing to speak for background only, I'd leave Victor Androvic's name out of the story until you've made your arrest. For all intents and purposes, you don't even need to be a part of the story at all."

"Then why are we even talking?"

"I need confirmation that Dr. Ford's research subject, the son of a multiple murderer, is himself a suspect in a violent crime. Victor Androvic isn't going to confirm that. According to Dr. Ford, neither will his mother. I need you to confirm it for me." Templeton paused, shrugging with feigned innocence. "Of course, I can probably convince my editor to let me go with the story anyway, to work around you as I write it. But I'd rather have your cooperation—work with you instead of against you."

De Marco regarded Templeton keenly. "For background purposes only?"

"If you'll just confirm that Victor Androvic is a strong suspect in the Bibby murder, I won't quote you or attribute anything to you until you give me your permission. And I won't identify Androvic by name."

"Not a word, not a fact—until I say it's time."

"I'll keep you completely out of it, until you say otherwise. I give you my word."

De Marco relaxed a little and favored me with a glance. "Mr. Justice, you'll have to excuse us."

"You're both adults," I said. "I guess you know what you're doing."

I left them sitting on a low wall along the sidewalk, De Marco lighting another cigarette while Templeton switched on her tape recorder and asked her first question.

Not twenty minutes later, Templeton found me around the corner, saying good-bye to Maurice and Fred, who were joining the long procession of vehicles to the cemetery for the interment. Templeton was ebullient as we sauntered back to her Thunderbird.

"I take it you got what you wanted?"

She nodded with enthusiasm, talking fast. "They've placed Victor Androvic at the crime scene through fingerprints found on Bruce Bibby's wheelchair. Androvic looks very good for the crime. No alibi, lied about where he was that night, previous felony conviction on the smuggling rap. They're just waiting for a detailed report from forensics before they make an arrest. All that's off the record, of course, until Detective De Marco gives me the go-ahead to use it."

"So you plan to hold off on filing the story."

Her eyes faltered, along with her voice. "Not exactly."

"What exactly does 'not exactly' mean?"

"I've got what I need to go with the story on Dr. Ford. The confirmation that Victor is a suspect—that's what I was after. The rest stays off the record."

"But you promised Detective De Marco you'd sit on the story if she talked to you."

"Not at all." The distant, detached tone of Templeton's voice made me uneasy. "I told her I wouldn't use any of her comments in my story or attribute anything to her, and I won't. I'll use what Dr. Ford told me independently. He gave me everything I need to go to print."

"Except the detective's confirmation about Victor."

"I'll attribute what I confirmed to an anonymous police source. No details will be mentioned, except what I already knew from Dr. Ford. I don't have a problem with it."

We'd reached Templeton's T-Bird and climbed in from opposite sides. She kept her eyes forward as she switched on the ignition, then busied herself worrying about approaching vehicles in her sideview mirror. She saw a brief opening, punched the accelerator, and shot into traffic.

"This isn't right," I said, "the way you're going about this."

"I'm a good driver, Justice. Don't worry, I'll get you home safely."

"I'm not talking about your driving, and you know it."

She swung right after a few blocks, drove down to Santa Monica Boulevard, and turned right again past the convivial gay lunch crowd at the French Market Place, pointing us back toward City Hall. "I promised De Marco that I'd use her strictly for background, off the record. She's confirmed that everything Dr. Ford told me is on the money. He's my primary source, not De Marco, and I'll keep her name out of it. Technically, I'm honoring my agreement with her."

"You tricked her," I said.

"I'm not planning to name Victor Androvic as the suspect. I'll keep his identity out of it as well."

"But you'll use the Bruce Bibby case as your hook."

"Of course. That's the point." Templeton clenched a fist with excitement, as if everything I'd just said was insignificant. "This is going to be such a great story. Page one, fantastic angle, color photographs. I can't wait to write this one up."

"And after it hits the streets, you sit back and wait for the TV stations to call you in for an interview. I'll bet you've already got your résumés out to every network affiliate in town, don't you?" She kept her eyes fixed on the traffic ahead. "You can't do this, Templeton. It's not right."

She shot through a yellow light, her voice frosty. "Of course I can do it. The public has a right to know."

"Please, Alex. Sit on the story awhile."

"Sorry, Justice. There's no way I'm not going to run with it."

I felt sick in my gut, sick in my soul, and thankful for the Prozac that offered emotional ballast. "That's City Hall, just ahead on the left. Let me out at the light, will you?"

"Why don't we grab lunch first, at Hugo's? It's still early. My treat."

"I've got a lot to do." I smiled with effort. "Thanks for the ride."

She checked her rearview mirror and pulled over. I climbed out, took a deep breath, and steadied myself. Then I crossed Santa Monica Boulevard with the green light, trying to convince myself that Templeton's behavior was none of my business—that my only business was the work waiting for me on my City Hall desk.

SEVEN

I ate lunch that day where I sat—a sandwich from Hamburger Mary's down the street, which someone in the office was kind enough to bring back for me—while I examined the plans for the third and final addition to the Pacific Design Center.

By West Hollywood standards, the PDC was a massive structure—two sections, six and nine stories high, with more than a million square feet of floor space—that loomed over Melrose Avenue and Santa Monica Boulevard across from West Hollywood Park. Opened in 1975 to serve the city's thriving interior design trade, the first building was vaguely rectangular with fascinating angles and curves, further distinguished by a striking blue glass exterior that had earned it the nickname the Blue Whale. In 1988, a taller green extension with dramatic triangular touches had its opening. Now a sweeping, wedge-shaped red extension was planned, to be built over seven years, the final piece in a monumental sculpture garden, completing the bold vision of the acclaimed architect, Cesar Pelli. These breath-taking structures had found their home on the sixteen-acre site of the old Sherman rail yards, whose redbrick barn, iron foundry, and other railway buildings had been torn down in the early seventies to make way for the PDC. Given its international stature as an architectural masterpiece, it seemed worthy of a special place in the brochure I was putting together, perhaps toward the end, I thought, with an eye toward the future.

At half past six, feeling as if I was finally finding some shape in

Bruce Bibby's endless data, I shut off my computer and slipped out of a darkened City Hall, on my way to a workout and steam at Buff.

Buff occupied the same space across from Tribal Grounds that had once been taken up by its fancier predecessor, Le Gym, which had catered to a wealthier and more pampered crowd. The piped-in Streisand and Donna Summer tunes were gone, along with the fresh-cut flowers in the lobby and the French cologne dispensers in the locker room, replaced by more free weights, more-affordable memberships, and longer waits for the most popular fitness machines. The name Buff might have been a throwback to the seventies, but the gym was as current as the latest high-priced protein powder. It was also ideally located across Santa Monica Boulevard from Tribal Grounds, where appreciative men could sit out front with their coffees and ogle all the pumping and flexing through Buff's second-story floor-to-ceiling windows.

"Justice, I didn't know you worked out here."

It was Tony Mercury, coming out of an aerobics dance class on the first floor, his powerful chest heaving as he patted his five o'clock shadow with a towel. He was dressed in a form-fitting tank top and Spandex shorts so snug they left little to the imagination, least of all why his brand name was the Greek Stallion.

"I'm pretty new at this," I said. "Still trying to get into shape."

He looked me up and down as he gulped water from a sports bottle. "I'd say you're getting there pretty fast, at least to my eye." His tone shifted almost imperceptibly. "So, how's the work coming on the brochure?"

"Getting there a little slower."

"Maybe you're being too thorough, worrying too much about getting everything in." He stroked one of his well-shaped biceps with the towel, then ran it across the thicket of moist hairs on his upper chest. "It's all about choices, isn't it? What to include, what to leave out. Seems to me you should focus on the most important historic sites and forget everything else."

"Forget the Sherman cottages, you mean?"

"I would, if it was my project." He slapped me on the butt. "Let's have lunch next week and talk about it." He turned up the stairs to the second-floor workout stations, while I headed the other way, down to the locker room to change. A few minutes later, I was on the second floor myself, mixing with the usual assortment of fitness devotees and muscle freaks, and the less active who liked to look at them. The crowd was mostly male with a scattering of women, as they made their rounds of the free weights and workout machines, grim determination etched on their glistening faces. My membership had been a Christmas gift from Maurice and Fred, and I was still getting accustomed to gym culture after avoiding it with a vengeance since my college wrestling days. Several months later, the workout rooms still felt like an exotic and alien landscape. There was no denying my attraction to a trim and muscular physique, if it wasn't exaggerated to the point of grotesque caricature. Yet I'd always been put off by the rampant narcissism and unspoken elitism among so many in the gym crowd, as if it was an exclusive fraternity to which only the best-looking and most accomplished were admitted. To be sure, there were friendly people and pockets of camaraderie at the gym, which was as much a social club for some as it was a place to work off cellulite and get toned. But if you looked closely, you noticed that fat people or those with bad haircuts generally worked out alone.

The consistent exception seemed to be the Asian men, who generally pumped and lifted with serious discipline but found just as much time to laugh and gossip and enjoy each other's company, as if they were all part of an extended family, with Buff the evening gathering place. It was in one of these groups that I noticed Trang Nguyen that evening, as I went through my stretching routine on a warm-up mat. Seeing him there, only minutes after I'd run into Tony Mercury, reminded me that in Boys Town all roads eventually lead to the gym. Trang was dressed in a sleek, one-piece Spandex workout suit and stylish Puma rock-climbing shoes that fit his narrow feet like gloves, chatting with several other Asian men of various shapes and sizes. I was surprised to see him smiling and laughing on the same day his good friend, Bruce Bibby, had been laid to rest. Then I remembered Trang's chilly words to Cecilia Cortez on the day she'd introduced us: *Maybe not such good friends.*

As I took in Trang's lean, well-cut frame, his dark eyes came around and found mine. They held for a fleeting moment before darting to a nearby abdominal machine. He went to it, straddled the bench, settled back, adjusted his arms under the lift bars, and began his repetitions—short, tight crunches, perfectly executed, that accounted for his rippling abs. He didn't look at me again, not just then.

Over the next hour, as I moved from machine to machine, forcing myself through my routine, I watched Tony Mercury and Trang Nguyen avoid each other like recent divorcees at a badly planned cocktail party. Trang stayed close to his friends while Mercury worked the room. He seemed to know everybody, dispensing handshakes, slapping men on the back, signaling others from across the room, or stopping by the aerobic apparatuses to chat with men pedaling or stair-stepping the pounds away. The one person he didn't approach, however, was Trang Nguyen. They seemed to have developed a careful choreography, constantly dancing away from each other, while each man used the ubiquitous mirrors to chart the other's position. Mercury, the polished politician, was more adept at watching Trang surreptitiously, while Trang's uneasy eyes gave him away, coming back to the mirrors again and again to make sure Mercury was keeping his distance.

Eventually, Mercury drifted off to another room, and Trang seemed to relax a little. He was midway through his reps on a chest-and-shoulders machine when I sauntered over to see if I could break the ice.

"I saw you at the funeral service this morning, Trang. I should have said hello."

His eyes remained straight ahead, and he continued his reps without missing a beat. "Yes, I see you there, too."

"It was a sad day. I don't imagine it was easy for you." There was no reply, so I asked him if he'd known Bruce Bibby long.

"I know Bruce two year," he said, "when I come to work at City Hall."

"Cecilia Cortez suggested that you and Bruce were pretty close."
He said nothing, bearing down as he neared the end of his routine. "It was an emotional service this morning," I added, recalling his stoic face. "Your composure was remarkable."

Trang grunted out his final reps, clenching his teeth, the cordlike muscles of his upper body straining and taut. When he was done, he exhaled with a grunt, still not looking at me. A bead of perspiration appeared at his temple, trickling down the side of his smooth face. His silence stretched out to half a minute or more.

"I should probably let you get on with your workout." I tried to find his eyes, without success. "You seem very serious about staying in shape." I glanced at the rest of him. "It shows."

His eyes came up briefly, his smile tight. "No pain, no gain."

Then he looked away, letting his smile fade. His message—for me to get lost—couldn't have been more unambiguous.

I ran into Tony Mercury again in an adjacent room as I searched a rack for a set of thirty-five-pound dumbbells. I'd been doing curls with thirty pounds for several weeks, and it seemed like a good time to increase the weight. Or maybe I was doing it more for Mercury's benefit than my own.

"Always hard to find what you need on a busy night like this." Mercury sidled up beside me, close enough that our shoulders touched. "Sometimes I come early in the morning, on the way to my law office, when it's less crowded. But I make a point of dropping by at least one or two evenings a week. Gives me a chance to talk to people, get some face time with my constituents."

"Not a bad idea," I said, "with an election coming up."

He gripped a sixty-pound dumbbell in each fist, took a step back, and began doing alternate curls, his biceps ballooning under the weight.

"I didn't see you at the service for Bruce Bibby this morning," I said.

"Wasn't there."

"You were the only member of the City Council who didn't show."

"Had a court date. Couldn't break it."

The veins in his thick neck swelled, and his skin flushed as he braced to finish out his set, pumping the dumbbells in his meaty fists.

"I imagine his murder must have been quite a shock," I said. "Nice guy like that, young as he was, apparently living a quiet life."

Mercury let out a roar as he powered his way through his final rep. He dropped the dumbbells back on the rack with an iron clang.

"Every murder in West Hollywood is a shock to those of us who serve the city." Mercury's eyes met mine in the mirrored wall. "Not that we have that many, thank God."

"You must have known Bibby fairly well."

He used his towel to mop his face and neck. "Why do you say that, Justice?"

"He was writing up the brochure you've taken such an interest in. It occurred to me that you might have talked to him about it, as you have with me."

"We might have had a couple of conversations."

"This brochure seems to be awfully important to certain people. You, Lydia Ruttweller, Lester Cohen."

Mercury chucked me on the arm. "Let's finish this discussion over that lunch we talked about. I've got another half hour of free weights ahead of me." He patted my stomach. "Put some extra work into those abs, Justice. You're almost there."

He made his departure walking slightly up on his toes, just enough to flex his well-developed calves, while showing off his shapely ankles with low-cut socks—carrying himself with a faint air of self-consciousness, as if most of us were watching his every move. Of course, most of us *were* watching his every move. As I let my eyes linger a while on his sculpted body, I awaited that powerful sexual response that would have rippled through me not all that long ago; when it didn't come, I tried to find it, tried to will it into being. It was useless; the appreciation of Tony Mercury's beauty was there, but no impulse to act on it, no physical desire. Exasperated, I turned away, only to see Trang Nguyen stretched face-first over the dome of a padded apparatus, bobbing up and down in his form-fitting one-piece, the muscles of his bubble-shaped behind flexing with each rep. Again, I waited for a reaction in my groin instead of my head; again, nothing came. There was no heat anymore, nothing to stir my blood or make my cock twitch or cause my heart to flutter the way it once had. It was as if I'd left my libido downstairs in my locker and forgotten the combination to the lock.

An hour later I was on my way home, still thinking about the naked men I'd just mingled with in the shower and steam rooms, and what little response their wet bodies had triggered in me. Even in the Jacuzzi, when the hand of the chiseled blond next to me strayed underwater to my thigh, my body had registered nothing. It wasn't that I expected an erection every time I came into contact with a good-looking man, but it would have been nice to at least feel something, even for a guy copping a feel amid the swirling jets of a Jacuzzi.

A block from the gym, I cut up a side street, wanting to get off Santa Monica Boulevard and avoid the busy Boys Town social scene. I wasn't depressed or panicked—Prozac wouldn't allow for that—but I didn't want to subject myself to the heady buzz of romance along the boulevard just then either.

As I climbed the hill, finding an alternate route home, I realized that the man up ahead—still in gym gear, towel around his shoulders—was Tony Mercury. As he neared the next corner he veered right, and out of sight. When I reached the same spot, I saw him cut across the intersecting street and into an alley so dark and narrow it was rarely used by anyone but hustlers doing a cheap trick or transients looking for a place to pee. I couldn't imagine what reason he might have for going there. Curiosity overcame me. I followed, quickening my step.

Just into the darkened alley, with little room to spare on either side, a white Bentley sedan was stopped, facing up the hill. The license plate was a custom vanity special: GOLDEN OLDIE. Someone in the backseat pushed a rear door open and reached out. In the light from the open door, I could see the glint of gold cuff links on French cuffs, a fancy watch on the wrist, a ring with a showy gem on one finger. Someone with money, I thought, who didn't mind letting it be known. Mercury reached to grasp the welcoming hand, which pulled him inside as he yanked the door closed behind him. Through the tinted glass of the rear window, I glimpsed the silhouette of two men kissing. The Bentley pulled away, up the narrow alley, swallowed by the darkness.

I stood watching the taillights disappear, wondering why a politician and former porn star like Tony Mercury, so open and uninhibited in so many ways, would seek a rendezvous in such a dark and inconvenient place. Unless, of course, the romance had a touch of the illicit about it, and the risk of getting caught—that intoxicating whiff of danger—was part of the excitement.

EIGHT

Templeton's story about Dr. Roderick Ford's research into "killer genes" broke the next morning in the *L.A. Times,* positioned front page below the fold and illustrated with the brain scan images Ford had shown her with such pride at lunch on Tuesday. It seemed awfully fast to get a piece like that written up and into the paper, which suggested Templeton had composed much of it even before she'd spoken with Detective De Marco. It made the whole thing stink just a little more, at least from where I stood.

I read the article over coffee at Tribal Grounds, while the young novelist Christopher Rice sat outside with a window between us, looking impossibly fresh-faced and earnest. In one hand, he held an open copy of Raymond Chandler's *The Little Sister,* which he studied like a dedicated college student cramming for a serious exam; nearby, next to a pack of cigarettes, was a copy of James M. Cain's *Double Indemnity.* While he reached for his cigarettes, I turned back to Templeton's article on Dr. Ford.

As promised, she linked his studies to Bruce Bibby's murder through Victor Androvic, the young suspect whom she carefully avoided naming, while including all the details on the Bibby investigation that she'd gleaned from Ford. As I finished the long piece, I tried to gauge how Detective De Marco might react to Templeton's calculated betrayal. It seemed a dangerous turning point for Templeton, not just in her evolution as a reporter but also as a person. It struck me as a bad choice that didn't bode well for her future—not unlike a decision I'd once made that eventually brought my world crumbling down around me. Templeton was a loyal friend and a first-rate journalist, but she was also human, subject to all the weaknesses, lapses in judgment, and temptations the rest of us face every day. The difference was, as a frontline reporter for a major newspaper, covering serious issues and events, she was held to a higher standard, dependent on the public's trust because of the unusual responsibility she'd sought and been given.

Grief, I figured, had eroded her self-confidence and sense of right and wrong, causing her to look too hard for recognition to replace what she'd lost when a vicious killer had robbed her of Joe Soto and their future together. Another worry had also started nagging at me: that Templeton might be too eager to pronounce a murder suspect guilty, convicting him in newsprint, to assuage the rage she rightfully felt after Joe's death. The problem was that reporters with Templeton's stature and influence don't get a pass on ethics because life is treating them badly, or they're in a funk. Maybe they get counseling, or take a leave of absence, or switch to writing softer features for a while. But jumping a story like this one into print too soon wasn't an option, not with so much at risk that involved other people's lives and reputations. I guess I'd been counting on Templeton to be stronger and more dependable than I'd been when I'd faced my own crossroads; I'd hoped that she might learn from my unforgivable mistakes, that she might carry on with integrity and professionalism in a vital line of work that I'd dishonored and betrayed. Maybe I'd been counting on her more than I should have.

In the background, Melissa Etheridge sang "When You Find the One," while I sipped my dark roast and stared out the window, wondering if my friendship with Alexandra Templeton would ever be the same again.

I entered City Hall a few minutes past eight to find people buzzing about Templeton's front-page story. I tried to ignore the chatter and get down to work, hoping to finish an outline for the brochure by the end of the day.

By early afternoon I was still at my desk, eating lunch and poring through Bruce Bibby's documents, making a list of areas where I felt I needed more data. During the week, I'd come to realize that Bibby had kept many of the details inside his head, with nothing on paper or in the computer, at least not that had been given to me. One area that he had documented meticulously was the Sherman district and its Plains cottages, taking note of what seemed like every board, brick, and bit of mortar used on the properties when the dwellings were built back in the early 1900s. At least that was one aspect of my assignment that would require no further research, much to my relief.

Shortly before five, when I figured Trang Nguyen would be leaving for the day, I headed down to his basement cubicle to get some help opening a document in my files that was giving me trouble. I could have messaged him over the computer, of course, through the City Hall communications system, and both of us could have worked through the problem without ever leaving our desks. But I was acutely aware of my attraction to Trang, even as I realized how cerebral and inaccessible it was, and how shallow the sexual impulse connected to it; it was there, but only faintly, like a sputtering signal from a satellite in outer space whose radio transmitter is running on its last reserves. I yearned to be next to him again, to see his splendid face, perhaps to touch him innocently, if only to keep that sputtering signal alive. With my wide-ranging taste in men, I had similar yearnings for the more brawny Tony Mercury. Yet despite Mercury's openness and seductive nature, I found Trang more vulnerable and approachable. The more he pushed me away, the closer I wanted to get.

As I entered his working quarters, he was staring blankly at Templeton's article; the newspaper was wrinkled, suggesting he'd read the story more than once, maybe even taken it with him to lunch. When he heard me coming in behind him, he quickly folded the paper and thrust it into a desk drawer. I explained my problem with the document and apologized for being such a dunce about computers. He found the document among his files, asked me to take a chair beside him, and took me through a few simple steps, converting the document so that I could open it with my existing software program. I pulled my chair close, taking a moment to study Trang more keenly—the clean slope of his neck, his dark and delicate lashes, the way his hair fell across his forehead like that of a guileless schoolboy. When our bare arms inadvertently touched, he quickly shifted his chair, putting more space between us. Yet I also noticed him steal a glance or two of his own, down at my hairy forearm, across to my craggy face. And when he moved his chair, it was only an inch or two, a token gesture at best.

"Yesterday, at the funeral service," I said, "I noticed that all the council members were there. Except for Tony Mercury."

Trang kept his attention on the computer screen, his fingers on the keyboard. "You see how easy it is to convert the document? You just do what I show you, and you have no more problem with it."

"What's going on between you and Mercury, Trang? I know it's none of my business, but—"

"No, it not your business." His voice was sharp. "It between him and me, like you say."

"What's he done that's so terrible?"

His eyes flashed. "You tell me you come here to get help with your work. I help you."

"It's connected to Bruce Bibby, isn't it?" Trang dropped his eyes, but he didn't stand or move away; tension tightened his neck and jaw. "Maybe it's connected to all three of you."

Trang glanced over his shoulder, saw that we were alone, then said straight out, "Tony touch me in way I no want him to do. It cause bad problem between him and me."

"Touched you—sexually?"

"He put his hand on me, down between my leg. I say, 'Please stop, Mr. Mercury,' but he very drunk. He not stop."

"When was this?"

"February, we go on trip. Six of us, from City Hall. Bruce, he also go. To San Diego, to see how they set up computer system to keep all their old records, all their photos, the things from very long ago."

"A city-sponsored field trip?" Trang nodded. "And Mercury forced himself on you when he was drunk?"

"We in bar that night, after we do our work. He drink too much, act stupid. He grab me in my private place. I tell him no. He no care what I say. He try to do what he want with me." Trang slapped his knee with his open palm. "So I hurt him, between his leg. Bang, with my knee. That stop him pretty quick."

80

I grinned. "You kicked him in the balls?" He nodded, but didn't smile. "Since he's a council member, and you're a city employee," I said, "what he did amounts to sexual harassment."

"That what Bruce say, right after it happen. He want me to make report, get lawyer. He say he back me up on what he see."

"Bruce Bibby witnessed this?"

"He see everything. He tell me I should file lawsuit against Tony, make trouble for him, get some money."

"You could probably get a nice settlement from the city, out of court. It wouldn't help Mercury's political stock, either—not if the city had to write a fat check at taxpayers' expense, all because a council member couldn't hold his liquor."

"Tony, he come to me later, he apologize. He say to me, please, do not make trouble. I tell him I not sure what I do. I tell him to stay away from me, that I do not want him near me no more."

"And that was the end of it?"

"Bruce, he keep after me to file lawsuit. I think because his friend, Mrs. Ruttweller, she want me to get Tony in trouble."

"Lydia Ruttweller was using Bruce to pressure you to file the lawsuit?" Trang nodded. "Did Mercury know this?"

"He know, because she say nasty thing to him about it. They no like each other, those two. Tony, he very nervous about this, that I make trouble with a lawyer before the voting time come."

"Were there any other witnesses when Mercury groped you?"

"No, just Bruce. Nobody else see."

"So now it's your word against Mercury's. It's been three months since the incident. He's up for reelection. Politics are involved. If you filed a lawsuit now, I'm not sure it would hold much water."

He regarded me with confusion. "Hold water for what?"

"Sorry—figure of speech. It means your case wouldn't be as strong now, that you might not win. It might look like it was politically motivated."

I asked him how long he'd been in the U.S. Nine years, he told me, after coming here when he was eighteen. "I sorry about my English," he said. "It still not so good."

I nodded at his PC. "You know the language of computers,

though. No problem there. I'd say you've done pretty well for your-self."

"I do OK." An uncomfortable silence followed, and he glanced at his watch. "My work over. Time for me to go. You OK now, you get everything you need?"

My next words came impulsively, out of the blue. "I could use a partner for dinner."

"Dinner?"

"My way of thanking you for your help."

He shook his head forcefully "Sorry, Mr. Justice. I no date older Caucasian guy no more."

"I'm not exactly asking for a date, Trang."

His smile was thin, almost insulting. "I know about you older white guy. You like pretty Asian boy for fun."

"Maybe I'm different. Maybe I just want some company."

He shook his head again, his smile like a razor, cutting back and forth. "You all the same. Rice queen looking for Asian boy toy. I know what you think. In dark, with lights out and no clothes, we all feel like little boy. I hear white guy say that once, and I finally under-stand. You have your fun with us, then you want some new boy, to play with and get you off."

I pushed my chair back and stood. "You're an angry man, Trang. A very angry man."

"Maybe I get hurt too many time by older white guy. Maybe I smarter now. Maybe I no get hurt again."

His eyes were bright and fierce, no longer such a mystery. I was reminded that delicate beauty like his didn't necessarily mean that he was weak or fragile or without the means to take care of himself.

"Thanks for your help, Trang. I'll try not to bother you again."

I was almost out the door when he called to me. When I turned, he had the newspaper in his lap, open to Templeton's article.

"You are friend with the woman who write this story, yes?"

"How did you know that?"

"Some people here at City Hall, they say you her friend."

"Alexandra Templeton—what about her?"

"Maybe you tell her to ask question."

"What question is that, Trang?"

"The one who kill Bruce take only one thing from his apartment.

He take Bruce computer. Nothing else. Bruce computer very old, not so good, not worth so much money no more. So why he take that, and nothing else, when Bruce have other thing with much more value?"

"How do you know that was the only thing taken?"

"Because the lady detective, Miss De Marco, she take me to Bruce apartment. She know that I go there many time, because Bruce my friend. She want me to tell her if anything gone. I tell her the only thing that I can tell is gone is Bruce old computer."

"So you and Bruce *were* good friends," I said.

His eyes shifted away for a moment. "Maybe we friend, a little bit."

"And what was Detective De Marco's reaction, when you mentioned the computer—that it wasn't worth stealing?"

"She write it down in her notebook. She take her pen, and she make the line underneath, three time. Maybe you tell your friend, and she write about that. Maybe you tell her also about Tony Mercury—what he do to me, what Bruce see."

"Why are you so interested in what she writes?"

"That my business, my private stuff."

I smiled. "I misjudged you, Trang. There's a good deal more to you than I saw at first."

"We all much more than what people see, Mr. Justice. We all different inside from what people think they know."

"You think you know me, Trang. You've judged me. But maybe I'm different inside."

He had no answer for that, just a baleful glare and a chin thrust forward in silent defiance. Trang was one of those pretty, nonwhite young immigrant men who'd learned to claw for his identity and dignity, the kind that get used by older gay men the way so many straight men objectify young women, wanting little more from them than their lovely bodies. For self-preservation, Trang had developed a tough hide, to protect his heart from further bruising, to hold on to the self-respect he'd forged through disillusionment and pain. That much was pretty clear to me now.

If there was something soft about Trang Nguyen, something tender, he wasn't about to let me see it.

NINE

I was halfway home, in the heart of Boys Town, when Templeton reached me on my cell phone, asking if she could buy me dinner.

She realized how insensitive she'd been the previous day, she said, and wanted to make it up to me. She also wanted to tell me about a rental she'd found, since her condo had sold, and she wanted to leave Santa Monica for West Hollywood as soon as possible. I accepted her invitation with mixed emotions, feeling reluctant to be so chummy after the stunt she'd pulled in the *LAT,* but relieved at not having to eat alone that night. We agreed to hook up at Boy Meets Grill at six, before the evening crowd grabbed all the tables.

I arrived a few minutes early, got a deuce in a corner on the sidewalk patio, and ordered lemonade while I waited. It was Happy Hour on a Friday evening, which meant that Boys Town was swarming with hundreds of young men with little more on their minds than a good time, driven by the promise of another heady weekend. Shorts and tank tops were in abundance, at least on the bodies worth showing off, along with a dazzling display of muscular arms, shapely legs, and Palm Springs tans. I was reminded of a bitter comment I'd heard years ago, from a pockmarked, overweight, self-avowed sissy in his forties: *If you're old or fat or ugly or female, Boys Town can be the loneliest place on earth.* I wasn't sure things had changed all that much, although I did see Bruce Vilanch, the portly comedy writer and actor of *Hollywood Squares* and *Hairspray* fame, holding court at an inside table and having a pretty good time of it.

The tables around me were slowly filling up with chatty groups of friends playing catch-up or couples holding hands and laughing across their tables. I glanced at my watch, hoping that Templeton would be on time. She wasn't. At a quarter past six, she called again, this time to apologize for breaking the dinner date she'd made only half an hour ago.

"I really don't want to eat alone tonight, Templeton. Can't you at least stop off for a quick bite? I've even got a sidewalk table, for people watching."

"I hate to do it to you, Justice, but something's come up."

"Find a better dinner partner?"

"Don't get pissy. You and I can have dinner any night."

"Except tonight, apparently."

"Look, I'll make it up to you. Tomorrow night I'll take you to a really neat place I just heard about. A restaurant critic at the *LAT* tipped me to it. I've already made the reservation."

"Maybe I'm busy tomorrow night."

"Do you want to enjoy a nice dinner with me tomorrow night, or would you rather spend another Saturday night alone, listening to your old jazz tapes and feeling sorry for yourself?"

"OK, I'll take the dinner. So what's suddenly come up that's so important?"

"If I tell you, you'll just say something nasty."

I thought about it for two seconds. "Let me guess. You're having dinner with Dr. Roderick Ford."

"Smart-ass."

"So I'm right?"

"Lucky guess."

"He's married, Templeton. You told me that yourself."

"Separated—for several months now. The divorce is imminent. He was very careful to inform me of that."

"And they say chivalry is dead."

"Our dinner meeting is strictly professional. Dr. Ford wants to thank me for the story I wrote. Besides, I have more questions for him."

"He liked your article?"

"He was very complimentary."

"That should tell you right there that it was too soft."

"See? I knew you'd say something like that. Anyway, he's promised new details on Victor Androvic, that Russian boy who's about to be charged with the Bibby murder."

"Possibly to be charged," I said.

"I want to keep Dr. Ford on a string, wring as much out of him as I can. This story isn't over yet. So we're on for tomorrow night?"

"Sure, if I don't have to wear a tie."

"At least look nice. I'll pick you up at half past seven."

Before I could reply, I heard her click off. I still wasn't sure I wanted to break bread with Templeton, but I figured it might give us another chance to explore some issues I felt she was avoiding. The waiter returned, I ordered a steak and baked potato, and watched the passing parade of men with a nagging disconsolation. Prozac doesn't end one's loneliness; it just takes the edge off enough so that you don't feel like slitting your wrists or drinking yourself to death as a cure. Two lovebirds at a nearby table were making eyes at each other and exchanging air kisses, the kind of West Hollywood twinks who've been in love for about a week and are already mulling names for the baby. When they started wrinkling their noses at each other I stood up, chased down my waiter, and asked him if it was too late to cancel my order. He said no, I offered to pay for the lemonade, and he said to forget it. I left two bucks under the saltshaker for his trouble and headed home, grabbing a Philly cheese steak takeout on the way.

I walked fast and determinedly, past the bars with their open doors and windows, where the clinking of glass could be heard and all the attractive young men kept their eyes on each other as they sipped their martinis and Heinekens, letting anyone with the wrong look know not to waste their time. Not a good place for an ex-drinker facing middle age to linger, so I didn't. Half a block north, as I waited for the light to change at Santa Monica Boulevard, I felt fingers busy at the back of my neck. I turned to find a slim young man standing just behind me, fiddling with the neckline of my shirt.

"Your label was exposed," he said in a light voice, smiling pleasantly. "All fixed now."

There were unwritten codes among us, unspoken rules, a communal language, secret signals, a shared understanding that covered a million things and united us in strange and invisible ways, from the most ridiculous to the most profound. The light changed and I crossed, with my shirt collar rearranged, thanks to a stranger on the street whom I'd probably never see again. As they say, only in West Hollywood.

Maurice and Fred were out to the movies, and the house on Norma Place was dark, save for a light in the kitchen and another over the door on the broad front porch. I trudged up the drive to the garage and climbed the stairway to the little apartment I'd lived in alone for nearly fifteen years, where Jacques had lived before me.

When I checked my e-mail all I found was the usual spam trying to sell me photos of naked ladies that didn't interest me, mortgages I couldn't use, home employment opportunities I didn't want, penile enlargement I didn't need, and Viagra. I had to concede that the Viagra promotions were starting to have a certain appeal.

I logged off and sat staring at the blank screen, knowing I should put in some work on my memoirs. I opened a recent letter from my editor, looking for inspiration. In succinct fashion, she'd reminded me of the major points I was expected to cover, for the sake of scope, content, and promotional value.

Dear Benjamin,

Just a quick note to clarify the essential elements of your personal story that will be of such vital interest to readers, as detailed in your outline and discussed more recently in our phone conversation of April 28.

These would include: your early childhood in Buffalo under the domination of your police detective father; the growing impact of his drinking and violence on you, your little sister, and your mother; your sexual initiation at age twelve by your family priest; the tragic homicide in which you killed your father at age seventeen when you caught him molesting your eleven-year-old sister; your decision not long after to study journalism and devote yourself to investigative reporting; the premature deaths of your mother from alcoholism and your sister from a drug overdose; your hiring at the *Los Angeles Times* not long after; the death of your lover Jacques from AIDS in 1990; the Pulitzer you won later that year; the scandal that ensued, when the winning series of articles was exposed as a fabrication, forcing you to return the prize; your rape several years ago and the HIV infection that followed; finally, in more abbreviated fashion, your involvement in solving a number of sensational murders in the Los Angeles area, working with your friend, Alexandra Templeton. Be sure to briefly include the loss of your left eye in that horrific assault you suffered earlier this year, connected to Joe Soto's death.

It's all such wonderful story material, so don't be afraid to make the most of it! Of course, you'll address your own issues with alcohol, anger, violence, and depression as appropriate, per your outline and our previous discussions.

I trust the manuscript is coming along nicely. Let me know if there's anything you need to discuss along the way.

With affection,
Jan Long

Seeing my eventful but miserable life laid out in such perky and orderly fashion did nothing to encourage me to write about it; if anything, I felt less disposed than ever to wade into the manuscript and try to give the sluggish narrative some badly needed momentum. For no particular reason other than procrastination, I decided to open a new document and type a list of everyone I'd met or had contact with that week since starting my new job, jotting down their phone numbers and e-mail addresses as well, if I had them. It was an old habit, making lists to find some order in the chaos of my life. When I was done, my latest list looked like this:

Cecelia Cortez
Tony Mercury
Trang Nguyen
Lydia Ruttweller
Colin Harrison
Ted Meeks
Dr. Roderick Ford
Detective Mira De Marco

Eight names, people who hadn't been in my life five days ago. I studied the list, assigning a role to each: *director of publications, prodevelopment council member, computer systems manager, historical preservation activist, landlord, property manager, research psychologist, sheriff's detective.* Each person, I realized in retrospect, had a connection to Bruce Bibby, however slight. Why that mattered to me I wasn't sure. I had no interest in Bibby or his murder, I reminded myself, only in finishing his work and getting back to my own. Still, before I closed the document, I saved it.

For an hour or more, I played old jazz tapes and paced the floor, trying to find a way back into my memoir that might get it moving in the right direction. The tapes I'd chosen were on the mellower side: Art Pepper, Bill Evans, Paul Desmond, Chet Baker, and Miles Davis during his *Kind of Blue* period. After shifting gears with Prozac, I no longer had an ear for the more frenetic, improvisational sounds of John Coltrane, Ornette Coleman, Thelonious Monk, and some of my old favorites; at times, I even felt edgy and uncomfortable listening to them, as if I'd lost that part of myself that responded to the personal joy or anguish they often expressed so brilliantly in their music, if you could connect to it while you connected to something deep in yourself.

Finally, as the clock neared nine, when I couldn't think of any other valid diversions or excuses, I sat at my desk again, entered my memoir file, and opened the outline document, looking over the roughly forty chapter headings I'd delineated as the skeleton of my unwritten book. For someone who had knocked out more than a thousand articles in his day, producing a manuscript of roughly a hundred thousand words seemed a reasonable goal; the trick, I figured, was not to think of it as a book, as an intimidating mountain to be climbed, but to focus only on writing one chapter—then another, and another, building the book chapter by chapter until it was done. But I'd been at it for a few months now, with nothing more to show for it than several lackluster chapters that laid out facts from my life in a dull and desultory fashion. As I sat there staring at my outline, I felt a creative numbing overtaking me, as if someone had given my imagination a shot of Novocain. What I needed instead was an injection of adrenaline, of pure emotion; if I could just get that, I told myself, I'd be on my way and have the damn manuscript finished in a matter of months.

I scrolled through the outline, past less pungent moments in my life, looking for something that might provide the necessary rush. I stopped on the night five years ago when I'd been raped by a demonic ex-cop and infected with the virus. If anything were to get me going, I thought, it would be that horrendous incident, and the vengeful rage it had produced. So I sat at the keyboard, typing and rewriting and deleting lines, trying to find the voice I needed to tell my story with the authority and passion it demanded. But nothing came. It was like trying to sculpt with dense, arid clay that crumbled in my fingers. No matter how much I pushed the words around, no matter how much I prodded and reworked them, they never came to life.

After nearly three hours, I erased everything I'd written and closed the document, feeling maddeningly frustrated and mentally exhausted. Without my Prozac, I might have ripped the PC from its moorings and heaved it against the nearest wall. As it was, I sighed deeply, rubbed my temples, and considered alternative approaches. A minute later, I was back on-line, intending to do some research on the subject of male rape to see if that might give me better material to work with, something concrete and tangible until I found my voice and the right words started flowing onto the page.

I engaged my search engine and typed the words *male rape* into the keyword window. A moment later, an index page appeared. After that came more pages, listing hundreds of choices, with each Internet source printed and underlined in blue for instant access. Many of them were links to books or published articles on the subject, with description lines indicating serious written content. But just as many pointed to a different kind of presentation, one that targeted not researchers or victims looking for information or assistance, but instead the sexually motivated, people for whom the notion of male rape was a turn-on, especially if visual images were involved.

Hard-core porn had never appealed to me much; I'd always preferred the real thing to the make-believe, and had never needed visual enhancements to get aroused. Still, despite my limited exposure to it,

I wasn't so naive that I didn't know how available it was. There was no end to the unwanted spam that flooded my e-mail box each day offering me photos and video of *hot pussy, fantastic tits, mouth-watering clit, cock-sucking babes,* and *naked virgin chicks under eighteen guaranteed.* It was enough to make one worry that heterosexuality might be a serious threat to the American family. For me, the Internet's chief attractions were for research and exchanging e-mail; for years I'd ignored the siren call of cyber porn, happy to have the Internet to assist me in my work.

That night, however, as I scanned the index of porn sites geared to male rape fantasies, I didn't turn away. It's funny how temptation works at us, ever present and all around; it beckons to us, hoping we notice just enough to be enticed, to come a little closer, try a taste, hoping it catches us at just that moment when an emptiness in our lives or hearts feels so gaping and full of ache that we're desperate to fill it with something, anything, that excites us or just feels good. It might be a temptation as simple as a chocolate bar or a cigarette, advertised with cunning, or as easy as moving the mouse on the mouse pad, placing the cursor on the blue underlined lettering of an Internet link, clicking, and entering a world of images that are fascinating, thrilling, frightening, forbidden, endless. Which is exactly what I did that night.

I'd never imagined that there could be so many sites with so many links to so many other sites, devoted to seemingly every variation of human sexuality, and so readily accessible. Hundreds of images, thousands, of men and women, men and men, women and women, each of them claiming *All Models Over Eighteen* but some clearly featuring boys and girls younger than that, if you looked hard enough or plowed so frantically and blindly into the depths of cyberspace the way I did that night that you stumbled upon these illicit sites by accident. My focus became relentlessly homosexual: *Hot smooth twinks, military studs, locker room fantasies, slim Asian boys, big hairy bears, black men in action, East Euro boys, wild gay orgies, fraternity JO, naked boys in bondage,* and on and on, approximating if not quite equaling the plethora of hetero sites.

I sat there jumping from link to link, transfixed by the images, unaware of time passing, though never physically aroused. Finally, feeling oddly spent yet hopelessly unsatisfied, I forced myself to log off. When I glanced at the clock, I was amazed to see that it was nearly 2:00 A.M. Without realizing it, I'd been lost in cyberspace for hours.

I brushed my teeth, took my late-night meds, and crawled into bed, embarrassed and just a little ashamed, vowing never to log on to an Internet porn site again. Lulled by my Prozac, I slept deeply and well.

TEN

The area of town Templeton and I were to dine in Saturday night was known as the Avenues of Art and Design, a chic neighborhood of galleries, design studios, boutiques, and restaurants in the southwest corner of the city, where ivy, wrought iron, and the design trade flourished, and everything—even the leaves—looked carefully arranged. Just the kind of neighborhood Templeton loved but where I rarely ventured.

"This restaurant must be awfully swank," I said, as Templeton arrived to pick me up at half past seven, punctual to the minute. "Given its address south of Melrose."

She plucked a piece of lint from a shoulder of my blue blazer and fastened a button on my shirtfront that I'd missed. "That's why we're dining there, Justice. I'm determined to broaden your horizons." She stood back and looked me over. "You could do with a new pair of shoes, but you're presentable."

It was a pleasant evening, so we left her car and strolled down from Norma Place. As we crossed Santa Monica Boulevard, it was coming to life with the older crowd that arrived early to dine and drink before abandoning Boys Town to the more energetic younger set. Our path took us along San Vicente Boulevard, past the sheriff's substation, then the looming blue-and-green glass structures of the Pacific Design Center, where ground would soon be cleared for the third and final red extension. That put us in the Avenues of Art and Design, with Melrose the primary thoroughfare. It was one of West

Hollywood's four primary districts, the other three being Sunset Boulevard, Santa Monica Boulevard, and the studio district, which included most of the city and hundreds of entertainment-related businesses, from small labs to sprawling studio lots.

We arrived at our destination a few minutes before eight to find valets scurrying to open the doors of luxury cars, mostly black with deep paint jobs polished like fine onyx. The restaurant was called Miss Chatelaine, which might have tipped Templeton to its special clientele if she'd been aware of the song by k.d. lang, which she wasn't. She got her first clue as we stepped into the lobby to find ourselves among a throng of diners who were mostly female. They were uniformly well-groomed and dressed on the elegant side, in keeping with the setting, although many of the women favored stylish pantsuits, short hair, and understated makeup and accessories, and pumps or flats in lieu of high heels. There was an ease and intimacy to the gathering that one doesn't usually find in a public setting, as if we'd stumbled into a sorority with its hair down, or a convivial dinner party thrown by a wealthy lesbian.

We were greeted hospitably by a stunning redhead on the statuesque side, who wore a body-hugging evening dress of green satin and three-inch heels. Clutching menus, she led us past a dimly lit cocktail lounge where Jo Stafford could be heard singing "Haunted Heart" in the background. Women in couples or small groups sat at scattered tables or on stools at the well-stocked bar, sipping cocktails from fancy, retro-fifties glasses, not a few looking like they yearned for a forbidden cigarette. Along one wall was an enormous aquarium filled with an array of exotic fish, casting its undulating light over the room and a few bare shoulders mixed among the more conservative attire. We left the sultry voice of Jo Stafford behind and traveled through a brief passageway to enter the main room, where a live combo played a tune evoking smoky Argentine nightclubs of the thirties. Out on the floor, several female couples were engaged in sensual tangos, while a spotlight followed their languorous movements, switching from couple to couple so deftly it was almost unnoticeable. Nearby on a small stage, a group of female musicians in white ties and tails performed under a spotlight of their own. There might have been a half dozen men in the place besides me—not counting the serving staff, which was mixed—but I didn't see more than that as we passed through. The few looks that went Templeton's way were appreciative but discreet, while the ones directed at me seemed more curious, even suspicious.

"I believe someone's played a joke on me," Templeton whispered, obviously referring to the restaurant critic at the *L.A. Times* who'd sent her here, and not sounding pleased about it.

"Maybe she's just trying to broaden your horizons," I said, and Templeton sliced me with a glare.

We were seated at a deuce off to the side, where we had a nice view of the room. Around much of the perimeter, plush chenille booths shaped like clamshells gave the room a feeling of cozy elegance. In one of the booths, I recognized Sheila Keuhl, the state senator, chatting animatedly with a graying couple I believed to be Betty Berzon, the author and psychotherapist, and her longtime female partner, Terry DeCrescenzo, a prominent social activist. The linen and silver on our table was of high quality, the crystal fine, the yellow roses and baby's breath fresh. Glittering chandeliers overhead had been dimmed to a faint shimmer, allowing the spotlights on the dancers their special distinction. I hadn't been to a place this posh in a long time, and said so.

"Frankly, I'm surprised I got in without a tie."

"I see more neckties on the women than the men," Templeton said, sounding a bit churlish.

"Relax, Templeton. No one's going to assault you. You're much more likely to get your butt pinched at one of the straight dives up on the Strip."

Templeton ordered a cocktail, which she usually didn't, while I made do with a bottle of Hildon sparkling water. She slid her eyes this way and that, clearly unsettled by the situation. Under her breath, she asked, "Why do I feel like they're all staring at me?"

"Because you're self-conscious," I said.

"I've never been self-conscious."

"I've seen you act like a flustered schoolgirl, with certain men you find attractive."

"Not for years."

"For some reason, you're self-conscious now."

"Because they're staring at me." She lowered her voice almost to inaudibility. "Some of them, anyway."

"And if they weren't? You'd be asking me why not."

"I would not." Quickly, she added, "Maybe we should go."

"Not on your life. You promised me this dinner, remember?"

Eventually, we ordered; the food, nicely prepared and presented, was served by well-trained waiters in bow ties and waistcoats. As we ate, I attempted to steer Templeton toward the subject of her article on Dr. Ford and Victor Androvic, hoping to get her to see things my way, but she seemed too spooked by the clientele to follow my lead. Instead, she peppered me with endless questions about "lesbian culture"—what percentage of the general population they might comprise, why they weren't more visible or politically active in greater numbers, if they tended to form long-term relationships more than gay men, if it was true, as she'd heard, that breast cancer affected lesbians at a higher rate than other women. I was able to answer a few of her queries reasonably well but not most, which failed to dissuade her from asking more.

"You talk about lesbians as if they're an alien species," I said.

"The idea of two women—" She broke off, making a face. "Never mind. Let's just eat our dinner."

"I never knew you were so homophobic, Templeton."

"I am *not* homophobic. I'm very liberal. It's just that—"

"They disgust you."

"They do not disgust me."

"You're obviously uncomfortable."

"I apologize, Oh Politically Perfect One." She sighed. "It's strange, that's all. I'm not used to being around this many gay women all at once. I prefer them one or two at a time, I guess, like chocolates."

"Feeling like a minority?"

Her retort came quickly. "A black woman always feels like a minority. That never changes, no matter what the setting." Suddenly, her eyes lifted from mine, toward the entrance to the room. "Am I wrong, or is that Mira De Marco?"

I turned to see the redheaded hostess leading a group of six women in the general direction of our table. Detective De Marco was among them, the tallest of the bunch. She'd exchanged her efficient dark business suit for a nicely cut silk pantsuit of periwinkle blue, which was set off with tasteful silver accessories that complemented the streaks of premature gray in her hair. The hair was short-cropped, as before, but with a wave to it, softening her angular face just enough to transform it from severe to handsome. She moved on low-heeled pumps with her customary sturdy gait, but also with grace and confidence, which went well with the rest of the package.

"That's Detective De Marco, all right," I said. "Looking very attractive, I might add."

Templeton shrugged. "In a boyish kind of way, I guess."

"It worked for Katharine Hepburn."

At that moment, as a busboy cleared our plates, De Marco spotted us. Her eyes quickly zeroed in on Templeton. As they did, the merriment went out of them and the set of her jaw got tough. She spoke briefly to the other women in her group, who continued on to their table without her, while De Marco veered directly toward ours.

"I think she's coming over," Templeton said. "Why would she be coming over?"

"Probably wants to compliment you on your article." I folded my arms across my chest and sat back. "This should be fun."

"For you maybe." Templeton raised her chin and drew back her shoulders, as if bracing herself for combat. "What are the odds of running into her on a Saturday night out?"

"West Hollywood's a small town." I smiled smugly. "One of its charms."

De Marco pulled up, looming over the table. Templeton beat her to the punch, speaking first in a chilly voice that belied her false smile.

"I didn't think deputies could afford to eat in places like this, Detective."

"It's my birthday," De Marco said. "Number thirty-eight. My friends are taking me out."

"Nice friends," I said. "Happy birthday."

De Marco kept her eyes on Templeton. "I'll make this short and sweet. Your article in yesterday's paper has caused some problems. It's got me in hot water with my superiors, but I can deal with that. What pisses me off is the way your story screwed our investigation."

"I was very careful in the way I wrote that piece, Detective."

"Not so careful that it didn't tip Victor Androvic that we were narrowing in on him as a suspect."

"I didn't mention Androvic by name, merely the Bruce Bibby murder."

"It was pretty obvious to anyone close to Androvic that he was the suspect you were talking about. Including Androvic himself, of course."

"You've heard from him?"

"Just the opposite. No one's heard from him since your story broke, including his probation officer. They were supposed to meet yesterday afternoon, as scheduled. But Androvic didn't show. Didn't call, hasn't checked in, can't be found."

"I see." Templeton's voice had lost some of its spunk.

"No, Miss Templeton, you don't see. Victor Androvic has taken off, gone into hiding. We don't know where he is. You promised me you'd hold off on printing your story. I guess that was my mistake, wasn't it? Trusting you like that."

"I told you I'd keep you out of it, Detective. I didn't tell you I wouldn't go with what I'd learned from Dr. Ford."

An unpleasant smile creased De Marco's face. "You think you're pretty clever, don't you?"

"I think I'm a conscientious reporter, who knows a good story when she sees it and recognizes the public's right to know the facts." Templeton lifted her chin again, regaining some of her resoluteness. "Anyway, you'd already questioned Victor Androvic. He knew that you were on to him. You told me that yourself."

"We told Androvic he was being questioned because he'd once made deliveries to Bruce Bibby's neighborhood, which we knew about from the previous investigation into the caviar-smuggling operation. We told him we were questioning anyone with a criminal background who'd been seen on Bibby's street recently and gave him the impression that he might be in the clear. He had no idea that we'd tied him to the crime scene through fingerprints. He didn't know we'd caught him in a number of lies that make him our best suspect. Thanks to your story, now he does."

"I didn't specifically write—"

"It was implied." De Marco leaned down, flattening her hands on our table, fixing Templeton with her angry eyes. "You gave Victor Androvic the heads up, and now he's on the lam. I asked you to sit on the story a little longer. You gave me the impression you would."

"I didn't exactly tell you—"

"You deliberately misled and used me." De Marco's words pounded like a sledgehammer. "And now you're cowering behind a pile of bullshit."

"If you misunderstood, Detective, I—"

"Law enforcement is a tight-knit community, Miss Templeton. Word travels fast about reporters like you. You could see a lot of sources dry up in a hurry."

Mira De Marco started to turn away but held up as Templeton spoke again. "Perhaps I could make it up to you." The calculation in Templeton's voice was unmistakable. De Marco waited, saying nothing. "If you were willing to officially name Androvic as your prime suspect," Templeton went on, "to go on the record, we could run his photo in Monday's paper. Alert the public that he's wanted, help you bring him in."

De Marco smiled again, not as ugly as before but not pretty, either. "And get another exclusive for yourself? You don't quit, do you?"

"If it would make you feel better, Detective, I'd run the story without my byline. Or turn it over to another reporter."

De Marco shook her head. "No, thanks. We'll make do without your help on this one."

"Suit yourself," Templeton said.

De Marco started off, toward the table where her friends waited. Templeton turned to me, looking unsettled and trying to hide it. "You heard my offer. I was willing to help her. If she's going to be stubborn, that's not my problem."

Before I could reply, De Marco was back at our table, her hands on her hips, keying on Templeton again. "One question, Miss Templeton."

"All right," Templeton said evenly.

"If Victor Androvic commits another murder before we find him, maybe a couple of murders, will you be covering that story as well?"

Templeton's hesitation spoke volumes. She cocked her head uneasily. "I beg your pardon?"

"You didn't hear me?" De Marco raised her husky voice. "I should speak louder?"

"I can hear you just fine," Templeton said.

"According to your article, the idea that Victor Androvic might kill again, perhaps soon, seems like a definite possibility, wouldn't you say? Father was a multiple murderer back in Russia. Killer gene in the circuitry of his brain. Felony conviction on his record. Now a suspect in a brutal murder. You made the case in print that Victor Androvic is one bad dude, a danger to the public."

"I made it clear that he's a suspect." Templeton was stumbling right into De Marco's trap and didn't even know it. "There's no proof that he's committed violence, no real evidence yet."

"No there's not, is there? So why did you print the story, Miss Templeton? If our case against him is so flimsy, as you seem to be claiming now to save your pretty ass, why didn't you wait until you had something more concrete?"

"I don't think my anatomy belongs in this discussion."

"I don't give a fig what you think. You're very nice to look at, Miss Templeton. It's a shame it's only skin-deep." Templeton opened her mouth, but no words came out, so De Marco hammered the nails deeper. "You don't give a damn about the damage you've caused. You don't give a damn if Victor Androvic takes another life or two while he's on the run. You don't give a damn if he leaves a trail of grief and tears behind him. Not as long as you get your front-page exclusive."

"That's not fair." Templeton's voice cracked, and I felt a stab of sympathy for her. I could only imagine what was roiling inside her at that moment, especially with the murder of Joe Soto so raw in her memory. Maybe what Detective De Marco was saying *wasn't* fair— not precisely—but Templeton was smart enough to know it was close to the mark.

"The only thing you care about is advancing your career," De Marco went on. "The only thing you care about is yourself, and to hell with our investigation or public safety or potential victims."

Templeton's façade had completely collapsed; she looked stricken. "I'm sorry if the timing of my story—"

De Marco cut her off again, relentless. "Maybe Victor Androvic will make a bloody mess of his next victim, Miss Templeton, and you can get an exclusive on the pictures, too. Before the coroner covers the body and carts it off to the morgue to be hacked up for autopsy, while a cop has to call the next of kin. I just hope I'm not that cop."

She turned on her heel and was gone again. This time she didn't come back.

Templeton sat very still, avoiding my eyes, her chin trembling. Finally, quietly, she said, "I guess I'd better ask for the check."

We walked home from Miss Chatelaine without speaking. It was close to ten, and the old-timers were heading home to bed or thinking about it as they had a nightcap in the cozier bars and restaurants where the mature set hung out. Out on the sidewalks, lines of younger men were forming outside the clubs where the clientele was attractive and the energy high, some of it natural, some pumped up with crystal meth or the plethora of designer drugs snorted or swallowed in restrooms or the darker corners of the busy dance floors. At times, I felt the only place of interest left for me in Boys Town was A Different Light down the street, where I could always find a worthwhile book, and I didn't feel like a gasping dinosaur at the age of forty-five. I was happy to get off the boulevard as we wound our way through side streets into the Norma Triangle, where I gave Templeton an obligatory hug and watched her drive off in her shiny T-Bird.

It was nearly half past ten when I was back in my apartment, shedding my sport coat and slacks and intending to get to bed early and make up some of the sleep I'd lost the previous night while surfing in cyberspace. I brushed my teeth, swallowed my meds, pulled back the blanket and sheet, and stripped to the skin. As I was about to climb in, I glanced across the small room to my desk, where the dark computer screen sat staring at me from the shadows like a giant eye, unblinking.

A moment later, I was sitting in front of it, booting up, finding the Internet icon with my cursor, using my mouse to gain entrance. A moment after that, I was scanning an interminable list of gay porn sites. I selected one, entered, sampled its gallery of photos and streaming video, then hit its list of links to other sites, looking for a name or a description that sounded more promising. *Hot hunks getting off, teen boys in action, hung studs fucking hard, gorgeous twinks like you've never seen.* From time to time, as the hours passed, I'd stumble by accident into a hetero site, reminding me that the universe of straight porn was just as vast and lurid as the one serving lonely and sex-starved queers. All it took was a click of the mouse, and I was out of that world and back into more familiar territory, jumping from link to link, taking the free tours, part of me wanting to stop, another part urging me on, demanding more. *Hard pecs, huge cocks, hungry mouths, tight holes, bodacious buns. Thai boys ready to serve your every need! Young Russian guys eager to please! Amsterdam's hottest escorts guaranteed!*

My eyes settled briefly on men of every size, shape, and color before quickly moving to the next site, eager for the next image, looking for the one that might spark a physical response, plummeting forward like a man searching frantically through teeming streets for someone whose face he can barely remember.

ELEVEN

"Benjamin!" I heard Maurice's insistent voice, then a tap on my door. "It's almost ten, a beautiful Sunday morning. Why don't you come down and have breakfast with us? Fred's fixing buckwheat cakes."

I struggled out of bed on a few hours sleep and opened the door. "My goodness," Maurice said, looking me over, "naked as a jaybird." He let his eyes linger a moment before raising them. "Not that I'm complaining, mind you."

I yawned, squinting to hold off the light. "What time did you say it was, Maurice?"

"Nearly ten, dear boy." He pressed his palm to my forehead, checking for fever. "Are you feeling OK?"

"Late night, that's all."

"We saw you come in early last night. Working hard on the book?"

I glanced over my shoulder at the computer. "Something like that."

"You'll join us for breakfast?"

"Sure. Give me five minutes, will you?"

I took more than that, using the extra minutes to shower, shave, and jump into fresh clothes. Trotting down the steps, I saw Maurice watching for me from his kitchen window. When I got there, I found a stack of Fred's buckwheat cakes waiting, with the butter already melting on top. Maurice drenched the stack in hot maple syrup right off the stove, and put a steaming cup of fresh-brewed coffee in my hand. Fred sat on the other side of the breakfast table, his hairy gut hanging over the waistband of his sweat pants and his nose stuck in the sports section, as usual. He wasn't in terrible shape for a guy pushing eighty, just sloppy and looking his age, a retired trucker who had no use for sit-ups, push-ups, or aerobic exercise. Maurice—a retired dance instructor bred of more gentility—tugged at Fred's T-shirt, enough to cover most of his furry paunch.

"We have a guest," Maurice scolded him, "in case you hadn't noticed." Fred glanced at me, grunted, and went back to his paper. "And it wouldn't hurt you to shave for one Sunday in your life, either. Especially since we're going to the cinema this afternoon, and meeting friends for dinner afterward."

Maurice eased his slim frame into a chair closer to me and began peeling an orange. "I've been thinking about this brochure of yours, Benjamin, the one you're writing at City Hall. It seems to me you might take a walking tour of the city. Observe the more prominent historic sites firsthand, the ones you haven't seen already. You've been very keen on walking lately, as part of this new fitness regimen of yours. And today's an absolutely lovely day, don't you think?"

I sipped more coffee. "When I wake up, Maurice, I'll let you know."

"Are you sure it was work that kept you up so late, Benjamin? You didn't sneak out after we went to bed, did you? Find a congenial fellow and get into some late-night mischief?" He glanced at Fred with a wink, and a little smile opened up Fred's heavy stubble, before he went back to his scores. "Not that that's a bad thing," Maurice went on. "We just want you getting your proper rest, that's all. Taking care of yourself the way you should. Now that you have this fabulous new career opening up with the city."

"It's a freelance assignment, Maurice. A few weeks, at best."

"Still, one mustn't let opportunity slip away."

I reached for my fork. "I was in all night, Maurice, chained to my desk, eyes glued to my computer screen. I promise you."

"Then a brisk walk about town is just what you need!" He pushed a sheet of paper across the table toward me. "I've put together a list of the essential neighborhoods, along with the notable historical buildings in each—a checklist, so you don't miss anything important."

"You're not going to give me a lecture about the importance of the Sherman cottages, are you, Maurice? I've had quite enough of that."

Maurice popped an orange section into his mouth. "I'm an ardent preservationist, and I have no desire to see more McCondos rising up to obliterate the character of West Hollywood. But to be quite frank, I'm rather ambivalent about the necessity of saving the Sherman cottages."

"You're the first one I've come across. The people I've spoken to seem either to love them or hate them."

"It would be nice to save them, I suppose, if the money were available to move and renovate them, and if a good location was available. But I'm not entirely convinced of their architectural significance, and that land they sit on is worth a fortune." Maurice sighed, chewing thoughtfully. "I just don't think we can save every single old building in the city. We have to pick and choose, and make the best use of our limited resources."

"I imagine Lydia Ruttweller has a few bucks at her disposal. She's managed to keep her nonprofit going all these years and put up a fight with Colin Harrison over the cottages. And she talks about restoring those cottages, which would cost a pretty penny. She must be very adept at fund-raising."

"CUP has done wonderful work," Maurice said, "and helped save countless treasures that were threatened. But I'm afraid with that tongue of hers, Lydia alienates as many potential allies and donors as she attracts."

"She's obviously getting funding from someone. As a retired schoolteacher, she can't have much of her own, can she?"

"I imagine she got a nice settlement in her divorce decades back. Mr. Ruttweller was quite successful in real estate, you know. And I'm sure Lydia invested well, at least what she had left after her wastrel son siphoned off the rest."

"Chas Ruttweller, the musclehead I saw at the funeral service."

Maurice clucked his tongue. "We mustn't be too hard on him. He hasn't had it easy, that one, with the upbringing he's had. Can you imagine being raised by Lydia Ruttweller, with no father around as a buffer? Tsk, tsk." Maurice got up to warm my coffee, fussing over me in his affectionate way. "But that's another story, for another day. Eat up, Benjamin! It's too fine a morning to spend indoors with a nattering old queen. I'll pack you a nice lunch to take along on your walk. And be sure to wear proper shoes. We don't want blisters, do we?"

Within the hour, after changing into decent walking shoes and grabbing my notebook, I was hiking east, following Maurice's checklist and taking notes along the way. My first stop was close by, at 8811 Santa Monica Boulevard, a 1922 building that had housed the First National Bank of Sherman but now served as a sound-recording studio. So intent was I in studying its crumbling decorative façade that I barely paid attention to an unusual number of unmarked sheriff's cars speeding past along the boulevard, sirens off, heading in the same direction.

Not quite an hour later and a mile east of City Hall, as I crossed Fairfax Avenue, I found myself entering the heart of West Hollywood's Russian immigrant community. From here nearly to La Brea Avenue, another mile east, one frequently heard Russian spoken along with English in the streets and shops; here and there, the commercial signage was in Cyrillic, the squat, blocky lettering of the Russian alphabet. The neighborhood was equally homosexual—gay bars on the seedier side were scattered along this stretch of the boulevard, along with the venerable Tomkat Theater, which specialized in male porn, and the Pleasure Chest, which offered all things erotic. But one saw more and more businesses these days catering exclusively to Russian émigrés.

West Hollywood had received its first Russian wave during the late 1970s, when Russian Jews had fled severe religious persecution in the Communist U.S.S.R. and been welcomed by a city with a sizable Jewish community whose roots went back to the early years of the movie industry. Most of the refugees had been from small towns in the Ukraine and experienced serious culture shock in their new surroundings; not just language and economic differences, but the sudden reality of living in a city where lovers of the same gender commonly displayed their affection openly and without shame, which sometimes caused sparks. Through the years, as the immigrants grew more accustomed to gays, and vice versa, their differences diminished in importance, and the Russian section of town grew and thrived. The most recent census put the Russian population in WeHo at about ten percent, based on language, but insiders believed the number to be perhaps twice that, because so many Russians sought to be identified as American, studying and practicing their English with an almost religious fervor. At night, older Russians, including many grandparents, filled ESL classes at the nearest high school or during the day at Plummer Park; gathering each day to learn their new language, it was said, was a social event nearly as important to seniors as attending the local synagogue each Sabbath.

I was approaching the park now, or at least the neighborhood around it. Maurice had included the Plummer Park Apartment Grouping on the list of historic sites he wanted me to visit, and I'd come across reams of information about it in Bruce Bibby's files. I found the five brick buildings in the eleven hundred block of North Vista Street, along the western border of the park. Built in 1929 on several parcels of land purchased from Eugena R. Plummer, they took their inspiration from the Andalusian region of Mediterranean Spain—graceful arches, wood balconies and shutters, casement windows, three-bay façades, and tiled roofs that featured abbreviated towers—giving the block its own special quaintness and appeal. Standing there, taking notes in the quiet of a Sunday morning, it wasn't difficult to imagine a different quality of life back then. The sturdy balconies on each building must have offered fine views of surrounding ranches and the rolling hills to the north, while the old Red Line Trolleys clattered slowly past on the Pacific Electric Railway tracks, carrying passengers along what was now busy Santa Monica Boulevard.

Suddenly, as I lost myself in pleasant nostalgia, sirens shattered the Sunday morning quiet. All around Plummer Park, sheriff's vehicles, both marked and unmarked, raced through the streets, lights flashing and tires squealing as they careened around corners. I trotted back to Santa Monica Boulevard, where I saw more of them coming from different directions, all of them turning into the same side street a block west. The mingling of sirens grew to an unholy wail that quickly subsided, suggesting a point of convergence just down the street, where something very serious was surely taking place.

I stood still for half a minute, listening to the sirens fade as the regular traffic along the boulevard got moving again.

There was no reason for me to follow those sirens down that side street, I reminded myself. I was out for a long walk and some note taking, a couple of hours of exercise combined with work, nothing more than that. I still hadn't surveyed all the buildings in the Plummer Park Apartment Grouping, the way a conscientious writer would. But that old instinct was still alive inside me, that curiosity that had driven me as a reporter, that compulsion to chase the action, ask questions, witness some drama if I could. I darted across through traffic, down the boulevard, and around the corner.

Half a block down, a young man stood in the middle of the residential street, surrounded by uniformed officers and plainclothes detectives. Several of them had their pistols out, and others were armed with batons and stun guns. Detective Mira De Marco was among them, advancing slowly while holding her pistol in front of her with both hands. As I drew closer, I could hear her speaking to the boy, coaxing him in a firm but nonthreatening voice. *Raise your shirt, Victor, so that we can be sure you have no weapons. Do it slowly. Everything's going to be all right, Victor.*

The boy was lean, blond, barely out of his teens. He swiveled his head this way and that, his blue eyes wild. Sweat soaked his Limp Biskit T-shirt and streaked his flushed face. I stopped at the edge of the police perimeter, watching him closely, recalling Dr. Ford's photograph and realizing I was looking at Victor Androvic.

To my left, on the sidewalk in front of one of the old apartment buildings, a woman who might have been his grandmother was wailing and weeping, and calling out his name and some foreign words in a thick Russian accent. Two officers, one male, one female, kept her from running to him, but not without considerable effort. Slowly, a look of abject resignation and despair reshaped the boy's face. He reached down to his waist and lifted his T-shirt slowly until it was just above his chest, dropping his eyes as if embarrassed to be exposing himself that way in front of the older woman and the crowd.

Detective De Marco spoke again, her voice calm and reassuring. *That's good, Victor, that's very good. Now lower your shirt and lace your fingers on top of your head. Kneel down slowly. Lay facedown on the street. Put your hands out to your sides where we can see them. It's going to be all right, Victor. Just do as we say, and you won't get hurt.*

He lowered his shirt and slowly raised his trembling hands. Detective De Marco inched her way toward him, repeating her orders, while he complied. He knelt, lay facedown, spread his hands as he'd been told. A moment later, several officers were on him, cuffing his wrists behind him, patting him down, searching his pockets, dragging him to his feet, leading him in my direction toward a patrol car stopped at an angle in the middle of the street.

I tried to match the frightened face with what I knew about Victor Androvic: age twenty, probationer, son of a multiple murderer executed a few months earlier in Russia. The wailing woman, I figured, was not his grandmother but Tatiana Androvic, who'd given birth to Victor in her late thirties, and whose hard life had aged her beyond her years. The anguish in her voice should have been enough to tell me that; it was a mother's pain that erupted from her, a sound like no other, a cry of desperation from deep in a mother's heart. I'd heard it in my own mother's voice, when I was seventeen, pleading for me to stop, as I fired round after round into the lifeless body of my violent and rapacious father, from the barrel of his own gun. It was a sound that you don't forget.

Victor Androvic suddenly resisted as the cops led him away. He pulled up, clenching his body, refusing to move another step. Then he drew back toward his mother, straining and twisting, even though getting free was impossible, and he had to know that. Still, he was able to stretch a few inches in her direction as the officers clutched him more tightly, contorting his upper body until the muscles in his neck corded up as if they might snap. I couldn't see his face now, but I could hear him clearly as he cried out to her. The language was Russian, which I didn't speak or understand. Yet I felt I knew what he was saying, without translation: *Mama, Mama! I'm innocent! Mama, I swear I didn't do what they say I did! Mama, Mama!*

I had no way of knowing if those were actually the words Victor Androvic spoke at that moment. It was just a gut feeling—instinct again—triggered by the anguish I heard, a sound so raw and wrenching it was hard to believe he could have been saying anything else. Except perhaps: *Save me, Mama! Save me, save me.*

Words I'd never spoken as a boy, never cried out myself, but so many times wished I had.

TWELVE

A deputy drove Victor Androvic away, with another patrol car following, and the crowd began to slowly disperse. I approached Mira De Marco as she stood scribbling in her notebook, a study in calm and concentration.

"It looks like you got your suspect, Detective." She looked up briefly, nodding once, without a word. "He wasn't behaving like a guilty man," I said.

"They usually do," she said, without glancing up, "but not always."

"You staked out his mother's apartment?"

De Marco closed her notebook and tucked away her pen, finally making eye contact. "What's your sudden interest, Justice? You told me you were keeping your nose clean these days."

"Trying."

"Not too successfully, apparently."

I smiled a little. "I guess not."

"Just happen to be passing by?"

I told her about my visit to the Plummer Park Apartment Grouping; she accepted it with a skeptical look. I asked her again if she'd had Tatiana Androvic's apartment building staked out.

"As you saw," she said, "Victor Androvic is very close to his mother. We figured he'd come around sooner or later."

"You're booking him for murder?"

She shook her head. "Probation violation, evading arrest. He missed an appointment with his P.O. on Friday, then took off half an hour ago when we caught up with him here. Led us on a pretty good chase. We had some fun."

"Doesn't sound like you have much in the way of criminal charges."

"Enough to keep him behind bars for a while, until we put a better case together on the Bibby killing."

"So you're not sure he did it."

"Never said I was."

"Still, he went into hiding after Templeton's story hit the streets. I suppose that's an indication of guilt."

"I'd say it qualifies, although his mother has a different slant on it." De Marco glanced toward the apartment house, where a male detective questioned Tatiana Androvic. "She claims the kid panicked because of his earlier conviction in the smuggling case. Says he's scared to death of the justice system, because of his experience back in Russia, and what happened to his old man—the execution. Says the boy thinks he's being railroaded, because of who his father was."

"Understandable."

"I suppose."

"You've still got his fingerprints, though, from the crime scene. No alibi, false statements. Doesn't look good for him, does it?"

"You fishing, Justice? For Templeton? So she can update that piece of garbage she wrote for the *Times* last week?"

"I don't blame you for being angry with her, Detective."

"I don't get angry. I get even."

"By bad-mouthing her around town and giving her freezer burn for the rest of her career?"

"It's happened to reporters who've done less."

"For what it's worth, De Marco, I tried to convince her to hold off on that story. You can believe it or not, but I told her she should sit on it, that jerking you around like she did was wrong."

De Marco studied me a moment. "You going to call her when you're finished talking to me, tip her to what just went down?"

"I was thinking you should do that."

De Marco laughed, but she didn't sound amused. "You're joking, right?"

"Victor's arrest will be in the *Times* tomorrow one way or the other. It's public record. You can't keep a lid on his connection to the Bibby murder much longer. It's to nobody's advantage if you and Templeton keep feuding. Frankly, I think she feels bad about what she did."

"What a damn shame, her feeling bad like that."

"I think she'd like to apologize, get it behind her. Her pride's getting in the way."

"That's her problem, isn't it?"

"Maybe you can move things along, De Marco. Make contact with her, turn the situation in your favor. She could be useful to you down the road, when you need a reporter on your side."

"Sure, I could do that. If I could trust her half as far as I could throw her."

"She's not a bad person. She's really not."

"Could have fooled me."

"She's been going through a rough time. I'm not excusing what she did. I'm just saying there's a reason."

De Marco was quiet a moment. When she spoke again, some of the edge was gone. "You're talking about that boyfriend of hers, Joe Soto. The columnist who got knocked off last year." I nodded. De Marco regarded me thoughtfully for a moment. "As I recall, that was a rough time for both of you."

"Rougher for Templeton than for me. They were going to get married, you know. He was just about everything to her."

"I know how that goes. I lost someone myself, not all that long ago."

"So maybe you cut Templeton some slack, Detective, give her another chance."

"You two must be close, the way you're standing up for her like this."

"I'm worried about her, to tell the truth. I think she's at a turning point that could go either way." De Marco shifted her gaze to Tatiana Androvic, as the other detective finished with her. I kept my eyes steady, hoping De Marco's eyes would come back to mine. When they did, I said, "Suppose I give you Templeton's cell phone number, in case you change your mind."

Mira De Marco took a long moment before making a decision,

as if gauging how much she should trust me, or maybe what I was worth to her. Then she opened her notebook and wrote down the number I recited from memory.

A few minutes later, after smoking furiously on a cigarette, Detective De Marco took off in an unmarked car with her male partner. When they were gone, I stood in the middle of the street, which was empty and quiet again, eerily so in the wake of what had taken place in the past hour and the impact it was sure to have on a number of lives.

I heard someone sobbing and turned to see two middle-aged women consoling Tatiana Androvic. All three women were wide-hipped and thick-limbed, with heavily styled hair colored in various shades to camouflage the gray; their attire looked off-the-rack from discount stores, designer knockoffs that fit them uneasily but seemed quintessentially middle-class American. Of the three, Mrs. Androvic was the only blue-eyed blonde; the features of the other women were darker. They put their arms around her and walked her down the sidewalk and through the arched entrance of a two-story apartment house, a Spanish-style place built around a courtyard lush with philodendron and banana palms. I stepped into the entryway to see them disappear around a corner on the far side. I followed in that direction, to a row of apartments in back, on the lower floor. The two women huddled in the doorway of an apartment toward the end, as if hesitant to leave Mrs. Androvic alone, yet unsure if they should go in. A minute passed as they murmured to her; then they were backing out, turning away, making large gestures of sympathy and support. As they encountered me, passing, the sadness on their faces turned quickly to suspicion, and I could feel their eyes on my back as I continued on to Mrs. Androvic's door.

I hesitated a moment, took a deep breath, and looked in. She sat across her living room, hunched on a sagging sofa while she wept into her thick hands. I raised a fist to rap my knuckles on the door but stopped before I made a sound. The moment was too private, too intimate, I decided, her anguish too raw for me to deal with just now. I started to turn away when she looked up.

"Yes? What is it you want?" Her accent was heavy, but the pronunciation good.

I suddenly realized how fragmented I felt, how uncertain. "I'm not sure," I said.

"You are the police?"

I shook my head. "I work at City Hall. I—I shouldn't really be here. I'm sorry I intruded."

Again, I started to turn away. She was up off the couch, crossing the room, reaching out to me. "You know my son? You are a friend of Victor?" She clutched my arm, so tightly I felt her nails press the flesh. "I know he has older friends. Sometimes, they call here. You are a friend of my Victor?"

I shook my head again. "I saw what happened in the street. I heard your son crying out to you. It reminded me of someone else—another mother, another son, a long time ago."

"You said you work at City Hall?"

"Sort of. Not really." I threw up my hands. "Temporarily. I don't know."

"You know important people there?"

"I suppose. One or two."

She clutched at me more fiercely. "They can help my son?"

"I don't know, Mrs. Androvic. Your son seems to be in a lot of trouble."

"Victor did not hurt this man as they say he did. He is not a bad boy. I know my son. He could not do what they say."

I thought: *Every mother says that about her accused son. Cops with airtight evidence hear it from naïve mothers every day. Jeffrey Dahmer's mother probably thought he was a good boy, just a bit confused, with odd culinary habits.*

"What makes you think he's innocent, Mrs. Androvic?"

"Come in, come in." She turned back into the room, wringing her hands. "I know, that's all. I know who my son is. I know what is in his heart."

I took a few steps inside. "Victor must be a very angry young man. His childhood in Russia, religious persecution, a brutal and abusive father who killed how many women in cold blood—a legacy Victor has to live with for the rest of his life."

She turned, looking almost angry herself. "Victor is not like his father! It is not the way they said in the newspaper, not the way Dr. Ford said. Victor and his father are nothing like each other. Nothing!"

"Dr. Ford seems to think differently. His research—"

"His research is wrong!" Her eyes blazed, and tears reappeared. "He had no right to talk to the newspaper. He promised that his studies with Victor will be private, con—confidence."

"Confidential."

"Yes, confidential. He promised that, back in Russia when he first came to talk to us, when we signed his papers." She sneered, brushing back her tears. "Dr. Ford, he wants a monster. He chose Victor. Victor is his monster. But you cannot blame a boy for what his father has done. This is not fair. This is not how it should be in America. In America, every person gets a chance to have a new life, to be innocent until the proof that he is guilty."

"Victor's been in trouble before, Mrs. Androvic."

"That was not what you think." She explained to me that Victor had been working for a local Russian grocery store, making deliveries, when he'd innocently gotten caught up in an interstate scam that passed off eggs taken illegally from domestic fish as high-priced Russian caviar. I'd read about these cases from time to time: Since the fall of the Soviet Union, the Russian caviar trade had become subject to Russian Mafia control, which had opened the Caspian Sea to overfishing. The resulting scarcity had made commerce in American caviar highly profitable, with the wholesale price climbing to as much as fifty dollars a pound. Poachers in Kentucky and Tennessee were harvesting eggs from paddlefish and sturgeon, supplying an illicit network of traders from New York to Los Angeles, a multimillion-dollar operation that fed the growing Russian demand for cherished caviar from the homeland. It was all part of a burgeoning Russian Mafia presence in the U.S. that had infested West Hollywood as well, where increasing numbers of innocent Russian émigrés were being victimized in all kinds of ways.

"Victor did not know what he was delivering," Mrs. Androvic said. "He was just a boy, driving a truck, making a little money to go to college. Doing what his employer instructed him to do."

"He was found guilty, Mrs. Androvic."

"He told them he was guilty, to stay out of jail, to get his probation. His lawyer said he should do that. And that is why Victor is so afraid now. He believes he will be found guilty again. Only this time, they will end his life, like they did his father back in Russia. So when he read the article in the newspaper, Victor ran away."

"Not for long. He was back today, to visit you."

That triggered another outburst of tears, causing Mrs. Androvic to excuse herself as she disappeared into a hallway. When she didn't return right away I took the opportunity to look around the sparsely furnished apartment. A bookshelf was devoted to photographs of Victor, as well as pictures of friends and family I presumed to be loved ones back in Russia, judging by the clothes and backdrops. He'd been a cute, towheaded child with a sweet face and blue eyes, developing into a young man with a narrow, boyish face that bordered on handsome. There were a number of photos of Tatiana and Victor together as he grew up, but none that I could see of an adolescent Victor with a girlfriend, confirming my impression of him as an unrepentant mama's boy. There was nothing wrong with being a mama's boy, I thought—Italy was a nation of them—but it didn't mean you couldn't be a cold-blooded killer, too. Tatiana had devoted one wall to Victor's academic and athletic accomplishments: American high school report cards pinned up in chronological order, showing mostly As and Bs; medals for swimming; certificates citing perfect attendance; others proclaiming his membership in math and science clubs. There was a picture of a local swim team, and another of Victor standing alone in a Speedo, a medal hanging from his neck, water droplets spotting his lanky body. Hanging on another wall was an American flag and a photograph of the Statue of Liberty, clipped from a magazine and set in a cheap frame.

The only other notable decoration was a small wooden doll on a shelf in the dining room, roughly eight inches high, shaped like a miniature bowling pin and colorfully and intricately painted with female features and peasant clothing. I recognized it as a Russian *matryoshka* doll, the kind that's hollowed out to open in the middle; inside the largest doll is an entire family of identically shaped and painted dolls that descend in size down an inch or less nesting one inside the other.

"Victor's father carved and painted that, with his own hands."

I glanced back at the sound of Mrs. Androvic's voice just behind me, to my right, on my sighted side. She set aside a box of tissues she was holding and picked up the doll, which she screwed open to reveal a slightly smaller doll within. As she talked, she kept opening more dolls, standing them in a line along the shelf like pretty little peasant girls all in a row. I was reminded of something Dr. Ford had mentioned over lunch: that Victor's father had killed young women in the Ukrainian countryside, burying their bodies in the surrounding woodlands.

"I kept these dolls," Mrs. Androvic said, "to remind Victor that his father had a good side, that he recognized beauty, that he could create something pretty and lasting. That he was not just an evil man who could only create violence and terror."

"They're lovely, Mrs. Androvic."

"They're quite valuable, this particular set. The craftsmanship is special. Victor's father was known for that." She laughed sadly. "Today, they make these in factories with machines. Thousands and thousands of them. But these—these are what you Americans call 'the real thing.'" Her voice became subdued, distant, almost as if she were talking to herself, convincing herself of something. "They could only be made by someone with good feelings inside him, a man with a good heart, not all bad. This is what I tell Victor about his father."

"Still, the man murdered at least fourteen young girls. He beat you and Victor. He made your lives hell."

Her voice came back to me, back from wherever she'd been for a moment. "Victor is different. This I know." Then, stepping around to face me directly, she said, "Will you help Victor and me, with the people you know at City Hall?"

"The city has a Russian Advisory Board, Mrs. Androvic. I would think they might be of more support than I."

"But you are here, are you not, in our home? You are talking to me, about my son. Something brought you here, did it not?"

"I'm not sure, Mrs. Androvic."

"What is your name please?"

"Benjamin Justice."

"Maybe you will think of some way to help us, Mr. Justice. Maybe you will hear something that is important, and tell us please."

"The police asked me to do the same thing."

"I see." Her eyes fell for a moment; she attempted a smile. "Well, you will do what you feel you need to do, won't you?"

"I probably should go now, Mrs. Androvic."

"Wait just one moment, please."

She disappeared into the kitchen, while I used the seconds to study the nesting *matryoshka* dolls one more time. When she returned, she clutched a pair of wooden spoons. They were shaped like deep, oversized soup spoons, and elaborately painted with floral designs in red, black, and green against a background of gold. "We call these *khokhloma*, Mr. Justice. From each village, they look different. The color, the pattern, is distinct, depending on its region."

"And the the dolls, the *matryoshkas*?" I asked. "It's the same for them?"

"The *matryoshkas* get their special look from each family that makes them." She picked up the largest doll, regarding it lovingly, lost for a moment in the peasant girl's gently rounded shape and delicate features. "Not like the machines in the factory. Those are not true *matryoshkas*." She set the doll back on the shelf, turned to me, and pressed the two wooden spoons into my hands. "Take them, please—my gift."

"Why, Mrs. Androvic? We barely know each other."

"Friendship, Mr. Justice." Her steady eyes fixed on mine, with a look of silent pleading. "I give them to you for friendship."

THIRTEEN

The next morning, the arrest of Victor Androvic made the front page of the B section in the *L.A. Times,* where local and regional news was printed. Templeton had the byline.

Accompanying the story—again, front page—was Androvic's most recent mug shot, snapped the previous afternoon. In it, he stared malevolently into the camera, the softness and tears I'd seen in his blue eyes the previous day replaced by what looked like icy rage, his mouth an ugly snarl. Away from his mother, and in the clutches of the law, the monster seemed to have emerged, or at least the face of one.

In her story, Templeton recapped Dr. Ford's research, using two brain scan photos from those she'd run before. This time she named Victor as the research subject and linked him to his demonic father, Leonid. She also quoted Detective Mira De Marco several times, on the record. De Marco confirmed Androvic as a suspect in the murder of Bruce Bibby, while emphasizing that he was only being charged for the moment with lesser, unrelated crimes, while the investigation continued. The detective was circumspect in her remarks, framing them carefully, but it was clear that she'd decided making Templeton an ally was preferable to having her as an enemy. For her part, Templeton had managed the proper neutrality in her tone and approach to telling the story. Still, if I'd been the average reader, I might have come away from the article assuming that Victor Androvic was guilty, with a trial a mere formality at this point, and probably a waste of good taxpayer money. The evidence against him seemed that strong.

I pushed the paper aside, trying to get Victor and his mother out of my head. For the rest of the day, I worked on my outline for the brochure, completing it in the late afternoon and beginning my research for details I couldn't find in Bruce Bibby's notes and documents. I quit at half past six, keeping a promise to join Maurice at a special public hearing called by the City Council. At issue were the Sherman cottages and whether the council should grant a permit for their demolition and development of the site for condominiums, should Colin Harrison decide to sell the land to the developer, Lester Cohen.

"Quite a turnout," Maurice said, as we stood at the back of the West Hollywood Park auditorium, which the city used for special council meetings and public hearings when the topic was controversial or of widespread community interest.

The fate of the Sherman cottages clearly qualified as a big draw. Maurice and I looked out at an audience of several hundred residents sitting restlessly in folding chairs, along with several members of the press. Up on the stage, the five City Council members were lined up in a row, with the mayor in the middle; to the side, armed with laptops, documents, and reference books, sat the city attorney and several city department heads. In the middle of the auditorium, on a small platform, a video camera operator captured the proceedings for live broadcast on the city's cable channel, which was standard for City Council meetings. Citizens and other interested parties who planned to speak pro or con had already signed up for their two minutes at the podium.

"There he is," Maurice said, "the catalyst for this brouhaha." He pointed a bony finger in the direction of a stout gentleman in a white linen suit, with a smoothly shaved head and a thick gray mustache that would have done a walrus proud. He was standing off to the side, against a wall, chatting with two other men in darker suits and ties, who were as pale and bookish as the bald man was tan and robust. "Mr. Lester Cohen," Maurice went on, "old Money Bags himself. I imagine he's lined up any number of people to speak on behalf of his condo project tonight. Those two would probably be his chief attorneys."

"Do I see a faint resemblance to Daddy Warbucks?"

Maurice slapped at me with a soft hand. "Benjamin, you're right! I never thought of it until you mentioned it just now." He bent close to my ear, covering his mouth, while keeping his eyes on Cohen. "Lester looks to be in awfully good shape for a man of eighty-plus, doesn't he? Personally, I find the shaved head rather sexy. When he's not wearing his nice suits for the public, Lester's very much a Leather Daddy. He was a regular at the Eagle and the Spike in the old days, on the lookout for boys with hairy chests and muscles who liked a beefy man to crack the whip."

"I take it you and Fred frequented the Eagle and the Spike as well."

Maurice rolled his eyes. "More Fred's kind of place than mine. Although I do admit, a man in assless chaps still gives me a thrill. Just for fun, I bought Fred a pair for his birthday once, but he couldn't fit into them. The poor man nearly suffocated!"

The mayor opened the discussion, bringing everyone in the auditorium up to date on various findings and opinions; the city attorney and department heads weighed in, including the housing manager for the city's Rent Stabilization and Housing Department, who spoke about the city's continuing need for low-income housing, to maintain some economic diversity. After that, citizens rose to speak at the podium in the order they'd signed in. As they made their varied arguments, I spotted a number of familiar faces moving about the hall, bending to whisper into the ears of seated allies or others gathered against walls, no doubt plotting strategy and organizing their forthcoming remarks. Lydia Ruttweller was the most active, striding about on her long legs, gesturing urgently and scowling; from time to time, she collected two or three allies and herded them outside like a stern mother taking her disobedient children out to the barn for a hiding. Tony Mercury was there, of course, up on stage and arguably the most handsome of the council members; Mercury was also the most sharply dressed, in a loose-fitting, beige Armani jacket and a haircut that had surely set him back a hundred bucks or more. Ted Meeks had taken a seat near the rear, on the far side, where he was inconspicuous under his floppy hat, his small frame hunched to make him seem even smaller; only occasionally did he lift his head to peer up at the proceedings, before ducking again to stare at his hands or shoes.

"I don't see Colin Harrison with Ted," Maurice said, clucking. "I've heard rumors that he isn't well. Goodness, it's hard to imagine Ted speaking in Colin's place. He's not the most confident or outgoing fellow. He's always depended on Colin for that."

"He seems quite sure about Harrison's right to sell the cottages," I said, "and Cohen's right to tear them down and build condos. I gathered that the day I met him at Harrison House."

"Oh, yes, he'd be with Colin all the way in that respect, or anything else for that matter. Colin's always called the shots."

It was at that moment that I recognized one more face, the only one that surprised me. Detective Mira De Marco slipped through a door near the stage to stand in the shadows, just behind the American and California flags. It was impossible to know what had drawn her to a council meeting in which no law enforcement matters were scheduled for discussion. She took no notes, never spoke with anyone. She just stood inconspicuously in the shadows, silent and attentive, her keen eyes scanning the stage and the audience, as if checking every face.

It was after eight when the heavy hitters started coming to the podium.

Ted Meeks, as Maurice had predicted, spoke on behalf of Colin Harrison but without the bluster and authority for which his absent partner was so well known; in a hurried, snippy manner, Meeks touted free enterprise and a property owner's right to make a profit on an investment, and suggested that to restore the dilapidated cottages to their original condition would be costly and of questionable architectural value. Lester Cohen was considerably more forceful and articulate, pointing out that the land on which the cottages sat had been wasted for years, with the buildings empty and boarded up; not only would the land be put to good use as a site for condominiums, Cohen said, it would add thirty new residential units to the existing eight when the three-story complex was completed and the units sold.

Then Cohen dropped a bombshell that drew a collective gasp from the audience: He offered to provide—at his own expense and at the urging of Tony Mercury—another twenty-two units of affordable housing in an apartment building he was renovating on the city's more affordable east side, at no cost to taxpayers, in exchange for the council's approval of the land sale, demolition, and development.

Both Ted Meeks and Lydia Ruttweller reacted in a way that suggested they were as surprised and stunned as everyone else by Cohen's gambit.

"It will be my gift to a city that has given me so much," Cohen said, in a rich baritone, and with a grand sweep of his pudgy hand, his gold rings and cuff links glinting in the media lights.

Many in the audience burst into applause, despite the mayor's earlier request that all reaction be withheld. Lydia Ruttweller stood in the midst of the crowd, absolutely livid, exhorting them to be silent, but with little effect. She was up next, and as the din died down, her name was called. As she made her way to the podium, the crowd hushed, although whispers and titters could be heard here and there among the regulars who knew from past experience what was surely coming. Nearby, a man whispered her nickname wickedly— "Lydia Rottweiler"—but Maurice quickly shushed him.

Mrs. Ruttweller adjusted the microphone for her height, drew back her shoulders, and let go with a blast of vitriol. "Listen up, people," she said in a haughty voice, "and maybe you'll learn something for a change."

"Oh, God," Maurice murmured. "Here she goes again."

Lydia Ruttweller's points were generally reasonable and well argued, stressing the need for the city to preserve what it could of its special character and flavor in the face of rapid change and depersonalization. Creating more low-income housing was a worthy goal, she conceded, but not at the risk of destroying a historical site that added a measure of quality to the lives of present and future generations. If the city failed to save the Sherman cottages, she insisted, slipping into hyperbole, then every unprotected historical building in West Hollywood was in jeopardy. As she spoke, she became increasingly shrill and arrogant, finally denouncing Cohen's proposal as nothing short of blackmail, a sweetheart deal brokered by prodevelopment factions on the council whom she characterized as "bribe-taking vermin who bring corruption and shame to our fine city." A few people cheered or applauded, but more began to hiss and boo, while the mayor repeatedly called for order. At one point, Mrs. Ruttweller referred to Lester Cohen as "that conniving pig who dares to come here tonight offering us crumbs from his overflowing trough," causing the blood and color to rise in Cohen's neck. By the time she'd finished—taking several minutes instead of the limited two, and ignoring the mayor's warning to step down—I understood why she'd earned herself a nickname that suggested a vicious canine; she'd done everything but foam at the mouth.

After hearing all the arguments, the council decided to table the matter for more study for another month, when it would decide whether to grant a demolition permit or not, causing another chorus of boos and grumbling.

"That makes your brochure that much more important," Maurice said. "It will be out by then, distributed to every household in the city. I imagine how you treat those old cottages may have an influence on the outcome of all this."

As we were leaving the auditorium, Maurice invited me to La Conversation for pastry and tea. Ted Meeks scurried past us and out the door without a word, looking distressed, which I attributed to his weak performance at the podium; he must have felt that he'd let Colin Harrison down, which I found touching, even if I didn't care for Meeks all that much. Lester Cohen followed a short distance behind, and I caught him looking me up and down with a lascivious eye.

"I told you he liked hairy-chested men with muscles," Maurice said. "Although I'm not sure you qualify as the submissive type."

"No," I said, "crawling on all fours on a collar leash was never in my oeuvre."

We were almost to the door when I reached out to stop him.

"What is it, Benjamin?"

Across the floor behind us, as city workers folded up chairs and the crowd dispersed, Lydia Ruttweller was lambasting Tony Mercury in a voice capable of loosening the rafters. He absorbed her blast with a pained smile, glancing at his watch and nodding mechanically. But it wasn't Mercury or Mrs. Ruttweller who'd caught my attention. It was Detective Mira De Marco. She stood at a distance from them, quiet and observant, studying one or the both of them with such rigid concentration that people had to step around her to make their exit.

"It's nothing," I told Maurice, smiling, as I slipped an arm around his shoulders and guided him out the door. "Let's go and get that pastry, before the café closes."

FOURTEEN

La Conversation was always busiest for breakfast and lunch, and generally closed its doors around eight for the nightly dinner crowd. But there were still diners dawdling over their meals when Maurice and I arrived around nine, and the friendly owners, Michael and Steven, admitted us for pastries and tea.

The Latin pop star Paulína Rubío was there with a bunch of friends, apparently celebrating something, which perhaps explained the delayed closing time. Even with the effervescent celebration, the charm and intimacy of the place was intact. Maurice and I had just placed our orders when I spotted Templeton at a side window table. She was engaged in animated conversation with Dr. Roderick Ford, laughing as the light from their candle flickered across her remarkable face, causing her brown eyes to sparkle in a special way that I hadn't seen since the death of Joe Soto the previous fall. Between them was an empty wine bottle; I suspected that Dr. Ford was tossing out some calculated compliment or clever *bon mot* intended to erode what was left of Templeton's resistance after the alcohol had washed away the rest. Templeton was an adult and had as much right as I did to get involved with the wrong men. But Joe's death had left her uniquely vulnerable, fragile, and needy, and I couldn't sit by and let a cad like Dr. Ford take advantage.

I excused myself to the restroom and cut a path that deliberately took me close to their table, catching her attention with my eyes on my way past. Half a minute later, she'd also excused herself, and followed me into a short hallway leading to the restroom.

"I know what you're going to say, Justice, so don't."

"The guy's as oily as a cheap pizza, Alex."

"It's not a 'date' date. We're here to discuss Victor Androvic's arrest and what that might mean to Rod's research. I'm softening him up, so he'll be an easier interview."

"Trust me, Templeton, Rod's anything but soft right now."

She showed me her best smirk. "He's promised me that he'll come to me first with any new developments worthy of news coverage."

"And where better to discuss that than one of the city's cozier restaurants, over a candlelight dinner and a nice bottle of cabernet?"

"He suggested a glass of wine to relax after a long day's work."

"At what point exactly in the conversation did he remind you that he's divorcing his wife and open to new relationships?" She glared hotly, but with just enough discomfort for me to know I'd struck a nerve. I lost some of the edge in my voice. "All I'm asking is that you take your time with this guy, and be careful, OK? You've been hurt enough recently. I don't want to see you hurt again for a while."

She laid a hand on my cheek and smiled fondly. "For what it's worth, I appreciate your concern."

"It's worth a lot," I said, "because *you're* worth a lot."

"I promise to keep my guard up. OK?"

"I guess it'll have to do."

She glanced over her shoulder. "I should get back. Don't be mad if we leave without stopping by your table to say good-bye. He's not your biggest fan."

"Is Alexandra dating again?" Maurice asked, as I returned to our table and took my seat. He glanced across the room toward Templeton and Dr. Ford. "She seems to be having a most convivial dinner with her handsome gentleman friend."

"Dr. Roderick Ford," I said, and explained who he was and why I didn't like him.

"That university professor who found the genetic link between that Russian boy and his loathsome father," Maurice said. "My goodness—to think that Bruce Bibby might have lost his life to such a twisted individual."

"You're speaking of the Russian boy or Dr. Ford?"

Maurice gave me an odd look. "The Russian boy, of course." He shivered audibly. "Just the thought of it gives me the chills."

"Speaking of Bruce Bibby," I said. I reached into my shirt pocket, pulled out a folded page I'd printed off my computer, unfolded it, and handed it to Maurice. "These are people I've run into over the past few days. They all have some connection to Bibby. These names mean anything to you, Maurice?"

He pushed aside his pastry and pulled his chair around, spreading the paper on the table between us: *Cecelia Cortez, Tony Mercury, Trang Nguyen, Lydia Ruttweller, Colin Harrison, Ted Meeks, Dr. Roderick Ford, Detective Mira De Marco.*

"Of course, everyone knows Cecelia. Sweet person, very competent at her job, from all accounts. Tony Mercury—well, we all know who he is, don't we? People say he's quite well put together, though I haven't seen his movies."

"I was thinking more of his role at City Hall, not his porn flicks."

"Of course," Maurice said. "Very prodevelopment, as you know, allied with Lester Cohen on the issue of the Sherman cottages."

"What about his relationship to Bruce Bibby, prior to Bibby's death?"

"Don't know much there, Benjamin. Should I?"

"If you hear any gossip, pass it on, will you?"

"Don't I always?" Maurice moved his finger down to the next name. "I can tell you that Tony Mercury and Lydia Ruttweller are archenemies. And she and Bruce were like this." Maurice raised his crossed fingers. "She'd do just about anything to get Mercury off the City Council, I can tell you that."

I glanced at the list. "Trang Nguyen?"

Maurice shook his head. "Name means nothing to me."

"I'm well acquainted with Lydia Ruttweller," I said. "And you've already filled me in about her son, Chas. What about the next two names, beyond what I already know?"

"Colin Harrison and Ted Meeks? Joined at the hip, those two." Maurice smiled wistfully. "Kind of like Fred and me."

"What else can you tell me?"

"They go back together longer than Fred and I do—close to sixty years, I'd think. They met when Colin was in his early twenties and Ted just starting college, right after the war. They'd both seen combat in Europe. Colin was wounded, I believe."

"You and Fred knew them back then?"

"We met them in the fifties, when they'd already been together for some time. It was a fairly small group of queers back then in WeHo. We all knew one another, or knew who we were. Colin and Ted were devoted, deeply in love. I'm sure I've got a photo of them from those days, back at the house, if you're interested." Maurice dropped his finger to the next name. "Dr. Roderick Ford. You'd know more about him than I would, Benjamin."

I glanced in the direction of Templeton's table to see Dr. Ford pulling out her chair as she stood. "Not as much as I'd like to." They made their exit without stopping by our table, although Templeton blew me a covert air kiss as they passed. I watched Ford hold the door open for her, then check out her legs and ass from behind. "Somebody that slick—I don't trust the guy, not for a second."

"This last name, Benjamin—Mira De Marco. Isn't she the detective quoted in Alexandra's article this morning?"

I nodded. "Name mean anything to you?"

"Can't say that it does." Maurice pointed a finger thoughtfully under his chin. "I did know a man once named Rocky De Marco, if that means anything." His gaze drifted off wistfully, as if Rocky might have been more than just a passing acquaintance. "I haven't thought of Rocky De Marco in years—haven't heard from him in decades. I don't think anyone has, not anyone that I know." Maurice sipped his tea and studied me across the rim of his cup. "You seem to be taking a rather keen interest in this Bruce Bibby business, Benjamin. Having a change of heart, are you?"

I smiled wanly. "That's one way of putting it, I guess."

He nodded at the sheet of paper on the table. "In that case, there's one more person you need to add to that list, isn't there?"

"Two, actually." While Maurice called for the check, I found a pen and scrawled the names at the bottom: *Victor Androvic* and *Tatiana Androvic.*

As we strolled back to Norma Place, I found myself feeling impatient to get home, and knew exactly why: At the top of the stairs, inside my apartment, was my computer—the gateway to that other world. As we turned off Doheny onto Norma, all I could think about was logging on to the Internet and losing myself in its alluring images again. I'd given up pretending to be blasé about its vast inventory of porn; the pull was too insistent, with me almost every waking moment, nagging like an itch I couldn't scratch. But as we reached the house, Maurice prevailed upon me to stop in, at least long enough to look at a few snapshots from one of his old photo albums. I mounted the front steps with him, feeling restless and on edge, yearning to be alone with my PC as soon as possible.

"There's a building you should see, Benjamin, connected to your work at City Hall." He unlocked the front door, called out to Fred, and we stepped inside. "Some of us would like to see it designated and protected as a cultural resource. The City Council could do it with the stroke of a pen, though it doesn't seem likely."

He sat me on a sofa and crossed the cluttered living room to a shelf laden with photo albums. Fred stuck his head out from the hallway, asked how the council meeting had gone, then went back to the rerun of a boxing match he'd missed over the weekend. "Fred loves to watch sweaty, muscular men in shorts go at it," Maurice said, as he pulled an album from a shelf and opened it. "I certainly understand that part of it. It's all that hitting that spoils it for me." He turned, holding open an old album and beaming. "Here it is! Here's the snapshot I was looking for. Colin and Ted, in front of the supper club where they first met."

Maurice sat close beside me, balancing the open album across our knees. It was an old leatherette model, overstuffed and cracking along the spine. "Fred gave me a Brownie camera as a first anniversary present," Maurice said. "I was always shooting pictures of our friends, any chance I got." Maurice pointed to a square, black-and-white snapshot, low in contrast, its white border serrated around the edges. It showed two young men with their arms around each other's waists, beaming in front of a nondescript, two-story building lodged on the slant of a hill. The taller, heavier man was clearly Colin Harrison, broad-shouldered and barrel-chested, with a healthy head of red hair and a thick mustache, and handsome in a hearty, ruddy way. Meeks was less recognizable as the wiry, irritable old man I'd met at Harrison House and seen again tonight at the public hearing. In the photo, Meeks was slim, blond, clean-shaven, and rather pretty, in a wide-lapel jacket with a silk scarf knotted nattily around his slender neck.

"That was taken in front of Café Gala," Maurice said, "due north of here, just above Sunset. Colin and Ted met there not long after the war. Many decades later, with a good deal of remodeling, it became Wolfgang Puck's first Spago restaurant, across from Tower Records. Back in the forties, it was a genteel supper club, a favorite gathering place of movie stars and wealthy bohemian types. Quite elegant, from what I hear, and one of the few queer-friendly clubs in West Hollywood in those days. Some of us old-timers think of it as the first gay club in town, even though it wasn't truly a gay bar. The queers who patronized it had a system, and the management looked the other way. Wink, wink."

"A system?"

"The unwritten rule was that one must always arrive with a lady friend, which, of course, often meant a lesbian. Gentlemen who wished to meet other gentlemen made discreet contact in a rear bar. If you were seen alone back there, and had a roving eye, others knew what was up. It was too dangerous for men to be seen leaving the restaurant together, and they didn't dare be caught at home or at a motel in a compromising position." Maurice raised his eyebrows knowingly. "Not surprisingly, many of them were prominent, married, or both, given the pressure in those days to hide who and what they were."

"Then how did these men hook up?"

"After finding a partner, one left the restaurant alone, sauntered innocently down the hill to the filling station on the corner, got the restroom key from the attendant, and tipped him generously. After a minute or two, one's new friend arrived for a few minutes of stolen intimacy, while the attendant kept watch for the cops. Not the most romantic setting to be sure, but one took what one could get in those days. At least it was a connection, the chance to be held for a minute or two, and find a bit of fleeting pleasure in another man's arms."

I studied the old photo more closely. "And this was where Harrison met Meeks?"

Maurice nodded. "They were so taken with each other they found the courage to meet later under more favorable circumstances. From what I understand, it was their mutual enjoyment of chess that drew them closer." Maurice smiled knowingly. "Ted was the more skilled but frequently allowed Colin to beat him, which probably helped the relationship—Colin's the dominant type, you know. At any rate, their friendship blossomed, deepened into love, and they've been together ever since." Maurice glanced over. "I don't suppose you'd consider mentioning Café Gala in your brochure, would you, Benjamin? I'm sure Bruce Bibby kept photographs of it from its heyday, before it underwent so many transformations."

"Let me think on it, Maurice. I'm not sure its architecture warrants inclusion, but it might qualify as a cultural resource."

He patted my knee and began turning through the album's pages. "So many wonderful friendships Fred and I made through the years. We've outlived most of them, you know. Isn't that the way it always is, with older couples who stay together?" Suddenly, he perked up, pointing excitedly at another snapshot. "Rocky De Marco! There's the man I spoke of, when you mentioned that lady detective with the same last name, the one who seems to interest you so much."

Maurice turned the album at an angle, affording me a better look at the snapshot of two men standing side by side but not touching. "Here he is, back in the early seventies, with Lester Cohen." The man on the left was clearly Cohen—close to fifty, I guessed, with longish hair descending from the fringes of a bald spot and a solid build that might have been left over from more youthful football days. He wore a paisley shirt open at the chest under a modish outfit of flaring cuffs and square-toed boots, looking very much like an older man who'd missed out on the social revolution of the sixties and was trying to grab hold of what was left. The man next to him looked to be in his late twenties—lean, dark-haired, crew-cut, and tough-looking in a sexy way, with dark stubble covering his granite jaw and a cocky squint to the dark eyes. Without question, it was the same face I'd seen in Mira De Marco's wallet, when she'd opened it to give me a business card in the parking lot at City Hall. In the fuller shot that Maurice was showing me, the man was dressed in jeans and work boots but no shirt, leaning on a garden shovel with a sly smile less in the manner of a hired workman than a rake. His build was tight and naturally muscular, the hard body of a man who made a living with his hands and his back, doing the kind of labor softer men don't. At the bottom of the photograph, someone had written: *Lester Cohen and Rocky De Marco, 1973.*

Maurice flushed, fanning himself. "My, my, how odd it feels to see Rocky's face again after all these years. I'd forgotten all about these photos." Maurice smiled with what looked like self-deprecation, mixed with longing. "I'm sure he's quite forgotten me, wherever he is."

"Decent-looking guy," I said.

"Decent-looking? Benjamin, Rocky could have been a movie star! Dark, Italian looks, rugged, chiseled face, a body to die for. We were all quite taken with him when he hit town in 1972. He began turning heads right away—not just the boys, either."

"He was a switch hitter?"

Maurice nodded. "And masterful between the sheets, from what I gather. I know for a fact that he was on Lester Cohen's payroll for at least two years, and I doubt that the only thing Rocky was doing all that time was cleaning rain gutters and repairing drywall."

"Who else besides Cohen?"

"Lester was Colin Harrison's attorney in those days. Rocky ended up working for Colin as well—Colin, Lydia Ruttweller, lots of others around town. I even hired Rocky once when I needed some help moving things, and Fred was away on one of his long trucking drives. Men and women who had no use for a handyman were known to find something for Rocky to do, particularly on warm days when he might strip to the waist and give them an eyeful of that physique." Maurice glanced toward the hallway to make sure we were alone, then lowered his voice. "I was devoted to Fred, but I must admit, when I was around Rocky, something came over me. It was almost as if he cast a spell on us, with his understated charm and seductive smile, and the way he had of giving off sexual heat without trying. There were times when I felt helpless, drawn to him against my will, dangerously so, like a moth to a flame."

Maurice suddenly slapped the album shut, as though he needed to shatter the hold Rocky De Marco still exerted on him. His tone became cooler, almost dismissive. "Personally, I think Rocky was just looking for an easy score, either financial security or a small windfall before moving on. He was especially attentive to the lonely—as long as they had money, of course."

"Did he ever get what he was after?"

"That I couldn't say. There was talk that Lydia Ruttweller might have given him money, beyond his handyman's wages, but I can't swear to the truth of it."

"De Marco and Lydia Ruttweller were bedding down together?"

"There was talk. I really shouldn't repeat it. It's been so many years now. Who knows what really happened?"

"Lydia Ruttweller, for one."

"That would be her business then, not ours. Perhaps we should leave the subject alone."

"It's just that I have trouble picturing Lydia Ruttweller with a guy like this, that's all."

"We're all subject to weakness at times, Benjamin. Lydia was facing forty when she hired Rocky, nearing the end of her safe child-bearing years, still without offspring, and on the verge of a divorce from an inattentive husband, from what I understand."

"This was before her son, Chas, was born?"

"I've really said more than I should, Benjamin. It's not fair to Lydia, to be talking like this."

"I suppose not."

Naturally, Maurice went right on. "She didn't have it easy, you know. Her husband left her shortly after she gave birth to Chas. That was 1974—the same year Rocky decided to move on, without so much as a word to any of us."

"You sound a bit hurt."

Maurice laughed with a scoffing that sounded forced. "Goodness no, I barely knew him. No one did, really. He was a drifter, after all, without family connections that any of us knew of. He simply vanished that year, never to be seen or heard from again."

Maurice pressed the flat of his hand to the album's cover and kept it there, as if wanting to touch something or someone inside, to feel some long-lost heat, if only for a moment.

"Rocky seems to have left an impression just the same," I said.

Maurice said nothing, just rose without looking at me and returned the photo album to its place on the shelf.

Minutes after I climbed the steps to my apartment I was on-line, searching the Internet for images of a different kind. These men were completely unclothed, frequently erect, and doing more than gripping a garden shovel and grinning slyly for the camera as a means of seduction. They were the Rocky De Marcos of the Internet age, and there were hundreds of them, thousands, tens of thousands, filling the screen with each new link, each new click of the mouse.

Gay fetish.

The words caught my eye as I surveyed the links on a site devoted to muscular black men, and the men of all colors who admire them. I'd already run through the gallery of thumbnail photos available for free sampling, and was ready to move on, like a spoiled kid turned loose in a candy store, unable to make up his mind.

I clicked the gay fetish category. A list of choices immediately appeared: *military, S&M, B&D, extreme pain and torture, slave, medical, hidden webcam, uniforms, nudist camp, massage, locker room, feet, golden shower, scat, spanking,* a few others.

I hit *medical.*

I'd always found certain medical situations from life to be tinged with eroticism, particularly if the doctor was on the attractive side and disrobing was part of the process. There was something inherent in the exposure and vulnerability of the patient, and the enforced propriety and repressed sexuality that professional protocol demanded, that made it all the more erotically charged. It was the hothouse effect: As with so many taboo subjects that society deems embarrassing or unmentionable, its clandestine nature only added to its power and allure. My response to the erotic undercurrent of the examining room and hospital setting was hardly extraordinary; so many heterosexuals were similarly titillated that a worldwide cottage industry catering to their overheated fantasies had mushroomed, from movies of the fifties like *Carry On, Nurse* to *Playboy* cartoons with big-breasted nurses and sponge bath gags to countless Web sites offering salacious videos of nurses and doctors doing all kinds of things to patients that obviously aroused all kinds of straight men and women. My fantasies just happened to be of the gay variety, without the big-breasted nurses.

Medical offered me a number of subcategories: *military exam, sports physical, hernia, enema, white glove, catheter, stethoscope, circumcision, injections.* I was restless, so I hit the first link on the list.

The military exam link provided more choices: *Boot camp physical, Marine sergeant checkup, Navy group exam, Russian army physical, VD training film, drafted at seventeen.*

I hit the first link, intending to work my way systematically through the bunch, looking for the most realistic or imaginative treatment of the subject. A moment later, I faced a thumbnail gallery of a dozen photos featuring a lanky young blond kid, college freshman age, in various poses, from fully clothed, reaching for the top button of his shirt, to clad only in his Calvins, lowering the waistband just enough to reveal a teasing glimpse of pubic hair. On the same page was a link to a streaming video that promised a thirty-second sample from a full-length video titled *Eric Joins the Army.* I clicked on the link, clicked again to start the video, and turned up the volume on my computer speakers. The video focused on the blond boy as he stood in line with other young recruits, being asked to drop his shorts by a military doctor. He pretended to be confused or embarrassed—an obvious ploy by the director to amplify the tension and suspense, but effective nonetheless—before lowering his briefs. The video ended just as the doctor was reaching for the boy and telling him to cough. I replayed the video sample several times, less interested in the model's lithe body than his all-too-familiar face.

Victor Androvic—I was almost certain of it.

I clicked out of the video and back into the gallery of photos, sought out the thumbnail that offered the clearest shot of the model's face, then double-clicked on that to maximize the photo. When it filled my screen, I had no doubt that I'd stumbled on to the image of Victor Androvic among the thousands I'd scanned in recent days.

I clicked again to access the full gallery and found a name at the top that was obviously a model's pseudonym: Eric. The name was in blue and underlined, indicating it was another link that would take me closer to Eric, or at least to information about him. I double-clicked on the name, which took me to another photo, which froze a shirtless Eric just as he unbuckled and opened his pants, looking into the camera with a smile that was part innocent boy, part savvy hustler. Below the photo was a brief description: *Eric is a beautiful blond boy of eighteen, with a slim, smooth body, and very eager to please. Eric enjoys skiing, volleyball, movies, working out, and romantic evenings in bed. If you're visiting Southern California, he'd love to spend some time with you, making sure your every fantasy and need is fulfilled.* A chart of his personal data followed—birth date, height, weight, penile length and girth, circumcision and HIV status, preferences regarding sexual roles and positions, what he was or was not willing to do, how far outside Los Angeles he was willing to travel for a "date"—everything a consumer would want to know before placing an order. Below the chart was another link, this one for the Hot Boy Escort Agency, with instructions for access, membership, prices, and using a credit card to acquire Eric's services.

So now I knew: Victor Androvic—aka Eric—was a prostitute, one of the countless men and women who plied their trade via the Internet, easily reached by anyone with a credit card and an Internet connection but generally beyond the reach or interest of law enforcement. Given how devoted Victor was to his mother, how hard he'd worked to please her and make her proud, I wondered to what lengths he'd go to keep her from finding out what he'd secretly been doing for money.

He wasn't just in the closet, this kid. He was deep in a double closet, encased in shame and secrecy, and further damned by his connection through blood to a monstrous father. It was something I knew about myself, that awareness that no matter how far you run, how deep you hide, the father who raised you is always with you, *inside you.* I stared into Victor's eyes, trying to get a sense of him, trying to figure him out. The longer I sat there fixed on that screen, on that face, on those eyes, the more I saw myself.

FIFTEEN

I staggered to work the next morning on a few hour's sleep, arriving half an hour late to find an e-mail message from Cecelia Cortez waiting for me, asking for a meeting and a progress report on the brochure.

As I made my way to her office up the stairs and through the beehive of City Hall cubicles, there was a sense that the shock and sadness following Bruce Bibby's death was starting to wane. Bibby had been murdered on May 1, a Saturday; ten days had passed, and City Hall had pretty much returned to normal. I still saw memorial photos of Bibby displayed on desks and file cabinets, some with a vase of fresh flowers beside them, but I also saw employees getting on with their work and their lives. They gathered in chatty groups at the watercooler to gossip or pored over forms and documents at their desks with renewed focus or traded quips and laughed as they passed in the halls. City Hall was humming again as its workers got back to keeping the city functioning.

It's said that a work environment reflects management, that workplace attitudes trickle from the top down; in West Hollywood, the unique makeup of the city shaped the atmosphere at City Hall as much as the managers chosen to run it. Here, there were men and women in roughly equal numbers, with equal status and responsibility, of a wide age and ethnic range, most without that dour or drained look so common among institutional employees. A few were transgendered or—in keeping with the city's nondiscriminatory dress code—attired in businesslike male or female drag, without seeming odd or out of place, or even slightly distracting. If anything, the work seemed to go more smoothly and productively with the broad mix of personal styles and self-expression, a well-engineered machine oiled by tolerance and mutual respect. I'm sure working at City Hall had its drawbacks, not the least of which was the numbing routine of regularly assigned work. There must have been a few petty rivalries, personality conflicts, and nasty squabbles to foul the atmosphere. And there were no doubt outsiders who would condemn City Hall as a haven of licentiousness and depravity for its fostering of individualism and human rights. But what I saw was a large, congenial family engaged in a common goal in a comfortable environment, where one could be oneself without fear of being judged, ridiculed, or ostracized. As I approached Cecelia Cortez's office, I wondered how many other city halls operated with that kind of harmony.

Mrs. Cortez welcomed me in, offered me a seat, and asked straightaway for a status report. I told her I'd just started writing the brochure, but was missing some details, and wondered if I might visit Bruce Bibby's apartment to search his personal archives for what I needed. She agreed to arrange it with the sheriff's department and his family, if she could. Then she asked me for a target date for my first draft, and seemed satisfied with the one I gave her.

That evening, after writing copy covering the Plummer Park Apartment Grouping, I set off on foot to Lydia Ruttweller's house to pick up some photographs of the old rail yard that she'd promised me earlier that day on the phone.

Mrs. Ruttweller lived in a two-story bungalow in the city's historic Craftsman District, which was comprised of North Hancock Avenue and adjacent North Palm Avenue, just above Santa Monica Boulevard. Although homes in the post-1910 Craftsman style were scattered across West Hollywood, it was here that one found some of the finest examples, among them the Ruttweller house. It featured a deep front porch behind a solid wood railing, with stone columns supporting an extended roof, off a large lower window that offered a view of the yard and street. The front yard was modest in size and design: a tidy lawn split by a stone walkway, a fruit tree on each side of the walk, and well-trimmed shrubs fronting the house, with ferns filling in the ground below; a low white picket fence that looked freshly painted surrounded the yard, with a latch gate front and center. It was just the kind of efficient, straightforward house, proud but unostentatious, that one might expect in a residence occupied by Lydia Ruttweller.

Long driveways are among the chief Craftsman characteristics, and Lydia's led me along the north side of the house to a smaller porch that served as an alternative entrance. Just beyond, to the right, I could see the edges of a rear yard under a sprawling shade tree; directly at the end of the drive was a single-story detached garage that had probably been built with the house eighty or ninety years ago.

The early May evening was warm and on the humid side, and I was bathed in perspiration as I prepared to knock. Before my knuckles touched the door, a sharp exchange of voices inside caused me to hold back. I pricked up my ears, stepped down from the shallow porch, and followed the sound to a first-story window roughly five feet above ground that looked into a kitchen.

"I'm tired of writing checks for you, tired of your wastrel ways! It's time you grow up and stand on your own two feet and make something of your life!"

The voice was clearly that of Lydia Ruttweller—sharp, judgmental, condemning. As I took a step back to the middle of the drive, I could see her through a scrim of gauzy curtains standing face-to-face with her son Chas. Her pointy chin was thrust forward with righteous indignation, while his—massive and elongated in the manner of a hard-core steroid addict—jutted out with ugly menace and machismo. He was wearing a tank top that revealed a neck, torso, and limbs inflated to ridiculous proportions, while his skin was prickly and pink, as if he were cooking from the inside out.

"One fucking check," he shouted. "That's all I'm asking for. You know you've got the money."

"Yes, and you're not going to get another penny of it. Not unless you straighten out your life and get a real job. Not until you start behaving like the decent young man I raised you to be."

"I've got a job!"

"A bouncer at Skin Deep, that tawdry club up on Sunset Boulevard. That's no position for a Ruttweller."

A nasty smile appeared, making his face even more sinister. "But I'm not a Ruttweller, am I, Mom? Not really." She blanched, uncharacteristically silent. "I don't know who the fuck I am. I never even met my old man, because you didn't want him around. Because you're ashamed of what you did with him. Because you're ashamed of me."

"That's not true, Chas." She looked stricken. "I've explained all that, so many times before." She reached for him, but he took a step back, just out of her reach. "What's happened to you, Chas? What's happened to my little boy?"

"I'm not your little boy! I'm thirty years old, for Christ's sake!"

"Then why don't you act like it?" Her voice was filled now more with pleading than judgment. "You inject those awful drugs and spend all day lifting weights, and most of the night up at those clubs, picking up young girls, 'partying.' " She spoke the word as if it was poison on her tongue. "Is this what you want to do with your life?"

"Would you be happier if I was a faggot, like your dead friend?"

Her voice regained some of its edge. "You mustn't speak of Bruce that way. He was a fine young man. I miss him very much."

"He was a fag." Chas thrust his words at her like a stiletto. "Your little queer friend in his wheelchair, that you kept around like a pet, someone who wouldn't talk back, someone you could feel sorry for."

She stepped forward and slapped him across the face, hard enough that I heard the crack of her hand from the drive. Almost immediately, she burst into tears. "It's those horrible drugs you take," she said, "those steroids. That's what's making you this way. Look at you, Chas. Look what they've done to your body." Her voice quavered as the tears flowed. "They've turned you into this creature I hardly recognize."

"I'm big, Mom. I'm strong. Not like that cripple you spent all your time with."

"Bruce was a special young man. Our relationship was special."

"You wish he'd been your son instead of me."

She shook her head, shaking off tears. "No, that's not true."

"You never wanted me. I was a mistake."

"Chas, stop." She swiped at her tears and reached for him again, but he sidestepped her, refusing to let her touch him. She seemed to give up at that point; her shoulders sagged and the emotion went out of her voice. "How much do you need this time?"

The tiniest smile tugged at the corners of his mouth. "A thousand would be nice."

"That's too much."

"Then why did you ask?"

"What's it for, Chas?"

"An investment opportunity."

"In more steroids? Are you selling them now?" He said nothing. "Promise me you'll make some changes in your life. Promise me you'll stop taking these chemicals before they destroy your body, before they kill you."

"I like my body this way." He ran his fingers over his comic book biceps. "There are guys who dream of having a body like this."

"You used to be such a good-looking boy, so well proportioned."

"You going to write that check or not?"

She sighed, turned, and rummaged through her purse on the counter. A moment later, she bent over her checkbook, scribbling with a pen. She tore off a check and held it out to him. He took it confidently, as if this scene had played out a hundred times before, in much the same way.

"It's the last one, Chas, unless I see some changes." She squared her shoulders, pulling herself erect. "I'm warning you, I won't go on being used like this, not when you're throwing your life away." She paused, then continued in a cooler, more assured voice. "I wasn't going to tell you this just yet, but perhaps it's a good time."

His tone grew wary. "Tell me what?"

"A few months ago, I made changes in my estate plan. Everything I own went to Bruce. Not to you, Chas, because you'd only use it to destroy yourself."

"You gave everything to that little fruit?"

She nodded perfunctorily. "Now that Bruce is gone, I plan to change my estate again, making Citizens United for Preservation the sole beneficiary. It's something I've been considering since Bruce was—taken from us."

"You wouldn't do that. You wouldn't leave everything to that fucking organization, to save a bunch of old buildings."

"Just try me, young man. You're going to see how serious I am."

"You bitch."

"I love you, Chas, but I won't be a willing partner in your self-destruction any longer. You either make changes in your lifestyle, or nothing of mine will ever be yours. Not this house. Not my savings or investments. Nothing. It will all go to CUP. Do I make myself clear?"

His look grew surly again, hateful. "Maybe I knew about what you did, giving everything to Bibby. Did you ever think about that?"

She stiffened, confused. "What are you saying?"

"Maybe I heard you on the phone, talking to your lawyer about making Bibby your beneficiary. Maybe I saw some papers in your office." He let out an acidic laugh. "Maybe I had the little fucker killed, so I'd be next in line to get your dough."

Concern rose in her voice. "Chas, don't talk like that."

"Or maybe I did it myself, Mom. Maybe it wasn't that Russian kid they arrested the other day. Maybe it was me who beat your little pet to death, just to hear him whimper and beg for his life before I finished him off."

"Stop, please. You don't mean what you're saying." She reached out, trying to touch his face. "What's happened to you, Chas? How did you get like this?"

He turned his head, but not so far that she couldn't make contact. Briefly, he closed his eyes, only for a second or two, while her fingers grazed the stubble on his florid face, as if he wanted to feel her touch but loathed it at the same time. Then he pulled away, out of the frame of the window.

Her hand remained outstretched, while she pleaded with him one more time. "Won't you stay for dinner? I'll cook something nice. Lots of protein, low carbohydrates, just the way you like it."

"I'm outta here."

She deflated, looking filled with despair. I heard the side door being opened and stepped back over to the small porch. Chas appeared, pulling up as we came face-to-face.

"Who the fuck are you?"

"My name's Benjamin Justice. I'm from City Hall. Your mother has some photographs for me."

He glanced toward the window. "How long have you been out here?"

"To be honest, I wasn't watching the clock."

"You're a smart-ass, aren't you?"

I shrugged. "I've been called worse."

His massive jaw jutted and the big vein in his thick neck was pumping. "I don't like people sneaking around, getting into our business."

I glanced at my watch. "You want to tell your mother I'm here, or do I do that?"

He glared a moment, before hollering over his shoulder. "Mom, you got company! Some fruit from City Hall." His eyes came back to me, filled with contempt. "You are a faggot, right? Like the rest of them down there?"

"Why, are you lonely?"

His nostrils flared, and he clenched his fists at his sides, while I wondered if he was going to redesign my face. Just then, his mother appeared.

"Mr. Justice—I wasn't expecting you quite so soon." She smiled awkwardly. "You've met my son?"

"We were just getting acquainted, Chas and I. Charming boy."

Chas fixed me one last time with his malevolent stare before stepping from the porch and brushing past me, making sure he caught me on the shoulder, hard enough that I felt it. Then he stomped down the driveway like a man with enough rage in him to hurt someone, for no other reason than to validate his perverted sense of manhood.

SIXTEEN

To the surprise of just about everyone, Victor Androvic was out of jail on Wednesday, three days after his arrest.

"He made bail late last night, got out this morning," Templeton said over the phone, just before lunchtime. "All they had him on was a missed probation meeting and evading arrest. The judge disallowed a more serious probation violation. I'm putting the story together now."

"Who coughed up the money?"

"His mother rallied the Russian community, came up with a fund. Mira De Marco's not too happy about it."

"You've already discussed it with her?"

"She phoned me early this morning, at home."

"She's got your home number now?"

"I thought you'd encouraged her to contact me."

"I did. I'm just surprised how far it got so fast."

"I told her she should call me anytime, if something's breaking and she wants to share it with me."

"She must not have much of a case against Androvic on the murder, or the D.A. would have charged him, put the bail at a million or more."

"You sound like you've taken his side, Justice."

"Trying to be objective, that's all."

"Androvic fled when they tried to arrest him, remember?"

"He's worried about being railroaded, after his previous conviction on the caviar deal. That's what his mother says."

"You've spoken with his mother? When was this?"

"Sunday afternoon, after they took him away."

"You're getting awfully close to the Androvics, aren't you?"

"I ran into his mother, that's all. Had a chat with her."

"And she thinks sweet little Victor is innocent." There was a mocking tone in Templeton's voice that I hadn't heard before. "Gosh, it must be true then."

"All I'm saying is, the evidence isn't there, or he'd still be locked up. Healthy skepticism, simple as that."

"Be careful, Justice. You might be falling for another pretty face, another young man in trouble. It's been your downfall more than once."

"Sometimes they're worth saving."

"Not this time," Templeton said. "Not the way I see it."

"Maybe that's the problem."

"Reporters are allowed to have opinions, as long as we keep them out of the story."

"Is that what you're doing?" Before she could respond, I said quickly, "Listen, I've got work. So do you. We'll talk later."

I hung up and returned to my rough draft, but without much success. I didn't like cracking heads with Templeton like this; it wasn't good for either of us. But I figured it would continue until this nasty business with Victor Androvic was resolved one way or the other. With that in mind, I jumped aboard a city-operated Dash minibus out on the boulevard, took a seat, and a few minutes later was stepping off in the Russian neighborhood.

The one person I didn't expect to see coming out of Tatiana Androvic's apartment house was Dr. Roderick Ford. He'd told Templeton and me that he'd cut his ties to Victor after Victor had tried to use him as an alibi during the investigation into Bruce Bibby's murder. But as I approached Mrs. Androvic's building, I saw the professor coming out a side gate, moving quickly with a cautious look, brushing at the shoulders of his sport coat like a man with a bad dandruff problem.

I stepped out of sight and watched him hurry to a black Chrysler parked at the curb, keeping his head down and ducking quickly into the car. As he sped away, not more than ten feet from where I stood in hiding, his eyes looked uneasy.

I entered the same gate to see what might have caused him to choose that route rather than the front entrance. The path alongside the building was narrow and unpaved, while the vines of lacy asparagus fern made passage difficult and dirty with their thorns and debris. I figured the only advantage to going in or out this way was not being seen. A half minute later, I was tapping on Mrs. Androvic's apartment door and brushing myself off as Dr. Ford had done. I knocked harder, but there was still no answer.

Mrs. Androvic's neighbor to the south, a small man with a soft belly and a little mustache, opened his door and looked out curiously. In a thick Russian accent, he informed me that I could find Mrs. Androvic working at nearby Plummer Park. He wasn't sure just where and suggested I check in at the administration office.

Years ago, Plummer Park had been a notorious nighttime hangout for male hustlers, drug dealers, and vagrants, where robbery and violence had been almost routine. These days, with new landscaping and buildings and better lighting and police patrols, it was a bustling center for community and cultural events, from a weekly farmer's market to classes of every kind, and public forums on social and political issues that were often well attended. More than anything, though, the park served as a gathering place for seniors, including an elder day-care center that provided social, mental, and emotional support, and a public kitchen that offered meals priced according to what one could afford.

At the administrative office, I learned that Mrs. Androvic volunteered in the Russian-language library, and that she'd be free to see me at the end of the hour. I decided to kill some time visiting the Russian folk art exhibit that was set up in a small auditorium, where Mrs. Androvic could find me when she had a break. The exhibit was modest in size but the handicrafts on display were attractive and interesting. Especially eye-catching were the hand-carved soup bowls, candlesticks, and jewelry boxes that were painted in the manner of the wooden spoons Mrs. Androvic had given me a few days earlier as a gift of friendship.

Another section was devoted to *matryoshkas,* nesting dolls like the set I'd seen in Mrs. Androvic's apartment. Unlike many of the other objects, these were locked in glass display cases, so I assumed they were more valuable. Mrs. Androvic had told me that each family of artists had its own distinct style, its own special use of pattern and color, and I could see that now as I surveyed the various sets of dolls. Below each set was a card providing the name of the family, its region or village of origin, and the special meaning conveyed by that particular set. The dolls of the Vasileva family, for example, were intricately painted with tea ceremonies to symbolize the importance of tea in Russian life and culture. The Lebedeva doll set featured an elaborate but less intricate design, with its ladies dressed in traditional Russian costume, including babushka shawls. Even the expressions and delicate features of the faces varied from doll to doll among different sets.

One set bore the distinctive design I'd seen on the *matryoshkas* in Mrs. Androvic's apartment. I recognized the rich floral pattern of the costume, heavy with pinks and lavenders, and the pixieish features of the face, with its wide eyes and fine lashes and deep blush to the cheeks. I was studying the family name on the information card below when a rabbi in orthodox dress approached, asking me if I was a *matryoshka* collector.

"Not really," I said. "Just happened by for a look."

I asked about the craft and he explained that *matryoshkas* were originally made as simple toys for children. Through the centuries, he said, the trade had developed into a fine art, with the dolls thought to bring good luck and prosperity to their owners. Authentic dolls like these, he added, were made from birch or lime wood that had been dried and cured for two years. By custom, the husband in the family was the skilled carver, while the wife completed the complex and minutely detailed painting; together, they handed down their artistry from generation to generation, although mass production was threatening the tradition.

"So you see," he said, stroking his gray beard, "there's a good deal more to these little dolls than at first meets the eye."

"And these," I said, indicating the *matryoshkas* with the design so similar to the set in Mrs. Androvic's apartment. "What special meaning do these convey?"

"These beautiful dolls, with their happy faces and their arms around their babies, symbolize the incomparable love of a mother for her child, and the vital role she plays in Russian life."

"And in this particular family, did the mother do the painting, following tradition?"

He adjusted his spectacles and peered down at the information card. "That's correct. According to this, the father did the carving, the mother the painting, in the traditional way." He looked up. "That's usually the case, but not always."

"Thanks for the insight, Rabbi."

"Thank you for your interest, young man."

As he turned away, Tatiana Androvic appeared in the doorway. She approached, but pulled up when she noticed the *matryoshkas* on display. Her eyes went from mine to the set of dolls behind me, the ones I'd just been studying.

"I've just gotten an interesting lesson about *matryoshkas*," I said.

She wrung her hands uncomfortably. "Why have you come here, Mr. Justice?"

"I came as a friend, with questions about Victor." Her eyes darted back to the *matryoshkas* before she suggested we speak more privately. She took my elbow and turned me away from the display, with a sense of urgency. When we were standing alone out on the lawn, she said tersely, "Victor's attorney told us we must not speak to anyone."

"The other day, you requested my help."

"Yes, I know. But it is best that you go now and not come to see me again."

"Perhaps you can answer a question about the *matryoshkas* first—in particular, the set of dolls I was just looking at back there."

Her eyes got jumpy, her voice more anxious. "Please, go away now, and forget anything I might have said in my foolish way."

"You told me that Victor's father had carved the *matryoshkas* in your apartment."

"The *matryoshkas*, they mean nothing." She shrugged haphazardly, with a forced smile. "They are just silly dolls. Pretty, silly dolls."

"I find them fascinating, Mrs. Androvic. You open them up, and each time you find something else hidden within, like peeling away layers of a well-kept secret."

Her eyes flickered with distress. "I told you, Mr. Justice, I have been advised not to speak about Victor with anyone."

"But we weren't speaking of Victor just now, were we? Just some pretty, silly dolls."

"Please, go, leave us alone." She turned and fled, scurrying across the lawn on her short legs, without looking back.

I left the park and caught the Dash back to City Hall, staring out the window at the passing landscape of the Russian community—the shop selling books in Cyrillic, the kosher market, the fire station, the discount car wash, the little hardware store famous for having every possible item needed to fix a plumbing problem. Staring out and wondering why the *matryoshkas* symbolizing a mother's love so closely resembled the ones in Tatiana Androvic's apartment, while bearing a different family name.

SEVENTEEN

By half past noon on Thursday, I'd roughed out another section of the brochure, pleased with the overall progress I was making.

This portion covered the Lingenbrink Commercial Grouping on Holloway Drive, which includes rare examples of commercial buildings designed by the noted architect Rudolph Schindler, better known for his early Modernist homes. I was about to reposition a paragraph and cut two others when Tony Mercury appeared, asking me to lunch. He had the thousand-megawatt smile going, looking drop-dead gorgeous in an off-white silk suit, with his shirt collar open to reveal a glimpse of unfashionable chest hair that made him that much more attractive.

"Sure," I said, pushing back my chair and trying not to stare too brazenly at his open collar. "A guy's got to eat."

"I thought we'd drop in at the Argyle," Mercury said, as we shot up Crescent Heights Boulevard in his gold Lexus convertible, past a cluster of vintage churches and synagogues. "Very nice restaurant up there." A lively spring breeze had come up, chasing the pollution and leavening the heat, and he had the top down. A George Michael tune pulsated from the quadraphonic speakers, making me feel like I was out for a casual spin with my boyfriend, the porn star. "I've asked a friend to join us," Mercury said, a little too offhandedly. "I hope that's not a problem."

"As long as I'm not buying," I said, "I'm not complaining."

He laughed, gave my knee a playful squeeze, left his hand there an extra moment, then swung left onto Sunset Boulevard, past the Chateau Marmont, and into the heart of the Sunset Strip.

The Argyle was a stunning, English-style residential hotel on the south side of Sunset, which had opened in 1930 as a swank apartment building known as the Sunset Tower. Rising fourteen narrow stories, it was one of those dozen structures in West Hollywood listed on the National Register of Historic Places. The white tower's lower portion was a striking example of Zigzag Moderne, with Streamline Moderne visible nearer the top; plaster friezes on the façade incorporated a decorative tangle of plants, fruit, animals, mythological creatures, zeppelins, airplanes, and Adam and Eve—arcane details I'd gleaned from Bruce Bibby's research. Famous as a setting in countless films, new and old, the Argyle had also served as a residence for dozens of stars. Down the street, the gothic Chateau Marmont— where a young Paul Newman had courted Joanne Woodward and the comic John Belushi had died of an overdose—was known as the hotel for celebrities who liked their surroundings comfy but subdued. Those who preferred more elegance and extravagance stayed three blocks west at the Argyle.

A parking valet took Mercury's convertible along the short circular drive out front. Moments later we stepped into a lobby of spotless marble floors and dramatic art deco brass railings. Using old photographs—the original plans couldn't be found—the current owners had meticulously restored the interior to its original splendor; I felt as though I'd been transported into a black-and-white thirties movie or a photograph by Hurrell. A hostess in the first-floor restaurant seated us at a window table on the south side, overlooking a narrow patio and swimming pool that appeared to be hugging the edge of the world, with an unobstructed view of the Los Angeles basin beyond. Within the minute, our third party was joining us. Tony Mercury stood and introduced us.

"Benjamin Justice, I'd like you to meet my good friend Lester Cohen."

The wealthy developer extended two pudgy hands, gold cuff links flashing on his French cuffs and showy gemstones on his fingers. He clasped my outstretched hand in both of his, shook it firmly, and said, "What a treat to meet a man with such an extraordinary background. I feel like I'm meeting a celebrity."

"If I were a celebrity, Mr. Cohen, I'd be rich, which I can assure you I'm not."

"No shame in that, my boy, no shame at all." He winked broadly. "Although there's nothing wrong with having money, either, is there? Please, sit, sit!"

I thanked Cohen for the gift basket he'd sent welcoming me to my new job. He waved it off as if it were nothing and launched into a discussion—more a lecture, really—on the Argyle's colorful history. He mentioned the cow John Wayne had once kept in his penthouse suite, and various eccentricities of other famous guests of the past—Howard Hughes, Paulette Goddard, Frank Sinatra, Errol Flynn, and the gangster Bugsy Siegel, who'd purchased hand-tailored suits down the street by the dozen. Cohen proved to be a warm, good-humored fellow, with a vitality and force of energy that belied his years. After taking charge of the conversation, he didn't let go, yet controlled it so effortlessly and with such congeniality that I didn't mind. He even ordered the starters without asking our opinion—oysters on the half shell and crab cakes that came with watercress, roasted red peppers, and sweet corn sauce—insisting that I had to try them because the restaurant prepared them just the way he wished. I told him politely that I wasn't in the mood for shellfish and ordered the soup of the day, which seemed momentarily to displease him.

When the waiter went away, Cohen steered the conversation to the subject of the Argyle's status as an architectural treasure and historic site worthy of official protection. By then, I had a pretty good idea where he was going. He didn't surprise me.

"You look at a place like this," he said, "or the Granville around the corner on Crescent Heights or the Colonial House over on Havenhurst, and you understand the need to preserve these beauties for posterity. This is art, genius, history. What's not to like?" He laughed good-naturedly, stroking the smooth dome of his head. "Then you look at those poor, broken-down cottages on Monette Avenue, and you say to yourself, 'Oy vey, these are nothing more than shacks, a nice meal for the termites but hardly deserving of designation as historic landmarks.'"

"You're speaking of the Sherman cottages," I said, "that stand on the land you want for your condominiums."

"I'm not thinking of myself," Cohen said. "Oh, sure, I'd like to put my little homes there. It's a nice location, nice view, close to everything. What's not to like? But you want to know what troubles me about this whole mishegoss, Mr. Justice—may I call you Ben?"

"Anything you'd like, Mr. Cohen, except putz. I never liked putz."

He roared with laughter, clapping his chubby hands together. "And you'll call me Les, because we're all friends here. I had an uncle named Benjamin, lovely man. Good name, solid, strong. So I'll tell you what bothers me about giving special treatment to those dumpy little shacks in the Sherman district. You do that, then you degrade the meaning of historic preservation, you make a mockery of it. If those little rattraps deserve protection, then why not everything? And if everything, then why not nothing? You see my point, Ben? You've got to set a high standard, be selective, if historic designation and preservation are to have any value at all. These Sherman cottages, these are piffle, these are not worthy of all this kvelling. We should look elsewhere around this fine city at all the genuine treasures and focus our attention on what truly matters."

He pointed out the window at various buildings among the more than two dozen already protected by local individual designation—the Normandie Towers on Hampton Avenue, the Emser Tile Building on Santa Monica Boulevard, the Beau Sejour on Fountain. "These are like fine gems, preserved in their proper setting, while the city continues to live and grow around them, as any city must to stay alive."

"I had no idea you were such an aficionado of vintage architecture, Mr. Cohen."

"Les—call me Les." He threw up his hands, beaming. "I love old buildings! And I love new buildings, when they're designed with imagination and skill. New ideas, new styles, new approaches to living. There must always be room for change, for a fresh vision. And that's what I plan for Casa Granada on Paul Monette Avenue—an architectural masterpiece that will live on after I'm gone, worthy of its own designation and protection as a cultural treasure when its own time comes."

He mentioned a famous architect, identified the style, boasted of the fine materials that would go into the construction. "First-class all the way, no expense spared. This building will be of such magnificence, the tour buses will put Casa Granada on their itineraries, like that cemetery east of here where all the dead movie stars are buried."

"You're quite the salesman, Les. You've got the pitch down cold."

Cohen elbowed Mercury. "He's not so easy, this one, is he?"

"A tough cookie," Mercury said, winking at me. "But I appreciate a guy with balls."

Cohen leaned closer across the table. "Tell me, Ben—what do you plan to do after you finish this little job, this brochure you're writing?"

"I've got a contract to write a book about my life."

"Making much money from this book?"

"Not all that much, given the time and expenses involved."

"After this book, then what?"

"Hadn't thought much about it."

"As you can imagine, I've got excellent connections. There might just be something out there that could help you get back on your feet, in a big way. Could be something in one of my companies, for a smart guy like you."

"Even with my reputation, Les?"

He waved it away like a man chasing away a fly. "That's all in the past. I believe in the future, Ben. I believe we all deserve another crack at the brass ring. I have my own reputation, my own past—the bathhouse issue. Left it behind years ago. Moved on." His smile faded, and his eyes narrowed keenly. "So what do you say, Ben? What is it you're looking for? What's out there that you'd like to have a piece of?"

"Is this brochure really that important?"

"Who said this has anything to do with that?"

"Let's not jerk each other off, Les. Not in such a nice place like this."

"I can think of worse ways to spend my time." I didn't laugh, and he threw up his hands. "You need to lighten up, Ben, relax a little."

"About the brochure," I said.

"OK, this brochure." He smoothed the ends of his walrus mustache with a thumb and forefinger, as if buying a few seconds to find just the right words. "This brochure is a small but vital piece in a larger construct. I'm a builder, Ben. I believe in laying every stone carefully, driving every nail straight and true. One weak link can weaken the entire enterprise. To that extent, yes, this little brochure matters."

I glanced at Mercury. "When Tony learned that Bruce Bibby's notes had survived the theft of his computer and backup disc, he seemed concerned."

"Surprised," Mercury said evenly. "That's different than concerned."

"Surprised or concerned, you definitely reacted."

Mercury's look grew darker. "What's your point, Justice?"

"Why the surprise?"

"Natural reaction, under the circumstances."

"Bibby was dead and his notes had disappeared. That wasn't exactly bad news for you, was it?"

"I'm not sure what you're implying, Justice."

"Boys, boys," Cohen said, putting a hand on Mercury's shoulder and gesturing to include me in an imaginary embrace. "We're having a pleasant lunch among friends. Talking about business, opportunity, the future."

"Is that what we're talking about?" I asked.

Cohen folded his hands in front of him and looked me straight in the eye. "That's what *I'm* talking about. Golden opportunities that come once in a man's lifetime and rarely present themselves again. Opportunities that can change a man's circumstances forever. Or not, if he's foolish enough to let them slip away."

"Did you offer Bruce Bibby similar opportunities?"

"Bibby's situation was different."

"He wasn't faced with the limitations that I am," I offered. "He didn't have a public scandal in his past. He had steady work. Is that what you're saying?" Cohen raised his eyebrows, along with the corners of his mouth, then his shoulders in a shrug that said what he had to say. We'd clearly come to a crossroads in the conversation, one that I didn't want to face, at least not yet. "Let me think on it, will you?"

"Of course—one should always think these things through." Cohen smiled benignly. "Just don't think too long. If I'm not mistaken, that brochure is due for completion in a matter of days."

When the starters arrived, Cohen relaxed again, as if buoyed by the sight of the food. As he sampled the oysters, then the crab cakes, washing them down with a fifty-dollar bottle of sauvignon blanc, he waxed nostalgic about his early days in West Hollywood, after setting up his law practice here in the early sixties because of the advantages afforded by county tax codes.

"I understand you were Colin Harrison's attorney back then," I said.

He paused with his fork in midair. "How did you know that?"

I explained that Maurice had filled me in on some local history, mentioning his full name when Cohen failed to remember him.

"God, I haven't spoken to Maurice in a good twenty years," Cohen said. "What a character." Mercury asked who Maurice was, and Cohen filled him in. "We go way back, Maurice and me," Cohen said, "more than thirty years."

"So you did handle Harrison's legal affairs back then?" I asked.

"I took care of Colin's business contracts, and a few personal things. He was just getting started in the property business. I'd been around by then, kept him out of trouble with the fine print. I still advise him now and then, when he asks for it. Saw him last month, as a matter of fact. Power-of-attorney matter."

"He doesn't seem in the best of health."

"Healthy enough to sign papers."

"In his right mind, you mean?" Cohen nodded, so I pressed on. "He signed his power of attorney over to Ted Meeks, giving him control of the properties?"

"Ben, please. That would be between me and my client. You know that."

"And Ted Meeks," I said. "If he was granted power of attorney."

"Which I'm not discussing, as I made clear. What's with the questions, anyway?"

"I've always been the nosy type. I can't seem to help myself."

"Let's put it this way," Cohen said. "I advised Colin to get his affairs in order. This is something anyone should do, I don't care what your age. You can get hit by a truck, a piano can fall on your head, anything can happen."

"A burglar can break in and bash in your skull," I said, glancing over to include Mercury, "the way it happened to Bruce Bibby."

"Sure, that, too," Cohen said. "So, yes, I suggested Colin update his papers. Now tell me about my old friend, Maurice, this goy I haven't seen forever. He still with that truck driver, what's-his-name?"

"Fred. Yes, they're still together."

"What a pair, those two. Maurice, you couldn't stop that queen from talking. Fred, hardly a word. Still together. Who'd ever figure?"

"From what Maurice tells me," I said, "you shared some mutual friends back in the old days. Colin Harrison, Ted Meeks, Rocky De Marco."

Cohen stopped chewing, regarding me curiously. "Rocky De Marco. That's a name I haven't heard in thirty years."

"You'd forgotten him?"

"I didn't say I'd forgotten him." Cohen nudged Mercury with his shoulder. "Rocky De Marco wasn't the kind of guy you forget. Not if you had an eye for rough trade, which some of us did in those days."

"Maurice showed me a photo of the two of you together."

"No kidding."

"From what Maurice tells me, Rocky also worked for Colin Harrison."

Cohen used his napkin to swipe at a bit of crab in his mustache. "Rocky worked for a lot of people."

"Even Lydia Ruttweller, according to Maurice."

"Like I said, Rocky got around."

"And then he just up and disappeared. Seventy-four, wasn't it?"

Cohen shrugged indifferently. "Something like that. It was a long time ago."

"You never heard from Rocky again?"

"Nobody did, as far as I know. Eat your soup, before it gets cold."

"It's gazpacho," I said. "It's supposed to be cold."

Cohen smiled again, but the warmth was gone. "So eat it anyway."

It was after two when we finished our meals. Following my gazpacho, I'd chosen roasted salmon and marinated tomatoes, with tropical sorbet terrine for dessert, the kind of lunch I could enjoy only if someone else was paying. Lester Cohen dropped an extra fifty on the table as a tip, making sure I saw it, and a minute later we stood out front in the towering shadow of the Argyle, waiting for Tony Mercury's car to be brought around. Cohen's long, white Bentley sat at the curb, gleaming like a shark's tooth, with a liveried driver behind the wheel.

"You need to understand something," Cohen said to me, rocking in his polished Italian loafers. "I'm in a position to change things for you. I'm also accustomed to having things go my way. And I can afford just about anything I want."

"I'll remember that, Mr. Cohen."

"Les, call me Les."

Mercury's convertible came up from the garage, and the valet parked it behind the Bentley. Cohen waved Mercury off and tipped the valet himself, putting a twenty in his open palm and getting a tip of the cap in return. We climbed in, while Cohen leaned on the doorframe, close to my ear. "These opportunities don't come along all that often, Ben. Not for most people and certainly not for someone with the problems you've had."

"Thanks for lunch, Les. I don't get to eat in places like this very often."

"That could change, kid." He straightened up. "Buckle your seat belt. You can never be too safe." He nodded in the direction of Mercury. "Especially when you're riding with the Greek Stallion."

As Mercury eased the Lexus away from the curb, my eye went to the rear of the Bentley. You didn't see that many white Bentleys around West Hollywood, and only one with vanity plates bearing the words GOLDEN OLDIE, since they were customized and sold on an individual basis by the state. I'd seen it myself just once before, in a dark, narrow alley near the gym, as Tony Mercury had climbed into the backseat for a clandestine rendezvous with his octogenarian lover.

Mercury pulled onto Sunset Boulevard, out of the Argyle's shadow and back into the West Hollywood glare, while I pondered the conflict of interest inherent in a secret affair between a developer and a council member, with the fate of the Sherman cottages and millions of profit dollars hanging in the balance.

EIGHTEEN

That night, I dropped by Buff to work off my expensive lunch.

I didn't see Tony Mercury in the workout area, but I did run into Trang Nguyen. He was performing curls with a twenty-five-pound dumbbell in each hand, checking his form in the mirror—body erect, shoulders drawn up and back, chin tucked toward his chest, like a guard at Buckingham Palace. I noticed that he isolated the work on the bicep without cheating by swinging his body for momentum, the way I would have. He was dressed again in a one-piece Spandex tight that left little doubt about how much power he packed into his deceptively slim frame. My guess was that he was also quicker than a cat.

"You're very disciplined, Trang."

He found my eyes in the glass, feigning surprise, although I'd caught him reacting moments earlier when he'd glimpsed me approaching from behind. I studied his body as he finished his set, his hard biceps bunching up like a baseball each time he raised the weight. In earlier years, bolder times, I would have fondled the bulging muscle as he lifted, to cop a cheap thrill and gauge his attraction to me, even at the risk of offending him. Now, I simply watched. It wasn't that I was all that much more genteel or proper. The sexual impulse simply wasn't there, as much as I longed for it.

"Discipline is all in mind," Trang said, setting the dumbbells back in the rack. "We can all do, if we want. Too many lazy people, that the problem."

"Is that how you approach everything in life, Trang? Strict discipline? No room for emotion, purely from the heart?"

"That private matter. I no talk of private matter, only with close friend."

"Maybe we could become friends, you and I, if you gave me a chance."

"I already tell you, I no trust older white guy no more." He was trying hard, but the conviction was slipping from his voice. "I got plenty good friend, Asian guy, they honest with me."

"Was Bruce Bibby honest with you, Trang?"

His eyes registered something too fleeting to decipher. "You please excuse me," he said, stepping well around me so our bodies never touched. "I got workout to do."

I saw Trang one last time that evening, soaping down in a shower stall, his back turned to reveal his long, slender body and a beautiful behind that would have made a Hollywood starlet jealous. When he turned to rinse off, facing me as I shampooed in the stall across the way, I got a full glimpse of his rippling muscles, which weaved an impressive pattern up and down his smooth torso and legs. Sensual, coltish, with a stunning face, he must have been an object of desire for countless other men; more than a few stole glimpses of him as they passed through the shower room on their way to the Jacuzzi. Yet as I stood there studying his flawless face and body, I was acutely aware once again of how little real lust I felt, and how long it had been—several months at least—since I'd felt a powerful sexual attraction for anyone at all. It was as if my appreciation for Trang—as for Tony Mercury—came not from real desire but from my recollection of it. I found myself at that uneasy juncture of memory and emptiness, nagged by a gnawing hunger but without the appetite to eat. As we stood there gazing across to the other's shower stall, I noticed his cock start to rise; he turned his back to me again, rinsed off quickly, wrapped a towel around his waist, grabbed his shampoo, and hurried toward the locker room stairs without another glance.

As I stood there with the water pouring over me, my frustration as an unapologetic gay man grew painfully acute. As homosexuals—my tribe, if you will—we'd been singled out and judged by our sexuality; our sexual feelings and actions were the root cause of all the ridicule, condemnation, and violence society had heaped upon us for as long as we could remember. It wasn't that we defined ourselves as individuals by our sexuality. That definition had been forced on us by others. To claim any pride, our only choice had been to embrace it without shame. It was what we had that others didn't—what set us apart, made us different, shaped our culture, brought us together, defined us as a group. We'd held on to that identity fiercely, those of us who'd been willing to stand up and fight for it, as if we'd been fighting for our very survival. *Without my sexuality,* I wondered, *who am I? What am I? What will I become?*

I shut off the shower, made my way to the steam room, and found a corner on the third tier of the tiled bleachers where the steam was heavy and the light dim. I was aware of two or three other men in the steam-filled room. Over the next minute or two, one by one, they left, until I was alone. That was when Tony Mercury happened in.

He entered with a yellow terry-cloth towel around him and even through the mist he looked magnificent, pleasing patterns of thick, dark hair adding special texture to his fine, strong frame. After a quick survey of the otherwise empty bleachers his eyes came around to me. I saw his white teeth as he smiled in my direction. A moment after that, he was sitting beside me.

"We have it all to ourselves," he said, without looking around again. "Not often that happens."

"I'm sure someone will come in any moment."

"But there's no one in here now, is there?" He touched my knee, then ran his big hand up my thigh until it rested at the crest, his fingers curling deep between my legs, just below my testicles. "Good, strong legs. I like that in a man."

I reminded him that Buff employed a young man full-time whose sole purpose was to detect and deter inappropriate behavior in the wet areas. The Penis Police, we called him—a cop wannabe eager to report rule breakers and score points with management. "A man in your position," I said, "can't afford to get caught in a compromising position, can he?"

"Maybe I'm a risk-taker." Steam and perspiration coated Mercury's face, dripping from his solid chin into the damp hair of his belly and crotch. He reached up, pinched my nipple gently, then harder, enough to cause me to hiss through my teeth. He glanced down. "Nothing happening down there?"

"I guess I'm just not interested, Tony."

"I don't believe that." He ran the back of his hand down my furry chest, then fondled my cock, while he kept one eye on the frosted glass of the door, watching for an approaching silhouette. He kept at me for a while, but my penis lay limply in his hand like a sleeping baby. "What's with you, anyway, Justice?"

"I told you, Tony, you just don't turn me on."

The line of his mouth was grim. "That's not something I hear very often."

"Unless I'm mistaken, you heard from it Trang Nguyen, during that city-sponsored trip down in San Diego."

Our eyes were locked, inches apart. Mercury didn't blink. "That's between Trang and me."

"Is it?"

Someone pulled open the door. Mercury removed his hand and shifted to put some space between us, while keeping his eyes on mine a moment longer. A well-built black guy wearing nothing but a cock ring entered and stood by the window, near the hissing steam. Mercury slid away, stepped down, and went out without looking back. The muscles of his neck and back were bunched in angry knots.

I'd always found anonymous sexual encounters with hard-bodied men in strange places to be a powerful aphrodisiac. But even that wasn't working for me any longer. I left the steam room quickly, showered again, and dressed. Minutes later, with the images of Trang Nguyen and Tony Mercury vivid in my brain, I fled the gym and all the lovely men whose beauty seemed so sadly lost to me, now that I'd traded away my more primal instincts for the safety net of drug-induced stability and composure.

I returned to an empty apartment feeling dreadfully alone. The wise thing would have been to go down and talk about it with Maurice, empty my angst into my memoir, or call Templeton to spill my guts. But loneliness is a powerful emotion that temptation can quickly sharpen to a razor's edge, and temptation was only a click or two away that night.

162

I tossed my gym bag on the bed, went straight to the computer, and logged on to the Web site where I'd discovered Victor Androvic advertising himself as Eric. A minute later, with a few clicks of the mouse, I was using my credit card to place an order with the Hot Boy Escort Agency. By chance, Eric was available, possibly because it was a weeknight and probably because the price—three hundred dollars—dissuaded many potential clients from following through. My three hundred bucks got me an hour with Eric and just about anything I wanted—only his ass was off-limits—with his visit set to commence at 10:00 P.M.

I waited at the window, staring down the drive to the street, trying to understand what exactly it was I wanted from Victor Androvic, what it was I needed. It wasn't just another test of my sexuality, enhanced by the illicit commercialism and the lurking threat of danger, which could always be a turn-on; if it had been that, I could have gotten it cheaper and more quickly on the street or in a nearby bar that catered to hustlers, where one or two always had a look about him that suggested the possibility of violence. It wasn't companionship I was after; I could have gotten that from Maurice and Fred, or Templeton, or from a man closer to my age over a game of pool down on the boulevard at Trunks. Victor had something I needed, and it wasn't just his youthful face and body, which didn't really interest me all that much, anyway; he was more than a boy but not quite a man and still too insubstantial in too many ways to make me seriously want him. The answer lay somewhere in that wail I'd heard from him on the street, as he'd cried out to his mother before the cops had taken him away, and in his eyes, whose emotions veered so wildly from helplessness to rage. At moments, I felt as if I almost had the answer, but I couldn't put my finger on it, couldn't put it into words.

I was still grappling with it when Victor showed up twenty minutes late. He sauntered up the drive trying hard to look cool and detached in the manner of hustlers who need to feel in control and above everything that's about to happen, because deep down they don't really want to be doing it. He was dressed out of an Abercrombie & Fitch catalog, his lanky frame draped with baggy clothes designed to look grungy and tattered that must have set him back a few hundred bucks, if not more. On his big feet he wore Converse hightops, the kind I'd worn as a kid and my father had probably worn before me, which apparently were still in fashion. His blond hair was gelled and arranged to appear casually spiked, but otherwise he looked squeaky clean. If I hadn't known what I did about him, I would have taken him for any other twenty-year-old growing up and trying to find himself along Melrose Avenue or the Sunset Strip, or even Santa Monica Boulevard, if he happened to prefer boys to girls.

I felt a surge of adrenaline as I heard him climb the steps, but it wasn't that old lightning bolt of lust I'd been longing for. The excitement now, I realized, had more to do with who Victor Androvic was and what he might have done, and what he might tell me about himself.

I pulled open the door, we exchanged awkward hellos, and I pushed open the screen to let him pass. His manner was curt, disconnected, as if what he was doing and who he was doing it with didn't matter to him in the slightest. I caught the trace of an accent in his speech, but he'd mastered it well, better than the general discomfort he worked so hard to conceal. He stood near the bed, looking at the single room and adjoining kitchen, at the sparse, plain furnishings.

"You own the place down there?" He jerked his head, indicating the house below. "You keep this place up here to hook up with guys like me?"

"This is where I live."

"Yeah?" He looked around again, as if trying to figure how a man in my situation could afford him. He shrugged for effect. "So what do you want me to do?"

"I'm not sure yet, Eric."

"I don't get fucked. You should know that up front. It says that on the Web site. Condoms for oral. No extreme pain. Those are the rules."

"Fine."

He slipped off his baggy denim jacket, removed a pack of cigarettes and a lighter from one of the pockets, folded the jacket neatly, set it on a chair, and put the cigarettes and lighter on a nightstand next to the bed. When he was standing in front of me again, he glanced down at himself self-consciously. I said nothing, so he pulled his T-shirt from his waistband and unbuckled his belt, letting the ends hang open like an invitation. I went to him and stared into his striking blue eyes; he had no problem staring back, and hardly blinked, as if he'd practiced doing it. I stroked the soft blond fuzz on his cheeks and chin.

"You didn't shave," I said. "Looks like a day or two."

"Some guys like that."

"You do dates with a lot of guys?"

"I get my share." He reached in a pocket of his T-shirt, found a business card, handed it to me. It identified him as Eric and had a cell phone number on it. "That's in case you want to call me again. You call me direct, we don't deal with the agency, I can give you a better price."

"And you get to keep the whole fee."

"We both benefit, right?"

"You always leave a business card with your clients?"

He nodded. "I'm building my own client base. I plan to go into business for myself. You got to be smart like that if you want to make it big."

"A real entrepreneur." I ran a finger over his lips, which were moist and waxy with lip balm. "Your accent sounds like Eastern European."

"Germany," he lied. "My father's a big doctor there. I'm just visiting the States. I go to UCLA. I'm studying business."

I brushed his soft beard with the backs of my fingers. "Is that why you need the money? For college?"

"My old man pays for everything. We're rich. But I need my own money to invest. I plan to make a lot of money, a real shitload."

I massaged one of his ears, concentrating on the lobe. If he enjoyed it, there was no indication. "Why's that so important, Eric?"

"You don't have money, you're nothing. I'm going to have a great house, a great car, tons of clothes, a million DVDs, everything I want. That's why I came to the States, to learn how you get all the stuff Americans have. Everybody here's got tons of stuff."

My eyes swept the room. "I don't have much."

He flashed a grin. "You got me, dude." He glanced at the Bulgari on his wrist. "For another fifty minutes, anyway. I can stay longer, but it'll cost."

"No other dates tonight?"

"Not yet." He pulled his T-shirt over his head and off, folded it with the precision of a retail salesclerk, and set it atop his jacket on the chair. Then he faced me again, showing me a lean torso with narrow hips, a flat belly, and the long muscles of a swimmer. "So what do you want to do?"

"To be honest, I haven't decided." When I brushed my fingers across his nipples they grew hard, which told me that he probably wasn't a straight guy doing gay men just for the money. "Lie down, Eric. Head on the pillow."

He settled onto the bed, lay on his back, stretched out with his hands at his sides, rigid as a board. I lay down on the pillow beside him, facing him, my head propped up on my elbow.

"Turn this way, Eric. Look at me."

He rolled over to face me, confusion in his eyes. "I can give you a blow job if that's what you want," he said. "I'm pretty good at it. Or I can strip for you, if that's what gets you off. I've done that a few times."

"I just want to talk for a while, Eric."

"Talk?" I nodded, peering into his nervous eyes. "About what?"

"About you."

He glanced at his watch again. "For how long?"

"As long as we need to."

He laughed weakly. "You got that kind of money?"

"Don't worry about that."

"Money matters, dude."

"The agency's got my credit card number. You'll tell them how long I kept you. Or maybe we can work something out between us, cut the agency out."

He shrugged like it was OK with him. "You mind if I smoke?"

"No."

He turned to grab his cigarettes, lit one, and lay down on his back, staring at the ceiling. I watched him smoke for a minute or two, letting the nicotine settle him. He flicked the ashes in his hand, then dumped them on the nightstand.

Finally, I said, "Your name's not Eric."

"Maybe not." He blew a series of smoke rings, watching them take form and slowly disappear. "Most of us don't use our real names. So what?"

"Your real name is Victor Androvic."

His eyes darted distrustfully in my direction. "You saw my picture in the newspaper?" I nodded. He took another drag on the cigarette, inhaling deeply; this time the smoke came out in a long, steady stream, while his eyes were somewhere else. "Is that why you wanted a date with me? Because of what you think I did? Does that turn you on or something?"

"I'm curious about a few things."

He looked at me again, angry now. "You a cop? Because if you are, man—"

"I'm not a cop, Victor."

"Prove it." His tone was tough, savvy.

I reached over, unzipped him. I slipped my hand into the waistband of his shorts, fondled him briefly, then zipped and buttoned him back up again.

"Do you believe me now, Victor?"

"I guess." He worked on his cigarette, looking sullen, but also troubled. I reached over, played with the silky blond hairs sprouting sparsely in the cavity of his chest, reminded of how young he was to be burdened with so much the way he was, remembering what that had been like.

"Your fingerprints were found in Bruce Bibby's apartment," I said. "On his wheelchair. How did that happen?"

He stared at the ceiling, but his eyes flared with suspicion again. "That wasn't in the newspaper, about the wheelchair. Only the cops know that."

"I know lots of things about you, Victor. But I'm not a cop."

"Like what?"

"Like how much you care about your mother. How hard you've worked to be a good boy and please her all these years. The swimming, the school clubs, the good grades. You play cool and tough, Victor, but it's all an act, a cover."

He abruptly sat up and swung his legs over the side of the bed to get up. I grabbed him around his waist and pulled him back, clutching him tight, my lips close to his ear. "We're not done, Victor. I still have forty minutes."

"You try to keep me here, I'll call the cops."

"I don't think so, Victor. Because then your mother will find out what you do for money, and I don't think you want that." He lay there in my grasp, tense, seething, but not making a move. "Give me the cigarette, Victor." He took a final drag, held the butt out. I took it, reached across him, and crushed it on the nightstand. Then I settled down beside him again, turning him to face me. "What's really going on, Victor? What really happened between you and Bruce Bibby?"

"That's my business, OK?"

"Bruce Bibby hired you for a date, didn't he?" His eyes slid to the side, giving him away. "You went to his apartment, once, maybe more. Left your fingerprints behind. They were on his wheelchair. Maybe you were kneeling, holding the handles, giving him a blow job. Was that what he liked, Victor?"

"Fuck you. I don't want to talk about it."

"You had a criminal record, so the cops were able to make a match with those prints. But you're too ashamed to admit why you were there. You don't want your mother to know. You don't want to shame her and your community any more than you've already done with your smuggling conviction. Not after she's worked so hard all these years to put some distance between her and your father, not after all the sacrifices she's made. So you lied to the cops, figuring they'd find the person who really did it, and all the trouble would go away. That no one would ever have to find out that Victor Androvic sleeps with men for money. But it didn't work out that way, and now you're in shit up to your eyeballs. Is that how all this played out, Victor?"

He looked at me again, more resentful than angry. "How come you know so much?"

"I have a knack for it." I shrugged. "A lot of it's luck, guesswork."

"Would you want your mother to know, if that's what you did?"

"My mother's dead, Victor. A long time ago."

"If she wasn't, would you want her to know?"

"You think your mother would rather know that you're queer and doing dates, Victor—or that you're locked up in prison for the rest of your life, convicted of murder? Which do you think would really break her heart?"

He swallowed hard. "Why do you care so much about my mother?"

"She seems like a nice woman. She loves you very much."

He pulled back in surprise. "You know her?"

I nodded. "So where were you the night Bruce Bibby was murdered?"

"Fuck," he said, clenching his teeth and lowering his eyes. When they came back up, they had that demonic look, the one from his mug shot that the *L.A. Times* had run. "You tell her what we did tonight, or anything else about me, I'll fucking kill you, man."

"You really mean that, Victor?"

"I could do it, man. Just like the newspaper said. You don't want to mess with me."

"You were servicing a client that night, weren't you?"

"Maybe. So what's it to you?"

"There's your alibi, Victor. There's the whole game, right there. Just tell the cops. It's possible your mother may not even have to know."

"Yeah, well it's not that easy."

"How's that?"

"It was a Japanese guy—a businessman. Some big hotel, I don't even know which one, I don't even know where. Maybe downtown, I'm not sure. He sent a car to pick me up. I waited for it at a donut shop over on Highland, so my mom wouldn't know. I fell asleep on the way and didn't wake up until we got there. The driver took me up to the room, through the garage. I don't know the hotel, the guy's name, nothing."

"The people who run the escort service could vouch for you. They'd have his name and credit card number."

"No way, man. Not those people. You can't get to them, anyway. They operate in secret, completely through the Internet. For all I know, they're based in some other country, a million miles from here. You can't get to those guys."

"That's tough," I said.

He chewed his lip. "Yeah, tough."

I glanced at his wrist. "You get the watch from a client?" He nodded. "Steal it?"

"The Japanese guy gave it to me. He liked me. Treated me OK. Said he'd call me again, when he was back in town."

"Maybe he'll call. Maybe he can be your alibi."

"Yeah, right. Like he'd admit anything like that to the cops. The guy has a wife and four kids back in Tokyo. He showed me their pictures, right after he sucked me off."

"I can see you've thought this through."

He glanced at the Bulgari. "We don't have much time left. You want me to get you off, or what?"

"No. That's not what I want." I reached for him, caressed his face, kissed him tenderly on the forehead. "I'm sorry about your father, Victor." His eyes grew keener, like he was really listening now. "I'm sorry about the kind of man he was, what he did, the way he died. It can't be easy for you." He bit his lip, glanced away. I turned his chin, made him look at me. "My old man wasn't so terrific, either. He didn't kill anyone, but I hated his guts—when I wasn't trying to figure out how to love him."

"He still around?"

"I killed him when I was seventeen."

He pushed himself up, staring down at me. "Bullshit."

"I shot him with his own gun. Nine times, until it was empty. If I'd had more, I would have kept firing."

"For real?"

"I'm afraid so."

"You go to jail?"

I shook my head. "Justifiable homicide. That means what I did was excusable, at least in the eyes of the law. I'd caught him messing with my little sister."

"Shit." He sounded shaken. "I never knew anybody who killed his old man." He shrank away from me a little more. "You aren't crazy or anything, are you? You're not going to try to do weird stuff with me, right? I had a date with a guy once who tried to shove a gun up my ass."

"I won't hurt you, I promise."

He turned his wrist up again to see his watch. "I really got to go." He hesitated, like a schoolkid waiting for his teacher to dismiss the class.

I took his hand, examined his long, slender fingers, thought about them clenched in pain and fury when he was younger and his hands were small, enduring what his father had dished out. "You never really get over it, do you, Victor?"

"What?"

"You never really get over what he did to you, or how he screwed up so much of your life." He averted his eyes, as if shielding himself from my words. "You still hear the rising sound of his voice when he started to get angry. You still see the look on his face when he closed his fist or stripped off his belt to use it on you. You still hear the sound of your mother's voice, pleading with him to stop, before he started in on her. You still think about how you loved him as much as you hated him, because he was your father and sons are supposed to love their fathers. Look at me, Victor." When he met my eyes again, his lower lip was quivering. "You try to forget, to shake off his shadow, but you never really do. Do you?"

Tears brimmed in his eyes. "No."

I opened my arms to him. "Come here."

He held back a moment, then reluctantly gave in, settling awkwardly down beside me. We slipped our arms around each other, and I drew him close. A moment later, I felt warm tears on my shoulder and the shudder of his weeping.

"Just a few minutes more," I said.

NINETEEN

My encounter with Victor Androvic on Thursday night seemed to clear my head and clarify some personal questions for me.

If nothing else, I thought, I had a keener understanding of why I felt so compelled to help him, and to help his mother. It had to do with fathers, and how difficult it is for some of us to love them, and what that does to us, and how we pass along our confusion and resentment and fear of loving and being loved to others, especially to our children if we have them, continuing a self-perpetuating cycle. I'd even begun to sense a possible connection to the barrenness I was experiencing sexually, how it might not just be the Prozac that was leaving my libido so lifeless but a much more complex web of issues that had to do with the relationships I fell into, who I loved and didn't, and why. That old refrain summed it up: *finding love in all the wrong places*. I'd been finding love—or at least looking for it—in all the wrong places for a long time. Templeton had reminded me—*warned* me—that I had a habit of getting involved with young men in trouble. Sometimes I ended up in bed with them, sometimes the relationship was chaste, sometimes it was combative, but I always seemed to be in love with them, at least a little, or for a little while. I was drawn to them like the proverbial moth to the flame that Maurice had spoken of, when the subject of Rocky De Marco had come up.

Maybe, in trying to help them work through their problems, I was trying to resolve questions of my own. Conventional wisdom has it that by the age of forty-five, which I'd reached, a man has had time to figure things out and drop his emotional baggage at one of the train stations along the journey, leaving it behind as the choo-choo chugs on down the tracks to Happyland. But experience tells me that most of us continue to lug much of it with us to the grave, without a convenient porter to shoulder the luggage for us. Maybe we numb ourselves with alcohol and other narcotics to make the load more bearable, or stash it in the locker of denial, or even balance it with strength and grace so it doesn't drag us down. But most of us are burdened by it nonetheless, one way or another, all the way to the end of the line.

I still wasn't sure how much of what I'd learned from Victor Androvic I should share with Detective De Marco. I didn't want to hurt Victor, to give up the secrets that shamed him so. But if a better suspect for the Bruce Bibby homicide didn't turn up soon, I'd have no other choice. Shame is a terrible coercer; it can drive us to all kinds of contortions to keep certain truths hidden, even to the point of self-destruction. There are people who would rather end their lives than give up their humiliating secrets, especially the young, for whom the judgments of others loom above all else in importance, often to irrational degrees. I decided to give Detective De Marco more time to make a better case against someone else before betraying Victor for his own sake, even though I couldn't be certain his explanations regarding Bruce Bibby would hold up or do him any good.

With that much resolved, I was able to concentrate all day Friday on my work. By early evening, I'd roughed out the section of the brochure dealing with the more than two dozen properties identified as potential cultural resources awaiting City Council approval, as varied as the Pacific Design Center, the Coral Gables bungalow court, Fire Station No. 7, and Tail o' the Pup, a fabled 1924 hot dog stand shaped and painted like a wiener in a bun, complete with yellow mustard.

Like they say, only in West Hollywood.

By seven, I was back on Norma Place, sitting on the patio with Maurice and Fred and a dozen of their friends, while the two hosts tended to the barbecue and the others danced to Maurice's scratchy LPs from roughly half a century ago. As corny and banal as it may sound, there's something about watching older couples waltzing cheek to cheek to "Moon River" that gives one hope in life after fifty and the human race. With the help of my Prozac, I was starting to think more along those lines. I was making a conscious effort to pay attention to the emotional ballast the drug afforded, for the inevitable moment when I'd have to wean myself from it, if I was ever to reclaim my inner fire and begin to really feel again. Along with my work at City Hall, the Prozac was also allowing me to calm down and appreciate West Hollywood in a different light—to see past its garish commercialism, beyond its snobby body culture and fixation with surface image, beneath the concrete and asphalt and pollution that covered it from end to end, like so many ruined cities. I was beginning to find WeHo's heart and soul, its unique character, the qualities that made it different and good. How many places, after all, could a group of queers like the one before me now gather to dance and hold hands and laugh in the moonlight, with the sweet scent of jasmine on the air, and without the slightest concern about who might see or hear them, as any human being should have the right to do?

During a lull in the dancing, when Fred was inside getting the dessert, Maurice drew me to a corner of the yard, looking solemn. "About the other night, Benjamin, when we were going through my old photos. You won't say anything to Fred about Rocky De Marco, will you?"

"Of course not, Maurice. Not if you don't want me to."

"I know how you feel about keeping secrets, Benjamin, given your family background and how you and your sister suffered because of them." Maurice smiled fondly, and fussed with my hair, pushing some loose strands behind my ear. "But trust me, dear one— some secrets are worth keeping, for the sake of another's feelings. Not everything needs to be told."

"Your secret's safe with me, Maurice. I promise."

He grabbed my hand. "Come get some dessert now, won't you? I've made a Boston cream pie that I believe has your name on it."

By 10:00 P.M. everyone was gone, no longer able to stifle their yawns, and I was bidding Maurice and Fred good night as well. As I climbed the steps to my apartment, leaving them alone on the patio, I glanced back to see them slow dancing to "A Summer Place"—the original Percy Faith version—with their heads close and their arms around each other, the way I'd seen them dance to that particular song more times than I could count. I watched them from the window until they'd danced themselves into a romantic mood and gone into the house holding hands, letting the cats scurry in behind them and shutting off the lights inside all the way to their bedroom.

I was restless, but my encounter with Victor Androvic had put the kibosh on any interest I had in the X-rated images available on the Internet. Having one of the models in my arms, in the flesh, had reminded me that these were real human beings, not inanimate objects devoid of souls and feelings; the notion of using them like inflatable dolls to satisfy one's masturbatory fantasies had lost what little appeal had been there to begin with. It's funny how we think we need something—how we're sure we can't live without it—until a dose of reality hits us, and the temptation vanishes as if it never existed at all.

If Victor Androvic had become less a mystery to me, along with Lester Cohen and Tony Mercury, Chas Rutweller remained an enigma, with his role in Bruce Bibby's murder still unclear. What I hadn't figured out was how much of his menace was male posturing, how much of it was real—and if he was truly capable of doing to Bruce Bibby what he'd hinted at in the volatile conversation with his mother that I'd overheard.

By half past ten, I was out walking, up toward the Sunset Strip and a club called Skin Deep, where I hoped to find him at the door.

Sunset Boulevard between North Doheny Drive and Crescent Heights Boulevard—the heart of the Strip—is always busy after ten, but especially on Friday nights. That's when it takes on a new intensity, a kind of feverish energy, as the clubs and crowds shift into a higher gear for the weekend.

I could feel the fever rising as I strolled past Johnny Depp's Viper Room, while a line of young people waited outside to get in, standing on the hard concrete where the young actor River Phoenix had died of an overdose on Halloween night in 1993. I continued on past Book Soup, where the latest Walter Mosley mystery was displayed in the window, with Tower Records just across the street. Across from the record store and up Horn Avenue was the old Spago building, which had once been the home of Café Gala, where Ted Meeks had met Colin Harrison nearly six decades ago. All around me, "tall walls" rose up—the exteriors of high-rise office buildings turned into giant, vertical billboards that served the entertainment industry, where a rock star's lips might occupy an entire upper story, while his hips rose above the lower rooftops, turning him into Godzilla with a guitar, towering above the boulevard. Out in the street, as traffic thickened, limousines competed for space with a glistening array of luxury cars, while young men and women shuffled along the side-walks like lemmings, desperate for action, diversion, anything to sat-isfy their truncated attention spans until the next bit of stimulus came along. I passed through Sunset Plaza, the Strip's oasis of class and re-spectability, where a slightly older crowd—thirties and forties—filled the sidewalk tables in the mild night air. I kept going until I was past the House of Blues and the Comedy Store and the Hyatt, where the rock stars regularly trashed the rooms, until Skin Deep was finally within my sights.

Last year, it had another name. Next year, it would probably have another. It was one of a half dozen clubs around L.A. that were cur-rently considered "hot," which meant they were filled most nights with young celebrities of the moment and their closest friends and as-sociates, and trashy but glamorous girls who wanted to meet celebri-ties and sleep with them. Outside were hordes of wannabes and hangers-on desperate to be admitted with the others, but who usually weren't. As far as I could tell, the primary reason the famous and semifamous flocked to these clubs was to be seen for the sake of being seen, to feel important while their moment in the spotlight lasted be-fore the inevitable decline to the status of has-been or never-quite-was. For hundreds of young people, getting into these clubs on certain nights was a mission, driven by an almost religious zeal. This gave the club doormen, the bouncers, enormous power over these rather pa-thetic young men and women. Their roles as gatekeepers—deciding who got in and who didn't—gave each bouncer his own little dictator-ship, a role for which Chas Ruttweller seemed especially well suited.

I spotted him outside Skin Deep at the sweet spot of the velvet ropes, the coveted place in line just outside the door, while a growing crowd extended between them down the sidewalk. From a vantage point near the curb, I watched Chas flirt with young ladies, admitting the prettiest and most scantily clad while ordering the others to stay back and not push. From time to time, a limousine or luxury car pulled up out front and a celebrity or two hopped out, causing a commotion among the wannabes before Chas hustled the chosen ones across the threshold and into the Promised Land. Sometimes, the fawning and gushing was directed at glitzy girls who'd never performed at all, unless you counted oral sex in the backseat of a limo, who'd become celebrities in their own right simply by being seen in the right places with the right people. The ubiquitous paparazzi were on hand with their cameras, maneuvering and elbowing their way for better angles and clearer shots of the stars, calling out to them, hoping to get a response, any response, which would make their pictures and footage more valuable.

Chas Ruttweller was clearly in his element, presiding over the crowd like a benevolent despot, lording it over the losers, while the most attractive females plied him with flirtatious glances and nibbled coyly from his hand. Each time he unclipped the barrier rope to let another past he did it with a bit of swagger, puffing up his already inflated chest, winking at the breathless groupie as she gushed her gratitude before rushing inside. I studied him closely, each overly pronounced gesture of masculinity, the need to flaunt his chemically induced virility, the way he craved power and control like a drug. Then I tried to picture him in a confrontation with Bruce Bibby, angered by something Bibby might have said, resenting Bibby's relationship with Lydia Ruttweller, enraged by her decision to leave her estate to Bibby instead of to her own son.

It wasn't that difficult to imagine a homophobe like Chas Ruttweller, his system flooded with artificial testosterone, hammering the frail Bibby with a blunt object grabbed in a moment of rage. I remembered his words, spoken to his mother in her kitchen: *Maybe it was me who beat your little pet to death, just to hear him whimper and beg for his life. . . .*

Suddenly, two other bouncers emerged from inside, dragging a boisterous drunk between them. Chas stepped over to help as they hustled the troublemaker out to the sidewalk, where they dumped him unceremoniously near my feet. That's when Chas saw me standing there, studying him the way a spectator gawks at a sideshow freak.

He didn't say a word, just switched his attention back to the drunk as he staggered to his feet, trying to get back inside. Chas grabbed the guy roughly by his shirtfront, slammed him to the ground, kicked him twice, shouted expletives at him while spittle foamed at the corners of his mouth. The other bouncers restrained him like someone pulling a snarling pit bull off a smaller, helpless dog. As they dragged Chas back to the club, he was no longer looking at the stunned drunk crumpled on the sidewalk between us. His furious eyes were on me, and his message couldn't have been more clear.

It was after midnight when I got back to Norma Place. As I left the drive to mount the steps, I noticed Maurice sitting on the patio with one of the cats in his lap, studying a photo album in the moonlight. I didn't have to take a closer look to know that it was the same one that held the snapshot of Rocky De Marco. The light remained out in the house, and I imagined that Fred was sound asleep, snoring like an old bear.

"It's interesting as we get older how we're unable to remember where we left our keys," Maurice said, as I approached, "but we can recall certain things so vividly from so long ago."

"Short-term memory loss, I think they call it."

"I've heard that just before death, some individuals recall things from childhood, even infancy, that they haven't thought of their entire lives."

"You must have been quite taken with him," I said.

Maurice asked me about the last name on my list, Mira De Marco. "Do you think there's some connection, Benjamin? Or is it just a coincidence?"

"It's no coincidence, although I'm not sure if it matters, or how."

"But you expressed some curiosity about her."

"I'm curious about most people, Maurice, when they're connected in some way to a murder investigation. My father was always like that, when he was on a case. He'd make lists of names and sit up with them late into the night, drinking and making notes."

"Did you want to become a detective, Benjamin?"

"Yes, but I couldn't."

"Why on earth not?"

"Because that's what he was."

"He couldn't have been all bad, your father, not the way he was so interested in getting justice for the victims in his cases."

"I suppose not." I offered the thinnest smile. "It might be easier if he had been."

Maurice studied the photo of Rocky De Marco in the album on his lap. "I wonder how things turned out for Rocky, if he ever found what he was looking for and settled down." Maurice smiled ruefully. "I hope he's happy, wherever he is, or at least not too terribly sad. Sometimes that's all one can hope for, isn't it, Benjamin?"

"You strike me as reasonably happy, Maurice. I can't think of too many people more content than you."

He brightened. "I'm not one to let losses or misfortunes get me down, at least not for too very long. No point in that, not that I can see. I prefer to recall the more pleasant memories, the joy we extracted from life while we could, at the moment it was there."

"Was Rocky De Marco a loss, Maurice?"

Maurice closed the album and slowly stood. "Fred is the great gift of my life, Benjamin. That probably sounds funny, especially to those who see Fred as an old grump, a stick-in-the-mud who's not that much fun to be around at times. But I know him differently, you see. I know my Fred, and he knows me the way only two people who have devoted themselves to each other for most of a lifetime can. That's the beauty of growing old, you know. The chance to experience a special kind of love that only comes with time." He briefly touched my cheek. "I'm tired, dear. I'll see you in the morning."

"Good night, Maurice."

TWENTY

I was up at eight the next morning, making good on my promise to help Templeton move into the rental she'd taken in West Hollywood's historic Harper Avenue District, while she continued her search for a permanent home.

"It's called Romanesque Villas," she said, as we gazed up at the imposing, four-story apartment building at the northwest corner of Fountain and Harper avenues. "Built in the twenties, like most of the finer buildings in the neighborhood. Nice, isn't it?"

"Nineteen twenty-six, to be exact," I said. "Leland Bryant was the designer—the same fellow who designed the Sunset Tower. The style is Spanish Churrigueresque."

"Know-it-all," Templeton sniffed.

"I can't help it if you've moved into a building that's featured in my brochure." I'd planned to position Romanesque Villas on the same page as the Villa d'Este, a spectacular garden apartment on nearby Laurel Avenue, perhaps the finest in the district. "I have to give you credit, Templeton, you definitely have taste. Although I'd hate to think about what you're paying every month, so I won't."

"I really appreciate this, Justice—you giving up your Saturday like this to help me move."

I glanced at her sideways. "Maybe we'll get a chance later to talk about a few things."

Suspicion weighted her voice. "What things?"

"Just things."

The movers arrived with their packed truck, and we got started. Templeton had taken a two-bedroom apartment on the top floor that came with southern light and views of the city beyond the palm trees. The ceilings were high, the rooms spacious, the detailing quaint and immaculate; the living room alone was larger than my entire apartment. The first thing she unwrapped was her colorful Romare Bearden collage, a Christmas gift from her parents long ago that she cherished. We hung it over the mantelpiece, where she placed a framed photograph of her mother and father, a handsome, dark-skinned couple who radiated the health and energy they'd passed on to their daughter. For the next hour, without a break, we dug into boxes, while the movers trooped in and out, and we traded information on the Bruce Bibby murder investigation.

"I can't believe you hired Victor Androvic for sex," she said, after I mentioned my encounter with him without giving away many details.

"Believe me, there was no sex involved. A sensual moment or two, I suppose, but no carnal acts to speak of."

"You weren't interested?"

"Let's just say I had other things on my mind." We stepped aside as two movers carried in a sofa. When they were past and out of earshot, I repeated Victor's alibi for the night of the murder, swearing Templeton to keep it between us and hoping it might diffuse some of her antagonism toward him. "I realize an innocent Victor Androvic doesn't fit in neatly to the coverage you've been giving the professor, this theory that Victor has his father's killer genes."

"You'd put more credence in what this boy says than the findings of a distinguished scientist?"

"I'm giving the kid the benefit of the doubt, that's all."

"You're sure it's not your savior complex working overtime?"

"He's had a rough life, Templeton."

"So did Jack the Ripper, I imagine. So did a lot of other people who never hurt a fly."

"Exactly! Genetics shouldn't be a pat explanation for evil. Too much inconsistency, too dangerous a road to walk in terms of crime and punishment, at least until the science is a hundred percent conclusive and ethics and the law have time to catch up."

"You're saying that a genetic background like Victor's shouldn't excuse what he's done—"

"Might have done," I said.

"OK, might have done."

"But it shouldn't be used to convict him, either."

"In Victor's case," Templeton said archly, "I imagine circumstantial evidence will be all a prosecutor needs."

"You're hell-bent on seeing this kid put away, aren't you?" I laughed bitterly. "If someone as smart as you can't be objective, he doesn't stand a chance with a jury."

Her cell phone rang before she could respond. She handed me a piece of Steuben glass she'd just unwrapped and took the call. I set the Steuben on the mantelpiece while Templeton grabbed a notebook and pen from her handbag. She began scribbling furiously, then asking the usual reporter's questions—who, what, where, when, why, how.

The call lasted several minutes, and I got enough of the drift to figure out that Detective Mira De Marco was at the other end. Templeton's face grew somber as their conversation continued. Several times she threw uncomfortable glances my way that suggested I wasn't going to be doing handsprings when she shared the news. Finally, she thanked De Marco in surprisingly friendly terms and shut down her cell.

"That was Mira. There's been a development."

"I gathered that."

"Another murder."

"Someone we know?"

"Lydia Ruttweller—bludgeoned to death."

I sat on the arm of the sofa, stunned. "Murdered just like Bruce Bibby. Same M.O."

Templeton nodded. "Blunt object, several powerful blows to the head. They found her body on the grounds of the Schindler House this morning."

"Is that the good news or the bad news?"

Her voice grew softer. "Depends on how you look at it, I guess."

"So what's the rest?"

She drew in a deep breath and began reciting. "They've arrested a suspect. He was seen driving away from the crime scene just before Mrs. Ruttweller's body was found. Two eyewitnesses have made positive IDs. Material evidence puts the suspect with the victim, right where she died. When they picked him up, he still had blood on his clothes. He admitted it was hers."

Chas Ruttweller. I remembered the ugly argument he'd had with his mother a few nights earlier and the steroid-driven rage that seemed constantly to consume him. I wasn't pleased to hear that Lydia Ruttweller was dead; no one deserved to die that way, and certainly not for being a passive-aggressive mother. Still, I felt an odd surge of relief that her son's involvement might also tie him to the murder of Bruce Bibby and clear anyone else who might be under suspicion.

But that's not how it went. Templeton rubbed my arm sympathetically and told me gently that the suspect they'd arrested was Victor Androvic.

I stood in the living room of Templeton's new apartment, staring out a window, while Templeton called her city desk to report the story and her intention to cover it, even on her day off. When she was off the phone, she asked me to stay behind and supervise the movers while she drove to the Schindler House to see the crime scene for herself. I politely declined, and said I'd be going with her. She told the movers to take a long lunch break at her expense, ordered a pizza delivered to their truck, and locked up the apartment. I'd come on foot, so we took Templeton's car, which was parked on the street. On the way I tried to adjust to the possibility—no, the extreme likelihood—that Victor Androvic was in fact the cold-blooded killer Dr. Ford had suggested, even though a part of me held out a small and probably foolish hope for his salvation.

Like it or not, I had to face the fact that there were now two brutal murders, both with Victor's fingerprints all over them, literally and figuratively. Circumstances like that weren't likely to ensnare an innocent man twice, so soon, and with such close connections; although why Victor Androvic might want Lydia Ruttweller dead had yet to be explained. Part of me despaired over the turn of events, but I was surprised by how calm I was, how I was able to deal with the turn of events in such a composed and rational manner. I reminded myself that I had no true ties to Victor Androvic; whatever happened to him now might be unfortunate, particularly for his mother, but it wasn't really my concern. This was how I needed to react, with cool reason and proper detachment; this was the Prozac at work, and it was important that I learn from it.

"I'm sorry the way things turned out," Templeton said, as she punched the accelerator, weaving in and out of Saturday morning traffic. "I know you cared about the Androvic boy. I realize you wanted it to be someone else."

"I misjudged him, that's all." I smiled for her benefit. "A good life lesson. It's like you said—they can't all be saved."

We arrived at the Schindler House within minutes. It was located on King's Road five blocks south of Santa Monica Boulevard, in a quiet, unassuming neighborhood of vintage homes, low-income senior housing, and utilitarian, three-story condos in the next block that stretched all the way to Melrose. The street had been cordoned off on both sides of the property, so Templeton backed up half a block until she found a parking place, driving fast and steering with the skill of a movie stunt driver. By the time we'd walked back, a uniform was stringing up yellow crime scene tape from tree to tree around the property. The lot was deep and heavily camouflaged from the street by a towering stand of leafy bamboo, the way the architect, Rudolph Schindler, had originally landscaped it when he'd built the famous house in 1922. A narrow dirt path ran alongside the south side of the property, leading from the street to the house; near the house, midway across the lot, we could see a criminalist from the coroner's team wearing latex gloves kneeling above a body slumped in the path.

Templeton used her press pass and got word to Mira De Marco that we were on the perimeter. After a few minutes, she came loping down the same path, dressed in a jogging suit and running shoes as if her weekend had been interrupted, like ours. Her face was free of makeup, and a fanny pack was strapped around her waist, while a detective's badge and photo ID hung from her neck. She circumvented the body widely to avoid fouling any evidence, and greeted us with a perfunctory, "Good morning."

"I'm surprised they've got you on this case so soon," I said, "before it can be definitely connected to Bruce Bibby. Especially on a weekend, when your overtime kicks in."

"I told my supervisor I wanted in on anything that might be related to the Bibby investigation, even if I have to work it on my own time."

"That's real dedication, Detective. You must have a personal interest in this."

"I have a personal interest in every homicide I investigate, Justice. It's the way I work."

"What else can you tell me for the record," Templeton asked, "in addition to what you gave me on the phone?"

De Marco informed her that Lydia Ruttweller routinely arrived early each Saturday morning to lead public tours of the Schindler House. Her body had been discovered shortly before 11:00 A.M., by another volunteer when she showed up to help out. Since Mrs. Ruttweller ordinarily came around ten, that put the killer's window of opportunity and time of death in the hour between. As De Marco talked, she remained at an angle, directing her attention more toward Templeton than me, almost as if I wasn't there.

I glanced at my watch. "You got here quickly. Johnny on the spot."

"I don't live that far away." De Marco barely glanced at me. She was back on Templeton in a heartbeat, relating details, while Templeton jotted notes. "Mrs. Ruttweller walks here for the exercise, enters up this dirt path like everyone else." De Marco indicated the Schindler House and grounds. "No one actually lives here. It's operated by a nonprofit as an art center." She paused for a moment to study the famous house, thirty-five hundred square feet that had been restored to its original state. "Not my style, exactly, but interesting."

"It's a classic," I said, gazing across the grounds to a deceptively simple structure that looked from our vantage point like a series of sunken, concrete walls staggered with hedges, framed with natural redwood, and draped with vines. I'd visited here years ago and knew that the most dramatic part of the house was to be found in the rear, where walls of glass looked out on sloping lawns and groves of trees. "You won't find many buildings that have had a greater influence on design than this one."

Of all the architectural icons in West Hollywood, Rudolph Schindler's early Modernist masterpiece was perhaps the most important, at least among aficionados. Despite its age—more than eighty years—it was the birthplace of the Southern California modernist movement that had revolutionized residential and commercial design, based on Schindler's philosophy that "the shape of the inner room defines the exterior of the building." Clean and simple yet striking to the eye, with all surfaces left in their raw state, the layout of the Schindler House encouraged social interaction inside while making full use of natural light; vertical and horizontal windows were built in wherever possible, and every room opened to a courtyard, connecting the interior to earth and sky. The style reflected Hispanic and Japanese traditions to create a building both primitive and futuristic, whose bold vision must have elicited shock in 1922.

"To have a murder take place here," I said, "seems almost sacrilegious."

"Every murder is sacrilegious," De Marco said evenly. "There's always someone left behind to grieve for the dead and live with the loss."

"In this case, that would be Chas Ruttweller," I said. "Although I'm not so sure he'll be grieving." I recounted the angry exchange I'd heard between Chas and Lydia, including his boast about killing Bruce Bibby and his mother's plan to disinherit him in the next few days. "If you're looking for motive," I suggested, "it would be hard to do better than a steroid-addicted bodybuilder who was broke and about to lose his meal ticket."

"My partner's checking up on Chas Ruttweller," De Marco said. "We're aware that Mr. Ruttweller was resentful of Bibby's relationship with his mother. We found a number of threatening messages left by Mr. Ruttweller on Mr. Bibby's voice mail. Mr. Ruttweller has been on our radar screen for some time." De Marco threw a glance in Templeton's direction. "This is all off the record."

To my surprise, Templeton closed her notebook without the slightest protest. "No problem."

"Obviously," De Marco said, "with these new developments, Victor Androvic becomes our prime suspect."

"Templeton said something about material evidence."

De Marco glanced at Templeton again. "Continuing off the record?"

"Of course," Templeton said amiably.

"You two sure closed the trust gap in a hurry," I said.

Templeton shrugged almost nonchalantly. "Mira and I decided working together is more productive."

De Marco fished a small plastic evidence bag from her fanny pack.

Inside was one of Victor Androvic's business cards, offering his special services, exactly like the one he'd left with me on Thursday night. "We found this next to Lydia Ruttweller's body," De Marco said. "When we caught up with him at his mother's place, he was in the laundry room, feeding his bloody clothes into a washing machine."

"So you know about Victor's line of work?" I asked. De Marco nodded. I tried not to sound anxious, but it was difficult. "Did he confess?"

De Marco shook her head. "Claims he got a phone call on his cell this morning, from a man who said he wanted a massage. According to Victor, the man gave this address. When Victor arrived, he found Mrs. Ruttweller down this path, beaten bloody. He bent over her, to see if she was alive. Says he's had lifeguard training, that he reacted instinctively. When he didn't find a pulse, he panicked and took off."

"It could have happened that way," I said, trying hard to convince myself. "It's not totally implausible."

"At any rate," De Marco said, "that's the kid's story, at least for now. The versions usually change a few times as trial approaches."

"And the witnesses?" Templeton asked.

"Married couple, man and woman, early thirties, arriving early to see the Schindler place. Androvic ran right past them as he fled. They saw the blood on his clothes, got a clear look at his face. When they found Mrs. Ruttweller a few seconds later, the husband ran back to the street and wrote down a plate number as Victor drove off." De Marco fixed me with her eyes. "Doesn't leave Victor with much wiggle room, does it?"

"Why would Victor leave his business card behind?"

"Maybe he dropped it in his haste to flee. Maybe it fell from his shirt pocket when he was beating the victim. Either one of those works for me."

"Lydia Ruttweller has all kinds of enemies. Over the years, she's alienated half the city. It's possible Victor was set up."

"Justice doesn't let go easily," Templeton said.

"There's something else," De Marco said.

I smiled painfully. "Isn't there always?"

"You can use this, Alex, if you want to." Templeton flipped open her notebook. "When we arrested Victor, we searched the apartment he shares with his mother. We found a computer. It was hidden in an

187

attic crawl space accessible through a small door above the closet in Victor's bedroom."

"A computer," I said, feeling my heart sink.

De Marco nodded. "It was the same computer that was stolen from Bruce Bibby's apartment the night he was murdered."

Templeton was scribbling like a madwoman. I understood her excitement but it sickened me just the same. I said to De Marco, "You sound pretty sure about that."

"We used the serial number to make a positive match. It's the stolen computer all right."

"I guess Victor's in pretty deep this time."

"I'm afraid so, Justice." De Marco glanced at the sports watch on her wrist. "Right about now, he's being booked for the murders of Lydia Ruttweller and Bruce Bibby. I hope for his sake he's got a good lawyer."

While Templeton finished up with De Marco, I wandered off by myself. From different vantage points, I glimpsed the fascinating Schindler House, with its imaginative design that made it appear, from the street, as if it were embedded in the earth. That's where Lydia Rutweller would be in a few days, I thought, rotting underground, unless she'd left instructions to the contrary; down the road, after the requisite number of years on death row, Victor Androvic would probably follow, interred in a pauper's grave behind a high-security prison, the way so many penal institutions handle the remains of the condemned. I wondered if they let mothers visit the graves of their dead sons.

TWENTY-ONE

We returned to Romanesque Villas, where Templeton spent the next couple of hours writing and filing her story from her laptop, and I supervised the movers as they hauled the last of her belongings into her new apartment.

Afterward, she offered to buy me dinner at the Formosa Café next to Warner Hollywood Studios. The creaky West Hollywood restaurant—originally called the Red Spot when it opened in 1925—had been a popular hangout for Hollywood stars in the thirties and forties. It sat on the same corner near the city's eastern border, dwarfed these days by a mammoth complex of discount chain superstores, only because the city had insisted the developer spare it from the wrecking ball. Glossy photos of its most famous patrons adorned the walls like wishful memories, their dead eyes staring at you while you sipped your overpriced martini or chewed your second-rate egg rolls, and the bar spilled over with Hollywood wannabes trying to look cool and maybe make a connection. Still, it reeked of nostalgia, which was why it had served so well as a setting for the Lana Turner scene in *L.A. Confidential.* I was pretty sure why Templeton wanted to eat there tonight: All the glossies and colorful barflies would give us something to look at and talk about, so we wouldn't have to discuss more somber subjects, like what life behind bars was going to be like for a nice-looking kid like Victor Androvic until he got the needle, or the despair his mother had to be feeling tonight, or what the last terrifying moments must have been like for Lydia Ruttweller as someone bashed in her skull in a location that must have been like a cathedral to her. I thanked Templeton for the offer but took a rain check, suspecting she was secretly relieved.

I picked up Thai takeout on the long walk home, ate without enjoying it much, took my meds, and tried again to pump some life into the manuscript of my memoirs, without success. At ten, I gave up searching for the right words and sat on the edge of my bed with the TV on, surfing through the evening news shows to see how the world would come to know Victor Androvic compared to how I knew him.

The first newscast I hit opened with Lydia Ruttweller's death and Victor's arrest, tied to the Bruce Bibby killing, while one of the anchors promised "sensational new developments that put a scientific spin on this tragic story of brutality and murder." For the next two or three minutes, I watched a segment that essentially reprised Templeton's stories on Dr. Ford's research, supplanted with freshly taped interviews and again identifying Victor as Dr. Ford's research subject. Dr. Ford had provided the station with a photograph of Victor's father, taken only days before his execution in Russia, which the news director displayed next to Victor's mug shot. Except for the demonic stare in both faces, I saw no particular resemblance between the younger and older man. Victor was blue-eyed and blond, with a sparse beard and boyish face; his father had dark hair and eyes, with a carpet of thick stubble and rugged features. If Victor took after anyone, I thought, it was his blond and blue-eyed mother, Tatiana.

During the newscast, the reporter spoke carefully, emphasizing that Victor was only a suspect, and had not been convicted of any violent crime. Dr. Ford did the same, although he went into considerable detail explaining the genetic similarities between father and son, as demonstrated in their brain scans, which he illustrated using the same color images he'd previously provided Templeton. He referred to his findings as a "dramatic breakthrough" in the field of criminology and genetic research, and predicted that in the next few years he would lead the way "to a new dawn of knowledge about the criminal mind and a future when society could protect itself from violent predators by identifying and treating them before they strike." The reporter dutifully raised the controversial issues of genetic selection and engineering, which Dr. Ford insisted was a worry being blown out of proportion "by well-meaning people who would thwart scientific progress out of a misguided and unwarranted concern for individual rights." Dr. Ford was poised, telegenic, and adept at giving the perfect sound bite—summing up his thoughts succinctly, articulately, and with flair, without hesitating, mumbling, or scratching his nose. It was a decent news package put together in a relatively short time, which couldn't have been done without Dr. Ford's full cooperation and support.

At eleven o'clock, the half-hour newscasts came on. I surfed through each of them to see if similar coverage had been scheduled. Dr. Ford appeared on every channel, although these versions were truncated and more sensational, hyped at the top of the show in a way that suggested Victor was a wild, wanton killer, plucked from the streets before he could commit more mayhem. There'd been a time when using the word "alleged" was mandatory when covering murder suspects—something we'd all learned in Journalism 101—but more than once a reporter referred to Victor almost casually as if he'd already been convicted. The coverage was brief, shallow, and rife with errors—ages, dates, places, even the spelling of names in subtitles varied from program to program—something TV viewers had long ago come to accept in local nightly newscasts. Still, I couldn't help but think: *If this is where Templeton is headed as a journalist, then God help us all.*

At half past eleven, I switched to CNN and found Dr. Ford being interviewed even there, with the network reprising all his colorful brain scan images that seemed so ideal and ready-made for TV. In a matter of a few hours, I realized, the man was in millions of households, looking and sounding like an authority on genetics and the criminal mind, with the kind of exposure publicists ordinarily work months to achieve. He even mentioned a book that he was writing on the subject, as well as a reality show he was discussing with TV producers that would put real-life criminals under a "video microscope" to try to find a scientific explanation for their pathology, while recounting their horrific crimes with news footage, archival material, and dramatic reenactments.

As I sat there watching him flap his lips, slicker than a Beverly Hills car salesman, I recalled a very different image of Dr. Ford—as he hurried out a side gate from Tatiana Androvic's apartment building, head down, eyes nervous, before driving hurriedly away. Then a thought struck me: *Take away the murders of Bruce Bibby and Lydia Ruttweller and nobody would be interested in this guy.*

I called Templeton on her cell and asked her if she'd watched the evening news.

"I'm still moving in, Justice. I won't get cable until Wednesday. What's up? It's almost midnight."

I told her what I'd seen over the past couple of hours—Dr. Roderick Ford on virtually every newscast, milking the Victor Androvic story for every drop of exposure he could get from it. "I'm assuming he has a personal publicist at this point. Otherwise, coordinating this kind of coverage would be next to impossible."

"There's no reason he shouldn't be giving interviews. It's a terrific angle on a legitimate news story."

"Templeton, he's all over the airwaves. And I'll bet he's in half the newspapers in the country by Monday morning. *Time* and *Newsweek* can't be far behind."

"If you were still a reporter, you'd be on him like a bloodhound for an interview. Admit it."

"I'd be looking just as hard at why he's so eager to use a research subject to put himself in the middle of the story. If he was serious about the science, he'd go about his research quietly and publish the results when the time was right, through the proper channels."

"And when would that be, Justice? When Victor Androvic has killed a few more people?"

"No, Templeton. It would be when Victor's convicted, not just accused. Tell me something. Are you going to be on all the cable talk shows next week, with all the lawyers and prosecutors and journalists, convicting and hanging the kid before he even goes to trial?"

"Of course not."

"I'll give you ten to one that your friend Dr. Ford already has himself booked on every one of those gabfests."

"I suppose that's possible. He likes attention. That doesn't make him a bad person."

"Why would a distinguished scientist run off and join the media circus instead of protecting the integrity of his work?"

"He told us that day at lunch. He needs to create more awareness of his research, so he can raise the necessary funding to continue."

"And you're going to swallow that, just the way he ladles it out?

Every story has its own dimensions, Templeton, its own complexity. That's the problem with TV. It doesn't bother with dimension or complexity. Couch potatoes tune out too quickly and hit the remote. It's all about pictures and bullet points."

"OK! I'll check a little deeper into Dr. Ford's background and possible motivations."

I could almost see her throwing up her hands, eyes wide in exasperation. It made me smile, but I kept at her. "Using other sources, who have no reason to protect or promote him?"

"Yes! Using other sources."

"Promise?"

"I promise. Now can I get back to my unpacking?"

"I'll make a reporter out of you yet, Templeton."

"Don't push it, Justice."

I didn't sleep right away. Instead, I sat on the edge of the bed, thinking about things—my unfinished manuscript, encrypted in my hard drive like a bloodless corpse; my diminished sex drive, which left me feeling like half a man; the way I'd come so close a few times to giving up on Victor Androvic, rationalizing that his problems weren't really my responsibility, willing to settle for a kind of mellow apathy in which life felt bearable, almost pleasant, and worrying about people like Victor really wasn't worth the anxiety or the trouble.

Prozac has a half-life of roughly two weeks. That means it takes that long after the first dose to start working and the same period following a final dose for its efficacy to fade away. I figured a person could learn a lot about himself in two weeks, about how he felt and behaved when his emotions were stable, if he really concentrated. I'd been trying to pay attention. I could try harder.

I unscrewed the cap on my vial of green-and-orange capsules, dumped them into the toilet, flushed it, and stood watching the water swirl down.

Prozac had given me six months of peace, of being able to get through the day without feeling overwhelmed by melancholy and dread. But it wasn't what I wanted anymore. I wanted to be able to write lines again that meant something to me. I wanted to experience sensuality again, to respond physically when a man touched me in a way that should have felt exciting and good. I wanted to care about someone deeply, to risk getting close as I once had, even if it meant doing it without a little pill to take the scary edges off. I wanted to reclaim myself, all of me, and start to feel fully alive again.

The bowl emptied, the capsules were gone, and the tank began filling up. I crawled into bed, pulled the covers up, and settled into another night of deep Prozac sleep, without nightmares but also without dreams.

TWENTY-TWO

Monday morning brought a late-spring rain, leaving the city wet and shimmering while mist rose from the pavement like steam.

I walked to City Hall listening to the splash of tires on the street as men and women hurried past under umbrellas, as faceless and disconnected as the drivers masked behind their wet windshields and the metronomic rhythm of their wiper blades. All day, Southern Californians would whine about the weather; the local TV news would be devoted to it, as if living here entitled one to a permanent pass from the inconvenience of nature. That was what earthquakes and wildfires were for, I thought, and the occasional deadly mud slide—to remind us every now and then that life is not a cinematic fantasy, with perfect lighting and smooth edits from scene to scripted scene.

I had two weeks to get accustomed to that reality again, I figured—two weeks to learn to roll with life's punches without Prozac to blunt the blows.

Shortly after lunch, I walked over to the twelve hundred block of North Flores Street to spend a few hours finishing my research in Bruce Bibby's old apartment.

The rain had briefly abated, but the sky was slate gray, with darker pockets that suggested the storm had more to unleash. Cecelia Cortez had arranged my visit through Bibby's older sister, who'd taken on the responsibility of sorting through his belongings but still wasn't up to getting started. I'd done some of that myself, back in the eighties and early nineties, when every few months another friend had died, sometimes at shorter intervals than that. If you were lucky, he'd have packed up everything and labeled it with a name or place where he wanted it to go, but sometimes it was less tidy than that. Sometimes you had to sit on the bed where he'd died—sometimes the same bed you'd once shared with him—and decide if his old sweaters were worth sending to the thrift store or should just be put out on the curb where the homeless could pick though them. Sometimes, it might even be a sweater you'd given him one year before the plague had come and changed everything. So I understood the desire of Bruce Bibby's sister to put off packing up her brother's life into boxes and shipping it off in parcels to loved ones and charity stores. I was also grateful for the opportunity to go through some of it myself, the city archives anyway.

Bibby's apartment was located halfway up the hill in the heart of the Courtyard Thematic District, which rubbed up against and even overlapped the Harper Avenue District, where Templeton now lived. Dating to the early twenties, the Courtyard district was known for its Spanish-style apartment complexes—stucco exteriors, dark wood railings, arches, red tile roofs—built around walkways and courtyard gardens that gave them a more communal feel. I found the street number I was looking for incorporated into the elaborate design of a broad, wrought-iron arch that served as a decorative entranceway. Some of the district's courtyard buildings were on the elegant side, designed around lavish fountain gardens, but this was one of the cozier and more humble models. Several adjoining, single-story apartment units faced each other across a single straight walkway planted simply with geraniums; at the far end was a separate, two-story unit comprised of a pair of two-bedroom apartments on each level. Bibby's place was on the first floor, to the left, with a solid wooden ramp constructed over a portion of the steps to accommodate his wheelchair. Faintly, from one of the apartments, I could hear an old recording—Louis Armstrong singing "What a Wonderful World"—but otherwise the place was quiet, as if time had stopped one drizzly day eons ago when West Hollywood had been less congested and cacophonous. It seemed the perfect residence for a nostalgia freak like Bibby, the kind of place seen in dozens of L.A. *noir* films from the thirties and forties, which also made it an ideal setting for murder, if one's imagination worked that way.

I glanced at my watch and saw that it was nearly two. Ted Meeks was to meet me on the hour with a pass key, so I turned up my collar and shoved my hands in my pockets to wait. I didn't have to wait long. Three minutes later, at exactly two o'clock, I saw him scurrying up the walkway in his crablike way, hunched under his floppy hat, a picture of efficiency. He covered the length of the walkway in a matter of seconds, remarkably spry for a man close to eighty, though he looked as driven by irritability as physical vigor. I stepped aside to allow him room under the porch roof, which wasn't much.

"I appreciate your dropping by like this, Mr. Meeks." I extended a hand, but he ignored it, slipping an aluminum key into the lock and giving it a turn. I reminded him that we'd met during my visit to the Sherman cottages a few days after Bruce Bibby's death, when he'd dropped by with Colin Harrison. "How is Mr. Harrison, by the way?"

He ignored that as well and opened the door a crack but no more, as if he owed me nothing beyond that.

"I remember who you are," he snapped. "You're the one writing that brochure for the city." I started to respond, but he cut me off and kept talking, while he eyed me suspiciously. "I'm not agreeable to strangers coming into a tenant's apartment, especially under circumstances like these. But since the family's given its permission, and the police are finished here, I don't suppose there's anything I can do about it."

"How long before the family has to have everything out?"

"Rent's up June 1. I told them to take whatever time they need and not to worry about the money. We'll give them another month or two at no charge, if that's what they need."

"Decent of you."

He waved the thought brusquely away. "Respect for the dead, that's all."

"Still—"

"We try to be good to our tenants," he snarled, as if I'd suggested otherwise. He pointed at the wooden ramp that covered part of the steps. "I built this for Mr. Bibby with my own hands, the day after he rented the unit. Made sure other special accommodations were ready inside. I tell our tenants, 'You respect us, we'll respect you.'"

"Admirable of you and Mr. Harrison."

"Not that it always works out, of course. That Russian boy, Androvic, the one that committed these murders. He's been a headache for us right from the start, I can tell you that. I pity his poor mother—first her husband, now her son. Good riddance to the both of them, that's what I say."

I cocked my head in surprise. "Colin Harrison owns the apartment house where Mrs. Androvic rents?"

Meeks glared at me like I was an idiot. "That's what I just said, isn't it?"

"Seems like quite a coincidence—a murder victim and the man suspected of killing him, both tenants with the same landlord."

"Psssh." He wrinkled his mouth and nose at my stupidity, causing his small gray mustache to twitch between them. "You obviously don't know much about Colin Harrison."

"I'm not sure I follow, Mr. Meeks."

"Colin owns twenty apartment buildings in the city. He'd own more, if the city didn't make it so difficult for income property owners, with all their damn rules and restrictions. That means close to six hundred tenants, by my last count. So I'm not sure how much of a coincidence it is, Colin collecting rent from Androvic and Bibby both." He glanced at the Timex on his wrist. "I've got better things to do with my time than stand here discussing things with you that are none of your business, anyway." He pointed at the doormat, then at the heavy copper handle on the door. "Wipe your feet before you go in, pull the door tight on your way out, and make sure it's locked." He peered at me skeptically again. "I guess the family trusts you not to take anything that doesn't belong to you. That would be their business. But I won't be held responsible."

I smiled a little. "Don't worry, Mr. Meeks, you can trust me not to steal anything."

He was already turning away, heading down the steps. "I don't trust anybody," he said gruffly, barely looking back. "Not a single damn one of you. Be sure to switch off the lights on your way out. We pay the utilities for these units."

I pushed the door open and stepped inside to the musty smell of old carpeting and drapery, and underneath that, the odor of mildewing paper. Behind me, I left the door open to let in some fresh air and because I didn't like the idea of being alone in an enclosed space where a man had recently been dispatched so violently. The drapes were drawn, so I switched on an overhead chandelier whose crystal was dull with dust, casting the front rooms in a pall that allowed for reasonable visibility, but not much more.

Both living room and adjoining dining room had been converted for Bibby's work, with his collection of photographs and documents obviously organized and stored for easier wheelchair access. Long, low double-decker file cabinets were positioned along the walls; here and there were teetering stacks of old newspapers and magazines that apparently had yet to be clipped and filed. The dining room table was given over to hundreds of photographs in neat piles, while framed movie posters dating to the thirties and forties hung on the walls. Near a desk in the living room, a copy of the *West Hollywood Independent* had been opened and spread on the carpeting to cover blood; some had seeped through the newsprint, staining a front page photo of Tony Mercury dedicating another tree along Santa Monica Boulevard to the memory of a city resident who'd died from AIDS, with the name of the deceased on a small bronze plaque embedded in the sidewalk. The bloody section of carpet was a few feet from a desk where Bibby's stolen computer console had been, judging by the monitor and other accessories that had been detached and left behind during the burglary. The desktop and other surfaces had been dusted by a sheriff's crime scene team for prints; I could see the residue they'd left behind. It occurred to me to look around for Victor Androvic's business card—he'd assured me that he left one with every client, after completing his services—but I quickly realized that Detective De Marco or her partner would surely have found it if it had been there, and bagged it for evidence.

Just beyond the desk was a fireplace that had been cleaned out; next to it, a wrought-iron poker, broom, and small shovel hung in a rack. Hanging above the mantelpiece was a large, framed, sepiatoned photograph of Sherman, circa 1907, apparently shot from one of the hills north of Sunset Boulevard. An electric trolley car could be seen clacking along the tracks that today was the median for Santa Monica Boulevard. Beyond the tracks was the sprawling Sherman rail yard, with its car barns, blacksmith shop, brass foundry, iron foundry, repair shop, and oil house, and a powerhouse that had been converted to a substation in 1905. In the foreground, the eight Sherman cottages rested on the slope of a hill, each looking freshly painted, surrounded by flower and vegetable gardens and white picket fences with all their slats intact. Up the hill and most prominent in the foreground was the largest cottage—later to be known as Harrison House—whose gravel pathways wound through flourishing gardens front and back. Palm trees towered above the dirt roadways, where vintage motorcars shared space with the horse-drawn carts of farmers. The landscape beyond appeared to be mostly orange and avocado groves, with the occasional ranch house here and there and telephone lines that looked strangely futuristic and out of place in such a rural area.

I needed to pee, so I stepped around the bloody newspaper and across the living room to a hallway, which led past a doorway on each side to a small bathroom at the end. Inside, a tub and shower had been rigged up for use by a paraplegic—special handrails on the walls, a low stool for sitting, a flexible shower hose and spray head within easy reach. The bathroom was as neat and tidy as the rest of the apartment, with Bibby's shaving and grooming gear still laid out precisely on a tray, as if he'd be getting up tomorrow and starting another day. Bibby had apparently been a fastidious housekeeper, within his physical limitations; everything roughly four feet and lower was spotless, while higher objects could have used a dusting. The dusting, I figured, was probably handled by a cleaning service or friends who came in to help. I unzipped and relieved myself in the toilet, staring at a framed lobby card for *The Front Page,* the 1931 version. It felt strange, pissing in the bathroom of a dead man without his permission, while his blood clotted the carpet fifty feet away. But I planned to be here awhile, so I figured I'd better get used to it.

I drank water with my hand from the tap, then went back to the two rooms I'd passed along the hallway. One doorway gave me access to a bedroom that was a world unto itself, with a four-poster bed and fancy dressing table worthy of an elegant women's picture from the forties, the kind in which Crawford or Davis always seemed to make up their extraordinary faces at least once before a mirror. In a closet, Bibby's clothes—mostly preppy in style, with a retro-fifties look—hung pressed and arranged by shades and colors on racks fixed lower than normal to the floor to accommodate his reach; laid out neatly on the floor were penny loafers, saddle shoes, and Hush Puppies, each pair reminiscent of another era.

The bedroom across the hall had been used for more filing and storage, all of it appearing to be meticulously organized like the rest. Instead of movie posters on the walls, shelves had been installed to display various items from the city's history, with small placards hand-printed with dates of origin and other vital data, giving the room a museum feel. My eye was drawn immediately to the memorabilia on the most prominent shelf, which is probably what Bibby had intended. About four feet from the floor, it would have been just within reach from his wheelchair for adding or removing items, though not so easily for dusting. It included one of the first spikes driven in the railroad tracks through Sherman in 1897, salvaged as a souvenir when the tracks were ripped up during the recent renovation of Santa Monica Boulevard; a highball glass used by Sammy Davis, Jr., when he'd helped break the Sunset Strip color barrier by performing at Ciro's in the early fifties; a framed photograph of an emaciated homeless man lying on the sidewalk, dying from AIDS, shot along a bleak stretch of Santa Monica Boulevard in 1983; and a placard reading "Fagots—Stay Out!," the infamous, misspelled sign that had hung in Barney's Beanery until 1985, following prolonged protest actions by gay activists and the passage of an anti-discrimination law by the new City Council. In between the railroad spike and the highball glass was an empty space on the shelf that measured perhaps eighteen inches; within that space a slightly smaller, rectangular outline was just visible in the accumulated dust, as if an object had been removed. A small card remained, hand-printed with the following:

*One of the bricks used to build the first car barn
in Sherman's railway yard in 1896, torn down in
1972 to make way for the Pacific Design Center*

I ran my finger within the rectangle, picking up a film of fine grit, which meant the object had been gone long enough for dust to begin settling in its place, a week or two at least. Then I headed back down the hallway to get some work done.

Beginning in the living room and working from a list I'd brought, I moved from file cabinet to file cabinet looking for the data I needed.

Bibby had cataloged his research materials carefully, organizing them alphabetically by subject area, with the subject divisions narrow and specific enough to help me focus my search, and the documents cross-referenced with other pieces in other files when appropriate. Still, his collection was voluminous and filled with fascinating tidbits, causing me to spend more time in certain sections than I should have. I found a trade paper clipping from 1919 on the birth of the Hollywood studio system with the formation of United Artists by Charlie Chaplin, Mary Pickford, Douglas Fairbanks, and D. W. Griffith, who erected their sound stages in West Hollywood at the corner of Santa Monica Boulevard and Formosa Avenue; a menu from classy Maxime's Café on the Sunset Strip from 1955, when the Strip was turning the city into a major tourist destination; a photo taken in 1965 as the Southern Pacific Railway—an engine, two boxcars and a caboose—made its final run down Santa Monica Boulevard; and on and on, as the hours ticked away.

By the time I'd finished in the dining room, checking off my list as I found what I needed, most of the light from the storm-darkened sky was gone. Through the open front door, I watched a warm rain come down in sheets, soaking the garden and pelting the windows beyond the heavy curtains. I glanced at my watch—a quarter to seven. I decided to take a quick spin through the final room down the hall, concentrating on my specific tasks and ignoring anything that didn't directly pertain to them. I left a small table lamp on but switched off the chandelier behind me, to save Ted Meeks a few cents on Colin Harrison's next utility bill.

My quick spin extended to more than two hours, which tends to happen when curious types like me find ourselves swimming in a sea of interesting information. It was after nine by the time I'd browsed most of the file cabinets, and I was beginning to feel light-headed from so many hours of mental concentration without food. As I closed the drawer marked X–Z, and prepared to switch off the light, a lone, remaining cabinet caught my attention. It sat off to the side, away from the others, a narrow, vertical, three-drawer model rather than the long, horizontal models I'd found throughout the rest of the house. Displayed on the face of the top drawer was a small label reading "Career 1976–1993." Inside were glossy eight-by-tens, newspaper and magazine clippings, scripts, and other keepsakes from Bruce Bibby's days as an actor.

The second drawer was marked "Personal," and the files inside were arranged alphabetically. Some were categorized by subject, such as Freelance Invoices, Medical Insurance, Screen Actors Guild, and Social Security. Others were labeled by name, including many I didn't recognize but five that I did: Tony Mercury, Lester Cohen, Colin Harrison, Trang Nguyen, Lydia Ruttweller. A quick survey indicated that most of the contents were personal letters, interspersed with news clippings in the files of the more public and prominent people. All the letters appeared to be photocopies, which probably meant that Mira De Marco or her partner had confiscated the originals as possible evidence, leaving copies in their place for Bibby's family. My knees grew stiff from kneeling, so I sat on the carpet as I pulled the five name files one by one and leafed through them. The letters to Cohen and Harrison were straightforward enough, pleas from Bibby to spare the Sherman cottages from sale and demolition. Only Cohen had replied, complimenting Bibby on his dedication to preservation but suggesting there were other buildings more worthy of his efforts. The letters and notes to Lydia Ruttweller were more casual and personal, a mix of friendly banter and business related to CUP, including a recent pledge by Bibby to personally raise five thousand dollars by the end of the year to help in the legal battle to protect the Sherman cottages. In a return note, Mrs. Ruttweller had thanked Bibby for his support, reminding him how desperate the organization was for funding. In a P.S., she'd scribbled: "Please keep the pressure on your friend Trang to go after Mercury. This is of the utmost importance. We're running out of time!"

The Mercury file contained a single letter from Bibby: a terse note suggesting that Mercury "reconsider" his public support of Cohen's condominium project and instead use his political influence to oppose it. If he didn't, the note implied, he'd risk "a serious public scandal involving more personal matters." Obviously a reference to Mercury's drunken groping of Trang Nguyen.

The file bearing Trang's name was the thickest. Inside, arranged chronologically, were dozens of notes and letters from Trang and a few responses from Bibby. Trang's missives came in the form of pretty note cards, funny gag cards, or e-mails that Bibby had printed out and kept. In the beginning, Trang's messages were cute and off-hand, as he attempted with humor to gently prod Bibby into a deeper relationship. Several complained that Bibby spent too much time with Lydia Ruttweller. As the dates moved forward, Trang's e-mails became more ardent and urgent, even anguished. The last few bore a darker and more accusatory tone, as Trang grew resentful of what he called "your fear of letting me love you the way I know you love me." His final message, dated a week before Bibby's death, ended with a line that one might interpret as ominous: "I try so hard to make you love me, but I give up. I think you afraid to let anybody love you. So this is the end." Bibby's replies were measured and polite, as he gently discouraged Trang's infatuation and tried to let him down as easily as possible. My guess was that these more personal e-mails between the two men were what Trang had been working so feverishly to delete from Bibby's files the first time I'd encountered him in his cubicle at City Hall. They confirmed a few suspicions and raised new ones.

I placed all the photocopied letters back in the file, shut the drawer, and switched off the light on my way out. I stopped in the bathroom for some water and a final pee, then flicked off that light as well. As I did, I heard the creaking of old floorboards down the hall. At the same time, I remembered how late it was and that I'd left the front door open when I should have closed and locked it.

I stepped cautiously into the hallway. A figure stood at the other end—male, I suspected—silhouetted against the faint lamplight behind him. In one hand he gripped a rod-shaped object. My mind went to the wrought-iron poker by the fireplace as I tried without success to make out his face in the darkness.

"Mr. Meeks?"

He said nothing as he started toward me down the hall. My mind raced and I glanced around for a way of escape, if it came to that.

There was a bathroom behind me, and two closed doors between us, halfway down the hall, but no easy way out.

"Who are you?"

He didn't answer, just kept coming, so I stepped back into the bathroom, prepared to lock myself in if I had to. I'd been a fighter once, the reckless kind who'd invited a challenge like this for the pure excitement that came with it. But I was forty-five now; I'd been beaten and broken in all kinds of ways, even blinded in one eye, and I didn't have much fight in me anymore. I reached for the inside doorknob, ready to slam and lock the door, when the stranger finally spoke.

"It is me—Trang."

I sagged with relief. "Trang, for God's sake. You scared me half to death."

"I sorry. I not mean to do that."

He stood before me now, shivering in a clinging wet T-shirt. In his left hand he carried an umbrella, still rolled up and fastened with a snap.

"What are you doing here? You're soaking wet."

"I out walking." He glanced at the unopened umbrella. "I not think about the rain. I have trouble in my head."

"What's going on, Trang?"

"I—I do not have the word I need."

"What is it you want to say?"

His eyes stayed down. "I feel bad, for something I do to Bruce."

"Feel bad—how?"

"I do something to him that is not right."

"You're feeling guilt? Over something you've done?"

He nodded, as his eyes came up. "Yes, that what I feel."

"What was it you did, Trang?"

"It private thing. Not thing I want to share with stranger."

I put a hand on the hard muscle of his shoulder. "But we're not strangers, are we?"

His dark eyes fell away again. "It not easy for me to talk with you."

I grabbed his chin, turned his eyes back toward mine. "You need to tell me, Trang. I need to hear the truth."

His eyes faltered once more, along with his voice. "I—I think about bad thing I say to Bruce before he die. It make me feel very bad. I take walk tonight, come here. I see the light on, the door open. So I come in."

"What was it you said to him that was so terrible?"

"I tell him he a selfish person, and that he a coward. Later, I want to say I sorry, but it too late. Somebody kill him."

"That's the only reason you're feeling guilty?" Trang nodded. "There's nothing more you want to tell me, Trang?"

"That all. That what make me feel bad."

I pushed the damp hair off his forehead, found his eyes. "You loved him very much, didn't you?"

Trang nodded, fighting tears. "I try to tell him that, many time, but he not believe. I want to be his friend, love him, take care of him, but he not want that from me."

"Maybe you weren't the right one for him. Maybe he felt you were suffocating him—trying to love him too much."

He shook his head. "No, we good for each other. We laugh, have good time, have private moment like lover, only no sex. So I know Bruce love me, but he cannot say it. He cannot accept that I love him, because of how he is."

"Paralyzed, you mean? In the wheelchair."

Trang nodded again, blinking back his tears. "I get close, he push me away. Because he not believe nobody can love him, with his body that way."

"I can't imagine it was easy for him, being a paraplegic in a world that places so much value on appearance."

"Not all of us that way." Trang's face grew solemn. "I not like that. I tell Bruce, I love you, we find way to make the sex good, it no matter about your leg. I say to him, I no care about that. I just want to be with him, just how he is. He beautiful to me, that what I tell him. But he not believe—he not feel good about himself."

"You say you loved him, Trang. But at his funeral, you never cried."

"Why you talk about that?"

"It seems unusual, no tears for someone you loved so much."

"I am Buddhist, from when I am little boy. When Bruce die, I go to the temple, I talk to the Buddha. I give him two gold ring I bring from Vietnam. I pray and talk to him. He tell me Bruce not dead, that nobody ever die, that life and death all part of the same. The Buddha, he say we all together, nothing separate from the other, nothing alone, all living thing is one, and all dead thing one with living thing. So I not feel so bad no more about Bruce. That why I not cry at the church. Because he with me now. He with me always."

"Where were you, Trang, on the night Bruce was murdered?"

"Why you ask that? You think I hurt him?" His eyes flashed defiance. "You think I do that to him?"

"Where were you, Trang? That's all I asked."

"The woman from the police, she already ask me that."

"Detective De Marco?" He nodded. "And what did you tell her?"

Shame softened his eyes. "I tell her I go to the gym, then I come here after."

"You came here that night?"

"I not come in. I stand outside. I wait, to see if Bruce go out, or someone come to see him."

"Why?"

"Because I so crazy about him. It stupid, I know. But I love him so much, I do stupid thing."

"What time was this?"

"I come about nine, maybe. Stay two, three hour. Then go home."

"You saw nothing out of the ordinary, no one go in or out?"

He shook his head, swallowing hard. "I do this many time before, come to watch Bruce, to see who he have come here. I see prostitute come sometime, be with him, for the sex."

"Victor Androvic, the man they arrested?"

"I see him once, many week ago. I see other guy come. I know what they doing. They stay maybe one hour, then they go. So I know he paying them for the sex."

"That must have hurt you very much." He clamped his jaw tight, silent. "It must have made you very angry, Trang."

His eyes grew cold. "You think I hurt Bruce, but I not do that. I tell Miss De Marco about what I do. She know I here that night. I not afraid to tell her."

"How did she react, when she learned you'd been here?"

"She say Bruce dead by then. That somebody kill him and go away before I get here."

De Marco would have checked Trang's alibi, I thought, since the attendants scan every membership card as the patrons enter. Still, a person could check into Buff and walk out unnoticed two minutes later, with a record of the entry but no record of the departure. So Trang's alibi wasn't much of an alibi at all. I didn't know how much of his story to believe. All I knew for sure was that any number of people had reason to want Bruce Bibby and Lydia Ruttweller dead. Trang was merely one of them, and not the most likely suspect at that.

He was shivering so violently now I could hear his teeth chatter.

"You're going to end up with pneumonia if you're not careful." I took his wrist, drew him into the bathroom. "Take off that shirt."

I found a fresh towel folded on a lower cabinet shelf. Trang stood where he was, clutching his arms, his T-shirt still on. I pried loose his hands and peeled the wet shirt up and off him as he submitted, raising his arms. Outside, the rain had let up and moonlight shone faintly through the frosted glass of a small window, casting his handsome face in a soft glow and transforming the dampness that covered his body to a lovely sheen.

"Listen to me, Trang, because what I'm going to tell you is important for you to understand."

"Tell me what?"

"You're a beautiful man, inside and out. There are plenty of others out there who'd be happy to have you take care of them, if that's what you want." I ruffled the towel through his dark hair, patted his face dry, wiped down the curves of his chest and back, while he stood passive and silent. Briefly, I touched his cool skin with my bare hand, like a nervous thief snatching something precious but putting it back, afraid of the consequences. "Plenty of men who'd be happy to love you in return."

His shivering had diminished, and his eyes were less resentful than they'd been a minute before. "Would you let me love you?" he asked. "If that was what I want?"

Our eyes were almost even, reminding me how tall he was. "I'm not the man you need, Trang. Besides, you're finished with older white guys. Isn't that what you told me?"

"What if I change mind? What if I like Asian for friend, but white guy for lover? What if that the way I am?"

"Then be patient, until you find the right one."

Tentatively, he reached out to touch my cheek, finding the traction of my beard, gauging the roughness of a face so different from his. "Why you have no lover, Mr. Justice? Good-looking guy like you."

"It's a long story, Trang."

"That mean you no want to tell me." When his eyes came up to meet mine, he seemed to be looking through me, as if I no longer existed to him. "I think maybe you afraid, too, like Bruce."

I heard a chill in his voice and thought about the love notes he'd sent to Bruce Bibby, each one more desperate than the last. I wanted to trust Trang, but I couldn't; there was still too much about him I didn't know, too many emotions inside him I couldn't quite measure or figure out.

"We can be friends, Trang. That's not so bad, is it?"

"I got plenty friend. I need lover now." He removed his hand, his look more resentful than hurt. "You like Bruce. You no want me that way. You too scared to be my lover."

I was more tempted than Trang knew. But he was also another young man in trouble, the kind I'd fallen for too often and too fast. When I said nothing, he grabbed his wet T-shirt and unopened umbrella and stepped past me out of the bathroom. I watched him glide down the dark hallway and out into the rain, the feel of his satiny skin sharp in my mind but everything else about him a confusing blur.

TWENTY-THREE

The next day I skipped lunch and stayed at my desk, determined to get back on track with the brochure. I plowed through a number of designated landmarks—Beau Sejour, the English Village, the William S. Hart House, the Tuscany. I was starting a new section on The Royal Gardens, trying to come up with a fresh first line, when I realized it was nearly seven, and my brain was fried.

I called Templeton to see if she wanted to stroll down the hill and meet me for dinner, although what I really wanted was an update on the two murder cases. Templeton already had plans, she said, and was on her way out.

"Dinner with Dr. Ford?"

"None of your beeswax, Mr. Busybody."

"So it is Dr. Ford," I said.

"I didn't say that."

I heard noise in the background and the faint murmur of Templeton's voice as she covered the receiver with her hand to speak to someone nearby. I wasn't boiling over with anger, but the thought of her dallying with Dr. Ford grated on me just the same.

"He's there now, isn't he?"

"We have a reservation, Justice. I really have to go."

"At least give me an update on the two investigations."

"I'm not sure I have anything new to offer."

"I'll take what I can get."

She sighed heavily. "I've learned that Lydia Ruttweller and Bruce Bibby had an exchange of e-mails on the afternoon he was killed. Chas Ruttweller discovered them. He turned them over to Mira De Marco."

"E-mails about what?"

"I'm not at liberty to say."

"De Marco showed them to you?"

"No comment."

"Do they involve Victor Androvic in some way?"

"No—I can tell you that much. I'm not quite sure what they mean. Neither does Mira."

"So she is your source."

"I really have to go, Justice."

"What else?"

"You can scratch Chas Ruttweller off your list of suspects, at least in his mother's murder. He's got an airtight alibi."

"He could have hired someone to do it," I said.

"Yes, I suppose he could have hired Victor Androvic."

"Don't be a bitch. It doesn't become you."

"I get this way when I'm hungry and on my way to dinner."

"How airtight an alibi?"

"Chas Ruttweller was in Cedars-Sinai Medical Center when his mother was killed. Intensive care, round-the-clock supervision, starting the previous night. His liver went on hiatus, due to all his steroid use."

"You know this for a fact?"

"Mira confirmed it. He's still at the hospital, out of intensive care and on the mend. That's where she interviewed him and learned about the e-mails he'd found at his mother's house."

"He was snooping around her office, before she was killed?"

"Apparently. Look, I really have to go. We're running late."

"You and the professor," I said.

She hung up without a reply.

I grabbed a quick meal at Bossa Nova, made a stop at Flower Power, then hustled half a mile down to Cedars-Sinai Medical Center and into the south wing. As I entered Chas Ruttweller's room, I was carrying a bouquet of small pink roses and white baby's breath, tied up with frilly pink ribbon and a pretty bow.

Chas lay on his back in bed, an intravenous line feeding into one of the fat veins in his massive arms. He'd lost some of his florid complexion, which had taken on a sickly jaundiced pallor, leaving him somewhere between puke yellow and Agent Orange. His eyes fluttered open as I stood over him. I'd seen healthier-looking men on slabs at the county morgue back when I'd been working the cop shop for the *LAT*.

"What the fuck are you doing here?" His voice was small, weak.

I held out the bouquet. "I thought these would cheer you up." He suddenly grimaced and turned his head, absorbing a stab of pain. I clucked my tongue. "Liver shutting down from all those steroids, is it?"

His sullen eyes came back around. "Fuck you."

"I won't stay long, Chas. I only need to ask you a few questions."

"Get the fuck out of here."

"You use that word an awful lot—fuck. Is that because you don't actually do much of it?" He snarled and tried to rise but quickly collapsed, gripped by pain. "Like I said, Chas, just a few questions. Then I'll be on my way."

"I got nothing to talk to you about."

"Sure you do. For one thing, you can tell me about those e-mails your mother was exchanging with Bruce Bibby the day he was murdered. The ones you turned over to Detective De Marco. I'm sorry about your mother, by the way. I mean that."

"Yeah, I bet you're real sorry. You didn't even know her that well, so fuck off."

"About those e-mails, Chas. Or I'll stay here for a while, just to piss you off. I've got lots of time, and you're not going anywhere, are you?"

He muttered another obscenity under his breath. "De Marco told me not to talk to anyone about that stuff. Anyway, you're not a cop. You're just some queer from City Hall writing up a stupid brochure. I got no reason to talk to you."

I unwrapped the bouquet, found an empty vase, filled it with water, and began arranging the flowers in it. "I've got a proposition for you, Chas. You can make nice and answer my questions, or I can wait here until some of your Neanderthal pals arrive for a visit and let them know what a flaming faggot you are."

"I'm no faggot!"

"Or maybe I'll pay a visit to Skin Deep tonight for a chat with your bouncer buddies." I set the vase on the tray next to his bed, affected a lisp, and rolled my eyes theatrically as I fiddled with the flowers. "Oh, the stories I could tell about what you do down in Boys Town on your nights off. I imagine word like that spreads rather quickly at the gym, doesn't it?"

"Fucker!" He tried again to rise and grabbed at me ineffectually before collapsing with a groan, clutching his side. "When I get out of here, I'll find you and kick your faggot ass."

I lifted the plastic urine bag that was connected by a catheter tube to his penis beneath the top sheet. "When you get out of here, Chas, you'll be lucky to take a halfway decent pee. You'll have enough trouble figuring out how you're going to live with yourself without your steroids and your mother's checkbook to prop you up."

He clamped his eyes shut. "I don't need this, man. I'm sick, you know?"

"So talk to me, and I'll leave you alone."

He pressed his clenched fists to his forehead, sounding truly bewildered. "Why are you doing this to me?"

"Because I need some answers, Chas. Those e-mails, between your mother and Bruce Bibby—what was in them?"

"Stupid stuff, that's all."

"I know it's a challenge for you mentally, but try to be a little more specific, could you?"

"Bibby was doing research for that brochure he was working on. He found out something about those old cottages they want to tear down."

"The Sherman cottages."

"Yeah, those. Bibby found out something about the main one, where that rich guy, Colin Harrison, lived a long time ago, with his little faggot friend."

"Ted Meeks."

"Yeah, Meeks."

"What exactly did Bibby find out?"

"That they'd made some change in the place, so it wasn't exactly how it had been when it was built. My mother was nuts about that shit—every little thing about an old house had to be just like it was a hundred fucking years ago."

"She'd learned that the building she'd been trying to save wasn't in its original state, wasn't authentic. Is that what you're telling me?"

"Something like that, yeah."

"What else, Chas?"

"Bibby said they needed to meet and talk about it. She e-mailed him back, and they made plans to get together the next day."

"Only someone killed Bibby that evening." He nodded. "In his e-mail, did Bibby say where he'd found this information?"

"I don't know, but he told her he'd put it on his hard drive, with all his other notes. I don't know what he was talking about exactly. I don't give a shit about that stuff. Can you leave me alone now?"

A nurse came in to check his intravenous drip, and told me that visiting hours were almost over. When she was gone, I said to Chas, "I was serious when I told you I'm sorry about what happened to your mother. Must be tough, losing your mom like that, even if the two of you were at odds a lot of the time." I watched his eyes closely, to see if they might tell me something. "On the other hand, you'll probably inherit most of what she owned, won't you? Since she died before she had a chance to change her will."

His eyes remained distant and sullen, and slightly glazed from whatever pain medication the doctors had him on. He struck me as someone who'd buried his feelings for so long he wasn't really sure what they were anymore.

"I've been thinking a lot lately about fathers and sons, Chas. I'll bet you've been thinking about yours, especially now that your mother's gone, since you're an only child."

He fixed his eyes on the ceiling and didn't look at me again. "I answered your questions," he said. "Now leave me alone."

TWENTY-FOUR

I resumed my work on the brochure early Wednesday morning, trying not to think about what arcane detail Bruce Bibby might have discovered in his research materials that had made a private meeting with Lydia Ruttweller so urgent.

The problem was that my accumulating information on their two murders seemed to be on a collision course with my City Hall deadline, pulling me in two directions. At one point, I even interrupted my work to phone Colin Harrison, hoping he might shed some light on a number of murky areas that had me bothered. Harrison wasn't listed in the phone book but Ted Meeks was, and since they lived together, I figured that number was as good as any. No one picked up when I called, so I left a message and tried to concentrate on my rough draft again. I was making reasonable progress until I got to the section on the development of the Pacific Design Center, double-checking dates in Bibby's files to make sure I had them all correct.

I sat studying them for several minutes, my mind going back through endless facts and figures that had flooded over me since I'd taken this job not quite three weeks earlier. Then I went to the restroom, rinsed my face at the sink, and stared into the mirror for a minute, trying to get my head around everything, trying to keep a bead on what I was after before it slipped away from me again. From there, I headed up to the office of Cecelia Cortez, bypassing the slower elevator and taking the stairs two steps at a time.

Cecelia was sipping tea and eating a fresh peach behind her desk, her large frame and voluptuous curves swathed in a pale yellow dress, with a floral-patterned silk scarf knotted loosely around her neck for an extra splash of color. She'd changed her dark hair since I'd last seen her, pulling it off her pale face, which further accentuated her large brown eyes.

Her lips stretched into a smile as I came in. "Had your fill of architecture and historic preservation yet, Benjamin?"

"I'll admit it's been quite a cram course."

She asked me how my research had gone at Bruce Bibby's apartment Monday afternoon, and I told her I'd learned a few things that might prove valuable. Then I inquired about which department I should go to for records regarding the salvage operations at the old rail yard during its demolition in the early 1970s.

"What specifically did you need?"

"I was hoping to find out what had happened to the bricks from the old buildings, in particular who might have salvaged them."

"That's an awfully small detail. You're sure you need it?"

"Curiosity, more than anything else. I don't plan to spend much time on it."

She regarded me with amusement. "You do have a reputation for curiosity, don't you?" She put the peach aside, wiped her fingers on a napkin, stood, and came around the desk on low-heeled pumps. "Tell you what. You keep working on the brochure, since that's top priority. I'll run down to records and put in the request myself."

"You're sure it's not too much trouble?"

"Not at all." She was already at the door. "I'm going in that direction on another errand, anyway. I'll let you know as soon as they get back to me with something. Be patient—it's a busy department and they're always backed up with requests down there."

I should have returned to my desk and resumed my work, but I didn't. Instead, I left City Hall and walked a half mile west along Santa Monica Boulevard until I reached West Knoll Drive, where I turned right and climbed the street as it curved west.

On my right, multistory apartment and condominium complexes were packed shoulder to shoulder, big modern boxes with narrow balconies and conventional landscaping, about as aesthetically interesting as a shoe box. On my left, the scene was much different, with that block of West Knoll serving as a demarcation line between past and present. A row of intriguing one-story homes in the Neoclassical and Regency styles of the twenties and thirties nestled along a small bluff like symbols of a bygone age, struggling to hang on before the relentless demand for housing pushed them over the edge into oblivion. Colin Harrison lived midway along the block, in a stately yet modest and unpretentious Neoclassical house with pillars supporting its domed porch. It was set back from the street by a freshly trimmed lawn and healthy ferns closer to the house; between the sidewalk and the lawn was a wrought-iron fence tall enough to discourage all but the most determined intruders.

I was about to ring the bell at the gate, hoping to chat with Harrison, when the front door opened and a male nurse in a white uniform appeared, carrying a medical bag and a dog-eared copy of Felice Picano's *The Book of Lies*. He was a trim, good-looking black man with braided hair and horn-rimmed glasses who'd given me a few sponge baths earlier in the year during my hospital stay, after I'd been carved up and lost an eye in the bloody mess that had cost Joe Soto his life. The nurse recognized me, and we exchanged greetings through the iron bars of the gate. I made a joke about his slow hands, we laughed, and he explained that he'd left the hospital to work in home health care.

"More personal this way, and the money's better," he said. "You're a friend of Mr. Harrison and Mr. Meeks?"

"I'm better acquainted with Ted, but I've met them both."

He glanced at the button beside the gate. "I don't think they'd hear you if you rang. Mr. Meeks just took Mr. Harrison out back for some air." He glanced at his watch. "I've got to run on to my next job. I don't think they'll mind if I let you in."

I offered my most convincing smile. "I can't imagine why they would. How's Colin doing, by the way?"

The nurse shrugged sympathetically. "Advanced Alzheimer's, final stages—not a pleasant situation, especially for Mr. Meeks. You might want to say your farewells now, although I'm not sure Mr. Harrison will know who you are or understand what you're saying."

"You don't think he has long then?"

"Another week or two—that's what the doctors have told Mr.

Meeks. He refuses to remove Mr. Harrison to a hospice. Insists he stay here to the end, in the final home they shared. It's very touching, seeing that kind of devotion."

"It certainly is."

He opened the gate, stepped aside to let me in, said good-bye, and scurried along the sidewalk out of sight. I closed the gate quietly and crossed the lawn past a concrete fountain and sculpted lion weakly dribbling water from its mouth. A paved drive led me along the east side of the house, toward a detached garage at the southeast corner of the property. A rear yard and a view of the city gradually opened up before me, along with a mass of commercial buildings and signage just below the property that lined Santa Monica Boulevard. A small gazebo sat in the farthermost corner of the yard, across a lawn split by a walkway that led to the edge of the bluff. If I squinted, I could just make out chess pieces set up on a wooden chessboard on a table in the gazebo.

Not ten yards from where I stood Ted Meeks appeared, slowly pushing Colin Harrison in a wheelchair along an adjoining walkway close to the house that led in my direction. I stepped back around the corner, behind a climbing wisteria, pressing myself against the wall, while I watched them through the vines. Meeks stopped, looking over as if he'd noticed my movement or heard something. He pricked up his ears and listened keenly for a moment. Then he bent his head again, pushing the wheelchair forward until he reached the main walk. Colin Harrison was slumped in his seat, his head hanging to one side, his eyes vacant, as if his slack body had been abandoned, leaving no one home. Meeks turned at the main walkway and followed it to the edge of the property, where he stood for a minute, gazing out across the city. Harrison remained slumped and inert, his chin on his chest, seemingly oblivious to it all. Meeks withdrew a small comb from his pocket, knelt in front of Harrison, and combed strands of red hair off his forehead. He did it precisely, tenderly, as if it was more a ritual of love than a necessary act. After that, he found a handkerchief in a pocket and wiped saliva from Harrison's chin, before turning the wheelchair and pushing it along an adjoining walkway to the gazebo. He parked the chair under the shade, locked the wheels, took a seat next to Harrison, and proceeded to begin a game of chess.

Harrison never responded, not with the slightest word or movement. Meeks moved a chess piece, carrying on a one-way conversation with Harrison as if nothing was amiss. After a minute or two, he reached over to Harrison's side of the board and moved one of his pieces.

"Colin, you scoundrel!" Meeks raised the brim of his floppy hat and scratched his white hair, feigning admiration and frustration. "What a brilliant move! Why didn't I see that coming?" He pondered the board for another minute or two, before reaching back to make a move of his own, after which he offered Harrison a smug expression. "Your move, Colin. Let's see how smart you are this time."

It went on this way for fifteen or twenty minutes, Meeks making Harrison's moves for him every few minutes, then pretending to be exasperated as Harrison's clever play gradually eliminated Meek's pawns and queens, until Harrison had won the game.

Meeks pulled off his hat and threw it to the ground. "Damn you, Colin! You've beaten me again! You'd think I could beat you just one time."

He studied Harrison's unresponsive face for a moment, growing solemn, then picked up his hat, dusted it off, and placed it back on his head. He walked alone back to the edge of the bluff, staring out, his hands shoved deep in the pockets of his wash pants. I tried to imagine what must be going through his mind as he realized these were the last days he'd spend with a man he'd lived with and loved for nearly sixty years.

There aren't many situations that will force me away when I'm looking for a confrontation or answers, but this was one of them. I edged quietly back down the drive, ashamed of my eavesdropping, crossed the lawn to the front walk, and headed for the gate. I was about to open it when a postal carrier appeared along the sidewalk, clutching a pack of envelopes as she approached the house. A glance at the top envelope showed me Lydia Ruttweller's name and address in the top left corner.

"I can take those in," I said. "Mr. Harrison's not feeling well."

She handed them through the gate with a smile. "Have a nice day."

When her back was to me and she was nearly to the next house, I glanced through the rest of the mail—bills and junk mail, except for the top envelope that had caught my eye. It was postmarked early

Saturday afternoon, the day Mrs. Ruttweller had been found dead, which meant that it had probably been posted that same morning, before she'd reached Schindler House, where her assailant had been waiting for her. I kept that letter out and dropped the remaining envelopes into the mail slot beside the gate.

Five minutes later, I was at Tribal Grounds with a cup of coffee, opening the envelope I'd retained. Inside, I found a handwritten note from Mrs. Ruttweller folded around photocopies of four checks, each made out by Ted Meeks to Mrs. Ruttweller for twenty thousand dollars. Also enclosed was a personal check from Mrs. Ruttweller to Meeks, made out for the same total—eighty thousand dollars.

The note, written in her precise script, was brief:

Dear Mr. Meeks:

As I mentioned on the phone this morning, it has come to my attention that alterations have been made to Harrison House after your assurances to me that it had been preserved in earlier years precisely in its original state, inside and out, with the exception of landscaping. This is most distressing to those of us who value so highly the historic integrity of the structures we're committed to protecting. The property may yet qualify for historic designation pending further and meticulous study, which I intend to personally undertake. In the meantime, I am returning your contributions to our preservation effort on behalf of the cottages, even though their loss is a severe blow to CUP financially. These donations will, of course, remain confidential, as you originally requested.

Yours truly,
Lydia Ruttweller

I read the note again, then folded it back up with the check inside, and slipped all of it back into the envelope. Ted Meeks might be an ornery and contentious old man, I thought, but his devotion to Colin Harrison seemed unquestionable, including his secret desire to protect and save the house where they'd shared their early years together, even as the more pragmatic and pecuniary Harrison had wanted it destroyed.

I finished my coffee, slipped the envelope into a pocket, and caught the Dash back to City Hall, more determined than ever to get on with my work. In the back of my mind, I intended to seal the envelope with a glue stick and drop it in Colin Harrison's mail slot the next morning, with no one the wiser about its delay. That was my initial intention, at any rate.

But as the Dash approached City Hall I stayed in my seat, continuing on through Boys Town, all the way into Tatiana Androvic's neighborhood for an overdue chat with Victor Androvic's mother.

TWENTY-FIVE

As the Dash rumbled toward my stop, life in the Russian community looked deceptively simple and straightforward.

Up and down Santa Monica Boulevard immigrants shuffled in and out of the stores carrying shopping bags they'd use over and over, still unaccustomed to the stunning excess and shameful waste so integral to America's disposable way of life. Old women strolled arm in arm along the sunny sidewalks, chatting in Russian or practicing their English, with the kind of contentment on their faces one rarely saw in other sections of the city. A middle-aged man in suspenders swept the pavement in front of the Russian Jewish Community Center, which occupied a fine old building with big, arched windows that had once housed a luxury automobile showroom, in the decades before the neighborhood had gone to seed with the passing of Hollywood's golden age. The Russian neighborhood had a leftover shabby look that could be misleading; it was a community on the rebound, thriving again with families and commerce, the way so many neighborhoods in the older sections of Los Angeles County reinvented themselves and came back to life every couple of generations with an influx of a new ethnic or immigrant group. They came with hope, a sense of rebirth, a willingness to work hard for what they might get, unlike so many who'd been born here to a sense of privilege and entitlement.

Tatiana Androvic had come with that kind of hope, especially for her son. But she'd also brought with her a secret meant to protect one man she'd loved that was now close to destroying another. I'd put together enough pieces from her fragmented life and lies to figure out that much; I also knew that the time had passed for her to come forward with the truth on her own.

As the Dash reached Plummer Park, I hopped off and followed a winding walkway to Long Hall, where the Russian-language library was temporarily housed, while the city looked for a new space to accommodate its more than twenty thousand volumes. The modest library, run by volunteers, was comprised of books that had been lovingly shipped ahead by aspiring immigrants a few at a time, each book approved for mailing by Russia's Ministry of Culture. Despite its history of political oppression, Russia was a country steeped in literature and a pride in reading; the little library in Plummer Park had become a lifeline for older immigrants trying to hang on to their heritage and culture, some of them riding the bus many miles each day from other communities to sit reading in Long Hall or to check out books for carrying home.

The library was open weekdays between 11:00 A.M. and 1:30 in the afternoon, and I got in just before closing. I found Mrs. Androvic sitting at a long folding table behind a Selectric typewriter, the kind of relic I hadn't seen since my early newspaper days, when the computer was about to doom the once-revolutionary Selectric to the junk pile, as electric typewriters had once doomed the Underwood. She was absorbed in her work, pecking out a list of recommended titles for a language student visiting from UCLA, reading each title to him as she poked at the keys. Next to her were a rotary telephone and a handwritten card catalog filled with the names and essential data on the library's nearly one thousand registered patrons. Along the wall behind her, long metal shelves held thousands of books in Russian, ranging from Tolstoy and Pasternak to Saul Bellow and Danielle Steele. The musty smell of bound volumes permeated the double-garage-sized room, where a few folding tables and chairs served perhaps two dozen readers.

As I stood there, Mrs. Androvic glanced up with an automatic smile that quickly disappeared when she recognized me. She returned more stiffly to her typing, becoming flustered and making an error, which she fixed by backing up the typewriter carriage, typing over her mistake with the white correction ribbon, then returning again to type in the correct letter from the Selectric font ball, before ejecting the paper and handing it to the grateful student. She waited until he was out of earshot before looking up at me again with a smile as tight as a line by Hemingway.

"Our books are all in Russian, Mr. Justice. I'm not sure you'll find anything that's useful to you here."

"I was looking for something with pictures, Mrs. Androvic."

"Pictures?"

"Photographs, drawings—renderings of *matryoshka* dolls that show the different styles and characteristics of the families who make them." I was especially interested in the work of one particular family, I told her, and mentioned the name—Komskaya.

Discomfort further strained her face. "I'm sorry. We don't have anything like that here."

"Maybe you can help me then. I just have a few questions."

"I'm not really an expert on *matryoshkas*."

"You showed me a lovely set in your apartment. Your husband's work, as I recall."

"It was just that one set. I do not know much beyond that."

"My understanding is that the husband customarily does the carving, while the wife does the painting."

"In traditional families, yes, that is usually the case."

Around us, library patrons were leaving their tables and returning books to the shelves. Some were already headed out the door.

"What about the Komskaya family, Mrs. Androvic—that beautiful set of dolls I saw last week at the folk art exhibit here in the park?"

"I do not know much about that family's work. As I said, I am not an expert in this area."

"Then you've never been a painter of *matryoshkas* yourself?"

She laughed uneasily. "Of course not."

"Then what about the *matryoshkas* that you showed me in your apartment? Those dozen little dolls nesting one inside the other? Your husband, did he do both the carving and the painting, since that's not your skill?"

"I told you, Victor's father—"

"Victor's father carved them, but he didn't paint them, did he?"

She glanced at her watch and abruptly stood, not quite looking at me. "I am afraid we have to close now. The rules—thirty minutes past one." She found her smile again, nodding as the last patrons filed out. When we were alone, she said, "Please, Mr. Justice—you must go."

She busied herself filing a few loose library cards in their box while I stood across the narrow table. "Victor's father carved the *matryoshkas* I saw in your apartment," I said. "But they were painted by his wife—Mrs. Komskaya. A rabbi who *is* an expert told me that the day I saw the other set of Komskaya *matryoshkas* at the exhibit."

Mrs. Androvic froze where she was, while her eyes flickered with something close to panic. "Why are you doing this, Mr. Justice? What do you want from me?"

"I want the truth about Victor's father."

She finished her filing in silence, but I could almost hear the pounding of her heart and the machinery meshing in her mind as it sorted frantically through the troubling possibilities I'd suddenly raised. "I won't leave you alone," I said, "until I have the truth." She spread a hand at her breastbone and gulped for air, starting to pale. I steadied her with my hand on her shoulder. "Perhaps you should get some fresh air, Mrs. Androvic, and a drink of water."

"Yes, I think I should do that."

"There's a drinking fountain outside. Then I'll walk you home, and you can tell me what I need to know."

We were out of the park, across Santa Monica Boulevard, and nearing her apartment before Mrs. Androvic spoke again.

"I have done a terrible thing to my son. Such a terrible thing for a mother to do. I have trouble speaking of it. Just to think about it causes me to cry with shame. Many nights, I lie alone and cry, especially now that Victor is in such trouble. To think, I have kept this secret for so long, and now you figured it out from a little set of wooden dolls."

"Would it help," I asked, "if I spoke the truth for you? If you heard it out loud, spoken by someone else?" She shrugged pitifully, but said nothing. I stopped, faced her, put my hands on her shoulders. "Victor's father was not the multiple murderer who was executed back in Russia, was he, Tatiana?"

She closed her eyes for a moment, shaking her head. "No."

"His father is Mr. Komskaya, the man who carved both sets of *matryoshkas*—the one in your apartment, and the one I saw in Plummer Park last week."

She resumed walking, while I followed. "Yes." Her voice quavered.

"You had an affair?" She nodded. "He was married, so were you. You let your husband Leonid believe the baby was his." Again, she nodded. "And you raised Victor to believe that Leonid was his father, never expecting that the man you were married to would turn out to be a maniac on his way to the gallows for killing so many young women."

Suddenly, her words came in a torrent. "I should have told Victor, when he became old enough to understand. But I was afraid, for many reasons. I was frightened of what my husband might do to Victor and me if he found out, and to Victor's real father—Leonid was a violent man, long before he was arrested for the killings. Mr. Komskaya had a family of his own. I loved him very much. I was afraid for him. He wanted to take his family to America, to start a new life. I did not want to ruin that for him. So I kept our secret to myself. I intended to tell Victor at some point but—"

"Things became complicated?"

"Yes, very complicated." Mrs. Androvic stopped outside the entrance to her apartment building, where she sat on a low wall, folding her hands in her lap. "When Dr. Ford contacted us in Russia, he seemed like such a good man, who wanted to help us."

"In what way, Mrs. Androvic?"

She looked up, her eyes full of pain. "He helped us to come to this country. He told us that if Victor agreed to participate in his research, he would help Victor get into the university. He promised a scholarship. He gave us money, to help us get started here. As refugees, we get help from the government, but it's not enough." She smiled sadly. "Victor, he's an American boy now. He wants so many things. He wants all the things so many other American children have. It's a wonderful country, the United States. But there is so much here, everyone has so much. Maybe too much."

If she was telling the truth—and my gut told me she was—then Dr. Ford was more Machiavellian than I'd suspected. "Dr. Ford must have doctored those brain scan images," I said. "It wouldn't be that difficult, not with all the new digital technology available." Almost immediately, a more chilling thought struck me: *If Dr. Ford was willing to do that to turn Victor into the vicious predator he needed to validate his studies, then what other risks might he take to frame him? To what lengths might he go to set Victor up, create victims, plant evidence, manipulate facts—to complete his scientific portrait of Victor Androvic as his father's monstrous offspring?*

"I know nothing of these images you speak of," Mrs. Androvic said. "Just what I see in the newspaper, which cannot be right." She shrugged haplessly. "Victor's real father was not a violent man. He was the kindest, gentlest man I have ever known."

"Yet you still said nothing. For years, you've allowed this lie to perpetuate itself."

She looked up, imploringly. "I did it to protect Victor, Mr. Justice. He is all I have now. All I care about, all I live for, is my son and his future."

"His future doesn't look too good at the moment, does it, Mrs. Androvic?"

"I never expected things to go this way, to become so complicated, so—"

She broke off as the front gate was pushed open and a familiar figure emerged. Ted Meeks scurried out, clutching what looked like a ledger in one hand; behind one ear, under his floppy hat and white hair, was a pencil. Mrs. Androvic nodded in his direction, he grunted and nodded slightly in return, and shot me a curious glance as he continued on to his old Mercedes station wagon at the curb.

"He comes for the rents," Mrs. Androvic said. "He works for Mr. Harrison, the owner."

"Yes, I know who he is." I watched Meeks pull away. "Mr. Meeks personally collects the rents?"

"Just the older people who have trouble posting their letters. He does not like us to leave the rent checks out for the postal carrier to pick up. Some checks were stolen once because of that. So now he comes around and picks up the checks himself from the old people who have trouble getting out." We watched the old station wagon sputter away down the street, listening to the ticking of its diesel engine. "He is very good to us, Mr. Meeks. He does not like to show it, but inside, he has what you Americans call a soft spot—a good heart."

I turned to look at her again. "You're an American, Tatiana."

She attempted a smile. "Slowly, I feel that way a little more."

"And Victor?"

Her smile broadened. "Victor wanted to leave Russia as far away as possible, as soon as he could. All he ever wanted was to be an American boy."

"Maybe it was to leave his father as far away as possible—or at least the man he believed was his father."

Sadness blunted the smile, dimmed her eyes. "Yes, I suppose that could be."

"He needs to know the truth, Tatiana. The world needs to know the truth. You have a son in jail, accused of two crimes he may not have committed. He's being portrayed as a coldhearted predator, like his father. You know that's wrong. You have no right to keep your secret any longer. You can't sacrifice Victor because of your own shame."

"Our lawyer told us that what Leonid did, all the killing, cannot be used in court against Victor. And these studies of Dr. Ford's—"

"Which are bogus, obviously faked, by an academic fraud."

"These studies have no bearing in court," she went on. "None of this can even be mentioned. So the truth about Victor's father—is it really so important now?"

I was staggered by her words. "Do you have any idea how tormented your son is?" She refused to look at me, keeping her head down. "He's driving himself crazy trying to be a good boy for you, trying to make up for the sin of being born to Leonid Androvic. Are you listening to me, Mrs. Androvic?"

"Yes, I hear you."

"But are you listening?" She raised her head; our eyes met. "Victor deserves to know the truth. And Dr. Ford deserves to be exposed as a fraud before he hurts someone else as badly as he's hurt your son. But you have to do that. You're the one who knows the truth, and can prove it."

"I don't know—after so much time."

"Is Mr. Komskaya still alive?"

She nodded. "In Chicago, with his family. They came several years before Victor and me."

"You've stayed in touch?"

"Oh, no. It would not be right."

"But you've kept tabs on him." She looked at me curiously, so I translated the slang. "You've kept current on where he is, what he's doing."

"Yes, a bit. It's hard to let go completely."

"You need to contact him, ask him to give up a DNA sample, convince him to let the truth be known. Maybe even have a role in Victor's life, if he's willing."

She looked away again, back up the street toward the busy boulevard. "I do not know, Mr. Justice. After all these years—I am not sure this would be the best course."

I spit my next words at her. "You don't love your son, Mrs. Androvic."

"Of course I do!"

"You love your lies more than Victor."

"No!" Her eyes were desperate, pleading. "You must believe me!"

"A mother who truly loves her child would never do this to him. A mother who truly loves her child would do what she knows in her heart is right."

She stared at me, tearing up again, but kept silent. I suddenly felt disgusted—with her, with my inability to reach her, with the whole stinking mess. I turned away, leaving Tatiana Androvic with her rationalizations and her shame, and hurried up to Santa Monica Boulevard, where I caught the Dash back to City Hall.

Waiting on my desk was a personal invitation from Lester Cohen to a campaign fund-raising event he was throwing the following Monday for Tony Mercury at the House of Blues. Tucked in with it were two complimentary tickets in case I wanted to bring a friend.

The man just doesn't give up, I thought, and tossed the invitation into the nearest paper recycle can.

A moment later, thinking twice, I retrieved it. I shoved it into a drawer along with Lydia Ruttweller's letter to Ted Meeks, figuring another meeting with Lester Cohen might be useful after all.

TWENTY-SIX

I spent the next two days in my City Hall cubicle working like a man possessed. Late Friday afternoon, I finally finished a rough draft of the brochure, meeting my deadline.

I was exhausted but hugely relieved to have it done. In the end, I'd devoted a third of a page to the old Sherman cottages, with most of that taken up by a photo I'd found in Bruce Bibby's apartment, circa 1905, showing the cottages when they'd still been in pristine condition, not unlike the one over his mantelpiece. In my copy, I established their place in West Hollywood's history in as straightforward a manner as I was able, mentioning the simple style of the Plains cottage design as well as the current dilapidated condition of the buildings. I ended with this line: *At this writing, the fate of the Sherman cottages is undecided.* I spent another two hours going back over my manuscript, reading each line aloud for its rhythm and pacing, adding and deleting words as I went, finding better word choices and sometimes omitting extraneous lines, much as I'd done in my old newspaper days, until I felt it was reasonably tight and well polished. In short, a respectable first draft worth turning in before I got Cecelia's notes and the serious revisions began.

I hit the save icon on my word-processing menu, made a backup copy on my CD, and sent another copy electronically to Cecelia Cortez as an attached document to an e-mail, even though it was Friday evening, and she'd already gone home. Then I went home myself, to have dinner with Maurice and Fred, at their invitation. We were finishing a dessert of Fred's fresh-baked brownies—heavy on the walnuts, the way he liked them—when I brought up the subject of Colin Harrison, in particular what they might remember about his temperament.

"He wasn't someone you wanted to cross," Maurice said. "He's a big man, as you know, and he was famous for his volatility. He'd turn red in the face and get blustery very quickly if you disagreed with him—tremble, shake his fists, bellow like a smokestack blowing off steam. More than once I wanted to haul off and smack that man, I can tell you. Thankfully, I'm more ladylike than that."

"He wasn't the type to hold it in then," I said.

"Oh, no—that was more Ted's style. How he put up with Colin I'll never know." Maurice slid his eyes playfully in Fred's direction. "He wasn't able to tame Colin the way I did Fred. If you're going to live with a lion, you've got to know when to crack the whip and remind them who the master is. Or in my case, the mistress."

Fred feigned a sweet smile, but he also reached for Maurice's hand, clasping it warmly. I told them what I'd learned earlier in the week about Harrison—that he was suffering from Alzheimer's, and apparently hadn't long to live.

"Oh, my," Maurice said, putting a hand to his cheek. "That explains why he wasn't at the public hearing the other night, when Ted did his best to fill in." He glanced at Fred, working up a pained smile. "There goes another one, sweetheart. Someone from the old days, about to leave us." Fred leaned over, kissed Maurice tenderly on the forehead, and departed silently for another room. Maurice followed Fred's exit fondly. "I'm so lucky I still have him, after all these years. I can't imagine what it would be like, if he should go before I do. Or you, Benjamin. You must promise me that you'll keep taking care of yourself, and outlive Fred and me, the way it should be. After all, you're like the son we never had. You know that."

"I'll do my best, Maurice."

He clucked, shaking his head. "Poor Ted. Not the nicest person to be around, but he'd do just about anything to keep Colin happy. Nearly sixty years together! That takes some work, I can tell you, especially when the whole world seems to be against you, telling you that two men mustn't love each other, that you mustn't feel the way you feel. Sometimes, it's remarkable that any of us queers manage to stay together at all, given all the forces trying to pry us apart." Maurice suddenly brightened, patting my hand. "I know what I'll do! I'll drop Ted a note tomorrow and tuck in a snapshot from the old days, just to let him know we're thinking about him. I think he'd appreciate that."

"I suspect you're right, Maurice."

That reminded me that I still owed Meeks a delivery of my own—the note Lydia Ruttweller had mailed to him, along with the check she'd sent. In my zeal to finish the rough draft of my brochure, I'd locked the envelope in a drawer at City Hall and forgotten it, which meant I wouldn't get to it until Monday at the earliest.

I helped Maurice and Fred with the dishes, thanked them for the good meal, and climbed the stairs to bed, reminding myself to get the letter into Colin Harrison's mail slot first thing during my lunch break Monday afternoon.

I began Saturday morning with a brisk walk in the hills above Sunset Boulevard, trying to clear my head and get some perspective on things. At the top, I spent a few minutes near a Neutra-designed house—walls of glass, jutting out dramatically from the hillside on stilts—while I caught my breath and took in the view, before starting back down. After a late breakfast at Duke's on the Strip, I decided to add another mile or two to my regimen before heading home. Minutes later, I found myself back in the Harper Avenue District, hiking east along Fountain Avenue until I reached Romanesque Villas.

I didn't kid myself that ending up in front of Templeton's apartment house was accidental. My last encounter with Tatiana Androvic was still eating away at me. I wanted to use Templeton as a sounding board for some things I'd learned in recent days and hear what she might have dug up in return. When I checked, I found her name and apartment number affixed next to an intercom button, which I pressed. A moment later I heard her voice through the speaker, asking who was there.

"It's me, Justice."

"Benjamin?" I heard the surprise in her voice. "What's going on? Are you all right?"

"I wanted to talk, that's all."

There was an awkward pause. "It's not really a good time."

"If you're still in your bathrobe and slippers, it's not a problem."

"How about lunch? I could meet you around one."

"I just had a late breakfast."

"Dinner then."

Suddenly, I got it. "Is someone with you, Templeton? Is that what's going on?"

"Come back in an hour. We can talk then."

"It's Dr. Ford, isn't it? He spent the night."

"Justice, please. Don't start."

"At least you can be honest with me, dammit."

"You seem a little edgy. Has something happened?"

"I stopped taking my Prozac, for one thing."

"Is that a good idea?"

"I guess we'll find out, won't we?"

"I don't like the way you sound, Justice."

"I had an encounter with Tatiana Androvic that didn't exactly cheer me up. I was hoping to share it with you."

"Like I said, it's not a good time."

"Fine, we'll do it later. Just do me one favor, will you?"

"If I can."

"Tell Dr. Ford I'm on to his game."

"He's not here, Justice, so stop worrying about that."

"Just tell him, Templeton. No, never mind. I'll tell him myself."

"I'm not letting you in, not when you're in a mood like this. Call me later, when you've calmed down."

I turned away down the steps, but the fury had already taken hold and wouldn't let me leave. I paced the walk, trying to picture Templeton and Dr. Ford going out to a romantic dinner the previous evening, then shacked up together in her big bed upstairs through the night. I envisioned them waking up to some sleepy morning foreplay that had probably developed into some good old-fashioned bonking before the requisite shared shower and the playful patter over coffee. I'd bet he had the routine down pat, all the right moves in the right erogenous zones and the murmur of sweet nothings afterward.

Dr. Ford's an academic fraud, I thought, *willing to sacrifice Victor Androvic for some cheap publicity. He's used Templeton as his dupe, and now she's slept with the son of a bitch.* Part of me was furious with her, and part of me deeply concerned: It wasn't just Templeton's emotional well-being that was at stake now; her career was on the line as well. But another, even more disturbing, possibility loomed: I'd seen Dr. Ford sneaking away from Tatiana Androvic's apartment ten days earlier, when she'd been away. Sometime after that, deputies had discovered Bruce Bibby's stolen computer in the crawl space above her son's bedroom closet. If Dr. Ford had planted it there to reinforce Victor's profile as a murderer, it raised some chilling questions: *How far would Dr. Ford go to make sure Victor looked like the brutal killer the fake brain scan images made him out to be? Was he that desperate? Why? And if he was the one who planted that computer, did he also set Victor up for the murder of Lydia Ruttweller, to frame him as a multiple murderer in the making, further validating Dr. Ford's research?*

I clenched my fists, feeling my bile rise along with my rage, something I hadn't experienced for half a year, since starting the antidepressants. Something my therapist had said resonated in me: *Depression is rage turned inward. You've got to control the rage, Benjamin, resolve it.* I took a deep breath, reminded myself that getting angry, losing control, would only be counterproductive, while turning it inward would wreak a different kind of havoc. I tried to remember the lessons of the Prozac over the last few months, tried to recall the patient way I'd handled upsetting situations when I'd had the drug to settle me down, the lack of panic and turbulence I'd felt. *This will be a good test,* I thought. *I'll wait here for Dr. Ford. When he comes out, I'll confront him with the truth, calmly and purposefully. Then we'll discuss his options and the best way to proceed, so that he can rectify the injustice he's caused. I won't scream at him, threaten him, or use him as a punching bag, the way I've too often handled vexing matters in the past. I'll behave like a normal man should, and help bring things to a positive resolution.*

So I stood outside the entrance to Romanesque Villas and waited. For nearly forty minutes, people came and went, out to play tennis or run errands or catch the late Saturday morning *shabbas* at the synagogue. Dr. Ford was not among them. I was thinking about leaving, and peered through the glass and across the lobby one last time, when I saw two people step from the elevator. One of them was Templeton.

They embraced briefly, exchanged light kisses, and said awkward good-byes with the blissful smiles of newly minted lovers. Templeton laughed, looking a bit embarrassed by the whole thing. Then she retreated into the elevator while her companion turned toward the doors, coming in my direction, with the strong set to the shoulders and the unmistakable sturdy gait so characteristic of Mira De Marco.

Detective De Marco walked briskly from Romanesque Villas and continued east along Fountain Avenue, while I emerged from hiding among the shrubbery.

I followed discreetly, intending to ask her some questions but wanting some time first to sort through my emotions and get my head together. For one thing, I was profoundly embarrassed for the vitriol I'd spewed about Dr. Ford over the intercom, only to learn that he wasn't with Templeton at all. I'd obviously given Templeton far too little credit for resisting his oily advances. I also felt immense relief that she'd be spared any heartbreak when she learned that Ford was such a fraud and scoundrel; finding out that she'd been used by him for publicity as she had would be a bitter enough pill for her to swallow.

Despite all that, I found myself smiling as I trailed Mira De Marco at a comfortable distance. The notion that Templeton, who loved men as unabashedly as I did, had fallen into the arms of another woman struck me as a wonderful blessing, one of those happenings in life that can leave one unexpectedly broadened and enriched, if the courage is there to appreciate it for what it is and not for what others judge it to be. Like so many of us, Templeton lived much of her life to please and impress people—her parents, her editors, her colleagues, her readers, even me. I was certain that was partly why she was so driven toward the false glory and hollow prestige of television, with its superficial rewards and journalistic bankruptcy. Perhaps a nice lesbian fling was just what she needed to ground her again, to remind her of what it was like to live life on one's own terms and not according to the expectations of others.

To my surprise, De Marco stopped at the Patio del Moro less than a block away. Familiar to anyone frequenting Fountain Avenue, the Spanish-style building had a distinct look and special charm; the owners had deliberately left its stucco exterior faded and in need of painting, allowing the old building proudly to declare its age and causing its decorative plasterwork, brickwork, and wrought iron to stand out in sharper relief. Constructed in the midtwenties, it was yet another West Hollywood building listed on the National Register of Historic Places, and one of the most photographed in the city.

As I approached, De Marco was slipping a key into the grated steel gate in the shadow of a dramatic arched entryway.

"Good morning, Detective. Out for a stroll?"

She glanced over, unperturbed. "Hello, Justice. Took you a while to catch up."

"You saw me?"

"The moment I stepped out of the elevator. I heard your rant over the intercom. You don't strike me as the type who goes away easily."

"It doesn't bother you, that I saw you and Templeton together?"

"Why, should it? We're both adults."

We stepped aside as another tenant came out. He and De Marco exchanged greetings, and he went on his way. "Rents can't be cheap in a place like this," I said. "How does a sheriff's detective afford it?"

"I got in years ago under rent control. Like a lot of folks in this town, I can't afford to move out."

"Maybe you and Templeton can find a place together. She's loaded, you know. At least her old man is. You could live in real style."

"I don't think that's going to happen."

"Why not? You two make an attractive couple."

"It wouldn't be hard to fall for Alex. She's a spectacular woman, in all kinds of ways. But I don't see her settling down with me, or any other full-blown dyke, at least not anytime soon. My guess is this is a one-shot deal."

"She must be attracted to you, Detective. Don't sell yourself short."

"Alex needs someone to listen to her, to give her comfort, to hold her in a way that most men don't understand. She's hurting, and I happen to be here."

"Awfully convenient, living just down the street."

"We bumped into each other one evening, realized we were neighbors, went out for coffee. One thing led to another." Her speech had become brisk, clipped; she was beginning to sound impatient. "What's on your mind, Justice? You must have followed me down the block for some reason."

"A few reasons, actually."

"Start with the one that's most interesting."

"How about Rocky De Marco?"

The name clearly caught her off guard, though she covered it well, with a cock of the head and a curious expression. "Who?"

"The guy whose snapshot you carry in your wallet."

She met my gaze straight on, without a blink, as if she was taking her measure of me, or what I might know. Then she said evenly, "Why don't we go inside, talk there?"

Mira De Marco's apartment was on the first floor, on the far side of a picturesque courtyard garden where the shadows were deep. A small dog came bounding to the door as she opened it, barking at me a few times before deciding to lick my outstretched hand instead. I used the bathroom while De Marco grabbed a plastic bag and walked the dog around the corner to do its business. When I'd finished mine, I made a quick survey of the cozy apartment, finding lots of polished hardwood floors and decorative tile, and not a stick of furniture that looked less than sixty years old, all of it restored, refinished, and polished to a fare-thee-well.

De Marco returned, brewed coffee for us, and invited me to settle with her in the living room. We sat facing each other in two fine old heavy wooden chairs that looked like they might have been discovered at one of the bountiful estate sales for which West Hollywood and the hills above Sunset were well known. The dog hopped up to drape itself over one of De Marco's legs after she'd crossed them.

"Rocky De Marco is my father," she said. "Is that what you wanted to know?"

"It's a start."

"My interest in Rocky is personal. I'd prefer to keep it that way."

"Why?"

"Because it's personal."

"You didn't seem reticent to discuss your relationship with Templeton."

"I'm a dyke, working in a department that has no problem with that, at least at the top. I don't make a show of it, but I don't conceal who I am, either. My feelings about my father are different. They go back a long way, and I haven't completely resolved some of them yet."

"How long have you been looking for him, Mira?"

She sat forward, looking intense. "How much do you know, Justice? And how much of that should I know?"

"I know that he disappeared in 1974, and nobody seems to have heard from him since. I know that you've ended up here, where he was last seen. The way you were studying faces so keenly at that special council meeting a couple of weeks ago makes me think you've been trying to find him, or at least trying to pin down which people in town might help lead you in his direction."

"You're assuming a lot, Justice."

"I think maybe you were keying on Lydia Ruttweller that night, because of her connection to your father thirty-odd years ago. Trying to connect some dots, maybe thinking about finally approaching her."

"Like I said, you're assuming a lot."

"You going to tell me I'm wrong, Mira?"

Her eyes flickered uneasily, and she reached for a pack of cigarettes. "You mind if I smoke?" I shook my head, and she lit up. "I'm trying to quit. The experts say it's harder than kicking heroin or cocaine, and I'm starting to believe them." She took a deep drag, held it in, then exhaled, looking less jittery though not quite relaxed. "How did you connect us—my father and me? Besides the photograph in my wallet, that is."

I told her about my landlords, Maurice and Fred, who'd known her father in the early seventies. I also mentioned the snapshot of Rocky De Marco and Lester Cohen that Maurice had shown me in one of his albums. "I've learned a few things about him," I said. "Not much, really, except that he was a good-looking guy who had a knack for making people fall in lust with him and probably used it to his advantage."

She settled back, sipped her coffee. Her eyes seemed to search beyond me, yet inwardly at the same time. Finally, she took a deep breath, and got started. "We lived in a small town in Missouri. Conservative, Bible Belt, dancing and rock 'n' roll strictly prohibited. My mother was a church person. My father wasn't."

"When was the last time you saw him?"

"Thirty-four years ago last month."

"Which means he disappeared when you were a little girl."

"I was four."

"He abandoned the family?"

"It was just the three of us. He left us in the spring of 1970, hit the road like a lot of young people were doing. I'd like to think he was coming back, at least to drop in now and then. It probably sounds foolish, but it would make a difference."

"You never heard from him after he left?"

"We got postcards—New York, New Orleans, Chicago, San Francisco. The last ones came from here. Scenes of West Hollywood, the studios, Sunset Boulevard, places like that. Sometimes he wired money. The cards stopped in 1974. That was our last contact with him."

"Did your mother try to find him?"

De Marco shook her head. "She said good riddance. Told me he had a bad streak in him, that the devil had gotten hold of him. Years later, before she died, she told me a little more. About the summer before he left, when I was three. We'd come out here on a vacation—Disneyland, the beaches, the usual sights. We also visited West Hollywood, although I don't remember anything about that. According to my mother, my father was never the same after that trip. She said he couldn't stop talking about the way people lived out here. You know, the openness, the freedom. Especially here in West Hollywood—'the land of fruits and nuts,' as my mother called it. She said he'd never been able to get the city out of his mind."

"So you followed him here, looking for him."

De Marco inhaled once more, then stubbed the cigarette in an ashtray and took up her mug again. "I was confused and hurt when he left us. No, that's not quite it—I was devastated, although I was too young to understand what was going on. It was as if he'd died, but there was no funeral, no grave to go to. Later, as I got older, I became angry about it. I hated him for abandoning us like that. I stayed that way for a long time. Still, there was a part of me that wanted to find him, have him back in my life. I ended up here in '85, thinking he might still be here."

"You did some investigating?"

"I started to, but didn't get that far. I got involved with a woman who resented my search for him. She'd been abused by her stepfather and an uncle and pretty much hated all men because of it. A hard-core separatist—there were a lot of dykes like that back then, who had put up with a lot of crap from men. For her sake, I stopped looking for him. She died last year of breast cancer."

"I'm sorry."

"We were going to have a baby, until she got sick. After she died, I decided I wanted to go ahead on my own, through artificial insemination. But I wanted to find my father first, to learn more about my medical history on his side of the family. So I started looking for him again late last year, not long after I made detective."

"You started to put some names together, people who'd known him?" She nodded, so I kept on. "Then this Bibby case came along, and you started to sense that your father might somehow be involved, given how many people were connected to both of them. That would explain why you've been so dogged about it, above and beyond the call of duty."

"I sense that Rocky's part of it, yes. I wish I saw it more clearly. I haven't given up."

"You spoke to Lydia Ruttweller about your father, before she was murdered?"

"My partner interviewed her about Bibby's death, but I didn't feel it was the right time to bring up her possible ties to my father. I wanted to keep my distance for a while, because of the same last name."

"You have some suspicions, though."

"I don't know quite what I've got at this point, but it can't all be coincidence."

"And now Mrs. Ruttweller's dead, along with Bruce Bibby. Who *have* you spoken to about your father?"

"Lester Cohen and Ted Meeks. Cohen admitted to employing my father but didn't say much beyond that. At one point, he cited attorney-client privilege, which didn't make sense, because he never represented my father legally. He conceded as much. Said it was just a slip of the tongue, then changed the subject."

"Interesting."

"I thought so."

"Colin Harrison?"

"By the time I got around to Harrison last week, he wasn't in his right mind. Meeks let me see him. He was actually very kind about it. But Harrison wasn't making any sense."

"I'm surprised you haven't spoken to Maurice and Fred. They both knew Rocky, especially Maurice."

"Their names came up. They're on my list of people to see." She leaned forward, shifting the subject. "So what's Roderick Ford done that's got you so upset?"

"I'll let Templeton explain that, after I've spoken with her about it. She deserves to hear it first."

"It's pertinent to the Bibby and Ruttweller cases?"

"Yes, but I'm not sure yet just how pertinent."

"I know you don't want to hear this, Justice, but right now, I don't see a better suspect than Victor Androvic."

"That's what bothers me."

"What do you mean?"

"It's all too neat, too perfect."

"We checked the Web site he gave us for the escort agency he claims he worked for. It's gone, erased from the Internet, virtually untraceable to anyone who might help him."

"Makes sense," I said. "The news that you'd arrested him for murder probably scared them into hiding."

"I suppose it's possible. It doesn't help him, though, does it?"

"Tell me something, Mira. Did you ever find one of Victor's business cards in Bibby's apartment? He told me he always left one behind with a new client, trying to drum up business on the side."

She shook her head. "We didn't find anything like that."

"You're sure?"

"Believe me, if we'd found more evidence that Victor Androvic had been at the crime scene, I'd remember it."

"That doesn't make sense. He said—"

"It makes perfect sense," she said. "He'd be awfully stupid to kill a man and leave a business card behind, wouldn't he?"

I faked an agreeable smile. "Of course. You're right. I hadn't thought of that."

"Victor may have been there on a date. But there was also a burglary, remember? That computer we found in his apartment. That may be why he was really there."

"Twenty bucks says there was nothing on the hard drive."

"It had been erased, yes."

"So a twenty-year-old kid who turns three-hundred-dollar tricks kills a man for an outdated computer that's not worth squat to anyone but Bibby. It turns up hidden in the suspect's apartment after he's arrested, with all the files wiped clean. You don't find that just a little bit odd?"

"I find it perplexing. That doesn't negate the evidence against Victor. He's still our best suspect."

"And if you don't come up with a better suspect, you go with the one you've got. The D.A. indicts him and puts him on trial, where the circumstantial evidence is overwhelming. It's a slam dunk for the prosecution."

"That's how the system works sometimes."

"He'll get the needle, Mira. If not for Bibby, then for Lydia Rutt-weller, because that one had to be planned."

"I said I've got a suspect. I didn't say I'd closed the case."

"What about that brick missing from the display in Bibby's apartment?"

"You noticed that, did you? We figure the perp grabbed it in a fit of rage and used it to crush Bibby's skull. The autopsy findings support that theory. The indentions in the skull, and bits of material embedded in the flesh. We assume he took the brick with him, to get rid of evidence."

"He went down the hall, selected the brick as his weapon, removed it from the shelf, came back to the living room, and used it to batter Bibby to a bloody pulp?"

"We think Bibby had the brick with him, next to his computer, when the perp showed up. Forensics puts it on the desk with a high degree of certainty."

"What would Bibby be doing at his desk with that brick?"

"Another interesting question," she said, "although I'm not sure how it figures into our investigation, or in the evidence against Androvic."

"Motive?"

"Homosexual rage, a young prostitute disgusted by what he's

just done, taking it out on the client. Not the first time it's gone down that way."

"That doesn't explain Lydia Ruttweller, does it?"

"Motive's nice, when you can nail it. But it's not a requisite for conviction." She paused, fiddling with an unlit cigarette. "Now you tell me something, Justice. What is it about this Androvic kid that has you rooting so hard for him?"

I smiled sourly. "Sorry, Detective—that's personal." I put my mug down and stood. "Thanks for the coffee and the conversation. It's been enlightening."

The dog jumped down as she rose to her feet. "I'd appreciate anything you can tell me about my father." When we reached the door, she added quietly, "It would mean a lot to me. An awful lot."

"I'll keep that in mind," I said.

TWENTY-SEVEN

Alexandra Templeton moved tensely about her four-poster bed, tucking in the sheet corners like a Marine recruit getting ready for inspection. I'd just filled her in about Victor Androvic's true parentage and Dr. Roderick Ford's duplicity, according to Tatiana Androvic's version of things.

Templeton hadn't responded. Instead, she'd busied herself with making up the bed, no doubt wishing her feelings could be as orderly. She pulled up the spread, fashioned a perfect fold at the top, fluffed a pillow, and arranged it carefully in place.

Finally, she stopped, staring across the room at nothing in particular. "If what you've told me checks out, I've made a terrible mistake. A stupid, unforgivable mistake."

"Some mistakes can be rectified," I said. "Think of it this way. You made Dr. Ford famous, and now you get to knock him down and kick him around for a while. Isn't that the way journalism's supposed to work?"

She looked straight at me. "It's not funny, Justice. If what Mrs. Androvic says is true, then I've hurt her son and allowed myself to be used by Dr. Ford. I've showed terrible judgment. Professionally, it's a disaster."

"He wouldn't be the first guy who lied to a reporter. You were just repeating what he told you."

Her smile barely registered. "Thanks for trying to cheer me up."

I patted the mattress. "So tell me, is this where you and Mira De Marco got down and dirty last night?"

"This is no time to be talking about things like that."

"You're embarrassed?"

"Not at all. What happened between Mira and me is private, that's all."

"So what's it like being with another woman, Templeton? You know I won't give up until you tell me."

Her look grew coy. "Let's just say I have a new appreciation for the shape and suppleness of the female form. As well as pleasurable alternatives to the penis."

"So men *are* becoming expendable."

"I can think of one I'd like to make expendable—Roderick Ford. Fluff that pillow, will you?" I did as I was asked, placing the pillow next to the other one, while she smoothed the bedspread. "I've learned a few things about him myself," she went on, "which may explain some of what he's done."

She wiggled her index finger, beckoning. I followed her across the hall to a second bedroom, which she'd set up as an office. She sat at her desk in front of her PC, calling up a document. "It came this morning attached to an e-mail from a source at the university. I opened it shortly after Mira left. Why don't you look it over while I fix myself something to eat? I'm famished."

"Who wouldn't be, after all that hot female-on-female sex?"

She punished me with a glare on her way out, while I took her place at the PC. The document on the screen ran to half a page, which I scanned in under a minute. Basically, it confirmed with specifics what I'd vaguely suspected: that Dr. Roderick Ford was not only desperate to get new funding for his research, but was also up for tenure as a professor, a controversial educator relatively new to the university and not terribly popular with his peers. To make matters worse, he was going through a divorce that was sure to cost him a bundle in alimony and child support. Unless he was granted tenure and the job security that came with it, he'd be in danger of tumbling into academic decline and personal bankruptcy. Motive enough to fake his research findings and use them to enhance his public image, I thought. But was it enough to drive an egomaniac like Dr. Ford to take two lives and devise an elaborate plan to frame an innocent man for the murders? It wasn't that farfetched; plenty of others had committed murder for far less.

"You've read it?" Templeton came back into the room, digging a spoon into a bowl of granola, blueberries, and skim milk. I nodded. "How could I be such an idiot," she asked, "to swallow his line so easily?"

"He was pretty persuasive. His science may even be sound. He's just in too big a hurry to get the right results and sell them to the public."

"You can say what you're really thinking, Justice. That I've been behaving selfishly, thinking less about the integrity of my reporting than making a move into television. That I've been arrogant and irresponsible, thinking what a hotshot I am."

"OK, you've been behaving—"

She pressed a finger to my lips. "You don't have to actually say it. The question is: What am I going to do about it? Should I just resign and get it behind me?"

"If you resign, you'll *never* get it behind you."

"Then what, Benjamin? I'm at a loss. I really am."

"Given that you're still a reporter, with the power of the *LAT* behind you, what would you like to do?"

She spooned some cereal into her mouth, chewing thoughtfully. "Put him back on the front page. Expose the bastard, even if it means taking my lumps." She came around behind me, bending over my shoulder to study the screen. "This memo mentions a symposium he's giving this weekend at the Bel Age. Maybe I should show up and offer him the kind of coverage he loves. Only this time, I'll be in charge of spin control."

I studied the date and time. "You'd better hurry. The symposium's today, and it started about an hour ago."

I felt her hand on my shoulder. "Thanks for being so good about this, Justice. You could have really rubbed my nose in it." She kissed my bald spot and made a hasty exit for the shower, while I printed out the document for her files.

Le Bel Age sat near the top of North San Vicente Boulevard just below Sunset, a modern hotel whose undistinguished exterior belied the refinement within, with unparalleled views across the city from its upper floors and rooftop sports bar. In addition to nearly two hundred residential rooms and suites, it served as the city's premiere conference hotel, only steps from the colorful Sunset Strip. A sign in the lobby announced Dr. Ford's symposium:

"PROBING THE VIOLENT MIND IN THE 21ST CENTURY:
GENETIC LINKS BETWEEN PARENT AND CHILD"
PRESENTED BY DR. RODERICK FORD
SATURDAY, MAY 22, 11 A.M., THE SALON ROYAL ROOM

We found the Salon Royal Room on the first floor, where the symposium had been moved at the last minute from a smaller room to accommodate a large media turnout. From a doorway, we could see Dr. Ford up on a stage behind a podium, a microphone just below his chin; his wavy, salt-and-pepper hair looked recently coiffed, and his European suit appeared to be the latest cut. Behind him, projected onto a Power Point screen, were the brain scan images of Victor Androvic and Leonid Androvic. Just as we arrived, Dr. Ford was winding up his presentation by taking questions from reporters with his usual bravura, as the still cameras flashed and the video cameras hummed.

"You could make mincemeat of him," I said, "skewer him while he's up there in the spotlight, getting all this coverage."

"Too early." Templeton's voice was firm, self-assured—she was starting to sound like her old, resourceful self again, taking charge. "I'd rather watch him climb as far out on a limb as possible before I chop it off. Let him make his claims and do his boasting for the record. When he falls, the landing will be that much harder."

"I like what I'm hearing, Templeton. You sound positively ruthless."

"Maybe I'm getting my chops back." She grinned. "It feels pretty good."

We waited another twenty minutes until the whole thing was over and the audience and media were filing out past us. Dr. Ford remained at the foot of the stage, chatting with admirers and media stragglers. His eyes lit up as he saw Templeton approach, although he looked less happy when he spotted me a step or two behind. He answered a few more questions, got rid of the laggers, and turned his attention to Templeton, flashing his fine dental work and turning on the charm. She removed a tape recorder from her handbag and asked if she might offer a few questions of her own, now that she had him all to herself.

"You can have me all to yourself anytime you want, Alexandra."

"Everything on the record, Dr. Ford?"

He chuckled. "For you, Alexandra, nothing less."

"Let's start with the fact that Victor Androvic was fathered not by Leonid Androvic but by another man."

Dr. Ford managed to keep his smile propped up, but the wattage dimmed considerably. "I beg your pardon?"

"Mrs. Androvic claims that Victor is the love child of an extramarital affair, that he's unrelated to Leonid Androvic by blood." Then Templeton took liberties with the truth the way cops sometimes do when interrogating suspects, to see what they might pry loose. "We're awaiting the results of DNA tests on blood submitted by Victor and the man who admits to being his real father."

Some of the color drained from Dr. Ford's salon-tanned face. "That's not possible. You must be misinformed."

"Why would Tatiana Androvic lie about something like that?"

"Obviously, to help her son, now that he's in trouble."

"And if the DNA checks out? What then, Dr. Ford? How will you explain these brain scan pictures you've been using to promote your research?"

"Surely, you're not going to write about this? On the word of a poor immigrant woman who has no standing of any kind?"

"Not until I see the DNA results and have conclusive proof."

"But, but—" A bead of perspiration trickled from beneath one of Dr. Ford's George Clooney sideburns. "This—this is all nonsense."

"You doctored the image from Victor Androvic's brain scan, didn't you?"

"Absolutely not!" He tried to muster some of his old authority, but couldn't quite manage it. "My research and my findings are above reproach."

"You'd be willing to submit all the original images for independent investigation, by technical experts selected by my newspaper? To prove, one way or the other, whether they've been tampered with?"

"I find this line of questioning insulting. It's beneath you, Alexandra."

She thrust the microphone closer. "So the answer to that one is no?" He stared at her like a man watching his life and career crumble before his eyes. Templeton's voice got tougher. "The game's up, Dr. Ford. It's a matter of time before the truth comes out." His eyes were everywhere by then, and he clasped his hands to stop their trembling. "I'm willing to cut a deal," Templeton went on. "Give me an exclusive interview right now, coming clean on everything, and I'll hold the story until Monday, giving you time to consult an attorney and prepare for the worst."

"They tricked me!" Dr. Ford's voice sounded pathetically desperate. "Victor Androvic and his mother used me. They took my money, my friendship. They never told me Victor had been fathered by another man."

Templeton turned, gesturing toward the brain scan images that rose ten feet high at the back of the stage. "Then you admit that these brain scan images *are* faked, that you doctored them to support the conclusions you wanted to reach?"

"Why would I do such a thing?"

"To get the tenure you desperately need and more funding to carry on your research."

He wrung his hands, looking disconsolate. "Yes, all right, I manufactured my results."

"How and where?"

"I used a digital lab here in West Hollywood, paid the technician to keep quiet about it." He named the lab and the technician, his voice quavering. "Victor and his mother duped me, don't you see?"

"So it was their fault?"

"I've been under extreme emotional distress. They saw that I was vulnerable, and they exploited that. You've got to remember, the boy's been convicted of a crime. Now he's been arrested for two murders. He never told me about his real father. They took advantage of me, and I made an error in judgment. Surely, you can see that."

"Victor never knew who his real father was," Templeton said. "He still doesn't. He knows only Leonid Androvic as his father."

"Yes, but—"

"As for Mrs. Androvic," Templeton went on, firing her words at him like bullets, "she's reluctant to admit the truth. She insists that you're the one who used them." She looked to the stage again, just as someone shut off the Power Point projector and the big images disappeared. "Explain to me how they've benefited from what you've done, Dr. Ford. I'll be happy to share it with our readers."

He swallowed with difficulty, found a handkerchief, patted away the perspiration on his forehead. "My God." He stared at her tape recorder, looking ill. "My children will read this. Please, I beg you, consider their feelings."

"Tell me everything, Dr. Ford. Like I said, it will buy you an extra day, give you time to talk to your kids, prepare them for what's coming."

"You know what this will do to me, don't you?"

"I have a pretty good idea."

I stepped forward, eyeball to eyeball with him. "Nothing worse than what you've done to Victor and his mother," I said. "Not to mention what you may have done to Bruce Bibby and Lydia Ruttweller."

Dr. Ford looked at me like I was crazy. "What?"

Templeton's expression was nearly as skeptical—I'd never broached with her the possibility that Dr. Ford might be more than just an academic con man.

"Think about it," I said, keeping a bead on Dr. Ford. "I saw you sneaking away from Tatiana Androvic's apartment last week. It wasn't too long after Lydia Ruttweller was murdered and Victor Androvic was arrested that deputies discovered Bibby's stolen computer in the Androvic's apartment."

"You think I had something to do with those murders?"

"You had reason to want Victor Androvic suspected, to help validate your findings. You're certainly cold and calculating enough to have set him up."

"For God's sake, I'd never kill anyone!"

"You've all but killed Victor Androvic with what you've done to him," I said. "You've destroyed his reputation, and certainly his spirit."

"I'm telling you, I had nothing to do with those two deaths!"

"What were you doing that day at the Androvic apartment?"

He turned away, ran his fingers through his hair, then turned back to face us, a picture of despair. "Tatiana called me that morning, upset about the media interviews I'd given about Victor. I'd promised them before I began my research with Victor that I'd never reveal his identity. She told me the truth about his real father. As you can imagine, I was stunned, shocked. I went to see her, to beg her to keep it to herself. I was prepared to offer them money, as much as I could get together, even if I had to borrow. That's the only reason I was there. When I found she wasn't home, I left by a side gate. For obvious reasons, I didn't want to be seen. That's the truth, I swear." He turned toward Templeton. "You mustn't link me to these murders, not even through speculation. I can't have my children read something like that."

Templeton never blinked. "Tell me everything, Dr. Ford. Every important detail." She glanced at her wristwatch. "You've got thirty minutes."

He started talking and spilled it all—his impending divorce, tenure troubles, financial problems, all of it. He told her exactly when he'd come up with the idea to fake his research findings, using Victor Androvic as his guinea pig, and how he'd accomplished it. Templeton was masterful, framing her questions to force complete answers from him, even picking up some pithy anecdotes along the way, which always make a newspaper story more readable. When Dr. Ford was done talking, he sat on the edge of the stage, sagging, staring at his fine Italian shoes.

"I'm ruined. My life, my reputation—all of it's gone."

"You'll survive," I said. "Once you hit bottom, it's all up after that."

He raised his stricken eyes, just barely. "How can you be so sure?"

"I've been there," I said.

From Le Bel Age, Templeton and I headed for the Russian part of town.

I drove so that she could stay on her cell, first to set up an interview with Tatiana Androvic, then to call the weekend news editor to discuss the article she wanted to break in Monday's morning edition. In past years, when Templeton had been on to an important exclusive like this, she'd be almost giddy with excitement, placing as much value on the personal glory of breaking the story as on the story itself, the way I'd often reacted when I was still green as a journalist. Now she seemed more grounded, more calmly professional, though no less determined to get the story and get it right. It looked like she was almost back from the long nightmare that had started with Joe Soto's murder, and maybe even stronger than before.

We parked on the street and crossed the courtyard of Tatiana Androvic's apartment house toward her unit located around the back. As we reached the corner, a woman's anguished cry pierced the early-afternoon quiet. Templeton and I exchanged a brief glance, dashed around the corner, and cut along the row of apartments at the rear until we reached Tatiana's door. It was a warm day and she'd left the door and all her windows open, allowing her ungodly wail to issue forth. Templeton and I stepped in to see Mrs. Androvic standing near the kitchen, still dressed for *shabbas,* clutching a telephone receiver to her chest, her mouth agape as her horrible scream went on unchecked. Before we reached her, several neighbors had rushed past us to her side, trying to calm and comfort her, and find out what was going on. She spoke to them in Russian, a flurry of words that meant nothing to us, beyond the obvious hysteria with which they were delivered.

Templeton took the receiver, carried the phone to a corner, and asked the voice at the other end what he'd just told Mrs. Androvic. As she listened, she opened her handbag, found a notebook and pen, and started jotting notes. A minute later she hung up and informed me that Victor Androvic had hanged himself that morning in his jail cell. He was alive, she said, but in a coma.

TWENTY-EIGHT

Victor Androvic's suicide attempt failed to make the local evening news, and ran only as a news brief in the B Section the next morning in the Sunday *L.A. Times*. If there'd been good video, of course, the local news stations would have led with it, replaying it for days on end, with a warning before each airing about how graphic the footage was to make sure viewers stayed glued to their sets.

I spent Sunday trying to get my head back into the manuscript for my book, while Templeton worked downtown at the *LAT* putting her big story together for the next morning's edition. I gave up in the late afternoon, plagued by images of Victor that emerged in my imagination; I kept seeing him hanging by a knotted sheet in his cell, turning blue, eyes bulging, crapping in his pants while his brain shut down from lack of oxygen, before finally hanging limp and nearly lifeless, another kid for whom the pain had become unbearable. I knew what it was like, wanting to die that young; I'd just never had the guts to take it as far as Victor had.

I put aside my memoirs and got out the list of names I'd fashioned a couple of weeks before, alphabetizing it to pass the time: *Tatiana Androvic, Victor Androvic, Cecelia Cortez, Dr. Roderick Ford, Colin Harrison, Ted Meeks, Detective Mira De Marco, Tony Mercury, Trang Nguyen, Lydia Ruttweller*. Between Victor Androvic and Cecilia Cortez I inserted the name Lester Cohen. Between Trang Nguyen and Lydia Ruttweller I added the name Chas Ruttweller. An even dozen, all linked, directly or indirectly, to Bruce Bibby.

As dusk fell, I was still studying my list, searching for closer connections or for something I'd overlooked, some obscure detail I'd stumbled across in recent weeks but had failed to see for what it was or might be, when I heard a knock on the door. When I opened it, Maurice was standing there in his gardening clothes, the pants soiled at the knees.

"We just got a phone call," he said. "Colin Harrison passed away this afternoon. Natural causes, from the Alzheimer's. I thought you'd want to know."

"I appreciate it, Maurice."

"We'll probably send flowers. Would you like us to include your name?"

"I don't think so, Maurice. I didn't really know the man."

When he was gone, I returned to my list, focusing on Colin Harrison's name. He was here a few hours ago, and now he was gone, forever. Gone like Bruce Bibby and Lydia Ruttweller, though without the terror and violence. At least now Ted Meeks had a chance to save Harrison House from the bulldozer, I thought, the way he'd secretly been trying to do—assuming Harrison had left the Sherman cottages to the man who'd cared for him to the end.

Templeton's piece exposing Dr. Roderick Ford as a sham ran four columns, front page center, in the Monday morning *LAT*. Her editors also gave her a generous forty inches of jump inside that included a reprise of Dr. Ford's brain scan images, which he himself now characterized in his taped interview as doctored and fraudulent. The tone of Templeton's article was exactly what was needed—straightforward and professional—and an admirable demonstration of journalistic self-control. She wisely let the facts and his admissions speak for themselves. For all intents and purposes, Dr. Ford was a ruined man.

A sidebar ran front page with the opening paragraphs, briefly mentioning Victor Androvic's suicide attempt and the fact that he remained in a coma, in critical condition. At midday, a distraught Tatiana Androvic called me at City Hall as I finished up the photo

255

captions for the brochure. She'd contacted Victor's father in Chicago, she said, and Mr. Komskaya had agreed to provide blood for testing, to prove his paternity; to her surprise, he'd also agreed to assume a role in Victor's life, if that was what Victor wanted.

"He finally has this chance to know his real father," Mrs. Androvic said, "and now he lies in a bed, unable to wake up or communicate."

She burst into tears, and I did what I could to console her. When she'd gotten control again, she told me how desperate she was to visit Victor's bedside, if only to hold him one last time before he died. The sheriff's department had denied her permission, she said, and she pleaded with me to help. I told her she was talking to the wrong guy, that I had no clout in that area. If anything, I said, my name was anathema to much of law enforcement, because of my disreputable past.

When I couldn't bear her suffering any longer, I eased out of the conversation and hung up, feeling more at odds with myself and further from my Prozac safety net than ever.

Evening fell with a pesky wind kicking up and a chill in the air that was uncharacteristic for late May. I zipped up my windbreaker and raised the collar as I hiked up Olive Drive to the House of Blues, where Lester Cohen was throwing his fund-raiser for Tony Mercury, with tickets going for a hundred bucks a pop.

The House of Blues was located on Sunset Boulevard, a few blocks northwest of Templeton's new digs and directly across from the Comedy Store, which had once been the legendary nightclub Ciro's. It was dusk as I trudged up the hill, with a hush broken only by the rustle of leaves and the occasional distant horn up on the boulevard. A car was coming down the hill as I hiked up, and Cecelia Cortez waved to me from the window on the passenger side as they turned into the parking lot behind a line of other cars. As I got closer, I saw her looking past me and turned to glimpse a figure across and down the street behind me, staring hard in my direction—male, I was fairly certain, although the dying light prevented me from seeing him more clearly. In a flash, he ducked behind a tree and into its shadows.

"Someone you know?" Cecelia asked, as I caught up to the car.

"I'm not sure." I glanced back again, but the figure was nowhere to be seen.

Cecelia introduced me to her husband, Reynaldo, a big man a couple of shades darker than she whom I recognized from the family picture in her office. He told her he'd park the car while we went ahead into the club and catch up with us on the dance floor. Cecelia climbed out, and we watched him descend to the big lot past a marquee advertising upcoming acts: James Brown, Chris Isaak, Melissa Etheridge, Reverend Horton Heat.

"It's so big," Cecelia said, looking up at the three-story building. "Have you been here before?"

"A few times, with my friend Alexandra."

The House of Blues was a hulking structure built against the hillside to resemble an old bayou shack, complete with a peeling corrugated iron façade and crude, hand-painted signage to add a touch of Southern swamp "authenticity." Templeton and I had dropped in over the years for the popular gospel brunch on Sunday mornings, but I'd never ventured up for nighttime events, when an eclectic mix of blues, funk, and rock drew a younger, harder-drinking crowd. Just to the east, a long block away, I could see the towering Argyle Hotel lit from all sides, its pale exterior frieze and terrace luminous like frosted Lalique crystal against the darkening sky.

"I had a chance to look at the rough draft you turned in for the brochure," Cecelia said, as we took the steps. "I think you did a first-rate job. We'll need a few minor revisions, mostly for format. But otherwise it looks terrific."

"I'm glad I got it right."

She squeezed my arm affectionately. "I think Bruce Bibby would have been pleased."

We entered the Music Hall to the lively rhythms of a *tejana* band that performed its Texas-flavored Mexican music from the stage, which fronted the dance floor. A minute later, Reynaldo caught up with us and immediately started moving his feet to the music, his big body jiggling; Cecelia waved a quick good-bye to me as he whisked her away to join several dancing couples, most of whom were gay. Three bars wrapped around the dance floor, with a series of intersecting walkways and standing areas between the bars that were filled at the moment with well-dressed men and women, mostly white and sipping cocktails, who probably didn't know a *tejana* from a fedora. The big room had been designed to look like a funky dance hall, with lots of unvarnished wood for the floors and railings and primitive folk art on the walls. Over the stage was a portrait of a yogi master hanging between two slogans: UNITY IN DIVERSITY and ALL ARE ONE. I recognized a state senator and a couple of assembly members milling about, along with a few reporters, who were probably there as much for the free booze as anything else.

I cornered Cohen near the dance floor, chatting up an assembly-woman who was with her husband. When he spotted me coming in his direction, Cohen quickly ended his conversation, turning deftly at the last moment to put his back to them and separate us with his considerable bulk like the Great Wall of China. He extended a hand, thanked me for coming, and asked me how the brochure was developing.

"Finished," I said. "Except for any revisions Cecelia asks for."

"I can't wait to see it. I'm sure you did a fine job."

"She seems to think it's OK. For what it's worth, I included the Sherman cottages, gave them a third of a page."

"Not a problem." Cohen waved at someone across the room, then blew a kiss to two fortyish men two-stepping on the dance floor, before returning his attention to me. "To be honest, the Sherman cottages no longer interest me."

The music was loud, so I thought maybe I hadn't heard him correctly, and said so. He assured me I had.

"Ted Meeks contacted me this morning," he said. "Colin Harrison left most of his property to Ted, including those in the old Sherman district. Ted's taking them off the market."

"Does that surprise you?"

"Not really. I knew Colin was seriously ill and that Ted has a sentimental streak. From what I understand, he wants to restore Harrison House and move back in, living where he and Colin first lived all those years ago."

"That must be quite a blow to you, given your plans to build Casa Granada on the site."

"It was, for about two seconds. I told you, Justice, I'm a man of vision, a man of the future. I don't get stuck in one place very long.

Anyway, Tony's talked me into putting my money into a new home for low-income residents with AIDS."

"You don't say."

"The city has nearly a dozen homes like that already, but they can use another one. There's this crazy notion that AIDS isn't killing anyone anymore, or driving them into poverty, but don't tell that to those who've had it for fifteen or twenty years, with the lost work time and the medical bills piling up." Cohen smiled mischievously. "Not all of them can afford to move to Palm Springs and live out their lives listening to show tunes and sunning around a kidney-shaped swimming pool."

"You sound quite serious about this."

"Oh, yes, I have grand plans for the Lester Cohen House. I intend to build something functional but also architecturally significant that will outlive me and, with any luck, outlive AIDS as well. I'll leave it to the city for posterity, to house people in need, so a part of me lives on with it."

"Very noble of you, Cohen."

"Bullshit. It's for my ego as much as altruism, and we both know it."

"So Ted Meeks is suddenly one of the major property owners in the city," I said. "I guess his undying loyalty to Harrison finally paid off."

"Fortunately, Colin had his affairs in order. I saw to that."

"You drew up the trust that just went into effect?"

"My involvement was minimal. Colin knew exactly what he wanted, and how he wanted the papers worded, for Ted's peace of mind, and his own."

"Meeks knew what he'd inherit?"

"Oh, yes. Colin made sure of that. He's always dangled his assets like the proverbial carrot." Cohen chuckled. "I learned that thirty years ago, when I drew up my first trust for him."

"That would have been 1974," I said.

Cohen hesitated, as if caught in a gaffe. "Sorry, I shouldn't have mentioned it—attorney-client privilege."

"Harrison's dead," I reminded him.

Cohen offered me a mollifying smile. "Yes, but not Ted."

"You're saying that thirty years ago Colin Harrison had an earlier trust drawn up that named Meeks as his beneficiary?"

"I didn't say that, no."

"If it didn't name Meeks as a beneficiary, whom did it name?"

Cohen shrugged innocently. "Someone else, obviously."

"Someone's who's still alive?"

Cohen's eyes had gotten jumpy; again, not like him. "Not to my knowledge."

"Then I don't see why attorney-client privilege is a problem, especially since the more recent trust rendered the older one invalid."

"It's not something I really care to discuss. I'm sorry I brought it up." He resurrected his smile and glanced around. "Have you spoken with Tony this evening? He'd be pleased to know you're here."

"I'm more interested in that trust document Colin Harrison had drawn up back in '74."

Cohen's smile was reptilian now. "Have some food, Justice. Enjoy the music. It's been nice chatting with you."

He started to go, but I grabbed his arm. "Talk to me, Cohen." My eyes scanned the room. "Or else I start talking to some of these reporters."

"Take your fucking hand off me." I removed my hand. "Just who in the hell do you think you are, Justice?"

"Someone with an interest in certain issues. Issues that make good copy—sexual harassment, conflict of interest, that kind of thing."

"Is that some kind of threat?"

"I don't know, Cohen. Do you or your candidate feel threatened by issues like that?"

"Tony's comfortable speaking on any of the issues."

"Then he won't mind discussing his drunken escapade down in San Diego, when he grabbed Trang Nguyen's privates. I imagine there are a few reporters here who'd be interested in that one. Sex always generates attention. Mix it with politics, and you've got yourself a front-page byline."

Cohen snorted dismissively. "If there anything to that, Nguyen would have filed some kind of complaint a long time ago."

"That's exactly what Bruce Bibby and Lydia Ruttweller were pressuring him to do. They wanted him to lodge a lawsuit against the city to embarrass Mercury. But they're conveniently out of the picture now, aren't they?"

"If you're suggesting—"

"I'm suggesting that as a lawyer and developer who does considerable business in West Hollywood, you've gone to great lengths to see that Tony Mercury gets reelected."

"I think he's an excellent candidate who's good for the city."

"And I'm sure you'd both go to great lengths to make sure nothing and no one interferes with that."

Cohen laughed. "You're suggesting we'd stoop to murder?"

"Do you both have alibis for where you were when the two murders went down?"

"As a matter of fact, we do."

"For the evening Bruce Bibby was murdered?"

Cohen cocked his head, his smile smug. "That's right."

"And the morning Lydia Ruttweller was found dead?"

"You'd better believe it."

"I do believe it, Cohen. I believe the two of you were in the sack together, doing what you do every Friday night and Saturday morning, after you pick him up in your sparkling white Bentley in dark alleyways that make it more exciting." Cohen's eyes burned with fury, but no words came from his mouth. "That would be a clear conflict of interest, especially if Mercury's been voting on projects that benefit you, and particularly if you've been giving him cash or other gifts." The color rose in Cohen's neck, but he still said nothing. "That's quite a story for an enterprising reporter, isn't it? Lester Cohen and Tony Mercury, carrying on a torrid secret affair, desperate to cover up their relationship, as well as an incident of sexual harassment that could damage Mercury's political standing. And the two people who most want the incident exposed—two people who opposed the sale of the Sherman cottages—are permanently removed as obstacles."

Finally, he found some words. "For you to suggest that we had anything to do with the murders of Bruce Bibby and Lydia Ruttweller—"

"The facts, as they stand, would be enough to at least fuel speculation on the eve of the election. I'm sure I could convince Trang Nguyen to talk to the media. Reporters can always use 'confidential sources' to cover themselves on your affair with Mercury. Forget about whispers of murder, Cohen. The sexual harassment and conflict of interest alone will sink your lover boy."

"West Hollywood's not a big enough city to warrant that kind of coverage."

"It is with a former porn star involved. Hell, they'd even be hashing it out on the cable talk shows, now that Bruce Bibby's national news."

Cohen showed me a clenched fist. "If I was a younger man, I'd beat the crap out of you."

"Smile, Cohen—people are watching, and Tony's coming this way."

Cohen lowered his fist and manufactured a smile as Tony Mercury came up. He shook my hand, thanked me for coming, and gave Cohen's shoulder a squeeze. We made some small talk as if our steam room encounter had never happened until Cohen suggested there were other people Mercury needed to talk to. Mercury thanked me again and moved on, playing the politician. I watched him make his way across the room, turning heads and shaking hands as he passed.

"Such a fine-looking man," I said, "so personable and smart, with such a bright future."

"He's a terrific guy," Cohen said. "He's reinvented himself, shaped a new life, made incredible progress. Why would you want to ruin that?"

"To save someone else, if I can." I pinned Cohen with my eyes. "So how is the Greek Stallion in bed, Lester? And what does it cost you to keep him there, when he's not off on city field trips, putting his paws on younger men?"

Cohen ran a hand over the smooth dome of his head, straightened his tie, buttoned his jacket. Then he said, "Not here. Outside, where it's more private."

The heavy door to the Music Hall closed behind us as we stepped outside, cutting off the festive *tejana* sound.

"This way," Cohen said.

I followed him up wooden steps that led past the second-level restaurant toward the members-only Foundation Room at the top. Just below us, to the south, was the parking lot; beyond that, the city lights. I zipped up my jacket against the wind that blew stronger up here, following Cohen to a landing just below the Foundation Room, where we were alone. He faced me, with my back against the wooden railing and a three-story drop behind that.

"So what is it, Justice, that's so important for you to know?"

"I told you—this trust Harrison had you draw up thirty years ago. I'd like to know the details—whom he named as beneficiary, why he later changed his mind, anything else that might be relevant."

"Relevant to what?"

"That's what I haven't figured out yet. I'm still fishing."

"Why?"

"I had an editor once named Harry Brofsky. He told me that if you went fishing enough in the right places, you were bound to reel something in."

"You're a strange man, Justice." He looked me over, letting his eyes linger. "Attractive, but altogether odd."

"You going for the bait, Cohen? Or should I go back down and start spilling the beans to those tipsy reporters?"

"There's something I want in return."

"What's that?"

"You'll find out after I've told you what you want to know."

"Not such a good deal for me."

"It's a small price I'll ask. Inconsequential, really."

"You don't really have much leverage here, Cohen."

"That's the point. I need to get something out of this. I'm a businessman, after all. I have my pride. Humor an old man, Justice."

I smiled, despite myself. "OK, Cohen. Now talk."

"It was early '74, a few years after the Stonewall riots in New York that ignited gay lib. Closet doors were flying open all across the country. We were organizing, marching in the streets, demanding our rights. The bars were filled almost every night. Clubs where men had never been allowed to dance together were finally getting dance permits. The bathhouses were packed with men who'd been forced their entire lives to repress their sexuality, to hate themselves for being attracted to other men."

"Which is where you made your money," I said.

"Why not? I saw opportunity, I went after it. It's the American way."

263

"Go on, Cohen, get to the point."

"It's hard for someone as young as you to realize what a heady time it was, how exhilarating. In certain neighborhoods, you could meet a man at the supermarket or on the street and talk to him openly. You could make a date, make a new friend, without worrying about losing your job or getting thrown out of your apartment or harassed by the cops. It was something queers had only dreamed about to that time but had never dared imagine might become a reality. It seemed like a fantasy come true, as if they'd unlocked the prisons and set us all free."

"It's interesting history, Cohen, but what's it got to do with Colin Harrison?"

"Colin came to see me that year about drawing up a living trust. He was worried that he might lose Ted Meeks to another man. Colin was the jealous type, incredibly possessive. Ted was a bit younger, quite attractive if you like the slim, pretty type. You have to realize, everyone was sleeping with everyone in those days, all the rules were being broken. Colin was facing fifty—a tough age for a man like him. His looks were going, his power was waning. He was terrified of losing Ted."

"I still don't see how—"

Cohen raised a hand to shush me. "Colin wanted me to draw up a fake document. Not exactly fake—a real trust, for appearances, but one that Colin never intended to sign. He made that very clear to me."

"Toward what purpose?"

"He named Rocky De Marco as his beneficiary."

I cocked my head in surprise. "Rocky De Marco?"

Cohen nodded. "De Marco had his eye on Colin. On his money, anyway. Ted knew that. He'd seen Rocky trying to charm Colin, and he knew how seductive Rocky could be."

"And Harrison, the domineering one, decided to use that to his advantage."

Again, Cohen nodded. "Colin had me draw up this trust naming Rocky as his chief beneficiary. He deliberately left it out where Ted would find it. He wanted to make Ted jealous."

"But Harrison never signed it."

"Of course not, it was just a ruse. Anyway, Rocky moved on, and that was the end of it. It apparently worked, because after that, Colin never seemed to doubt Ted's loyalty. They were closer than ever, and nothing ever seemed to come between them again."

"And no one ever heard again from Rocky De Marco?"

"I certainly didn't. I owed him a week's pay, but he never came around to get it."

"That doesn't strike you as odd?"

"He was a character. A drifter, the mysterious type."

"He had a wife and daughter, you know."

"Yes, Mira De Marco spoke to me about that."

"Don't you feel she deserves to know where her father is?"

"If I knew, I would have told her. But I don't."

"Are you sure about that, Cohen?"

He stepped closer, until I felt his big belly touching mine. "I just said so, didn't I?" I sensed the railing only inches behind me, and the open fall behind that. "I answered your questions, Justice. Now you owe me. We had a deal." I started to edge away, to get some space between me and the railing, but he shifted his feet, trapping me with his portly body. "I said there was a price to pay, remember?" He nudged me backward, until I could feel the rail press against my flanks. "I always want something for myself from any transaction. I'm afraid it's my competitive nature."

His hands came up suddenly, grabbing my face. I tried to ward him off but he pressed forward, pinning me tighter against the railing. Panic engulfed me; I grabbed for a post, something to hang on to, but couldn't reach it. A second later, he kissed me on the mouth, squeezing my face with his pudgy hands, making it last. It wasn't a bad kiss, all things considered; I'd certainly choose it over being pushed three stories to my death.

Just as suddenly, he let go and backed off, patting my cheek. "I've wanted to do that since the first time I laid eyes on you." His smile was small but satisfied. "One way or another, I usually get what I want."

I watched him trot down the stairs, straightening each cuff snappily like a Don Juan who'd just gotten laid.

"Benjamin, there you are!" Cecilia Cortez found me as I emerged from a restroom, after returning to the Music Hall. She rummaged in her handbag and pulled out a photocopied document. "I forgot to give this to you earlier. It's a copy of the receipt from the sale of the bricks you asked for—the salvage from the buildings at the old Sherman rail yard. Records sent it to my office late this afternoon."

I thanked her and told her I was on my way out.

"Going home so soon? I was hoping I could get you out on the dance floor."

"I'm afraid I've got two left feet, Cecelia. Thanks just the same."

She kissed me quickly on the cheek. "Thanks again for the great job on the brochure. I imagine we can find more work for you in the future."

She turned back to the dance floor, while I made my exit, past a volunteer who thrust a Tony Mercury campaign button into my hand. I found a bench under a light, left the button on the bench, and scanned the document Cecelia had given me. The sales receipt was dated 1972, and indicated that Colin Harrison had purchased the bricks when the railway barn had been demolished that year, to make way for the Pacific Design Center. From Bruce Bibby's notes, I'd learned that a hundred of the bricks had been set aside as historical souvenirs handed out to individuals with ties to the city, which would account for the brick in Bibby's apartment that had apparently been used to kill him. But that had left thousands of bricks unaccounted for and presumably still in Colin Harrison's possession, unless he'd used or unloaded them in the years since. I folded the paper into quarters, stuffed it into my shirt pocket, and climbed the drive up to Kings Road, pondering how to use it and what my next move should be.

That abruptly ended when I caught sight of Chas Ruttweller. He was standing directly across Olive Drive, no more than fifty feet away, staring at me like he wanted to pound me into mush. He didn't bother to hide this time, which afforded me a better look at him. He still had a sickly pall, as he had when I'd tormented him at the hospital, but some of his color was back. It also looked like his rage had survived his hospital stay, maybe even intensified after the grilling I'd put him through against his will. I could see it in the glower on his misshapen face and the coiled tension of his gorilla body and the clenched fists that hung stiffly at his sides, like the heads of two sledge-hammers that had eyes only for me.

This is not a good situation, I told myself. *Not a good situation at all.*

There was no point turning back into the House of Blues. I couldn't call the police. Chas had broken no laws, and there was nothing for which to arrest or even detain him; he worked in this neighborhood, after all, maybe even lived around here. I'd feel foolish asking for anyone's help, particularly Lester Cohen, or one of his event organizers. I didn't want to try to sneak out and drive off with Cecelia and Reynaldo Cortez, for fear of putting them at risk.

But I couldn't stand around all night, either, waiting for Chas Ruttweller to decide when he was going to pummel me to a bloody pulp. I could hear my heart thumping against my chest while my mind raced through my options, looking for a way out.

TWENTY-NINE

Conventional wisdom has it that when faced with the threat of physical harm, the target has two choices—fight or flight.

In my earlier, more reckless years, prodded by testosterone and foolish male pride, I'd usually opted for combat. But things were different now. I was older and wiser, and not in the best of health; I'd been battered, bent, and mutilated from too many such confrontations. True, I was only forty-five, which isn't exactly teetering on old age; but I was no match for a steroid-driven ape in his prime like Chas Ruttweller, either. My choices ran more along the lines of pee or flee.

That night, I fled.

The darker residential neighborhood below seemed problematic, so I turned quickly toward the hustle and bustle of Sunset Boulevard a hundred feet up. My plan was to dash across Olive Drive and head west along the Strip, past the magnificent Piazza del Sol—originally the Hacienda Arms, built in 1927—and into the well-lit Sunset Plaza district. Chas would be a fool to cause mayhem among the well-heeled shoppers and diners there; the cops would be on the scene in seconds, with a legitimate reason to arrest him. I figured that if I could lose him at Sunset Plaza, I'd continue on to the Strip's most famous and venerable clubs, the Whiskey-A-Go-Go and the Roxy. At that point, I could cut down the hill into the dark and angling streets of the Norma Triangle and get safely home.

But as I started across Olive, Chas charged brazenly up the street in my direction. So I turned abruptly back the other way, heading east. I dashed past the small shop where Zena, the clairvoyant and psychic, was advertising a ten-dollar special on a sandwich board out front, and continued down the long block past the Argyle. I glanced back to see Chas lumbering along the sidewalk, churning his Bluto arms as he closed the gap between us. Up ahead, on the other side of Sunset, the Chateau Marmont loomed in gothic profile, across from the tacky minimall where Nazimova's Garden of Allah had once stood. I took another look back and saw Chas so close that I could make out the grim expression on his face. He continued lurching forward but seemed to be tiring; his grimace appeared to be etched as much in pain and exhaustion as fury. All that extra muscle meant that his heart had to pump overtime to feed blood to those extra miles of capillaries, and it gave me hope. We'd covered only three blocks—a quarter of a mile—but Chas was clearly struggling, while my exercise regimen was paying off.

The next street ahead was Harper Avenue. I saw the street sign just beyond the Body Shop, the city's most popular straight strip joint, with its neon silhouettes of naked women. I broke into a sprint and angled around to Harper and down the hill. From the corner of my right eye I saw Chas make an effort to keep up, gasping and wincing as his big muscles cramped and taxed his overworked heart. Then I lost sight of him as I plummeted down the two blocks leading to Fountain Avenue.

I was pointed at Romanesque Villas, Templeton's place. If I could reach her intercom with half a minute to spare, I thought, she could buzz me in, and I'd be OK. I glanced back again but the street and sidewalk were too deeply shrouded in shadow to reveal anything clearly. I dashed past a succession of historic garden apartments dating back seven or eight decades—Casa Real, Villa Sevilla, Harper House, El Pasadero—dramatic structures rising with broad stairways above the street that looked like they belonged in Florence or Madrid. As I stumbled on, frightened and a bit deranged, their attractive forms became distorted in my mind, until they loomed over me, massive and menacing. The past bled into the present, dates and timelines collided, the façades of lovely old buildings blurred with the faces of dead people, anguished cries echoed among my footsteps, all of it somehow tied into these streets and this city, what I'd learned about it and what I still didn't know, creating a fearful landscape in my head. You think you know a place—a city, a neighborhood, a building— but they're no more knowable than people, as secretive as a false smile and a well-told lie.

Finally, across the street at the northeast corner of Harper and Fountain, the vine-covered walls of Villa Primavera came into view. Moments after that, I saw the outlines of Romanesque Villas just ahead, with its rounded upper balconies and antiquated fire escapes. I raced up the front steps and pressed the buzzer—five, six, seven times. Ten seconds passed, fifteen. I pressed the button again, more frantically. Half a minute that felt like hours ticked by. I pushed the buzzer in and didn't let up for several more seconds. No one answered.

Templeton, I thought, *why the hell aren't you home? Where are you?*

I edged cautiously back down the wide steps, up against a wall in the shadow of a hedge, and listened for footfalls on the pavement. All I could hear was the wind rustling the leaves and the soft rush of traffic passing on nearby Fountain Avenue. No footsteps, no labored breathing, no grunts from the muscle-bound lug who wanted to turn me into hamburger.

I ventured a few inches from the shadows. Glanced up the sidewalk, scanned the street. If Chas was there, I didn't see him.

I took a deep breath, stood up tall, feigned confidence, and stepped out to the sidewalk. I'd taken three or four steps when he sprang from a crouch behind an SUV parked at the curb. He grabbed me by the neck—both hands—and drove me back across the sidewalk through a ragged opening in a hedge until my back slammed against a wall, followed a split second later by my head. I pried uselessly at his hands, which felt like iron claws covered with flesh and fur. Panic started to overwhelm me as the air was cut off from my lungs and the blood from my brain. There are two places to go in a situation like that—the eyes and the gonads. I brought my knee up between Chas Ruttweller's legs like I was aiming for the moon.

His mouth opened wide and emitted a high-pitched squeal that didn't seem to have much air behind it. Then his hands loosened around my throat. For a brief moment he stood upright, staring at me bug-eyed, while the shock wheezed out of him. He doubled over and grabbed himself where the agony was focused in that unbearable way known only to men, then crumpled against the wall without quite going down, while I made my escape.

I stumbled across Harper Avenue, passing Villa Primavera, heading east again, trying to get my senses back. It didn't occur to me that Chas might be coming after me until it was too late. I heard his groans and looked back to see him staggering toward me on bowed legs, holding his crotch with one hand while the rage reclaimed him, driving him forward through his pain. He was on me again before I could break into a sprint, throwing me to the ground and missing with a kick as I crawled on my hands and knees into the cavelike entrance of Patio del Moro. I rose and tried the handle on the security door but found it locked before he spun me around and slammed me against the metal grating. He seemed to be taking his time, enjoying himself now that he had me trapped in a space the size of a small closet. I glanced to my right, ran my eye down the apartment numbers and the names until I saw Mira De Marco's. Before I could press the button, Chas seized my throat and pinned me to the wall, too close for me to bring my knee up again.

"You're dead meat," he said. "In your case, ground turkey."

"Really, Chas, we can't go on meeting like this."

"You're really funny, you know that?"

"Then why aren't you smiling?"

"I will be, when I rip your balls off."

My fingers crawled over the wall, found the button for De Marco's apartment. I pressed it and prayed.

Chas raised one of his sledgehammer fists. "I'm going to start with your face, and work my way down. You ready, wise guy?"

"You don't want to do that, Chas."

"Want to give me a reason why not?"

"I'm HIV-positive."

I felt him loosen his grip, just a little. "Bullshit."

"There's bound to be blood," I said. "Some of it will surely get on you. Maybe some of it already has."

He let go suddenly and backed away, staring at his hands, surveying his body. I heard Mira De Marco's voice through the speaker, asking who was there.

"It's Justice," I said. "Get out here quick. I'm in trouble."

Chas continued scanning his body like he hadn't heard a word between De Marco and me. He looked up, into my eyes, unsure of himself. "You're bluffing. You don't look like you got AIDS. You were moving pretty fast for a sick guy."

"You don't look like your liver's turning to jelly, but it is."

He raised a fist again to strike me, but hesitated. Next, he opened his hands at my throat as if to strangle me again, but hesitated once more. "You're fucking with my head, man."

"Why are you so angry, Chas?"

"What?"

"That rage that's eating you up inside. All that hatred, projected on to other people. It's all about your father, isn't it?"

"Don't you say a fucking word about him."

"You're hurting, aren't you, Chas? You feel empty, unfinished. Because you never knew him, never held his hand when you were a kid, never played ball with him. Never got a phone call, or a birthday card. And you know you never will."

His eyes roamed mine, wild but vulnerable, too. "What the fuck do you know about my father?"

"I'm an expert in fathers, Chas. I majored in fathers. You're not the only one, you know."

Again, he raised his fist, directly in front of my face, and I thought this time he might use it. "You fucking shut up, man."

"There's someone else, Chas. Even though your mother's gone, you've still got family."

He pulled his fist back, like he was cocking a gun. "What the fuck are you talking about?"

Just then, the door opened behind me. Mira De Marco stood there in a dark blue sweatsuit and running shoes, her gun in one hand, her badge in the other. Her eyes were on Chas and his cocked fist.

"What's going on here?"

"Mira," I said, "I'd like you to meet your half brother. Chas Ruttweller—Rocky's boy."

Chas Ruttweller didn't calm down right away. It took some soothing talk from Mira De Marco and some explaining from me, as he paced the sidewalk listening, while he decided if he wanted to risk arrest or getting shot so that he could finish manhandling me for all the trouble I'd caused him.

Finally, Mira spoke the magic words: "Is this any way to greet your half sister for the first time, after all these years?" The rage began to seep out of him after that, until he started to resemble a rational human being. We went inside. For much of the next hour, I sat in a chair across from Mira and Chas in her living room, while she sorted through a box of childhood photographs and told him what she remembered about their old man. I hadn't told them much of what I knew and didn't intend to, not just yet.

"If you know where he is," Mira told me, "you need to tell us, now. We've both been waiting too long."

"Before I do, I need a favor."

She sat next to Chas with her little dog in her lap and the box of old photos between them. "What's this favor that's so important?"

"Tatiana Androvic wants to visit her son. She's afraid Victor might die before she has a chance to say good-bye. I understand his real father's flying out from Chicago, to be there however it turns out. Problem is they can't get access."

"I just made detective last year. I don't have that kind of clout, Justice."

"You're respected. You're heading up a high-profile investigation. I imagine you might make some headway, if you really tried."

"It'd be a long shot."

"What if I have something else to offer?"

"I suppose that depends on what it is."

"Crucial evidence in two murder investigations."

She set the dog aside and sat forward. "Bruce Bibby and Lydia Ruttweller?" I nodded. Her voice took on an edge. "If you've got something, you'd better give it up. We're looking at obstruction of justice here."

Our eyes locked. "I couldn't care less about an obstruction charge, Mira. What I care about is that kid and whether he survives or not."

"You're playing with fire. You know that."

"If you want me to," Chas said, tensing up again, "I could beat it out of him. Give me a minute alone with him. He'll spill his guts."

De Marco smiled faintly. "Let's use that as a last resort, shall we?"

I stood. "Call me when you've got Mrs. Androvic and Mr. Komskaya cleared for a visit with Victor. Do that for me, and I'll tell you everything I know."

Hope flared in her eyes. "Including where we can find our father?"

"Sure, I'll throw that in."

"I'll see what I can do. No promises."

I made my exit, while Mira picked out a photograph of Rocky De Marco as a young man and handed it to Chas. He held it awkwardly in his big mitts, studying it with what looked like a mix of trepidation and longing. I figured they'd probably be sitting there awhile, late into the night, since they both had a lot of catching up to do.

THIRTY

I was at my City Hall desk, working on the revisions Cecelia Cortez had asked for, when Mira De Marco called the next afternoon. She informed me that Tatiana Androvic was in a deputy's patrol car with Victor's father, on their way to the jail ward at county hospital to visit their son.

"There's something else you'll want to know," De Marco said. "Victor Androvic came out of his coma during the night. They've upgraded him from critical to serious, and he's alert and stable. No signs of permanent brain damage that they can find."

"Thanks for going the extra mile on this one, Mira."

"Thanks for putting me in touch with my half brother."

"He's something of a mess. Think you can salvage him?"

"I can try. It might help if he knew where his father was."

"I guess that's my cue, isn't it?"

"You said you had some information for me."

"Don't plan on any fairy-tale endings, Mira."

She didn't respond for a long moment. Finally, she said, "I'm a big girl. I'll take what I can get at this point."

I asked her to meet me at the Sherman cottages in an hour, then called Templeton and suggested she join us.

It was nearly four when Templeton pulled to the curb in her Thunderbird convertible along Paul Monette Avenue in the old Sherman district. Nearly a month had passed since Bruce Bibby's murder, and May was heading to a close. June gloom was upon us early, casting the sky in somber tones and softening the shadows, which bled into the diffusive light.

Mira De Marco arrived a minute or two later, parking in a red zone the way cops get to do without worrying about tickets. She looked more intense than ever, her lantern jaw locked into place and her body stiff, as if she was preparing for something she'd already figured out, or almost. Templeton greeted her with a hug, but they didn't say much. Together, the three of us turned up the hill toward Harrison House, where an old yellow Mercedes station wagon sat in the drive.

"It looks like Ted Meeks got here ahead of us," I said.

Templeton glanced over. "Is that a problem?"

"I didn't plan it, but it's a nice confluence. I'm hoping he'll confirm a few things, clear up this whole mess."

We turned in at the gravel walk in front, then took another pebbly path that ended at the brick walkway leading to the rear patio and yard. Meeks was sitting on the edge of the circular fountain at the center of the patio, shoulders slumped, staring at the old house. He looked up from under his floppy brim as we entered the gate, but only for a moment, before his eyes returned to the peeling paint and weathered wood siding of Harrison House. When we got close he began talking, unbidden and out of character, sounding more genial and at ease than I'd ever heard him. The death of his longtime mate had apparently taken the starch out of him, which can happen.

"Colin and I lived here for twelve years," he said, keeping his eyes on the old Plains cottage. "Early in the spring of '67, that's when we moved in."

"It must have been an exciting time for you," I said.

"The first thing I did was put in a spring garden. Colin was on my case about that. He wanted everything unpacked and put away immediately, every item in just the right place. That's how he was. But I wanted flowers, color, and the scent of roses later when summer came. Every home should have a spring garden, don't you think?" He glanced up at me, with a countenance and manner that was almost warm. "I never wanted to move out, you know. I wanted to stay in this house forever, just Colin and me in our quiet little world."

I sat down next to him. "He wanted a bigger place?"

Meeks nodded. "Eventually, when he started to acquire more properties and make all that money. I didn't like big houses. I felt lost in them, found them rather lonely places. I worried that in a big house we might lose the intimacy we had, that it might escape into all the empty rooms. That probably sounds silly, doesn't it?"

"You're awfully talkative today, Mr. Meeks. Not like you, is it?"

"Colin and I always talked. He's gone. I have no one to talk to now. We didn't have a large circle of friends, Colin and I. It was pretty much just the two of us, which was fine with me."

I nodded in the direction of Harrison House. "It must have been difficult for you, leaving a place that meant so much to you."

Meeks smiled bitterly. "It's what Colin wanted. So out we moved."

"To the place you're in now, on West Knoll Drive?"

Again, he nodded. "It was something of a compromise—bigger, grander, but not terribly so. It's been a good home for us, but still—" His eyes returned to the weathered old house in front of him. "I would have liked it if we could have remained here, where we had our best years, when we were young and still discovering each other, building the foundation for the rest of our lives together."

I glanced around at the expansive yard, at the gravel walkways that started near the edge of the brick courtyard and meandered off among the untended and weed-infested gardens. "It must have been a lot of work, caring for a place like this. But then, you probably had help."

Meeks glanced over again from under his floppy hat. His eyes briefly studied mine before returning to the house. "I handled it all the first few years. I didn't mind. I was young, the labor was good for me, made me stronger. Colin had the money, you know. Taking care of our home was my contribution. Later, as I grew busier managing Colin's properties, I found it necessary to hire extra help."

"Rocky De Marco, for example?"

Meeks's eyes flickered in my direction, while he kept his face straight ahead. "A fellow by that name worked for us now and then, yes."

I glanced toward Mira De Marco. "I believe you've met Rocky's daughter, Mira, when she came seeking information about her father."

"Yes, we've spoken. And I spoke to her partner, the other detective, after the unfortunate matter involving Bruce Bibby."

"I believe Rocky worked for you until 1974," I said.

"Something like that. I don't recall exactly. He moved on without letting anyone know. He wasn't all that reliable, to be honest. No offense, Miss De Marco."

"From all accounts," I said, "he was quite handsome, almost irresistible."

Some of Meeks's snippiness returned. "I suppose, if one likes that type."

"Mira's also working the Lydia Ruttweller case, since it's tied to the Bibby murder."

"Yes, I read that in the newspaper when they finally arrested the Androvic boy."

"What a remarkable coincidence, don't you think, Mr. Meeks?"

"I'm not sure I follow."

"Mira's been looking for her father. She ends up here, where she runs into you, who knew him, and who also knew Bruce Bibby, Lydia Ruttweller, and Victor Androvic, the suspect in the two murder investigations."

"I imagine that's true of quite a few people," Meeks said, sounding irritable. "West Hollywood's a small town."

"I keep hearing that. Six degrees of separation and all that."

A moment passed in silence while Meeks let his eyes rove without settling. "I don't mean to be rude," he said, "but I came here to be alone." His voice grew solemn. "Colin's death—I'm sure you understand."

"You're probably thinking about renovations, now that you've decided to keep the place, rather than sell it to Lester Cohen."

"How did you know about that?"

"Cohen and I had a little chat last night."

Meeks studied the cottage again. "Colin wanted to sell it, for pragmatic reasons. I always supported him, of course. But now that he's gone, and the cottages belong to me—I've had a change of heart."

"If you supported him, Mr. Meeks, why were you secretly giving large sums of money to Lydia Ruttweller, supporting her preservation efforts?"

"That's preposterous. Why would I do something like that?"

"You tell me, Mr. Meeks." I stood, pulled an envelope from my rear pants pocket, and showed him the copies of the checks Lydia Ruttweller had mailed back to him. "You've given her at least eighty thousand dollars over the last couple of years to help her fight the sale and demolition of these cottages, including Harrison House. My guess is it was the bulk of her funding, essential for her legal battles with Cohen."

Meeks rose beside me, looking outraged. "Where did you get those?"

"A better question, Mr. Meeks, is why it's been so important to you to protect these properties from the bulldozer. So important that you'd oppose Colin Harrison behind his back, secretly funneling money to his most staunch adversary, and surely risking his wrath if he'd found out."

I handed the photocopies of the checks to De Marco, whose attention was riveted, along with Templeton's. Meeks watched the transaction, sputtering. "I—I love this old house. It's filled with memories. I couldn't bear to see it destroyed."

"You knew Colin was dying. You were trying to buy time, until he was gone. You figured he'd leave you the cottages, and you could put a stop to the sale."

He nodded rapidly, looking relieved. "That's right. Yes, exactly."

"You're sure there's not a less sentimental reason, Mr. Meeks?"

"I've answered your question. Why are you badgering me like this?"

I removed Lydia Ruttweller's note from the envelope and read it aloud. Templeton had her tape recorder on, picking up everything that was being said. When I'd finished, I reread the section in which Lydia Ruttweller promised a meticulous investigation into the Sherman cottage properties, particularly Harrison House.

Meeks grabbed for the piece of paper. "That belongs to me. Give me that!"

I passed it to De Marco, along with the envelope. "In his research, Bruce Bibby discovered something unusual about this property, something not quite right. That's what he and Lydia Ruttweller were going to meet and talk about. But he was killed the evening before their meeting, by someone who was terrified about what they might find out. Someone with something to hide, and paranoid enough to kill two people before it came to light."

"I have no idea what you're talking about," Meeks said. "Whatever it is, it has nothing to do with me."

"You went to Bruce Bibby's apartment on the evening of June 1 to pick up the rent, which was due that day. You made a habit of personally collecting the rent from tenants who had trouble getting out to post their checks. Bibby had just sent his e-mail to Lydia Ruttweller, informing her of a discovery he'd made of something amiss at Harrison House and asking to meet her the next day to discuss it. When you entered his apartment, he confronted you with what he'd uncovered. He even showed you the brick that had opened his eyes to what you didn't want him to see. The same brick you then used in a moment of panic to kill him."

"How dare you! I'm ordering you off my property." He pushed at me ineffectually. "Go, get off! All of you. You have no right to be here."

Mira De Marco stepped forward, nearly between us. "I think we should hear him out, Mr. Meeks. Why don't you sit?"

Meeks stared at her a moment, furious but slightly unhinged. Finally, he sat, hunching his shoulders, rubbing his hands together as if the weather were cold.

"Go on," De Marco said to me.

"Yes, please," Templeton said.

I paced the courtyard, pulling my thoughts together. "After you'd killed Bibby, you knew you had to cover your tracks. You're a smart man, Mr. Meeks, a skilled chess player able to think several moves ahead. You discovered Victor Androvic's business card in Bibby's apartment, advertising his escort service, so you knew he'd probably been there. You may have even found something on Bibby's hard drive with similar information. It's even possible that you'd seen him there on previous occasions, when he'd been servicing Bibby as a client. Victor's your tenant, after all. You may even have known or suspected that he was a hustler, and you certainly knew about his conviction in the smuggling case, which made him an ideal suspect for framing.

"You also knew you had to steal Bruce Bibby's computer. That's where he'd stored his data about the Sherman cottages containing the tidbit of information that you considered so damning and dangerous, as trivial as it was. You made off with the computer, making it look like a burglary. You took Victor's business card with you, because a killer wouldn't leave something like that behind. And you took the brick, not because it was the murder weapon, but because it's the central clue to unraveling this whole nasty mess, not realizing that it had been on a shelf in another room with a small information card to identify it after you were gone.

"A few days later, Lydia Ruttweller called to tell you she was returning all the money you'd donated and planning to personally investigate Bibby's claims herself. That was even more dangerous to you because she had a direct connection to the secret you'd worked for so many years to keep hidden. That was why you murdered her the next morning, when she arrived for her regular Saturday morning volunteer work at the Schindler House. Paranoid that you are, you were terrified that she'd already put two and two together, or soon would. By then, you'd called Victor Androvic on his cell and arranged for him to come to the Schindler House address for what he thought was a massage appointment. At some point, knowing he'd be arrested and his apartment searched, you used your master key to enter the Androvic apartment and plant the stolen computer in the crawl space above his closet. Of course, you'd already erased the hard drive and the damning data on it. Meanwhile, Dr. Roderick Ford had cast Victor as a monster, the son of a depraved murderer with the same genetic disposition, which fit neatly into your elaborate frame job. All in all, a brilliant series of moves that very nearly won you the game.

"The only problem was that I was hired to complete Bibby's work, and a computer specialist named Trang Nguyen was able to provide me with copies of the files you'd destroyed. Eventually, the same bit of data that Bruce Bibby had found so intriguing also caught my eye—after I'd literally stumbled over it on my first visit to Harrison House without really seeing it."

I glanced around the courtyard until I found one of the odd bricks dated 1896, pointing it out to Templeton and De Marco. "Notice the year?"

Meeks jumped up, red-faced and agitated. "Of course they're dated 1896! Why shouldn't they be? This house is pre-1910, you fool! It's a Plains cottage, not a Craftsman! What do these bricks have to do with anything? You're making no sense."

"In the original photos of these cottages, the paths were all gravel. There were gardens but no brick courtyards. Sherman was an undeveloped railway stop in those days. These were workers' houses, where bricks would be a luxury. These bricks came from the railway yard at Melrose and San Vicente." From another pocket, I extracted the copy of the sales receipt Cecelia Cortez had gotten for me from the records department at City Hall. "Colin Harrison purchased the lot of them as salvage when the railway buildings were torn down in 1972 to make way for the Pacific Design Center. You still had some around in 1974 when you needed them to build this courtyard and the walkway leading into it, hoping the dated bricks would fool people, since they appeared to fit into the same time period in which the cottages were constructed."

Meeks was trembling badly. "And why would I do that?"

"Because you had something to hide, Mr. Meeks, and you used these bricks to do it. Something you were afraid Lydia Ruttweller might uncover, given her relationship with Rocky De Marco and his sudden disappearance in 1974. You were afraid she might start thinking back to her torrid affair with Rocky and how he dropped from sight so mysteriously, and connect it to you and Colin Harrison."

Mira De Marco glanced from me to Meeks. "Is there something you can tell me about my father, Mr. Meeks?" Meeks shoved his trembling hands in his pockets and ducked his head, until his eyes disappeared beneath the brim of his hat. She stepped closer, lowering her eyes to find his. "Mr. Meeks?"

When he said nothing, I continued. "In 1974, Colin Harrison had a trust drawn up leaving all his assets to Rocky De Marco. Meeks saw it. He's the type who bottles up all his anger, who holds it in but finally explodes when his fuse burns down. When you saw that trust, it lit your fuse, didn't it, Mr. Meeks? It also struck genuine fear into you. You were terrified that you were losing the one thing that meant more to you than anything else in the world—Colin Harrison. You killed Rocky De Marco, buried him, and covered up the crime with a load of bricks whose date you thought would fool anyone who came around looking for a body."

De Marco stared at her feet. "My father's buried here? We're standing on his grave?"

The brim of the floppy hat came up as Meeks raised his head. His eyes had changed; they were no longer resentful or afraid, but filled with what looked like quiet resignation. He spoke softly, remotely. "Why did he have to come here? Why did he have to parade around, making eyes at every man and woman who had money, showing off his body, tempting them? He wanted Colin. He put his hooks into him. I could see it happening. Then I found that living trust, leaving everything to Rocky, and all my suspicions were proven correct."

"Then you did kill him," De Marco said. "You murdered my father."

He nodded, almost innocently, as if she'd surely understand. "He came by to do some yard work just as I was reading that document. Colin was away on business for a few days. Something came over me. His back was to me, there was a shovel. I grabbed it, swung it as hard as I could. I was surprised by my strength, by the force of the blow. It was just that one moment, when I lost my mind. I wasn't myself. Really, Miss De Marco, I wasn't."

"And the other moments," De Marco said. "When you crushed Bruce Bibby's skull? When you did the same to Lydia Ruttweller? Who were you then, Mr. Meeks?"

He sat back down on the edge of the fountain; his trembling had stopped, and a deep calm seemed to settle over him. He spoke as if everything he was saying made perfect sense. "Colin was still alive, you see, when Bruce Bibby made his discovery. Colin was even lucid from time to time. I couldn't have any of this come to light while he was still living. The shame, the scandal—it would have been unbearable for him. He was a proud man, you know." Meeks stared at the old house. "It was never about Colin's property or wealth for me. None of that really mattered. I only cared about it because it meant so much to Colin, because it kept me close to him. Colin was my life. Your father tried to take him from me. If you must blame someone for what's happened, blame your father, Miss De Marco. He caused it all."

"Not really," I said. Meeks's head came around slowly, as he regarded me curiously. "Colin had no interest in Rocky De Marco," I went on. "That trust he had drawn up was simply a ploy to make you jealous, to give you a scare and draw you even deeper into his control."

Meeks's eyes filled with disbelief. "What?"

"Colin was afraid of losing your affections. He had Lester Cohen draw up a document he never intended to sign. He left it where you'd find it and read it."

"That can't be possible!"

"Cohen told me himself, last night."

"Oh, dear God," Meeks said, tremulous again.

"You murdered Rocky De Marco over a worthless piece of paper. One small deceit that led to three murders and a lifetime of lies."

Mira De Marco stared at the bricks beneath her feet while the realization of what she'd just learned began to sink in. I was thankful Templeton was there; she put her arms around De Marco and held her for a couple of minutes, the way De Marco must have held Templeton during their night of lovemaking together. After that, De Marco pulled herself together, put Ted Meeks in handcuffs, and called for a backup unit and a crime scene team. She thanked me for helping her resolve the issue of her missing father, and I told her I was sorry I couldn't provide a better outcome.

"If you'll excuse me," she said, "I'd like to go find Chas and break the news to him before he hears it some other way. In a way, I was prepared for this. I imagine it's going to be harder on him than it is on me."

"At least he won't have to deal with it alone," I said. "I have a feeling that if anyone can help straighten him out, Mira, it's you."

She smiled a little and led Meeks out to the street, while Templeton used her cell to alert her city desk to yet another bizarre twist in the Bruce Bibby case, and to a murder confession she had on tape. While she scheduled a story for the next day's paper, I studied Harrison House, trying to envision it the way it had been when Ted Meeks and Colin Harrison had lived here—when the paint was fresh and the gardens blooming and the two men were forging a lasting relationship held together by jealousy, lies, and deadly violence. So many people were rootless these days, I thought, so disconnected and alone; families split apart, communities disintegrating, neighborhoods where residents didn't know their neighbors' names, unlike the good old days. But roots alone are worth nothing if they're poisonous, and the wrong connections can strangle as easily as they bind.

Templeton shut off her cell, slipped an arm around my shoulders, and tapped my bald spot. "So what's going on in that restless mind of yours, Justice?"

"I was just thinking that nostalgia's not all it's cracked up to be."

EPILOGUE

Ted Meeks lost his sentimental streak and sold the Sherman cottages to Lester Cohen after all, to raise quick cash for his defense against charges of first-degree murder. I guess that can happen when you find yourself facing the needle, or a slower death in a vile state prison.

For his part, Cohen returned to his plan to bulldoze the old cottages and build the most grandiose condominium complex in West Hollywood, while the city cut a deal for twenty-two low-income housing units on the east side in return, in addition to the AIDS housing Cohen had promised Tony Mercury. Mercury was reelected in a landslide, joined Alcoholics Anonymous the next day, and asked the forgiveness of Trang Nguyen as part of his twelve-step program, which seemed to lighten both their loads. A week before Gay Pride weekend, my brochure was published and widely distributed; people seemed to appreciate the information it provided and especially liked the vintage photographs, so I chalked it up as mission accomplished.

Victor Androvic recovered and was released from county jail, cleared of all murder charges. We were reunited when his mother insisted I come to the apartment for a Russian-style meal, and it was nice to see the kid looking almost happy, with the world off his shoulders. While we ate, he told me that the university had offered him a full scholarship, although he and his mother still planned a lawsuit for the way they'd been exploited so disgracefully by Dr. Roderick Ford. After dinner, Victor showed me a photo Tatiana had snapped of him with his real father, who'd promised that he'd become a meaningful part of Victor's life. I remarked on their close resemblance, and Victor commented on how he saw it, too.

My experiment with Prozac—getting off the stuff cold turkey—was a dismal failure. By the third week without my little green-and-orange capsules, I found myself slipping back into dark fits of serious depression and anxiety that seemed beyond my control. My therapist convinced me to wean myself gradually by decreasing my dosage ten milligrams every six weeks, under careful supervision, which is how I've been proceeding.

Frankly, I needed my emotional stability to deal with Trang Nguyen. He'd started following me around like a lost puppy, keeping a safe distance but studying me with sad eyes, and I knew I had a lovelorn stalker on my hands, going through his first real experience with grief and fixing on me as a replacement for Bruce Bibby. I finally took Trang aside and had a heart-to-heart with him, trying to convince him of the boundless future that lay before him. I told him how he was more likely to find the man he was meant to be with if he'd stop trying so hard and let it happen, in its own time and its own way—that it had happened for me that way years ago, even if the time we'd had together had been a lot shorter than we'd hoped for. Then I got a flash of inspiration and invited Trang to join me and some friends to watch the Christopher Street West Parade down Santa Monica Boulevard during Gay Pride weekend. Gay Pride always fell on the third weekend in June, concluding with the big parade on Sunday, which I noted with some irony was also Father's Day.

I hadn't attended the festivities in years. For one thing, I found it too big and grossly commercial—more than three hundred thousand people flooded into West Hollywood for the weekend, while the city cashed in on everything from beer and sexual lubricant sponsorships to vendors hawking all manner of tacky wares. To me, it was more a party than a political event, and I just wasn't interested. But Maurice and Fred always went, and Templeton was going this year because she was a new resident of the city, so I'd agreed to tag along. As a parade committee member, Maurice had seats in one of the grandstands along the grassy median where the Southern Pacific Railroad tracks had once lain, so at least we wouldn't have to fight for oxygen while wedged among the bystanders packed shoulder to shoulder along the sidewalks.

Unknown to Trang, I'd also invited Victor Androvic. Like Trang, he was single and nice to look at, and I figured it wouldn't hurt to throw them together and see what happened. If nothing else, I thought, they'd make a cute couple for a few hours, and Trang might gravitate away from me toward a more likely love target in Victor.

Everyone met at the house on Norma Place and we walked down to the boulevard from there. When we were in our seats, Maurice recalled L.A.'s first Gay Pride parade back in 1970, when a couple of hundred courageous women and men had marched down Hollywood Boulevard arm in arm, long before such demonstrations were fun, safe, or fashionable.

"In those days," Maurice said, "there were always people taunting, or spitting on us or throwing garbage from the sidewalk. The LAPD was supposed to protect us, but treated us like swine. We'd had to fight for our permit against the public objections of the police chief, you know. The cops smacked us with their batons or arrested us if we so much as put a toe over the white chalk line they'd drawn down each side of the street. The Christian extremists were there, of course, condemning us to hell. Walking back to our cars after the parade was quite dangerous—one never went alone, and we were frequently beaten up, especially the women." He sighed deeply, almost reverently. "Still, it was a glorious time. We were in the vanguard, there was change in the air, and we sensed it." He surveyed the massive crowds, the interminable line of floats and cars filled with dignitaries and celebrities, the marching groups passing with their banners and flags, the media covering the event from the ground and from the air. "But this is awfully nice, too." He put an arm around Fred, pulling him closer. "So many people, so much freedom, so much love right out in the open. Who ever would have thought, sweetheart, that we'd see this in our lifetimes?"

Tony Mercury rode by in his open Lexus convertible, sitting up on the seat with his shirt off and blowing kisses while giving the crowd a glimpse of his magnificent torso. A few minutes later, Detective De Marco appeared in another convertible with an openly gay male deputy and the sheriff, to advertise the department's nondiscriminatory hiring policy. She waved up at us, grinning, and we all waved back. I noticed Templeton staring after the car as it passed, and suggested her feelings for Mira De Marco might be deeper and more permanent than she realized.

"Actually," she admitted sheepishly, "I was staring at the hunky deputy behind the wheel, the one with the mustache."

An extravagant float rolled slowly by, carrying transvestites in full regalia and bronzed muscle men in thongs, followed by Gay Accountants United, two dozen men and women marching lockstep with briefcases, dressed in conservative business attire. But no group got a bigger roar of approval than the perennial favorite, the triumphant Dykes on Bikes. Maurice seemed to know most of the participants, naming them and waving grandly as they passed. "I just love living in a small town," he declared. "There's nothing quite like it."

Trang Nguyen and Victor Androvic had pretty much forgotten us by then. They were sitting close, off by themselves, and looked as if they'd hit it off. The way I saw it, Trang needed an unfettered companion, someone closer to his own age, to be there while he worked through his grief over Bruce Bibby's death, and maybe someone to take care of, which seemed to be his nature. Victor, I thought, needed someone to listen, to understand, to appreciate him just as he was, so that he might grow into manhood feeling OK about himself. I noticed they were already laughing, which is always a good sign.

For both of them, it was their first Gay Pride parade shared with someone they might just fall in love with; their sudden sense of place in a community of others like themselves, and the importance of that, seemed palpable, even though they might not have been consciously aware of its effect. As the crowd swelled, and the parade wore on, and the communal energy crackled in the June heat, Victor and Trang seemed to bask in a special aura, an unexpected state of grace, that only a gay man or woman who'd experienced it would truly understand.

Of course, one never knew for sure how it would work out between Victor and Trang. Maybe they'd just have a fling, and it would be over after a one-night stand or a couple of dreamy dates, before reality set in or temptations drew them apart, the way it so often is with youthful couplings of all kinds. Maybe they'd be together forever, like Maurice and Fred. The point wasn't how long it would last. They deserved a chance to find each other, to test the connection, to have the same shot at intimacy and happiness as anyone else. In West Hollywood, for all its silliness and superficiality, all its tawdry glitz and self-conscious glamour, all its attention to image and gratification, they were given that chance. Whatever its flaws, it was a city that let people be themselves and make their own choices about whom they loved and how, without judgment or condemnation or hatred. That was the point.

As I studied Trang and Victor off by themselves, I saw Victor take Trang's hand, as easily and naturally as taking a breath. In that moment, I realized why I'd stayed in West Hollywood so long, why it kept me here, year after year, even as I tried so hard to find a way to leave.

After a while, the four of us decided to walk back up to the house, leaving Victor and Trang to enjoy a moment in time that comes only once, and only to the young, or the young at heart.

Maurice served sandwiches and fresh lemonade out on the porch, while the cats curled up at our feet, and a rare summer breeze stirred the leaves along Norma Place. In the distance, we could hear the din, the blare of the music, the occasional roar of the crowd. Late-arriving men and women passed along the sidewalk on their way down to the parade and the festival in West Hollywood Park. On our way home, we'd seen rainbow flags adorning houses and apartments, along with the occasional AIDS prevention poster or a banner demanding the right to marry. There was a sense of history and significance in the air, an unspoken awareness of freedoms gained, friends lost, and more work yet to be done. Templeton had never lost anyone with whom she'd been truly close to AIDS, never suffered insults and humiliation for loving someone who happened to be of the same gender. But she had lost Joe Soto, and she still lived every day as a black woman fighting for every ounce of respect she could get, and I wondered if she wasn't sharing some of the same feelings swelling in the rest of us.

"I think I'm going to like living here," she said, as a female couple waved at us while pushing a baby carriage toward the parade. "It feels like a community, even if it's not exactly mine. I don't know just where that is yet, just where I'll finally settle down, but I'm sure I'll find it someday."

"Until then," Maurice said, "we'll do our best to make you feel at home."

"You've all done that already," Templeton said, and blasted us with a smile.

"Welcome home then, dear one." Maurice took her hand, pressing it to his lips, but slid his wise old eyes in my direction, as if he might also be speaking to me. "Welcome home."